What the critics are saying...

ꕥ

Hands On

"Ms. Burton has taken a simple plot of insecurity, lies, and misunderstanding and turned it into a great story, pleasurable to read. Lara and Mark are two strong individuals with opposite personalities and views, yet they complement each other perfectly. Tensions between them are highly charged and the sex is explosive and hot. This is a most delightful story that I would encourage readers to get their hands on." ~ *Coffeetime Romance*

"Hands On is simply scrumptious. Lara and Mark are great together. ...This well-paced story will touch all of your emotions and keep you hoping for that happily ever after ending. Get your "Hands On" this one and read it!" ~ *Just Erotic Romance Reviews*

"Hands On is erotic romance at its very best! Jaci Burton has written a steamy erotic tale which you will not be able to put down. The pace never flags, the action is sizzling and the sex scenes are scorching. Her characters leap off the page and readers everywhere will fall in love with Mark and will relate to Lara who is the kind of heroine you'd love to have as your best friend. Hands On is a truly irresistible story written by a master of this genre!" ~ *eCata Romance*

Coffee, Tea or Lea?

"Scorching hot sex coupled with fast and furiously funny dialogue!" ~ *Coffee Time Romance*

"Witty, fun characters and a fresh, new story line!" ~ *Romance Junkies*

Twice Upon a Roadtrip

"Jill and Ethan's story is a hoot! Their chemistry is hot, and Stacey's comedic timing is wonderful in this fast-paced read that delivers on all counts." ~ *Romantic Times BOOKclub*

"Shannon Stacey has given her readers a story that is lighthearted, but not at the expense of sensuality and heartfelt passion. TWICE UPON A ROADTRIP shines with touches of realistic human emotion between a man and woman who are attempting to resolve all questions as to whether they are willing to take a chance on love. I have no problem giving this book a very high recommendation." ~ *Romance Junkies*

"Shannon Stacey has penned a funny, hot tale that sizzles with witty dialogue. TWICE UPON A ROAD TRIP is one expedition few can only imagine. The situations Jill and Ethan get into might appear implausible, but it will keep readers in stitches. Definitely a book high on the entertainment scale. The love scenes are straightforwardly steamy and the sparks between them fly, but once their vacation fling is over, what happens next? I had fun reading TWICE UPON A ROAD TRIP and highly recommend it." ~ *Romance Reviews Today*

GOING the DISTANCE

Ann Wesley Hardin
Shannon Stacey
Jaci Burton

An Ellora's Cave Romantica Publication

www.ellorascave.com

Going the Distance

ISBN 1419954741

Edited by Briana St. James
Cover art by Melissa Waitley

Trade paperback Publication September 2006

Warning:

The following material contains graphic sexual content meant for mature readers. This story has been rated E–rotic by a minimum of three independent reviewers.

Ellora's Cave Publishing offers three levels of Romantica™ reading entertainment: S (S-ensuous), E (E-rotic), and X (X-treme).

S-*ensuous* love scenes are explicit and leave nothing to the imagination.

E-*rotic* love scenes are explicit, leave nothing to the imagination, and are high in volume per the overall word count. In addition, some E-rated titles might contain fantasy material that some readers find objectionable, such as bondage, submission, same sex encounters, forced seductions, and so forth. E-rated titles are the most graphic titles we carry; it is common, for instance, for an author to use words such as "fucking", "cock", "pussy", and such within their work of literature.

X-*treme* titles differ from E-rated titles only in plot premise and storyline execution. Unlike E-rated titles, stories designated with the letter X tend to contain controversial subject matter not for the faint of heart.

Contents

HANDS ON

By Jaci Burton

ஐ

Dedication

ꕥ

To Jamie, my wonderful friend, who told me about this really interesting annual event she'd read about which made

HANDS ON come to life. Thanks babe.

To my editor, Briana St. James, for hanging in there with me through all these books. Thank you.

To my pals for always being there with me through thick, thin and hysteria. You know who you are. Thanks for the coffee and your friendship.

And to Charlie, as always, for making me believe that anything is possible. I love you.

Trademarks Acknowledgement

The author acknowledges the trademarked status and trademark owners of the following wordmarks mentioned in this work of fiction:

K-Mart: KMART PROPERTIES, INC. CORPORATION

Chapter One

ഇ

"You're from where? And you want to do what?" Lara was certain she blushed all over. The event was supposed to have been an anonymous fundraiser. The tall, dark hunk of beefcake standing at her door had to be joking.

"*Total Man Magazine*. You're Lara McKenzie, right?"

She remembered a phone call from the magazine the other day, but she'd been too caught up writing her book to really pay attention to what they'd said. Now it clicked. Something about sending out a reporter. But wasn't that supposed to be next week? "I thought this was about my book."

His lips curled in a devilish smile that turned her knees to jelly. "No, it's about the fundraiser."

"The fundraiser isn't newsworthy."

"Sure it is. You came in first. That's big news."

He couldn't hide his smirk. This was the most embarrassing moment of her life.

Mr. Too-Sexy-To-Be-Legal flashed his driver's license and magazine ID. "My name's Mark Whitman. Can I come in and ask you a few questions about your, uh, win?"

Oh dear God, where was the nearest hole she could crawl into? "Why?"

He arched a dark brow, his whiskey-colored eyes making her wish he stood on her doorstep for any other reason than her winning the fundraiser.

"Have you ever read our magazine?"

"No."

"Trust me, what you did is a guaranteed sell-out."

Great. Just what she didn't want to hear. "What if I refuse an interview?"

He shrugged, leaning his broad shoulder against her doorway. "We'll write about it anyway, and then add our own comments."

Mortification ran rampant through her. The knowing smile on his face was enough to make her regret answering the door.

"It's nothing to be ashamed of, you know," he added. "It was for a good cause."

"If the shoe was on the other foot and I was here to interview you about…that subject, how would you feel?"

He shrugged, not in the least bit embarrassed. "I'm a guy. We're always bragging about our capabilities."

Lara blew out a breath. Who could she blame for entering that stupid contest, anyway?

Nancy, that's who. It was Nancy's fault. She made a mental note to kill her best friend. Maybe she'd been drunk when she agreed to do it. Unfortunately, she *did* have a lot of experience in that area. And she knew she could bring in a lot of money for the women's center. But she had no idea the results would be made public.

"Can I come in or should we do the interview right here?"

"My, uh, sex life is private." Yeah, right. Sex and her life had absolutely nothing in common. But Mr. Hot-As-Hell-Reporter didn't need to know that.

"If it's so private, then why did you do the fundraiser?"

She gave up. Maybe the article would increase sales of her books. Lara stepped aside and Mark walked in, his gaze darting around her living room. His perusal of her messy house only added to her embarrassment. This guy had to be from New York and this was small-town Pennsylvania. She lived in a tiny rented house filled with old, cheap furniture. Her research notes littered every mismatched table in the room.

"Sorry for the mess. I was reorganizing."

"You're nervous," he commented, casually moving a magazine aside. He sat on her ugly brown and orange sofa, pulling a laptop out of his backpack.

"Me? Nervous? Hardly." She swiped a loose curl behind her ear, hoping she didn't look as bad as she felt. At least she'd brushed her teeth this morning. And the plaid pajama bottoms and Penn State T-shirt covered her body, even though they didn't match. She sighed and plopped into the chair next to the sofa.

Why did it even matter how she looked? Someone like her could never attract a guy like Mark Whitman.

Mark smiled, his mouth bringing her attention to his dark moustache. His hair was raven black and curled at the ends. Well-worn jeans hugged his long legs and the black T-shirt stretched tight across his wide chest.

Didn't it just figure? Mark Whitman was the image of her fantasy man. The one she imagined when she wrote her books and thought about at night when she laid alone in her bed, masturbating and wishing for reality instead of fantasy.

"Ready?" he asked.

No. "Sure."

"How does it feel to have logged the most hours in the annual Masturbation-a-thon?"

She was going to die. Right here, right now. No, first she'd kill Nancy. Then she'd die.

She tried for nonchalant, knowing she failed miserably. The telltale heat creeping up her neck was a dead giveaway to her embarrassment. "I'm glad I raised a lot of money for the women's center."

"Yuh-huh," he said while typing. At least he wasn't looking at her. "Why did you enter in the first place?"

Because I'm so good at it? No, she'd faint dead away if she told him that. "Like I said, it was for a good cause."

He looked up and smiled at her, revealing two adorable

dimples on either side of his mouth. Damn, damn, damn. Why did he have to be so good-looking? Weren't all reporters supposed to be slovenly, old and bald?

"How often do you masturbate?"

He was joking, right? "That's really none of your business."

A laugh escaped his throat. Dark and sinfully sexy. She could imagine him making those sounds in her ear while they were entwined together in...okay, not good. *Mustn't think of Mark Whitman as a potential sex partner.* Now as far as her fantasies? Oh, yeah, he was going to be in her bedroom tonight. Definitely.

He leaned back against the couch and Lara's eyes widened when she realized she'd folded her laundry right there. Her purple panties were right behind him.

"You entered and won a fundraiser dealing with the number of hours you masturbate. Honey, it's public knowledge how much you did it in a month. I'm just asking if that's typical, or if you, shall we say, increased your average during that time period?"

Okay, so he had a point. Except she focused on the way he'd said *honey*, how it rolled off his tongue like an endearment she could never grow tired of hearing.

Focus, Lara, focus. "Daily."

One corner of his mouth curled. "Really."

"Yes." She examined her hands. Really should get a manicure. Maybe a pedicure, too. She made a mental note to add bread to her grocery list. And cat food. Where was that damn cat, anyway? Oh, that's right. She didn't have a cat.

"I can't believe you're embarrassed about this."

Oh, sure, easy for him to say. "How often do *you* masturbate, Mark?" She wondered how he liked having the tables turned.

"Daily. Unless I have a girlfriend who likes a lot of sex."

"Do you like a lot of sex?" She cringed as soon as the

question fell out of her mouth. Maybe if she was lucky she'd implode and end this mortifying conversation.

Mark set the laptop to the side and leaned back, his head resting against her underwear. Lord, she had to do better at housekeeping.

"Actually, I love sex. Daily, hourly, as much as I can get. It's hard to find a woman who wants it that much, though."

Maybe the air conditioner was broken. Something had to account for the sweat pooling between her breasts. His comment hung between them like the July humidity outside, thick and nearly tangible. She wanted to reach out and touch his words, touch him.

But she wasn't that kind of girl. If she were, she'd have fewer vibrators and more real sex. Daily, hourly, as much as she could get.

"Does it bother you that I'm so frank about sex?"

Of course it bothered her. Couldn't he see she was drowning in a puddle of heated perspiration here? "No, not at all. After all, it *is* what I write about."

He nodded. "Of course. You're a writer. Tell me about your books."

"I'm sure you'd find them dull."

"Not really. I'm a journalist, remember? I live for the printed word. Nonfiction books about sex, right?"

"Actually that's a fairly simplistic explanation of a boundless and complicated subject. I write books on female sexuality."

"Yeah, I knew it was something along those lines. My editor gave me some of your books but I haven't had time to read them. Care to summarize for me?"

She snorted, unable to help herself.

He arched a brow and asked, "Something funny?"

"Sorry. Yes, and no. I'm often asked to summarize my books, but really, they're too complex."

"I'm hardly a moron, Miss McKenzie."

"Call me Lara." Bad enough she was out of his league sex-wise. She'd die if he treated her like some homely basket case.

"Okay, Lara. Then tell me about your books in as much detail as you'd like."

"I don't want to take up any more of you time than necessary, Mark. Is it all right if I call you Mark?"

"Sure. And my time is yours right now, Lara. Go ahead."

He seemed sincere, but then many others had seemed that way, too. Except she'd later found out that they wanted to bed the professor of sex. Or even worse, wanted to use her knowledge to help them with their own research. She was so tired of being used for someone else's gain.

Someday, she might actually find a man who wanted her just for her. Maybe.

"Okay. As I said, I write about female sexuality. But more than just biological functions. My books explore how women's sexuality has changed from the early fifties until now."

"And how has it changed?"

"Women have thrown out the old customs of simply lying there while a man gets off. Now they can demand what they want, they can show their partners how to satisfy them. Really, all the new sexuality that's touted in my books is nothing more than teaching women how to communicate with their men."

He looked at her and nodded. "I'll drink to that. I can't tell you how many times a woman has given me that disappointed look and I felt helpless because I couldn't get them to open up about how to please them."

"Did you ask them?"

"All the damn time. Do you know how many women are afraid to let loose?"

"Too many, unfortunately."

"Why is that? I mean, here you have a scenario where two people have this great chemistry. And you know a guy's biology is a given. If he sticks his, uh, you know..."

"You can be as frank as you like, Mark. I've heard it all."

"Okay. So, during sex, a guy's gonna get off unless he has some physical malfunction. But with a woman, her physical makeup is so freakin' mysterious we need a road map to make her come."

She leaned forward and spoke with enthusiasm, barely able to form the words that her mind threw at her. This was her element, what she lived to talk about. This is where her comfort level came in. "All too common, I'm afraid. Women have struggled for years to gain the courage to tell a man what to do to make her come. Or, God forbid, actually show him."

"Now that I'd like," he said, a gleam in his gorgeous eyes. "Not only would it be educational, but hot as hell."

"Indeed it would be, for both you and your partner." Lara figured that previously wished-for implosion was right around the corner. Mark Whitman had fired her libido in ways that shocked her. She'd spoken frankly about sex with colleagues, students, even some of her readers. They all wanted to know how to charge up their sex lives.

She'd told them. Many times in very sexual terms. Not once had a discussion turned her on.

But this time it had, in a big way.

Her mind refused to stay grounded in the discussion. Instead, it wandered off into dangerous territory. Like demonstrating for Mark how *she* liked to get off. In graphic detail, naked and with props.

She licked away the perspiration on her upper lip and didn't dare raise her arms because she knew the sweat stains would show. Although she was tempted to take the magazine lying on the table next to her and use it as a fan.

She really needed a shower, followed by a good orgasm, because what was happening here was not good. Not good at all. She wasn't having a simple clinical discussion with Mark. This was foreplay!

"Um, are there any other questions?" *Please say no and get out of my house before I embarrass myself.*

"Yeah, if you don't mind. I could come back later if you're busy."

"Yes, that would be good. No, wait." Crap. She didn't know what was worse—having him stay and torment her further or letting him come back and start all over again.

What she needed was some time to get a grip on her emotions *and* her wayward libido.

He looked at her expectantly, no doubt waiting for an answer from the crazy woman who couldn't make up her mind.

"I could take you to dinner tonight, if that works for you," he said, no doubt to break the awkward silence.

"Dinner?" Was her voice squeaking?

"Yeah, dinner. You know, that place where they serve food. You do go out, don't you?"

Not this millennium. "Uh, sure. I just don't think, well, that is I'm not sure if we..."

"That's okay if you don't want to. We can just finish up now and I'll get out of your way."

"No, wait!" God, how embarrassing to be so socially inept. "Dinner would be fine. Is seven okay?"

"Yeah. You choose the place since I'm not familiar with the area and I'll pick you up here."

She watched him pack up his laptop, hoping her panties wouldn't somehow attach themselves to his clothing. Or worse, his head.

As she walked him to the door, momentary panic struck. She had to go out to dinner with Mr. Magnificent-In-Blue-Jeans. And there she stood, the plaid, pathetic one. Was she insane?

No, wait, it wasn't a date. It was an interview. Sometimes she amazed herself with her naiveté.

"See you at seven, then."

She nodded and pulled open the door to let him out.

"Oh, and Lara?"

"Yes?"

His gaze strayed to the sofa where her panties dangled over the edge, then back at her. Heat warmed his eyes, darkened them. "I like purple."

Chapter Two

ꙮ

It was obvious she had nothing to wear.

Jeans, sweatpants and pajamas made up the bulk of her wardrobe. That and pants suits or long skirts for professional appearances or lectures at the university.

But going out to dinner with a sexy man? No, there didn't appear to be anything in her closet to fit that scenario.

Fortunately she had Nancy, whom she'd called in a panic as soon as Mark left.

Nancy, the one she was going to kill. Later. Right now they stood in her bedroom with a pile of Nancy's sexy dresses.

"Dresses? You brought dresses? I don't wear those, Nance."

Nancy scrunched her pixie face and frowned. "Tonight you do. So, tell me about him. Is he gorgeous?"

Lara sighed and fingered the purple silk of a sundress that seemed to call to her. "Beyond gorgeous. Way out of my league."

Nancy groaned. "No one's out of your league, honey."

"Wanna bet? You know how I am with guys, Nance."

Lara stepped back from Nancy's shaking finger. "That's your own fault. You have a lot to offer, you just don't know it. You're beautiful, intelligent, have a witty sense of humor and guys look at you all the time."

"Yeah, right. I've never seen guys looking at me. I only see them looking at you." And what man wouldn't? With Nancy's perfect body, short, raven hair and stunning blue eyes, what man would notice Lara when the two of them stood together?

"That's because you don't pick up the signals. You know,

for someone who claims to have all this knowledge about the opposite sex, you sure suck at recognizing a man's interest."

"You're insane, woman. But I love you anyway. Now what am I supposed to wear to dinner?"

Nancy's lips curled in an evil grin that always made Lara wary. "Something hot and sexy."

"Business dinner, not prelude to a seduction."

"It could be, if you wanted it to."

"Forget it, Nance. He's a reporter, here for a story on that idiotic masturbation-a-thon you forced me to enter, and then he's outta here."

"Oh, but you're so good at masturbation, Lara. I knew you'd be a shoo-in to win."

She couldn't help it. One glance at Nancy's innocently batting eyelashes and Lara burst into laughter. "Gee, thanks. I think. Remind me not to tell you so much about my personal life anymore."

Nancy pulled the purple sundress out of the pile and held it against Lara. "Hey, you're the sexpert, not me. Can I help it if we've known each other since we were five years old and share every sordid detail about our personal lives, including sex? Or should I say, the lack of it?"

Smoothing her hand over the sinfully soft material of the dress, Lara shook her head. "*My* lack of it. *You* get plenty."

"That's because I recognize the signals men give off. You'd get more sex if you pulled your head out of your research and started focusing on the real thing."

Real thing? Sex? Bah. No such luck in that department. She'd already tried and failed miserably.

Besides, she got plenty of sex. It just so happened to be the do-it-yourself variety. And she was good at it. *Damn* good.

As if being an expert at masturbating was something to be proud of. How pathetic.

An hour later she was dressed in silk that clung to her body much too closely. Did it have to be purple? She should have chosen another one. Mark had said he liked purple, although he had been referring to the panty incident at the time. She didn't want him to think she'd worn the purple dress to impress him.

Not that he'd be impressed anyway, regardless of what she wore.

Nancy, who'd decided to hang around and get a peek at Mark, pronounced her sultry.

Lara just felt stupid and overdressed. And Nancy had insisted she pull her hair up into a clip and let her long curls sail down her back.

Ugh. She'd feel better having it braided so it wouldn't annoy her, but there was no fighting Nancy once she got an idea into her head.

When a knock sounded at the door, Lara's heart sank into her stomach.

"Don't answer it," she said when Nancy started toward the front door. "I've changed my mind. I don't want to go."

Nancy rolled her eyes and ignored her. "Coward. You're going, so don't bother trying to hide. I'll just drag you out here again."

Nancy graced Mark with her most cheerful smile as she threw open the door, shook his hand and let him in. "Hey there, you must be Mark. I'm Nancy, Lara's best friend."

"Hey there yourself, Nancy." Mark grinned.

Still in those jeans that looked as soft as a baby's blanket, Mark had changed into a white shirt that showed off his great tan. The room temperature increased by at least ten degrees and Lara was thankful the dress she wore was sleeveless.

Always comfortable around men, Nancy engaged Mark in an easy discussion that made Lara wish she had her friend's gift for gab.

Oh sure, the two of them hit it off like they were old friends. Maybe Nancy could go out to dinner with him instead.

"You look great," he said, finally noticing her standing there despite her best efforts to blend in with the furniture.

"Thank you." She cleared the squeak from her throat.

"Well, don't you two make a charming pair," Nancy stated, looking as satisfied as if she'd personally set Lara up on a blind date.

Lara glared at her and turned to Mark. "You ready?"

"Sure. Let's go. Nice meeting you, Nancy."

"You too, Mark. Have fun, honey," she said to Lara as they approached the door.

"Thanks, Mom," she whispered to her friend, hugging her. "You sure you don't want to come along?" *Please say yes.*

"No way. I've got a hot date of my own tonight. Enjoy!" Nancy winked and slammed the door shut, then hurried to her car while Mark led her to his.

Hot date, indeed. Mark would be so bored he'd have her back home in an hour.

She suggested a steak place downtown, which Mark readily agreed to try. Once seated at a booth in the restaurant, she waited for him to drag out his laptop or notebook and resume the interview.

"Nice place," he said.

"Yeah, it is." *Can I go home now*?

"Do you eat here often?"

She shrugged. "Sometimes. I don't get out much."

He arched a brow. "Why not?"

Because I have no reason to go out, and no one asks me out anyway. "Um, too busy with research."

"Sex research?"

Did he have to grin at her like that? His eyes reflected heat she was unprepared to handle. "Yes, sex research."

"Is all your research academic-related, or is there some, uh, hands-on?"

She spit her tea back into the glass. Not very ladylike at all. Wondering how long before this so-called interview would be over and she could go home and hide, she said, "Obviously, there's some hands-on research."

"So, that means you date a lot?"

Lara couldn't help the laugh that escaped. "Not really."

"Steady boyfriend then?"

"Sort of." She smiled behind her glass.

"Does he live around here?"

"Yes."

"What's his name?"

"Why do you want to know?"

Mark shrugged his impressive shoulders. "Just thought we might throw his name in the article."

"Oh, I don't think so."

"First name only, then?"

"Bob." Nancy would die when Lara told her what she'd admitted to Mark.

"Bob's a lucky guy, then."

Smooth talker, and as full of it as they came, too. "Thanks."

"Does he help you with the research for your books?"

She really should tell him who Bob was, but she couldn't bring herself to get any more personal than she already had. "Yes, extensively."

"Even luckier, then."

"So, do you have any more questions for the article?" *In other words, Mr. Smooth, get your mind out of my gutter and back on your job.*

He knew it too. She could tell by his sly smile.

They spent the rest of dinner talking about her background, education and books. Subjects Lara took an avid interest in. As opposed to her social life, which was nonexistent enough to cause a huge stop in conversation.

By the time he'd paid the check, she was more than ready to head back to her little hovel and hide from the world again.

She couldn't get out of his car fast enough. Unfortunately, Mr. Sexy-and-Chivalrous felt compelled to walk her to the door. Really, this was small-town Pennsylvania, not the streets of New York. She hardly needed an escort to the front door.

"Thank you for dinner," she said, rummaging through her purse for her keys and trying to avoid looking at him. As it was, his image would remain in her memory banks long after he was gone.

She couldn't wait to get inside and do what she'd thought about doing with him all night long. Too bad he wouldn't be there for it.

"You're welcome. Thanks for agreeing to the interview."

Clearly he wasn't going to go away until she looked at him. She turned, smiled and held out her hand. "Nice meeting you, Mark."

He tilted his head to the side and looked a bit confused. Then he leaned in, his face inches away from hers.

Oh no. Oh hell no! He wasn't going to do that, was he? Surely not. She wasn't his type at all. He was hot and sexy and she was just plain frumpy. She fought back panic as her thoughts ran rampant. His breath sailed across her cheek as he bent his head toward hers.

Then he shocked the hell out of her by brushing his lips against hers. His soft mouth teased and tormented.

Her toes curled, her heart pounded so loud she was certain he could hear it thumping against her ribs. This kind of thing never happened to women like her. Men like Mark Whitman didn't kiss boring, socially retarded professors.

But he did. Right on the lips, his breath tinged with the sweet wine they'd consumed at dinner. His mouth was soft, gliding ever so gently over hers.

She couldn't breathe. How long had it been since she'd been kissed?

Oh, hell. She'd never been kissed like this. One touch of mouth to mouth and she was heading for a coronary.

As quickly as it started, it was over. Lara had to right herself because she'd leaned clean into him.

He grinned and said, "Night, Lara. Good luck with your next book."

She watched him walk away and suddenly she felt like Ilsa saying goodbye to Rick in *Casablanca*. She was certain that wistful, I-wish-things-could-be-different look hung on her expression long after he'd driven off.

She was such a dork!

After slipping inside and tossing off her uncomfortable shoes, she headed straight for the bedroom.

Cinderella night was over. She hung up Nancy's sundress and returned to her ratty shorts and T-shirt.

Thankfully, that ordeal was over. But Mark's kiss still burned on her lips, making her feel hot, flustered and utterly foolish. How old was she, anyway? Fourteen?

"You're a moron, Lara. You really need to get out more. Your social skills are atrocious." And now she was talking to herself, a habit brought about by spending way too much time alone.

She plopped down at her desk and turned on the computer, blowing out a sigh of frustration. The computer wasn't the only thing turned on.

Why couldn't she be like other women? She was approaching thirty. Well-educated, sexually knowledgeable, with the sexual experience of the average teenager. Less, actually, if her research was accurate. Her few forays into sexual escapades had been one bomb after another.

Meanwhile, gorgeous, sexy men like Mark Whitman blew in and out of her life like a snowstorm.

Another one bites the dust, Lara, and all you got was a little taste of what could be.

Her work blurred on the screen, her body on fire from a simple peck on the lips.

No sense in waiting while the urge was so strong right now. Time to go find Bob and get a little relief.

She pushed away from the desk and headed into the bedroom, plopping down on the bed. Slipping off her T-shirt and shorts, she reached into the nightstand drawer. Toys of every shape, size and texture imaginable filled the drawer, making it look like an overstuffed toybox for the perverse. She giggled and wrapped her palm around Bob, the big boy.

Leaning back against the pillows, she closed her eyes and imagined Mark, his face and body coming into view quite clearly. Only this time he didn't just stand there and smile that sexy smile at her. This time, he stood at the foot of her bed and began to undress.

She planted her feet flat on the bed and spread her legs, flipping Bob's switch and smiling as he whirred to life. Just the sound of her favorite vibrator got her juices flowing.

Not that they hadn't been flowing all night long at dinner. By the time Mark had dropped her off her panties were soaked. Talking about sex always turned her on. Talking about sex with someone as hot as Mark Whitman had her ready to explode.

Snagging her bottom lip between her teeth, she slipped Bob between her legs, letting its soft vibration tickle her clit. She squeezed her buttocks together at the exquisite sensation, rocking her hips back and forth and moving Bob along her slit. Hot cream poured from her cunt and down the crack of her ass. She couldn't remember the last time she'd been this wet or this excited.

And she knew why. Visions of Mark standing naked before her crept into her fantasies. He arched a dark brow, crawling onto the bed and stopping between her legs. She watched in utter rapture as he bent down, pulled Bob away and planted his mouth firmly over her sex.

She shrieked at the heat pulsing through her. When he licked the length of her, sliding his tongue inside her pussy and licking up the cream there, she moaned, thrashing around on the bed like she was on fire and trying to escape the heat.

But she didn't want to escape. Instead, she slid Bob between her folds, imagining Mark's cock. Thick and long, it breached her tight entrance with one quick thrust, embedding him deep inside her.

She knew he'd fuck like a savage. Exactly what she wanted, what she needed. Rough, determined, well-practiced in the art of pleasing a woman.

His mouth captured hers, his tongue mimicking the movements of his tunneling cock. The knot of nerves at her clit exploded and she cried out, thrusting upward and against him, holding tight as she rode out cresting wave after wave until she collapsed, shattered and exhausted.

Shutting off Bob's switch, she closed her eyes and fought for even breathing.

That was good. Really good. And for the first time, despite her amazing orgasm, having sex with her vibrator just wasn't quite good enough.

* * * * *

Kissed her. Why the hell had he kissed her?

Mark emailed the article to *Total Man Magazine*, then shut down the laptop and packed up his things. He'd spent the majority of the night writing and in his estimation it had come out damn good.

Now to get the family stuff over with. It was a short drive to his uncle Roger's house, anyway. Might as well stay there and save the money *TMM* had fronted for his expenses.

It wasn't that he was trying to get as far away from Lara McKenzie as he could. After all, she was an interview—a means to an end. The end being money and a contract with the top magazine in the country.

No, he wasn't interested in her. She wasn't his type at all. He didn't go for redheads with more mind than body. He liked willowy blondes who enjoyed fun and games with no commitment. Not brainiacs like Lara. The only stimulation he wanted from women was the physical kind.

Lara stimulated him all right. Mentally *and* physically. In his book, that was bad news.

His career was his number one goal. And if this article came out as well as he thought it would, he could thank Lara for getting him the in to *TMM* that he'd wanted for years.

She'd been so out of her element last night it was painfully obvious. He'd nearly ended up apologizing to her for making her go to dinner with him. For a woman who claimed to be an expert in all things sexual, she didn't have a clue.

Yet there was something about her that drove him crazy. Innocence, maybe? God knows he'd met very few women as naïve as Lara. Miss Published Sexpert was not as experienced as she led people to believe. At least not practical experience.

The kiss had been his way of atoning for making her uncomfortable. That had to be the reason he'd done it.

The only reason. Except that innocent little brushing of lips had lit him up like a wildfire on dry tinder.

Maybe he'd been the one out of his element, not Lara. He wasn't used to women like her.

Good thing he'd never have to see her again.

Chapter Three

ꕥ

Slipping into the guest room to avoid the noise of his family, Mark pressed the cell phone to his ear. The call he'd waited two days for had finally come through. Jonathan Smitz, the senior editor for *TMM*, was finally calling about the article he'd done on Lara McKenzie.

"Jonathan, could you say that again?"

"The article is perfect, Mark. Fantastic job."

He grinned, smelling success. "Glad you liked it."

"I think we need to talk contract."

He pumped his fist in the air and tried to keep the excitement out of his voice. "Sounds great. I have a few ideas for a regular feature I think you might like. Like a monthly man's opinion. What I thought I could do is—"

"No, no, no. I already have an angle going."

Shit. Not what he wanted to hear. He'd had his own thoughts about a regular monthly article. But hell, if *TMM* was talking contract, he was listening. "What's your angle?"

"You and Lara McKenzie doing a monthly feature about opposing viewpoints on sexuality."

His excitement burst like an overfilled balloon. "Huh?"

"I think it would be great. With her keen insights into female sexuality and your arrogant male perspective, you two could have a helluva hot argument every month. Kind of like two sides to the same coin. The readers will go apeshit over it."

The readers might, but Mark thought it was the worst damned idea he'd ever heard. "Look, Jonathan, there's no way Lara McKenzie will agree to something like that."

He hoped. No, he knew it for a fact. It had been like pulling teeth just to get her to agree to the first interview. Even then it wasn't like she was eagerly forthcoming with information.

"Sure she will. Once you convince her. Think of the readership she'll gain for her academic books."

"She won't do it."

"She will, if you convince her."

"I'd have to lie to her, make something up, make this really appealing for her."

"Well, then make it appealing."

Right. And what would appeal to Dr. Lara McKenzie?

She had seemed to enjoy that kiss he gave her. And she was a bit awkward, socially. Maybe she didn't get out much.

"Great idea," Jonathan said.

Oh hell. Had he said that out loud?

"Take her out. Wine her and dine her. Do whatever you have to do with her, but get her to agree."

"You want me to compromise my principles for a contract?"

Jonathan laughed. "I know you, Mark. You have no principles. Besides, she can't be that hideous. Take one for the team, pal."

"Bad idea, Jonathan." He had to steer Jonathan away from Lara McKenzie. No way did he want to see her again. "Actually, I had a couple ideas for a different kind of feature that I think you might like. I'd love to run some ideas by you."

The silence on the other end of the line spoke volumes. He was screwed.

"Look, Mark. You're a great writer and all, but we've already decided what we want. You either get Lara McKenzie on board or we'll have to go in a different direction."

Different direction meaning he'd be out of a contract. "I'll see what I can do, then."

"Great! Go charm the panties off her. Call me when you have the deal."

The line went dead, kind of like how Mark felt. Nothing like going from soaring with the eagles to crawling with the snakes in a matter of seconds. He closed the cover on his phone and tossed it on the bed, not wanting to face his animated relatives just yet. In fact, he'd rather be at home in New York instead of Nowhere, Pennsylvania.

Worse, he'd have to go back and see Lara McKenzie again. Something he really didn't want to do, for a lot of different reasons. But she held the key to his future, and like it or not he had to get her interested.

He needed a plan before he approached her. Some way to get her to agree to write the articles.

Maybe a little romance wasn't such a bad idea. Not real romance, because he sure as hell wasn't interested in her that way. But she had seemed flustered around him. And if there's one thing he knew, it was when a woman was attracted to him. Not that he was stud of the year or anything, but any man who couldn't spot a woman's receptive signals had no business calling himself a man.

Plus, he wasn't that bad-looking and had a little charm. He'd never had any trouble getting a date. So he wasn't repulsive and she'd told him that guys weren't exactly beating down her door for dates. Although there was that Bob fellow. But she hadn't seemed too enthused about him, so maybe he had a chance.

Lara McKenzie was interested in him. That was his angle. If he could play on her attraction to him, get her to trust him, maybe even get a little romantically involved with her, she'd agree to do anything for him.

Guilt made his stomach clench. Okay, so it sucked that he'd have to lie to her. Deceiving women wasn't something he liked to do. The types of women he dated had no problem putting up with his I-don't-want-to-get-involved speech.

Lara wasn't that type of woman, so he'd have to lie.

Damn, he hated to do that. But in this case, it was necessary. His career was on the line. The brass ring was within his grasp. And if he had to lead Lara on a bit to get there, he'd apologize later.

He'd just make sure to keep it light and friendly and not let her get too involved. He might have to get her to like him a little, but he wouldn't let it go any further than that.

As secluded a life as she lived, she'd probably jump at the chance to get out and have some fun.

* * * * *

Lara assumed the knock at the door was the express courier delivering the books she'd ordered. She was right in the middle of a key passage in her book and refused to get up. He'd just leave it, anyway.

But the incessant tapping continued. Blowing out a sigh, she pushed her wayward hair out of her eyes and padded to the door, conscious of the fact she wore sweatpants with holes in the knees and a tank top without a bra. Well, she supposed she'd give the delivery guy his thrill for the day.

She chuckled at that and threw open the door, then immediately wished she hadn't.

Oh God. What was *he* doing back here? "Mark?"

He grinned and leaned against the doorway, looking too tall, too male, and too temptingly sexy. "Thought you'd never see me again, didn't you?"

Actually, he'd been her number one fantasy the past two nights. "No, I didn't. Why are you here?"

"Can I come in?"

Social skills, Lara. Gotta work on those social skills. "Sure."

She moved out of the way and he brushed past her, his shoulder connecting with her right nipple on the way by. It hardened. On the one breast only, of course. Now she looked deformed. And she couldn't very well pluck at her shirt without looking like she was masturbating in front of him.

Great. She crossed her arms and followed him into the living room.

And look at her house! Her clean laundry was everywhere again, newspapers on the floor and research books littered all over the furniture. Chagrin washed over her face. "Sorry. The maid is late today."

"Looks like the same one I use." He winked, then sat on the sofa next to her dirty socks.

"Um, is there something I can help you with, Mark?" *Like showing you the front door again*? She grabbed for her socks and stuffed them behind a pillow.

"I told you I was going to be in town for a while, right?"

Did he? Frankly she couldn't remember much of that humiliating experience. Maybe she'd conveniently blocked it out of her memory. "I guess you did."

"Well, my family has this annual reunion, and this year it's at my aunt and uncle's. They live in Breckenridge, just east of here."

"Uh-huh." Brilliant conversationalist. Where did she get her Ph.D. anyway? K-mart?

"It's pretty boring there. Thought you might be up for a night out. I just had to get away from family, and since we hit it off so well the other day I thought I could entice you into going out with me."

Was this some kind of alternate universe? Who exactly did he meet two days ago? Her doppelganger?

"No."

His eyes widened. "No?"

"I said no. Thank you, but I'm not interested in going out with you."

He frowned as if she'd given him the answer in French. "No?"

Surely she didn't have to spell it for him. She'd given him credit for being smarter than that.

"No. I'm very busy and don't have time to date."

The shock on his face was priceless. "You don't like me?"

Oh, hell. This had never happened to her before. "Of course I like you."

"Then why won't you go out with me?"

Because I don't know how to date, you idiot. Look at me! "I told you. I'm busy."

"It's because you're dating Bob, right?"

"No."

"So, you two aren't exclusive?"

"No, we're not." Which was a lie, of course. Bob was her nightly companion, just not in the way Mark thought.

"Okay, I get the hint. I'm repulsive."

Was he blind as well as an idiot? "You are not repulsive. You're sexy as hell." *And speaking of hell, shut the hell up, Lara.*

His eyes darkened. "Sexy, huh? So you *are* interested."

Where was Nancy when she really needed her? She pinched the bridge of her nose and closed her eyes, willing away a headache.

"Lara, look at me."

She did, then wished she hadn't. The look of sexual promise in his eyes had her wet in exactly two seconds. "Okay, I'm looking at you."

He scooted over and took her hands in his. Her sweaty hands.

"Look. This isn't a proposal of marriage. I just thought you might want to go out. I felt like we connected the other day, and thought you might want to explore that a little. I know I do."

Connected? Explore? Was this some kind of joke? "We connected."

"Yeah."

"You and me."

"Yeah."

"And so you want to take me out."

"Yes."

She stood and paced behind the sofa, wringing her hands together. She could just say no and be done with it. Then again, when would she have another chance to go out with a fun, gorgeous guy? She didn't attract guys like Mark Whitman. Not since…well, never. "Okay."

He stood and watched her, his lips curling into a smile. God, she wanted to lick that grin off his face. Then bathe the rest of his body with her tongue.

Uh-oh. There went her nipples again. Both of them this time. She crossed her arms over her breasts.

"Great. I'll pick you up at eight."

She followed him to the door. "Eight."

"Yeah, eight. Is that okay?"

No. None of this was okay. "Sure. Eight. Fine. See you then."

He walked out, then turned partway and said, "Oh, and wear something sexy. We're going dancing."

* * * * *

Three hours later she was sitting in Lamour, the town's best salon, with Nancy jabbering in her ear.

"Take a bunch of length off. And do something with her toenails, ugh. And those fingernails. Geez, Lara, when are you going to stop biting your nails?"

When I'm dead. Which she wished she was right now. She should have known better than to tell Nancy about Mark's return. Her friend had nearly burst her eardrum squealing over the phone, then raced over and dragged her out of the house, claiming she needed a total makeover.

She wondered if Marco, the stylist currently tsk-tsking over her hair, could do a complete personality makeover while he was at it.

Maybe make her vivacious, alluring, a witty conversationalist and an overall fun date.

She wouldn't know a fun date if she tripped over it.

"Dahling," Marco said, "What do you wash your hair with? This stuff is like straw. It has to go."

Nancy had assured her Marco was the best stylist in town. Right now he looked more like Dr. Frankenstein.

And Lara was the monster—his latest science project.

In less than two hours she'd lost a good ten inches of her hair and had her eyebrows waxed. *Bronze Babe* nail polish sparkled on her fingernails and toenails, and they'd taken so long to apply makeup that she probably looked like a hooker.

But when Marco turned her around to face the mirror, she smothered a gasp.

Who *was* that woman?

She looked over at Nancy's smirking face, Marco's self-satisfied one, then back to the stranger in the mirror.

Her. The one with short, wavy red hair that curled lightly against her chin, and green eyes that sparkled, showing off her heart-shaped face. Full lips were painted the lightest bronze color and shined with sparkles.

"Wow," she managed.

Nancy squeezed her shoulders. "*Wow* is right. Honey, we should have done this years ago. I've been telling you that you're a knockout."

Somehow she knew that at midnight she'd lose her glass slipper and turn back into the scullery maid she really was.

"Now, we shop for clothes."

She paid homage and a hundred dollars to Marco, thanking him for the miraculous transformation. He was no Dr. Frankenstein, the man was a freakin' genius!

Then, despite her protests, Nancy dragged her out of the salon and into the trendiest clothing store in the village. Every sexy outfit she said no to, Nancy said yes. They argued until Lara was simply too tired to fight any longer.

By the time they got home she wanted to take a nap, not get dressed.

But there she stood, in front of her bed where three outfits stared back at her, daring her to wear one of them on her date.

A date she didn't want to go on, anyway. How did she keep getting talked into doing dumb things? First the masturbation-a-thon, now this date with Mark. Was she a slug with no backbone? Why couldn't she just say no?

"I know what you're thinking."

She glanced in the mirror and saw Nancy behind her. "No, you don't."

"Yes, I do. You think you don't want to go out with Mark."

"Okay, maybe you do know what I'm thinking. But look at me, Nance. This isn't me. This is someone else."

Nancy stepped behind her and grasped her shoulders, hugging her. "No, sweetie, this *is* you. You just hide behind miles of hair and loose clothes because you're afraid if you step outside your shell, no one will love you."

"Ridiculous. You psychoanalyzing me?"

"I've known you since we were kids. You were the smartest girl I knew, with big green eyes and a full smile that the boys would drool over. But you never noticed. And eventually, they stopped drooling over you, because they knew they weren't going to get your attention."

She patted Nancy's hand. "You're delusional."

"And you're in denial. Now get that gorgeous body into one of those sexy dresses so you can strut your stuff and get laid."

"Nancy!" She pushed away and turned to her best friend. "I am *not* getting laid."

Nancy crossed her arms and smirked. "I'll bet you a million bucks he has his hand up your dress before the end of the night. And if you don't call me tomorrow and tell me he gave you an ear-splitting orgasm, I'll resign as the resident meddler in your life."

"You're on."

Hand up her dress. Ear-splitting orgasm. Nancy was full of it.

After Nancy left, Lara slipped on the short blue dress that sparkled in the light like the aurora borealis, then teetered into the living room on strappy blue sandals with heels that looked like they were made of thin straws.

She'd fall on her ass trying to dance in these things. But, she had to admit they made her legs look long and shapely.

By the time eight o'clock rolled around, she was hyperventilating and wanted to throw up. But she was bound and determined to go on this date, if for no other reason than to prove Nancy wrong.

No one was getting their hands up her dress tonight. And the only one giving her an orgasm later would be Bob.

A soft rap on the door had her heart catapulting into her throat. Sucking in oxygen, she opened it slowly.

Adonis. Well, it was Mark, but it could have easily been Adonis.

Black pants, gray shirt that molded to his impressive chest in a way that made her want to drool. Raven hair that her fingers itched to run wild through. And a killer smile that curled the ends of his moustache upward.

She'd never survive the night.

* * * * *

Mark stood in the doorway, his mouth hanging open.

Where had the frazzled little redhead gone? Who was this gorgeous siren decked out in a sinfully short wisp of a dress, with her hair cut and styled and showcasing a face that stopped his heart?

And her mouth. Holy shit, that mouth. Visions of those full lips wrapped around his cock had the snake coiling and twisting to life in his pants.

Not good. Not good at all. The objective here was to fool her, not fuck her. He was supposed to garner her interest, not get into her panties.

But damned if that wasn't what he wanted to do right now. Forget the date, forget the subterfuge. Just throw her over the nearest piece of furniture, pull that hot dress over her hips and slide into what would surely be a nice, tight, wet pussy.

Ah, hell.

"You look gorgeous," he finally managed.

The blush she wore on her cheeks only made her look more desirable. "Thank you."

"You ready to go? I'm anxious to get my arms around you."

At her shocked expression, he corrected, "On the dance floor, of course."

"Oh. Of course."

She closed the door and brushed past him, giving him a whiff of a soft and seductive scent. Vanilla with something a little wild mixed in.

Just like the woman. Sweet and innocent, but he'd bet his career that her innocence hid a lurking wildcat just waiting for someone to let her out of her cage.

Mark wanted to be the one to set her free.

He was in deep trouble.

Chapter Four

ஒ

Lara tugged at the hem of her dress for the umpteenth time, conscious of how the silky material rode up her thighs.

She was also fully aware of the way Mark's eyes darted to the skin exposed by the traveling material.

They'd been in the car for over a half hour and during that time he'd cast several glances in the direction of her legs. And cleared his throat a lot. Other than that he was mostly silent. Probably wondering how quickly he could get her back home.

Although he had seemed genuinely pleased with her appearance.

God, she was so inept at reading a man's sexual signals. And she called herself an expert? Yeah, right. Only if the subject in question wasn't focused on her.

She inhaled a shaky breath. Damn, he smelled good. Like the mountains. Crisp, clean with a seductive spice that made her want to search his skin for the location of that scent. Everywhere.

Which immediately brought about a vision of her nuzzling his balls. Damn.

She cleared her throat.

"Doin' okay over there?" he asked.

"Fine."

"You're fidgety."

"I'm fine."

"You don't get out much, do you?"

Was it that obvious? "Not really. I prefer working on my books and research."

"Real sex is more fun than reading about it."

Her gaze flew to his and he winked. "Well, it is."

Not the sex that she'd had. "I'll take your word for it."

"I could…"

He didn't finish his sentence. She couldn't resist asking, "You could what?"

Instead of answering, he turned into a parking lot filled with cars. "We're here."

Mark came around and opened her door, then led her to a one-story brick building. She heard the music from the parking lot. People milled outside. A neon sign blinked from the window, proclaiming the place as All That Jazz.

Smoke poured out of the dimly lit nightclub. Strains of a saxophone wailing from the stage filled her senses with a slow, seductive melody that sang through her nerve endings.

Mark led them to a table in the corner of the room. The place was packed tight, bodies undulating on the huge dance floor. The waitress brought them drinks and Lara sipped hers while watching the interaction of the couples milling about.

"So, what do you think?" he asked.

"I think this place is ripe for research."

He arched a brow and took a long swallow of his drink. "What kind of research?"

"Sexual."

"Oh yeah?"

She nodded. "Sexual behaviors of the young and single couples. I wish I'd brought my notepad. I could jot down some ideas or maybe even wander around and ask some questions."

His lips curled. "Oh yeah. I know they would love that."

Good point. "Okay, maybe just observing will give me some thought processes to go on."

"Tell me what you see."

"Look at that couple in front of us."

Mark's gaze followed hers. "The woman in the red dress with the really tall guy?"

"Yes. See how he looks *over* her, not *at* her?"

"Yeah. So?"

"He's not really interested in that particular woman."

"How can you tell?"

She smiled, feeling more comfortable now that she they were talking about her area of expertise. "His body language. He holds her loosely, his hands barely grazing her hips. And no body contact. They're at least six inches apart. The fact he isn't looking directly at her clearly indicates he's already scoping out another woman."

"Really. You can tell all that just by looking at them?"

She turned to him and nodded. "Yes."

With a shrug, he said, "You're probably right. Places like this are known to be meat markets. And some guys like to have a lot of women to choose from."

"Is that why you brought me here?" Stupid question.

"Nah. I said some guys, not all guys. Besides, I've got the best-looking woman in the place."

Lara snorted and turned to the couples on the dance floor, scanning for more interesting subjects. She'd have to keep her wits about her tonight so she could remember everything she saw. When she returned home, she could type up her observations.

"Tell me more. What else do you see?" he asked.

"The area over by the bar. That's where the male will size up available females before making his choice."

"Why?"

"Typical male response. Males are hunters. Their primary mission is continuation of their species. They always look for the most attractive woman in the crowd. If he captures her, if they have chemistry, he knows he can bond with her."

Now it was Mark's turn to laugh. "I can guarantee you that ninety-nine percent of the guys in here aren't looking for a wife."

She shook her head. "No, not a wife. A mate. Someone to have sex with. Good sex, at least to a man, equals a good mate and therefore continuation of his line. Doesn't mean he wants to spend all eternity with her. In fact, it's exactly the opposite. The male of the species deals in quantity, not quality. The more women he can spread his seed among, the more likely his lineage will continue."

"In other words, fuck 'em and go on to the next one."

"Exactly."

She could have laughed at his affronted look.

"Whoa. That's kind of harsh."

Lara smirked, knowing all about a man's ego and how easily it could be bruised. "But it's true. If you think about it logically, you'll know it to be true."

"So in other words, my taking you out tonight is because I want to have sex with you."

She choked and grabbed for her drink. "Um, no. That's not what I meant at all." She didn't mean the two of them. She and Mark were…well, whatever they were, it wasn't like that at all.

"Then you've just blown your theory right out of the water, professor."

At a loss for words, she watched the dancers, hoping Mark wouldn't ask her any more questions.

"You prefer that, don't you?" he asked, pulling her attention back to him. He leaned back and slung his arm over the top of the chair. The movement stretched his shirt tight over his chest. She hoped she wasn't drooling.

"Prefer what?"

"Watching, rather than participating."

"I'm an analyst. I love to survey the sexual interactions between people. It's what I do."

"Don't you miss joining in?"

She never had before. Content with her life for many years, Lara had convinced herself she didn't need a man to make her complete. She still felt that way, although if she were going to participate rather than watch, the man sitting across the table from her would be her first choice.

"Not really. I'm satisfied with my life."

"Satisfied, but not happy?"

Mark must have taken psychoanalysis lessons from Nancy. "I didn't say that."

"No, you didn't. Let's dance." He stood and held out his hand.

"I'd rather watch."

"Not this time, professor. This time you participate. C'mon."

She took a quick gulp of her cocktail and stood, hoping she wouldn't pierce his foot with her stiletto heels. Or even worse, fall on her ass.

Mark maneuvered them through the throng of bodies on the dance floor. The music was slow, sensuous, a wailing strain of heartache pouring from the saxophone. He stopped and turned, then gathered her into his arms and pulled her close. His hand rested low on her back. Damn Nancy and her choice of low-cut dresses.

And he could dance. Lord, could he dance. His body fit tight against hers, his fingers splayed on the skin of her back, softly moving up and down against her spine. Her legs wobbled.

"Would you relax? I'm not going to bite you. Unless you ask me to."

His teasing wink was not comforting. His gaze focused on hers and for the life of her she couldn't pull herself away.

Chemistry. Biology. This was the stuff she wrote about, but had never really felt with a man. This self-combusting ache that settled somewhere between her legs, making her breasts tingle, her body fire up in preparation for…

For what? For sex? With Mark? He'd laugh if she told him what she'd been thinking.

They were wedged tight within the throng of heated bodies surrounding them, all swaying to the music. Some men's hands rested on their women's buttocks. Considering they were in public, it was a free-for-all of sexuality that astounded her.

"No one cares," Mark said.

She refocused on his face. "Cares about what?"

"About who is touching who and where they're touching. Everyone's into the music, the moment, concentrating only on the body they're holding onto. Do you see anyone else studying the people around them?"

She scanned the room, realizing that the couples on the dance floor focused only on each other. Okay, maybe she'd been wrong. "No."

"Then look at me, Lara. Feel me, touch me anywhere you want. Let your senses come alive and get into the moment. Get into the reality."

The offer was tempting, but scared her to death. "I'm doing fine."

His lips curled in a delicious smile that made her shudder with a need she hadn't realized existed. "But I'm not."

Blazing a scorching trail of fire, his hands moved up her back to tickle the nape of her neck, then slowly, ever so slowly, traveled downward past the middle of her spine. Then lower, and even lower.

When he rested his fingers against the top of her butt, she gasped, but he held her firm. His fingers burned through her skimpy dress and flimsy panties, scorching her skin.

"Do you want me to stop?" he asked.

She almost blurted the *yes* that automatically hung on her lips. But his hands felt too good. "No."

"Then touch me. Anywhere you want."

Swallowing past the lump in her throat, she moved her hands over his shoulders, delighting in the feel of his muscles tensing against her fingers. Exploring further, she moved her palms over his chest. His heart beat fast and strong against her hand.

So did his erection. Nestled between her legs, he rocked his hips against her and sparks shot off deep inside her sex. He was hard. She turned him on. Holy hell, that was exciting!

"Feel what you do to me?"

"Yes."

"What are your thoughts?"

She didn't want to tell him what her thoughts were. But she couldn't help herself. "It excites me."

His whiskey eyes darkened, the sensual promise within their depths melting her from the inside out. "Good."

He pulled her close to his chest and her nipples beaded to hard points. They ached for his touch, his mouth, anything to douse the fire he'd started. He arched a brow and grinned, then moved against her, mirroring the dancing couples around them.

Each time he ground against her mound, she wanted to drop in a heap of arousal onto the floor. Her clit was in a knot, her pussy pulsing. Juices ran from her slit onto her panties, readying her for a sensual assault she truly wanted but knew she wasn't going to get.

Really, how could people take this sexual teasing? The academic part of her mind wanted to take notes, to jot down every thought, every sensation running through her body. The woman part of her wanted to rip Mark's clothes off and have her way with him right here, right now.

She was pathetic. One dance, one hot body rubbing against hers and she was toast.

"Let's go," he said, moving away from her and leaving her chilled and wanting.

She thought he was tired of dancing, but instead of

returning to their seats he led her out the door and back to his car.

That was it? One drink, one body-melting dance and they were done? Her body was aroused to the point of pain, her panties wet and her nipples desperately trying to bore a hole through her dress.

And now she was going home?

What a disappointment! She slid into the seat of his SUV, remembering now why she didn't date. The reality was never as good as the fantasy.

He drove her home in virtual silence, the tension between them palpable. Lara glanced over at him, hoping he'd smile or make some kind of eye contact.

Nothing. His jaw was clenched tight and he gripped the steering wheel like he was trying to maneuver through an obstacle course. By the time they reached her house, she was prepared for him to slow down, toss her out and speed away.

Instead, he parked, walked up the sidewalk with her and waited while she fished for her keys. When she got the front door open he fit his hand on the small of her back and gently propelled her inside, following her.

He shut the door. Locked it.

She turned around, planning to ask him what he was doing, when he grabbed her by the shoulders and pulled her against him. He didn't say a word, but his eyes spoke volumes. His pupils were dilated, his breathing heavy and erratic.

He brushed her hair away from her face and lowered his mouth to hers.

She expected a gentle touch of his lips, like the last time.

That wasn't what she got.

His lips crashed down against hers and he tightened his hold on her, slipping his tongue inside and licking the inner recesses of her mouth. He drank from her lips like a man in the throes of desperation. She welcomed the onslaught because she was insanely hungry for his touch.

Lara melted in his arms, grabbing his shoulders and then winding her arms around his neck to tangle her fingers in his hair. He groaned against her lips and kissed her deeper, harder, ravaging her mouth in a way that left her unable to take a breath.

Not that she cared. This was passion. Pure, unadulterated mating of two bodies with explosive chemistry. She'd never had it before, had no idea it could be like this.

Now that she'd discovered it, she wanted more. So much more.

His hands moved frantically over her body, heating her blood wherever he touched. His heart raced against her breast, the rapid staccato beat matching her own.

She tore at his shirt and pulled it from the waistband of his pants, sliding her hands under the fabric so she could make contact with his skin. His stomach quivered and his breath caught and held. She could entice that kind of reaction from him?

Wow. For the first time in her life, she felt wanton and desired.

Mark pulled his mouth from hers and rained heated kisses across her jaw and down her neck. She shivered, goose bumps popping up on every inch of her skin. When he sank his teeth lightly into that spot between her neck and shoulder, she whimpered and scraped at his back with her fingers.

His skin was on fire. Her body was fully engulfed in flames. She needed that inferno doused and now.

Mark tasted the sweet skin of Lara's neck again, his body hard and aching to sink between the soft flesh of her thighs. This he hadn't planned on, had no way to fight it. She fired him up hotter than a breaking story, and right now all he wanted to do was make love to her, article or no article.

The rest he'd worry about later.

Reaching behind him, he pulled her arms from around his

back and moved her a bit so he could look at her.

Her lips were swollen from his demanding kisses, her hair mussed from his fingers tangling in the silken tresses. Her nipples were clearly outlined against the flimsy dress, erect and begging for his touch. He wanted his mouth on the perky tips, wanted to taste her there. Hell, he wanted to taste her everywhere.

If he were polite he'd ask her permission, ask if she wanted to make love, ask where her bedroom was.

Fuck it. He wanted her and her body sure as hell was giving off the same signals. Without a word he swept her up into his arms and walked through an open doorway.

Ah. Bedroom. He laid her on the bed, taking a moment to admire the view of her long legs, gorgeous hips and breasts.

But he knew with Lara he'd have to tamp down his urges a bit. Throwing her dress up and plunging into her wouldn't be a wise choice. That might be exactly what he needed, but she needed much more. And he'd damn well planned to give her everything she needed, and then some.

He'd think about the whys of that later.

Easing onto the bed next to her, he let his hands roam freely over her body, not wanting her to change her mind at the last minute.

"You're beautiful," he murmured, burying his face in her neck and nuzzling against her soft hair.

"Am not," she whispered.

"Are too." He slid his hands underneath her and pulled her so they lay on their sides, facing each other. When he swept his palm over the material covering one breast, she gasped.

He caressed the distended bud through the thin material covering it, rewarded with her whimpering moan. When he closed his mouth over her breast, she cried out and threaded her fingers through his hair, holding him closer.

The taste of silk and woman was intoxicating. The taste of

Lara was intoxicating. More so than any woman he'd ever touched. He was in way over his head with a woman like her. Eagerness and innocence made her lethal, dangerous.

Wherever he touched, she responded fervently. Her whimpers and moans drove him crazy. His cock throbbed, insistent on having its way, and he was finding it difficult to win out over his demanding libido.

"Lara, look at me."

Her eyes tightly closed, she didn't want to open them. The sensations were indescribable, delicious and wicked, like her fantasies. She didn't want to open her eyes and find out none of this was real. But she did as Mark asked, shocked to see his darkly aroused gaze. When he thrust his hips against her, she gritted her teeth to keep from crying out in ecstasy.

"I want you."

She wanted to ask him to say it again, she'd heard it so infrequently in her lifetime. How did one respond to a statement like that? "Thank you."

He laughed. "Thank you? How about you want me too?"

"That's kind of obvious, Mark. You can tell by my body's biological response to you."

He'd show her a biological response or two. He slipped the thin straps of her dress over her shoulders and down her arms. Her bra followed next, revealing her small breasts. She fought the urge to cover them with her hands, but he pushed them away. Her tiny pink nipples were gorgeous. No way was he going to allow her to cover them.

"Your body's biological response, huh? You mean, like these hard nipples?" He petted one and it puckered and stood up as if reaching out to him.

"Yes."

"And are you wet for me, Lara?"

Oh, God. She couldn't answer that. "I…I…"

His fingers seared her leg, then blazed a forest fire up to her thigh. When he slipped his knee between her legs and ran his fingers further upward, she couldn't hold in the groan of pleasure.

He made short work of sliding her panties off. She was on fire, craving his touch, desperately needing his hands, his mouth, his body on her.

She thought it couldn't get any better. But it did. Right when he cupped her sex with the palm of his hand. She shuddered, her body writhing against him.

"Oh yeah, you're wet all right."

Mortification mixed with excitement as he slowly moved his hand over her aching clit. Sparks shot into her belly and she silently begged him to send her over the edge. She was close, so very close.

"I'll bet if I pet you a little bit you'd come all over my hand, wouldn't you, wildcat?"

He really was psychic. "Yes. No. I don't know, maybe."

"Shh, quit talking. Just feel, Lara. Let me please you."

Please her? He was damn near killing her! But she bit her lip to keep from saying anything more. Until he touched her again. Then she couldn't hold back her response.

"Oh Mark, yes. That feels so good. Right there, yes, there."

She couldn't help talking now, needing him to caress that magical spot.

"There? Tell me, wildcat. Do you like it when I touch you there?"

"Oh, yes."

"Soft, like this, or a little harder?"

His voice was as seductive as his fingers, both sending her spinning out of control. "Yes, like that. Now faster."

His husky laugh had her shivering and rocking against him.

"That's it baby, come for me."

She'd never done that before. Never had an orgasm in front of a man. But the roller coaster was heading downhill now and she could do nothing to stop it. His fingers coaxed a response she couldn't have denied if she tried. When he slipped two fingers inside her and grazed her clit with his thumb, she exploded, screaming as her climax raged through her like an out of control train.

She clung tight to Mark's arms as he continued his carnal assault. He didn't let up until she relaxed her hips and fought for breath.

Then he pulled her against his chest, his hard-on rigid against her thigh.

It had never been like that. She'd never seen stars when she came, she'd never told a man what she wanted, despite all her research.

Wow.

Not much of a vocabulary for a Ph.D., but it was the best she could come up with right now.

Chapter Five

ꕥ

Mark fought for restraint, his body coiled tight with the need for release. A release he was desperate to spill inside Lara.

He was right. Lara was a wildcat in disguise. Verbal and exciting and so goddamn sexual she nearly had him coming in his pants, something he hadn't done since puberty. Her whimpers and moans and the way she told him exactly how she wanted him to touch her was more stimulating, more arousing, than any woman he'd ever been with before.

The way she came apart in his arms made him crazy with the desire to rip off that flimsy little silk thing she wore and plunge deep and hard inside her.

And that's exactly what he was going to do.

Only a knock sounded at the door before he could. Lara's eyes flew open and she clenched his arms.

"You expecting someone?" he asked.

"Uh, no. It's late. I don't get visitors."

"What about Bob?" The guy Mark wanted to conveniently forget about, but obviously hadn't. Then again, Lara sure had.

She frowned. "Bob?" Then her eyes widened. "Oh, Bob! No, it wouldn't be him."

The pounding at the door continued. Lara stood and brushed the wrinkles from her dress, her face coloring. "I'd better see who it is."

"You do that." In the meantime, he'd do some math calculations…anything to make his throbbing erection subside.

And while he was at it, he should exit Lara's bedroom, just in case it was Bob at the door.

He stepped out in time to see Lara trying to shoo her friend Nancy out the door. The attractive brunette peered over Lara's shoulder and grinned, then waved.

"Hey there, Mark. How's it goin'?"

It was going fine until you showed up. "Great. How are you?"

"Sorry to interrupt, but I left my bag here earlier and I've got to have it for work." She brushed past Lara, winked at Mark and said, "I am so sorry for interrupting."

"No problem." Actually it was a huge problem. The huge part he was attempting to cover up right now. He jammed his fingers through his hair and blew out a sigh loaded with frustration.

Lara stood at the doorway, her lower lip firmly in the grasp of her teeth. She looked first to Mark, then to Nancy, and said, "Nance, wanna stay for some coffee or something?"

Bag in hand, Nancy shook her head as she headed for the door. "Are you insane? You two obviously want to be alone. I'm outta here."

Lara grabbed her arm. "You don't have to leave so soon. We were just—"

"I know what you were just doing and I feel awful for barging in. Now get back to doing it and forget I was even here." She hugged Lara and ran out, giggling with yet another mumbled apology.

By the time Lara closed the door and turned to Mark, he pretty much figured that ignoring Nancy's interruption wasn't going to happen. Whatever heat they'd exchanged had now cooled considerably.

"I'm sorry," she said, looking more at the furniture than she was at him.

"No big deal. It's late and I have a family thing to do tomorrow anyway." He stepped to the door.

"But you…that is, I did but you didn't and I…"

He laughed at her discomfort. "Don't worry about it. We'll

take care of that next time."

"Next time?"

"Yeah. I'm busy tomorrow, but how about Monday? I could come over, we could share a pizza, just talk a little. Or maybe you'd like to go out somewhere."

"Um, you want to go out with me again?"

Mark wondered who'd knocked the hell out of Lara's self-esteem. "Of course I do. That is, if you want to."

"I guess. I mean, sure, I'd like that."

"Great. Call you Monday." Before she could stutter out another sentence, he pulled her into his arms and kissed her, long, hard and so deeply that his cock sprang to life again. He'd better get the hell out of there before he did have his turn at release. This was all happening too fast. He had to be more subtle.

Logic warred with his brain, and since his brain currently resided in his aching dick, it was a helluva battle. But he finally pulled away. "Night, Lara."

"Night, Mark."

She closed the door and he slipped into his SUV. Sexual tension still clung to every part of his body.

Lara had surprised the hell out of him tonight. First, she looked nothing like she usually did. Not that there was anything wrong with her before, but he'd found that harried and frazzled look indicative of her scatterbrained personality. And actually kind of sexy.

Yet listening to her talk at the club tonight, so confident in her assessment of sexual mores and body language, impressed him. Maybe he'd have to sit in on one of her lectures, learn a little bit more about Dr. Lara McKenzie.

Only to play the game better, of course. Once she agreed to do the article with him, their relationship would be strictly business.

His main goal was his career. Success was just around the

corner, he just had to play his cards right.

Lara's innocence and naiveté should make that part easy.

And if he kept telling himself that, maybe he'd start to believe it.

* * * * *

Lara refused to watch the clock. She had work to do. Only a teenager would pace the house waiting for a boyfriend to show up. First off, she was way past the teenage years, and second, Mark wasn't her boyfriend.

Nevertheless, he'd been due to arrive a half hour ago and still hadn't appeared.

"Quit doubting yourself, Lara. He's going to show up."

She was going to have to stop talking to herself. But old insecurities had reared their ugly heads, making her doubt her abilities to attract a man. It had been a long time since she'd been involved with anyone, and certainly no man had ever given her the shattering orgasm that Mark had.

Nancy had been right, much to her chagrin. He had slipped his hand up her dress and given her an ear-splitting orgasm that night. Her body heated at the thought of what she'd allowed him to do, how easy it had been to take her over the edge.

And then he'd left without satisfaction. Unless he hadn't been as turned on as she had.

No, he had been. She'd felt it. Boy, had she felt it. Quite impressive too. Bob would be jealous.

A giggle escaped and she wound her arms around herself, feeling stupid for standing there dressed up at six o'clock on a Monday night.

She should be working. Okay, she'd tried to work all day. But work led to sexual thoughts, and sexual thoughts had led to images of her and Mark and the things they could do together.

How long had it been? Too damn long to remember. Not since that disastrous relationship in grad school. Larry Unger.

Tall, blond, good-looking. Sports star, too. Track or football or something like that.

He'd clung to her for an entire semester. They'd seen each other every day. He'd been so sweet to her, hugging her, kissing her, taking her places.

The lovemaking hadn't been spectacular, but that had been as much her fault as his. Still, she'd thoroughly enjoyed having a guy like Larry pay attention to her. They'd grown so close they even did homework together. She'd helped him with all his papers.

He'd graduated with honors.

And then she'd never heard from him again.

Lara vowed to never get involved with a man again after that disaster. And she'd held herself to that vow. Until she met Mark.

But Mark was different. She'd already given him the interview. He'd been the one to ask to see her socially. He had no ulterior motives other than interest in her as a person.

What a refreshing change. She'd like to be able to trust a guy. She'd been so dumb back then, so blindly trusting.

Nice not to have to worry about that happening again.

Lara jumped at the sound of the doorbell, her heart thumping against her chest. Really, this heart-pounding, sweat-inducing panic attack was ridiculous. A man coming over shouldn't thrill her this much.

But it did. She opened the door and sighed. A guy shouldn't be able to look so good dressed in a simple pair of blue jeans and a sleeveless shirt. Yet, Mark did. "Hey there."

"Hey yourself. You look gorgeous."

She looked down at her plain yellow sundress and wondered what he saw that she didn't. He was the one who looked good enough to eat.

And didn't that thought just gel in her mind and conjure up all kinds of wicked images? "Thanks. You look pretty darned good yourself."

Mark stepped in and pulled his hand from behind his back, producing a dozen coral roses. She stopped breathing.

"Thought you might like these."

Like them? No one had given her flowers before. Ever. With hands that had begun to shake, she took the flowers. "Thank you. They're lovely. I'll just go put them in a vase. Please, sit down and make yourself comfortable."

She rolled her eyes as she walked into the kitchen. She'd just sounded like a fifties sitcom wife. *Please sit down and make yourself comfortable*? She wondered if there were any books on how to carry on a social conversation without sounding like a moron.

"Would you like a drink?" she hollered, arranging the roses in a vase of water.

"Not right now."

Lara shrieked as Mark slipped his arms around her waist.

"You scared me!" She started to turn, but he held her tight.

"Don't move. I want to smell you."

When he pressed his lips against her neck and inhaled, she shivered and nearly dropped the vase. Setting it carefully on the countertop, she braced her hands on the sink, fighting back the desire that washed over her. His body pressed full-length against her back, denim jeans brushing her legs and setting her afire.

He moved his hands over her waist, down her hips, squeezing the flesh there until her legs shook.

"I didn't mean to start anything," he whispered, his voice husky and aroused. His erection nestled against her buttocks, creating a wet arousal between her legs.

"Yes, you did."

"Okay, maybe I did. Maybe I couldn't wait to get my hands on you. Want me to step away? We could sit down in the living room and talk about books and stuff."

Books and stuff? Was he insane? His body tucked against hers had her thinking myriad thoughts, none of which centered around sitting in the living room and talking about books.

Emboldened by his desire for her, she leaned back and cupped his neck. "I don't want to talk about books and stuff. In fact, I don't want to talk about anything at all."

"Good answer." He spun her around and pulled her against him. His erection brushed the sensitive spot between her legs and she nearly died from the sensations arcing through her.

When his mouth came down over hers, she grabbed for his hair and held him close, searching out his tongue with her own.

She was starving. Literally starving for this kind of intimacy. It had been so long…correction, it had never been like this. She'd never felt this way about a man before, and she welcomed every sensation, both deliriously sexual and profoundly emotional.

Her desire for Mark had become an all-consuming passion that threatened to swallow her up and leave nothing behind.

And she loved it. Wanted it. Needed this more than she needed to breathe.

He dragged his mouth away from her lips and kissed her neck, licking at her earlobe. He whispered, "Tell me to stop if you don't want this."

All the while his hands flipped open the buttons on her sundress, one by one. His knuckles brushed her breasts—how could that be so incredibly arousing?

With two fingers he deftly popped open the front clasp of her bra. When he cupped the globes in his hands, she gasped. "No. Don't stop."

His half-hooded eyes were nearly black. "Make sure this is what you want."

She stilled, wondering what he meant. Was he as insecure as she? No, it wasn't possible. And yet, he'd sounded that way. "This is exactly what I want. Now will you shut up and make love to me?"

A low growl escaped his throat and he kissed her hard, rocking against her sex. He bent down and slowly slipped his hands under her dress, raising goose bumps against her thighs. Her legs trembled when he reached her panties. She nearly fell to the floor when he slipped his fingers under the strings at her hips and pulled them down her legs.

"Wow. When I give a command you sure obey quickly."

His grin was lethal. Wicked and filled with sexual promise. She gulped back the nervous jitters and concentrated only on watching him pull his jeans and shirt off.

He hadn't worn underwear. Holy hell, that was sexy!

His body was magnificent. Tanned, muscular in all the right places, but not overly so. She wanted that body covering hers, wanted to feel his weight against her, inside her.

"We're in the kitchen, Mark."

"So? You can only do it in the bedroom?"

It was the only location she'd had sex so far. "I guess not."

"Ever done it on the kitchen table?"

She looked at the wobbly-legged, chrome and laminate table and envisioned a disaster. "Not sure that's a good idea."

"Fine. I have another idea." He scooped her into his arms and sat her on the countertop.

"My butt is freezing up here." She wriggled to get down, but he laid his hands on her thighs, his fingers tucked just inside the hem of her sundress.

"Not for long." He pushed her back and pulled her legs down over the edge, then kneeled.

"Oh God."

"Oh yeah."

He started at her knees, touching and placing light kisses against her skin until she wanted to scream at him to get up and fuck her. Then again, there was nothing more thrilling than seeing this dark-haired devil's face between her legs.

As he moved upward, he lifted her dress. Inch by agonizing inch. When he licked her inner thighs, she arched her back and let out a low moan.

"Talk to me, Lara," he murmured against her thigh. "I like it when you make noises."

Good thing. She wasn't quiet. Especially when he put his mouth over her sex. Then she wasn't quiet at all. She moaned, long and loud.

He chuckled, then placed his mouth on her clit and sucked. She nearly toppled off the counter. Gripping the edge with her fingers, she held on, her body tense with the need for release.

His mouth was warm, wet. His tongue was so magically talented that she wondered if he'd written the book on oral sex.

"Yes, Mark. Lick me like that." She gave instructions, letting him know exactly where to put his mouth, his tongue, his hands. He followed every one to the letter, taking her to the brink and then moving away.

"Dammit, I'm so close."

He stopped and she lifted her head to look at him. "Good. Now watch me."

She did, unable to tear her gaze away from the sight of him. His eyes stayed focused on hers as he moved his mouth over her sweet spot, then licked her like she was an ice-cream cone.

The visual coupled with the sensation was more than she could bear. She tensed, then toppled, screaming as she catapulted into a climax.

The orgasm rocked her. Quick and intense, she hadn't expected it to be like that. And yet one touch of his hot mouth against her sex and she went off like a firecracker.

"My, my, my, somebody sure needed that." He rose and stepped between her legs, a satisfied smirk on his face.

Lara fought for breath. She sat up and kissed him, the lingering taste of her still on his lips. Need built within her again. "I know someone else who needs a little release."

"Damn straight woman. Get to releasing me." He winked and pulled her down off the counter.

His tone was light and teasing, but Lara felt the tightly coiled tension through his arms and body. His erection was steely hard against her belly. He'd already made her come twice without getting off.

That was going to change, and right now.

"Come with me." She picked up his discarded clothes, grabbed his hand and led him out of the kitchen.

Chapter Six

ꙮ

Did the woman not know how sexy she was? Her hips swayed gently from side to side as she led him into her bedroom. Her yellow sundress with the big red flowers was half unbuttoned, and damned near transparent. The outline of her naked ass was clearly visible in the light shining from the lamp.

He still tasted her on his lips, sweet and musky and driving him crazy. His cock twitched, aching and filled with the need for release. Even getting himself off the other night after they'd been interrupted hadn't relieved his desire to plunge hard and deep inside Lara's wet heat.

She stopped at the edge of the bed and turned around. God, she took his breath away. Her lips were swollen from his kisses, her hair mussed up and the whole package was sexy as hell.

She sat and beckoned him toward her. He moved forward, his erection nearly touching her lips.

Glancing at his cock, she grinned, then looked up at him. "I missed tasting you the other night. I don't want to miss it now."

Oh, God. If she sucked him, he might not be able to hold on for long. That's all he'd thought about the other night. Her mouth on his cock, teasing him, taking all of him into that gorgeous mouth of hers until he went off.

She rested her head against his hip and wound her fingers around his shaft, slowly stroking from base to tip. He fought for breath.

Then she replaced her hands with her mouth, slowly covering the head of his cock with her lips.

"Christ, Lara!" he hissed.

She sucked him like she was a master, varying her tempo,

taking him to the brink and then pulling back to make eye contact with him.

It was the most erotic experience he'd ever had. She definitely wrote the book on blowjobs.

"Enough," he said, pulling away, afraid he'd come in her mouth and then pass out in delirium. "I want to come inside you. I want to feel your heat around my shaft."

Her eyes had darkened, her lips swollen. The wicked dress she wore had buttons all the way from top to bottom, driving him crazy with the desire to have her like that, still wearing that dress.

He intended to chase that desire. He pulled her upright, then wound his arms around her waist and lifted her. Moving around to the side of the bed, he deposited her on her back. Then he climbed up and knelt between her legs.

"That dress," he said.

She frowned. "What about it?"

"I want to fuck you while you're wearing it. It turns me on."

Her eyes widened. "It does?"

"Yup." The few buttons he'd undone earlier only made him crazier. So damn sexy.

He started with the button below her breasts, slowly popping it open so he could spread the material to the side. "You have gorgeous breasts, Lara."

"They're small."

He laughed, then showed her how much he liked them by leaning forward and capturing one tip in his mouth, laving it with his tongue until she was panting. Then he did the same to the other, squeezing the globes together so he could lick both nipples.

She grasped his hair, tugging him closer. Sensing she needed more, he grazed his teeth over her nipples and she cried out.

"Please, Mark, now."

He agreed. He couldn't wait any longer. He searched his jeans pocket and found a condom, quickly sliding it on. Pushing her legs apart, he slid her dress up over her hips, admiring her glistening sex, then settled over her.

He slipped inside her with one thrust at the same time he took her mouth in a searing kiss. She moaned against his lips and wrapped her legs around him.

Christ, she was tight. Virginal-tight, squeezing his cock in a vise of pure pleasure. He stilled, afraid he'd embarrass himself by coming immediately. But his balls were rock-hard and tight against his body, ready to shoot a huge load of cum inside her. He fought for control, breathing deeply through the sweet pulses of her pussy contracting around his shaft.

Being inside her was heaven and hell, sublime and torturous. She moved against him fluidly, perfectly, her moans taking him higher and higher. With unashamed abandon she touched him, caressed him, pulled him close and kissed him with such passion he was afraid he might go crazy.

How could a woman he clearly had no intention of keeping be so damn perfect?

Lara gasped at the unfamiliar sensations, emotion tangling with the purely physical reaction to Mark's lovemaking. With every thrust, he touched her deeply, drawing a response she'd never known she could give. She let it all go with him, like she never had before. Allowing herself the freedom to respond to his every movement was a liberating experience.

She'd fight the questions and doubts later. Now she just reveled in her body's response to this fabulous man making love to her.

"Harder," she commanded, pleased when he eagerly responded by quickening his pace and thrusting deeper. Whatever she asked for, he gave, time and time again.

"You keep talking to me like that, urging me to fuck you faster, I'm gonna come," he warned.

She grinned and kissed him, loving the feel of his heart racing madly against her breast. "Then do it. Fuck me harder, Mark. Make me come with you."

She'd never been this wanton, this open, this willing to tell a man exactly what she wanted. And yet with Mark, she was so at ease it almost frightened her.

So many thoughts ran through her mind. Thoughts of how it felt to have Mark inside her, what it meant to her, wondering what it meant to him.

Too many things to think about now. She'd deal with all that later. Now was the sensation, the culmination. "I'm close, Mark. I want it deeper."

With a dark grin he complied, his movements relentless as he pulled back and powered hard and deep, grinding his pelvis against the tight knot of her clit. She cried out his name as her orgasm washed over her, the pulses squeezing his cock tight, pulling him even deeper inside her. With a loud groan he followed along with her, clutching her tight while he jerked in release.

The room went silent, save for their rasping breaths. Mark moved to the side, still inside her, and threw his leg over her hip to keep her close. Lara rested her ear against his chest, listening to his heartbeat go from raging fast to normal.

He didn't speak, just held her and caressed her back. Lara started to worry when the minutes ticked by and he hadn't said a word.

It had been monumental for her. But what about for him? She hated to ask. Wouldn't ask. That would be too needy and she wasn't about to start their relationship requiring constant reassurance that she'd been acceptable in the sack.

Okay, maybe she *was* that needy. "Mark?"

"Yeah."

"You doing okay over there?"

"Yep."

"Anything you wanna talk about?"

Silence. She chewed her bottom lip, waiting for a reply.

Finally, he spoke. "This is one of those woman things, right?"

"Woman things?"

"Yeah. That whole afterglow thing where we're required to dissect the sex and talk about how good it was for both of us."

"Uh, no, not really." When would she learn to keep her big mouth shut?

"C'mon, Lara. It was great. I came, or didn't you notice?"

He couldn't really be serious. She lifted up onto her elbows and peered at his grinning face. Then he winked and she smacked his arm. "Jerk."

Laughing, he tickled her ribs. "Couldn't help it. You got all serious on me for a second."

"Oh please. Like men don't ask if it was good for us."

"This one doesn't. I heard your screams."

"I could have been howling from the agony of boredom."

He shifted, moving her onto her back and holding her arms up over her head. "You lie. You were in the throes of ecstasy."

Tossing out a snort, she shook her head. "I was on the verge of falling asleep."

He kissed her, his tongue torturing hers until warmth spread between her legs.

"Wanna bet? I can make you yell again."

If this was foreplay, she was all for it. "What's the bet?"

"Loser cooks dinner."

"You're on," she said, then sighed as his mouth covered hers.

Good thing she liked to cook.

* * * * *

Mark watched Lara laboring over the stove, feeling supremely satisfied with his ability to please her. Yeah, he'd made her scream all right. Long and loud, howling like a wild animal.

Damn, it had been good. So good it scared the shit out of him. Now, sitting here all domestic-like and watching his woman fix dinner, he was almost…dare he even think it? He was almost comfortable.

Visions of nightly dinners and him doing the crossword puzzle while gazing longingly at Lara over the table had him shuddering.

He shook his head to clear his wayward thoughts. This whole thing with Lara was a means to an end, a scam, and nothing more. He'd try to keep it as low-key as possible so that when the time came for him to end things, they'd have both enjoyed some fun and that would be the end of it.

"What are you cooking?"

She turned her head and smiled, warmth emanating from her clear green eyes. "Spaghetti. You like it?"

"Hell yeah."

How could watching her stir sauce be so arousing? He adjusted the growing bulge in his jeans. "So, about the differences between men and women…"

She frowned. "Huh?"

Great. And he called himself a writer? About as subtle as a bomb drop there. "Remember what we were talking about after sex? That need for women to be reassured?"

She sipped the sauce off the edge of the spoon and then nodded. "Oh yeah. What about it?"

"What do you think?"

"I think men like to be reassured about their prowess in bed as much as women do. They just approach it differently."

Now they were really cooking. "How do you mean?"

Lara leaned her hip against the counter. "Women want to

know that we've pleased our man. We also want to be held, stroked and cuddled. To know that we matter to the man who just made love to us. That he wants to be there, that he isn't already thinking of the football game that starts in ten minutes."

Good thing there hadn't been a game on today. Not that he'd have cared. What man in his right mind would trade great sex for sports?

"For a man, he wants to be told that he made the earth move for us, that we came. Other than that, they don't need anything else, and in fact they would prefer we just shut up and not say a thing."

"I don't agree." Even though he did. But the article would have to be a difference of opinion and how the different sexes think about things. This was as good enough a starting subject as any. "I think men worry about all kinds of things after sex. They just aren't as vocal as women."

"Men want to hop out of bed and forget about it as quickly as they possibly can," she countered.

"And women want to talk about every sexual episode for weeks on end."

The corners of her mouth lifted. "You may be right there."

Aha, agreement at last. He pressed the issue. "In fact, women will share every sordid detail of the sex act with their friends. How big was his dick, how long did he last, what he did with his hands, his mouth, how many times he made her come. Men just say they got laid and leave it at that."

"Wrong, bucko. Men are just as descriptive as women. They just don't couch it in flowery terms. They'll talk about her tits, her ass, her pussy, whether it was tight or loose, how good she is at oral sex, how much she participates when fucking." She pointed the spoon at him. "So don't give me that crap about how men just tell their friends they got laid. I've done my homework on that subject."

They argued throughout dinner, then washed the dishes together and argued more. But at no time was she irritated or angry. In fact, Lara seemed stimulated throughout their entire debate. She smiled, she laughed, she pushed her point home but always listened to his side.

Hell, if there were more women like her maybe he *would* think about settling down someday. And that thought made him want to run like hell.

It was late. He had to get out of there, regroup mentally, and then press home his attack tomorrow.

He planted a kiss on her nape, loving the way she purred against him when he touched her. "I need to go."

She wiped the suds from her hands and grabbed for a towel, then turned around and offered a bright smile. "Okay. I know you have family stuff to do. Sorry to take up so much of your time tonight."

"Hey. Would you knock that off? I loved being with you. Quit apologizing."

"Bossy as hell, aren't you?"

"Yeah. And I like you when you show a little sass, too."

She grinned. "I'll keep that in mind."

She opened the door for him. A summer breeze had picked up, signaling rain. The wind whipped her dress and lifted the skirt up to her thighs. She fought the dress and her hair. God, he wanted to grab her, kiss her and carry her to the bedroom. For a guy who rarely had sex with a woman more than once or twice, the desire he felt for Lara unnerved him.

He'd better leave and now, before he changed his mind and ended up staying.

Forever.

"I'll see you tomorrow, wildcat."

When he kissed her, she jumped back. "Oh, not tomorrow. I'm giving a lecture at the college."

He arched a brow. "Oh yeah? Where and what time?"

"Biology department's lecture hall. Room four twenty. At seven."

"Maybe I'll pop in."

She gazed at him as if he were some giant puzzle she couldn't quite fit the pieces to. "I'd like that."

After she shut the door, he nearly ran to his car, feeling safe once he'd gotten inside and locked the doors.

Lara McKenzie had woven some magical spell around him and turned him into a lovesick idiot. Already he missed her. He couldn't wait to see her again, to inhale her sweet fragrance and listen to the sound of her voice when she spoke. He wanted to touch her skin, feel her long legs wrapped around him and sink so deeply inside her that he'd never surface again.

Christ! He'd known her a week and he was pussy-whipped already. If it weren't for the articles he had to convince her to write with him, he'd be running as far away from her as he could.

Chapter Seven

ꟙ

Lara tried not to scan the crowd for Mark's face, but couldn't help herself. Unfortunately, the bright lights of the auditorium hid most of the faces from her view.

She cleared her throat and answered the question that had just been asked. "Human sexuality has always been a mystery. Both objective in the biological aspect and subjective in the personal or emotional aspect, you can look at a subject from ten different angles, ask any man or woman the same question and you will never get the same answer. Sexuality is as individualistic as appearance. No one short of twins looks the same as anyone else, and no one's sexuality can be summed up by any expert or study. The best you can hope for is an average. The experience itself is unique for every individual, every time."

Her answer reminded her of yesterday's lively argument with Mark. Heat raced through her body as she recalled every intimate moment they'd spent together. She'd even found herself dressing tonight to please him, hoping he'd be here. Where typically she'd wear ankle-length flowing skirts and a loose blouse, tonight she wore one of the trim designer suits Nancy had insisted she buy.

"Any more questions?" she asked, glancing up at the clock. Two hours of lecture, questions and answers. Not bad. And the room was filled to capacity.

When no one else responded, she said, "Thank you so much for your time."

Applause rang out and she smiled, spoke with a few people, then began to gather her presentation materials.

"You look sexy as hell in that suit."

She whirled around to find Mark grinning at her. Her

palms began to sweat and her heart jackhammered against her ribs. "I didn't know you were here."

"I figured wolf whistles during your speech would be inappropriate."

She couldn't hold back her smile. "Probably."

"But I thought about it."

His compliment warmed her. "So, how did I do?"

He leaned against the desk and crossed his arms. "I disagreed with most of what you said."

She smirked. "Then I must have done well with my presentation."

He laughed and slipped his arms around her waist, pulling her against him. "I missed you."

"I just saw you yesterday."

"Ah, casting me aside like a used rubber already, are you?"

Lara threw her head back and laughed. Who was this woman who laughed with a gorgeous man, who felt sexy as hell in her short skirt and thigh-high stockings? This wasn't the Lara McKenzie she knew.

And yet, she felt okay. Better than okay. Fantastic. Desirable, even. For the first time in her life.

"Hey, I need to ask you a question," Mark said.

"Sure."

"Have you told your boyfriend about us?"

Boyfriend? What boyfriend? "Huh?"

He rolled his eyes at her. "You know. Bob."

Oh, God. "Uh, don't worry about Bob."

"Oh, but I do. I don't want to be rolling around in your bed and have Bob storm in and catch us."

She choked back her snort. "That won't happen. Trust me."

"I think you should at least tell him you're dating someone else."

Dating? They were dating?

"I need to tell you about Bob," she said, wondering how she was going to explain this, and hoping he had a sense of humor about the whole thing.

Mark let go of her and sat on the desk. "Okay, tell me."

Where to begin. Should she laugh it off, or approach it seriously followed by an apology for misleading him? "There is no Bob."

He arched a brow. "Huh?"

"There is no Bob. He doesn't exist."

"You made him up."

"No. Well, sort of."

When his eyes narrowed, she knew he wasn't finding this amusing. Might as well get it over with. "Bob is an acronym."

"For?"

This was going to be painfully embarrassing. "Battery-Operated Boyfriend."

It took him a few seconds, then he threw his head back and laughed so loud she was afraid the other lecture halls were going to hear him.

"Your boyfriend is a vibrator?"

He laughed like a damn hyena, and wouldn't stop. Glaring at him, she said, "Really, it's not that funny."

"No, it's not just funny, Lara, it's goddamn hysterical! I can't believe you told me that. His, or rather, its name is going to be in the article, too."

Oh, hell.

"Care to explain why you told me you had a boyfriend?"

Not really. "You asked. I didn't want to seem, I don't know, like a loser." Which she really was and now he knew it.

"Just because you aren't dating anyone exclusively doesn't mean you're a loser, babe. I'm not involved with anyone, either."

Which meant he didn't think what was between the two of them could be classified as involvement. "I see." She tried to keep the disappointment out of her voice, but she could tell from the way he tilted his head that he read her body language.

"You're upset."

"No, I'm not." *I'm a child and I need to grow up. This isn't the man of your dreams, Lara, this is a guy you're fucking and having some fun with.*

"Yeah you are. You're tense."

"Long day. I just need to relax a bit."

"I can help you with that."

She met his lascivious gaze. Determined to block out her emotions and enjoy the moments she had with him, she said, "Ah, yes. I'll just bet you can."

"Need a ride home?"

"My house is only a block from here. I walked." In heels, too. Never again.

"Come on. I'll drive you."

She stuffed her paperwork in her briefcase, pleasantly surprised when Mark took it from her hands and carried it out to his SUV. She slid into the leather seat and crossed her legs, tugging the damned short skirt over her thighs. Nancy and her bright ideas about clothing.

Then again, she had to admit the clothes did something to her. Tonight she'd actually felt naughty. The silk stockings caressed her legs and the tops of the hose rubbed against her thighs. All she could think of during the lecture was Mark, kneeling in front of her, lifting her skirt and slowly rolling down her stockings.

Not a good mental picture when one had to remain composed in front of a hundred plus people.

"You look hot, Lara."

She glanced over at him. His eyes were hooded, half-closed and it was dark, but the way his gaze moved over her body told her what he was thinking.

"Thank you."

When he reached for her leg, resting his palm over her knee, she fought back a gasp. Arousal moistened her sex, readying her for him. Her nipples tingled against the barely there bra she'd worn under her silk blouse.

With a death grip on the armrest she watched his fingers move upward. Slowly, he walked them closer to the hem of her skirt. When he got there, he used the side of his hand to slide the skirt up.

Her breath hitched, stopping just short of a complete inhalation. She held it, waiting for his response.

Arching a brow when he reached the tops of her stockings, he said, "Thigh-highs?"

"Uh-huh."

"Damn, that's fucking hot!"

And now she couldn't breathe at all because he'd moved his hand further upward, between her legs, teasing at the edge of her panties.

"You're wet."

"Yes."

"You want me?"

"Yes."

"Now?"

"Now?" He couldn't be serious. They were in the parking lot of the Biology Department building. There were…she looked around. No cars or people in sight.

"Lara?"

When had she been adventurous in her life? When had she taken naughty little risks like this? When had she been more sexually stimulated by a man?

Never was the answer to all her questions.

"Push your seat back, Mark."

Other than their heavy breathing, the whirr of the electric seat was the only sound. She climbed over the center console and straddled him.

Mark's eyes widened. Not quite what he had in mind, but this would certainly do. Lara's wet panties pressed against his erection as she situated herself over him.

"God Almighty, Lara!" he hissed when she rocked against him. She shrugged out of her suit jacket, the buttery-soft silk of her blouse tickling his cheek. The crisscross cut provided a glimpse of the most tantalizing bra he'd ever seen. Hardly even a bra, actually. Just a wisp of see-through material that barely covered her nipples.

He wondered if her panties matched.

Her skirt stretched between her thighs, affording him a glimpse of decadent panties that, sure as hell, matched the bra.

"Get those panties off," he said, suddenly needing to be inside her.

She gripped his shoulders, her green eyes glassy with desire. "Kind of difficult in the position I'm in."

"Then I hope you didn't pay a ton of money for them, because they're coming off one way or the other."

Her swift intake of breath wasn't an objection. "Do it."

Keeping his gaze focused on hers, he reached for the string on the side of her hip and wrapped it around his fist, then yanked. She cried out when the elastic gave way with a single rip, then licked her lips, panting heavily.

The SUV was uncomfortable as hell, but damned if he was going to wait to get her home. He lifted the skirt over her hips, going mad with the sight of the tuft of red curls between her legs. He reached down and skimmed her flesh. She was as wet as he was hard.

"Lift up, babe," he commanded, then unzipped his pants and pulled out his aching shaft.

She didn't need instructions. She waited, arched above him,

as he grabbed a condom from the console and slid it on. Then she settled over him, moving so agonizingly slow he wanted to grab her hips and plunge his cock fast and hard inside her. Finally, she sat fully on him and began rocking, slowly at first, then picking up the pace.

He pulled her blouse aside, slipping it off her shoulders and burying his face in her breasts. He licked her nipples over the material of her bra and she whimpered, pulling at his hair.

When he tilted his head back to look at her face, she drew closer. Her lips ground against his, her tongue plunging into his mouth at the same time his hips rose to meet her.

The windows steamed. He panted, she panted. Clothes were pulled aside so that skin made contact with skin.

His little wildcat had gone feral on him. She bit his shoulder and pumped away at his shaft until he felt death was imminent.

What a way to go!

Reaching around behind her, he slipped his fingers between her legs, swiping some of the copious juices that seeped from her pussy. He massaged her slit, loving the feel of her bouncing up and down on his shaft, then drew his fingers upward, coating her anus with her own cream.

"Oh, God," she whispered, stilling completely.

"I want to feel inside that hot ass of yours, Lara," he said, desperate to slide inside that tight rosebud and sample her heat.

"Yes," she hissed, bending forward to give him access.

Sufficiently moistened, he slid one finger past the tight muscle of her anus. Her ass gripped him, pulling his finger deeper and deeper while her pussy quivered around his aching shaft.

"Christ, you're tight back there, baby. I'd love to fuck that ass some day." Just the thought of burying his cock deep into her hot, tight cavern had his balls tightening and threatening to explode.

He moved his finger in and out of her, drawing nearly

completely out, then plunging back inside again. Soon he was fucking her ass in earnest.

And she liked it. Man, did she like it. She dug her nails into his shoulders and rode him like a wildcat, tilting her head back and crying out in pleasure that had him ready to burst.

"Now, Mark," she cried, bucking furiously against him. His balls ached with the need for release and he pumped harder and faster. His groan and her keening cries mixed together as they both reached their climax at the same time.

Minutes passed and neither of them moved. He was sweating. So was she. He withdrew from her anus and grabbed one of the tissues on the console. That was as far as he got, though, because he couldn't move a muscle.

Hell, he didn't want to move. Her cunt continued to pulse around him. His crotch was soaked with the combination of her juices and his cum.

Damn that had been good.

"I'm stuck," she finally said.

He opened his eyes and leaned back, searching her face. "Stuck where?"

She smirked. "Well, other than being impaled on your dick, I'd say my legs are wedged pretty tight on either side of the seat. And my foot's asleep."

God, she was beautiful all disheveled like this. Her blouse was open, her breasts exposed. Her hair had gone wild, tumbling out of the clip she'd secured it with and her skirt was hiked high over her hips.

Appreciatively, his cock responded by hardening again.

Her eyes widened and she arched a brow, then lightly licked his lips. "No way in hell, bucko. Get me out of this position and take me home before you fuck me again."

"Is that an invitation?"

"Hell yeah. Now get moving. I'm ready for round two."

* * * * *

Lara tiptoed around her house, picking up pieces of discarded clothing. They'd certainly ripped their clothing off quickly last night, beginning at the front door and making their way through the rest of the house. By the time they'd fallen into bed, there was nothing left to take off.

Mark lay sprawled across her bed, sound asleep.

He didn't snore. A plus for him. The other plus was the sight of his naked ass.

She sighed, unable to believe this gorgeous Adonis found her attractive. Not only attractive, but seemed to really want to spend time with her.

After they'd made love again last night, they'd padded into the kitchen, both of them naked, and fixed peanut butter and jelly sandwiches.

Then they'd spent hours talking. About everything, from her work to his, to the differences in the male and female mind as it related to sexuality.

The fact he was so interested in her work and her thought processes made her smile. He was definitely different than any other man she'd ever known.

His shirt was strewn over his laptop and notes. She picked up the T-shirt and held it to her nose, inhaling the scent so unique to him. With a sigh, she added it to the pile of clothes she was going to wash, then began to tidy up his folders. One fell to the floor and she hurriedly picked up the contents to jam them inside.

But her name on the notes caught her eye. She scanned them quickly, feeling equal parts of guilt and curiosity. Really, she shouldn't be doing this. Then again, why was her name in his notes for *Total Man Magazine*? The article he'd written about her and the masturbation-a-thon had already gone to the publisher.

Lara flopped onto the sofa, her heart racing as she read

what he'd written. It was an outline for a series of articles for the magazine, with them as co-authors. They'd take a subject and he would write a man's viewpoint and she would write a woman's. The feature would run monthly.

Holy hell!

She stood, file folder in hand, and walked into the bedroom.

"Mark, wake up."

He groaned.

"Mark!"

She ignored his perfect body, including his prominent erection when he rolled over onto his back. Blinking one eye open, he smiled at her. "Mornin'."

"Don't you *mornin'* me. What is this?" She tossed the file folder onto the bed next to him.

With a yawn, Mark leaned up on one elbow and peered at the file.

Then his eyes widened. He looked up at her and she read the guilt on his face.

"You've got some explaining to do, Mark."

Chapter Eight

ꟸ

He was busted. Now what was he going to do? His mind wasn't coherent enough to come up with a pack of lies. "I can explain this."

"Then I suggest you get started." She crossed her arms and stared down at him.

He scrubbed a hand over his face and sat up. "It's not what you think."

"You have no idea what I think. Now tell me about those notes."

The tight tone in her voice told him she wasn't too damn happy about finding the outline. Visions of huge paychecks from *TMM* disappeared like a mirage in the desert. He was fucked, and not in a good way.

Best thing to do was to come clean about the whole thing and be done with it. "I'm sorry, Lara. I shouldn't have done it."

"No, you shouldn't have."

"I'll get my things and leave. I'm really sorry." Funny thing was, he meant that. He shouldn't have manipulated her this way. It had been a really stupid idea and he should have just come right out and been honest with her from the start, then lived with whatever her answer was.

He scanned the room for his clothes, hoping she wouldn't throw him out naked.

"Leaving? Why are you leaving?"

"Uh, isn't that what you want me to do?"

She sat on the bed and organized the papers in the file folder. "Of course not. I want to know more about this idea of yours."

Was there anything she did that didn't knock him on his ass with shock? "You do?"

"Yes." She looked down, her cheeks darkening that sexy coral color. "I'm...flattered."

"Huh?"

Her gaze met his, those guileless green eyes making him feel guiltier by the second.

"I said I'm flattered. I wish you had discussed your plan with me, but still, the fact you want to co-author a feature with me every month is quite a compliment."

Following her train of thought, he said, "I hope so. You *are* special. And I was going to talk to you about it. It's just that when we started talking about a few subjects, I got this idea and wanted to jot down some notes. I intended to ask you for your okay before I presented it to *TMM*."

"So, are we going to talk about it now?"

"Do you want to talk about it?"

"Of course. Granted, if I didn't know you as well as I do I would never even think about writing for a magazine like *TMM*. But since I do know you, and you did think of me when planning the articles, I suppose it's a good idea. The opportunity to reach so many male readers with some of my ideas is too good to pass up. I'm honored that you thought of me."

His plan had worked. Hook, line and sinker. She was his, she'd agreed. He should be ecstatic. Instead, he felt lower than dirt.

They ate breakfast, discussed the articles, and Lara excitedly shooed him away for the day so she could get started on the first month's subject matter.

After he left her house, he drove around for about an hour, feeling worse with every passing second.

Never having been one for scruples in the past, he sure as hell picked a fine time to develop some. This wasn't the first time he'd manipulated a subject to get what he wanted.

But Lara wasn't just any subject. She was special. She'd been honest and forthright with him from the beginning. He'd been underhanded and played dirty, manipulating her innocence in the worst possible way.

He was a bastard. And worse, a lying bastard. She deserved so much better.

She deserved a genuine, honest guy who wouldn't lie to and manipulate her. Someone who'd appreciate her intelligence, her humor, her passion, the way she gave one hundred and ten percent of herself to a relationship.

Relationship. That's what Lara thought she was having with him right now. An honest give and take, learning about each other. Even working together.

The excitement of writing for *TMM* had lost all its appeal. Eventually he'd have to tell Lara the truth. And once he did, his career with *TMM* would be over.

His relationship with Lara would be over.

And that hurt. Holy shit, that hurt!

Had he done something even worse than lying to Lara? Had he finally gotten caught in the trap that he swore he'd never get caught in?

Had he fallen in love?

No way. He didn't fall in love. He was too cynical, too damned busy, too focused on his career to let feelings for a woman sidetrack him from his goals.

Certainly it had never happened before.

And no way in hell was he going to let it happen now.

He was a user. Sometimes being a reporter meant people got hurt. It had never bothered him before, so why now?

Because it was Lara he was hurting. And like it or not, she mattered to him.

Fuck! No, she didn't. He wouldn't let her matter to him. He'd use her, do their articles as long as he could, and once he'd proved to *TMM* he was a great writer, they'd never let him go.

Of course once that happened, she'd dump him.

Wasn't that what he wanted? Cut all ties so he could be free?

That's exactly what he wanted. Except the thought of being without her made his gut ache in a way that had nothing to do with guilt and a helluva lot to do with his heart.

Yeah right. He had no heart. Just look at what he planned to do to her. Use her, then cast her aside.

"You are one great fuckin' prize, Whitman," he muttered to himself. She'd hate him when this was over.

Right now, he wasn't too damned fond of himself, either.

* * * * *

Lara grinned as she put the finishing touches on her part of the article.

Something about this felt so right. They were joined together both in work and in play.

Plus, she was giddy as hell and floating on air most of the time. Okay, all the time.

She loved him. How it happened, she couldn't say, but she knew for a certainty that she'd fallen head over heels in love with Mark Whitman.

And he had to feel something for her, too. He was still here. He hadn't gone back to New York after his family reunion. Instead, he had all but moved into her place.

In the past few weeks they'd written four articles for the magazine. More than that, they'd talked. They'd discussed. Even argued, although she preferred to think of it as debating a subject.

And of course, they'd made love. Lots and lots of love, each time more passionate and filled with tender emotion.

He'd surprised the hell out of her. Frankly, she'd surprised the hell out of herself, too. After the disastrous relationships in her past, she'd never thought she'd be able to trust a man enough to really let loose.

But with Mark, she held nothing back.

Now the big test. To tell him how she felt about him. And hope he didn't run like hell in the opposite direction. But they'd been honest with each other so far. It was only fair that she tell him she was in love with him.

* * * * *

Mark had to tell her. Guilt stabbed at him, every day getting worse and worse. He had to tell Lara the truth.

As much as he'd wanted to run away from his own truth, it stared at him every time he looked in the mirror.

He was a prick. A prick in love with a perfect woman.

Confession time. And once he confessed, he'd beg her forgiveness and ask her for another chance. Because he wanted this relationship with her, as strange and scary as these feelings were.

Sucking in a breath of fortitude, he knocked on her door.

Lara opened it, grinning. "We've got to get you a key. No point in knocking, you practically live here anyway."

Pang, pang, pang went the guilt in his stomach. "Good idea."

"I poured some wine. You want some?"

Yeah, a whole bottle. With a straw. "Sure."

He followed her into the kitchen, never tiring of the sexy sway of her hips. Even dressed in faded gray gym shorts and a skimpy little tank top, she exuded sexuality.

And so completely unaware of it, too. That's what made her so different than any other woman he'd known.

She handed him a glass, then sat at the table with him. "I finished my portion of the last article. Did you send in the first one yet?"

Bang, bang, bang. Remorse burned like a fire-breathing

dragon now. "Yeah. Few days ago."

"Any feedback yet?"

"No."

She wrinkled her nose. "Well, dammit, I'm dying to know what your editor thinks."

"They typically don't respond unless there's something that needs to be changed. If it's good-to-go as is, he'll just run it."

"Oh. Well, see how much I have to learn about the magazine business?"

Yeah. She had a lot to learn all right. Like how to be a lying prick and manipulate your way to the top. He could teach her about that. He was a goddamned expert at it. "You're doing fine."

"Good."

Silence permeated the room. Mark fought for the right way to broach the subject of what he'd done.

"Mark, I have something to tell you."

Good opening. "Okay. I have something I'd like to tell you, too."

Her eyes sparkled with her grin. "Wouldn't it be funny if we had the same thing to say to each other?"

Not a chance of that happening. "Yeah."

"Okay, give me a minute. I'm a mess here from cooking and I need to clean up a bit and change clothes. I'll be right back and then we can talk."

He nodded, pondering his glass of wine and wishing he could crawl into the bottle right now and pull a cork over his head.

Hiding out didn't seem to be an option. As soon as she came back he was telling her the truth.

* * * * *

Lara fussed with her hair and straightened the slinky little skirt and top, hoping it would have the desired effect.

Not bad for a dowdy professor. Tight black skirt, equally body-hugging spandex tube top. If anyone had told her a month ago she'd be dressed this way and about to tell a guy she was in love with him, she would have certified them as insane.

Then again, maybe she was the insane one.

She stood in front of the mirror. Okay, not bad. She might not be a fashion model, but she'd get a rise out of him.

The phone rang just as she was leaving the bedroom. She picked it up, annoyed that whoever was calling was interrupting her confession of love to Mark.

"Doctor Lara McKenzie?"

Lara didn't recognize the gruff voice on the other end of the line. "Yes?"

"This is Jonathan Smitz with *Total Man Magazine*."

"Oh, hello, Jonathan! I'm so glad to finally be able to talk to you!"

He laughed. "Me, too. I just wanted to thank you for agreeing to do the articles with Mark."

"It was my pleasure."

"See? I told him it wouldn't be hard to convince you. And he said you'd be a tough sell. It sure ended up easier than he thought it was going to be."

"Excuse me?"

Jonathan continued, laughter in his voice. "Well, he did say he'd have to get you to fall in love with him before you'd agree to write for our magazine. Glad to know he didn't have to resort to such drastic measures."

Lara's hand trembled and she fought for control of the telephone. "Fall in love with him?"

Jonathan's chuckle reverberated through her nerve endings. "Yeah. Hey, I told him to do whatever it took to get you on board. Glad to know our boy is so persuasive."

She felt sick. Whatever it took? No. She hadn't heard correctly. It couldn't be. Mark wouldn't do that to her. He was different than the other men she'd known. He had to be. His feelings were genuine.

"Anyway, I called to talk to you about your contract with *TMM*."

His voice was nothing more than a buzz in her ears. "I...I have to go, Jonathan. Nice talking to you."

Jonathan started to say something else, but Lara hung up, then plopped onto the bed. Despite the July heat, her entire body chilled.

She closed her eyes and fought back tears. Tears of stupidity that she quickly swiped away.

Humiliation burned in her throat and traveled down into her stomach. Mark had been using her. Using her! The idea to write the articles didn't happen after he'd gotten to know her. He'd come back here with the express purpose of getting her to agree to co-write with him.

He wanted something from her. Ulterior motives. Just like before. She hadn't grown any smarter in the ways of men and relationships. In fact, this one was worse than the first time.

Someone should stamp *gullible* in the middle of her forehead. Although it seemed she already wore it like a neon sign, probably emblazoned on her dumb ass.

How could he do this to her? She thought he cared about her, thought maybe he even loved her. If it didn't hurt so damn bad she'd laugh about that part.

She wasn't loveable. Never had been, never would be. She wasn't meant to have relationships. She should have stayed with Bob. At least Bob wouldn't have hurt her.

A desire to crawl under the covers and curl up into a ball of denial was nearly overpowering. But Mark still sat in her kitchen.

She had to get him out of her house.

Out of her life.

Out of her heart.

Right now.

Fighting for control, she smoothed her hair back and walked into the kitchen. Mark turned to her with a smile on his face.

His smile died.

"What's wrong?"

"That was your editor on the phone."

"Jonathan?"

"Yes."

A wary look crossed his face. "What did he want?"

She stepped around him and leaned against the counter, refusing to go anywhere near him. "Oh, he just wanted to commend you for blindsiding me so brilliantly."

He paled and swallowed, hard. "What do you mean?"

"I mean he told me, Mark. Told me you would have done anything to get me to agree to do those articles."

The chair scraped the floor as he pushed back and stood. Her heart pounded madly against her breast, but she refused to budge as he drew closer. "It wasn't like that, Lara. You've got to believe me."

"Oh, I've got to believe you? I don't think so."

"I wanted to write for *TMM*, I admit. Jonathan said that the only way I could do that was to bring you on board. So I got this stupid scheme in my mind that if I dated you, you'd get comfortable with me and agree to do the articles. But then I got to know you and—"

She held up her hand. "Oh, don't tell me. You got to know the real me and fell madly in love."

"Yes."

Refusing to believe the sincerity in his near whisper, she shook her head. "Too little, too late, Mark. You got what you wanted from me. Four great articles for *TMM*. You'll have to find another woman to write with you now, because our working relationship ends today. In fact, our everything ends right now. Get out."

"Lara, please. Let me explain. I'm sorry. I didn't mean for it to happen this way. I didn't know I was going to fall in love with you."

Her throat constricted with the struggle not to cry. "Do *not* tell me you love me. At least be honest now."

"I am being honest, Lara. I love you."

"Get out. Now. I mean it. Don't ever come back here again. Don't ever contact me again."

She brushed past him, hurried to her bedroom and slammed the door, needing that wall between them. With a shuddering breath she held the tears in while she waited for him to leave, holding back the emotions boiling within her until she heard the final click of the front door.

Only when she was convinced he was gone did she let it all out.

She wouldn't have been surprised if the neighbors heard her sobs.

Chapter Nine

ℵ

"Are you out of your mind?"

Mark stood firm against Jonathan's wide-eyed expression. "I'm serious, Jonathan. Pull the articles."

Two weeks after returning to New York, Mark wasn't any closer to forgiving himself for what he'd done.

There was nothing he could do to change Lara's mind about him. He'd tried to see her, but she wouldn't let him in. Wouldn't take his phone calls, either. No matter what he did or said, she'd never believe in him again. He didn't blame her.

But he could do one thing.

Jonathan's eyes widened. "You're joking. We're going to print in two days."

"Tough. Lara won't sign a contract and is threatening to sue if we run the articles."

"What the hell happened? I thought she was all gung ho about them."

He shrugged and tried to act nonchalant. "Who the hell knows? PMS, maybe? She changed her mind."

"Well, that makes no fucking sense."

Pushing the point home, he said, "She's a woman, Jonathan. They don't make sense."

"Godammit, the article was great. Did you try to convince her to let it run?"

"Yeah. She said she'd sic her attorneys on us if we even attempted to print the article without her permission."

"I thought you'd gotten her to sign the contracts."

Oh, he did. They were in his briefcase, soon to be run

through the shredder. "I thought she had signed them and sent them in herself. Then I found out she hadn't, and sure as hell isn't now."

With a sigh, Jonathan nodded. "Guess this means you're out of a job with *TMM,* Mark. Sorry. No go without Lara McKenzie."

And it was so much less than what he really deserved. "No big deal, Jonathan. See you later."

He walked out of the offices of *TMM,* feeling not the least bit upset about losing the prime opportunity to write for one of the best men's magazines in the country.

He'd get over it. There were other jobs.

But there was only one Lara.

* * * * *

Lara tried to smile for Nancy. She was certain it came out more of an apathetic grimace.

She'd hid it from Nancy as long as she could, but her friend finally figured it out and forced her to tell all about the disastrous episode with Mark.

"Honey, I'm so sorry. I just didn't see it."

Lara nodded. "Neither did I. But it's true."

Nancy grasped Lara's hand and sidled closer to her on the sofa. "You love him, don't you?"

"No."

"Lara."

"I don't." At Nancy's dubious expression, Lara added, "Okay, maybe I thought I was falling in love with him, but I wised up as soon as I found out the truth."

Nancy shook her head. "Just doesn't make sense. He seemed to sincerely care about you."

"Uh-huh. Don't they all? But they all want something."

"You're pretty cynical."

"I've earned the right. He got what he wanted. A series of articles from both our perspectives. Nothing I can do about the ones we'd already written. I did sign a contract."

"Maybe he'll get fired for losing you."

"Doubtful. He's very talented. They'd be crazy to let him go."

"When does the first article come out?"

"It's already out, I think."

"You gonna read them?"

"No. I don't want to be reminded about Mark Whitman ever again."

And yet, two hours later she was browsing the bookstore at the mall, immediately spotting the cover of *TMM*.

She wouldn't look. She wouldn't. Okay, maybe she would. She grabbed the issue and flipped to the table of contents, running her fingers down the titles.

That's odd. No article. And they'd specifically stated in the issue with Mark's interview of her that they'd be following up with regular features including the two of them.

Yet, nothing.

Maybe there'd been a delay.

But something nagged at her. She bought the magazine and took it home, then went through every page.

She found the retraction in small print under the editor's comments.

Correction—The new feature, He Said/She Said, with Mark Whitman and Dr. Lara McKenzie, will not run as indicated in our last issue. We apologize for any inconvenience.

The articles weren't going to be printed. But why? It didn't make sense. She'd had her part done already. All Mark had to do was finish up edits and turn them in. When he'd shared with her the payment for a regular feature, she'd nearly fallen out of the chair.

It was an amazing amount of money. And he'd been excited as a kid about becoming a feature writer for *TMM*.

So where were the articles?

Before she could analyze her reasoning, she picked up the phone and called Jonathan Smitz at *TMM*.

"Doctor McKenzie," he said, his voice filled with caution. "We didn't run the articles, just as you'd dictated."

What the hell was he talking about? "I didn't say not to run the articles."

"Yes, you did. Mark told us you threatened a lawsuit if the articles ran. We canceled the series."

Canceled the series? "I don't understand, Jonathan. I never asked Mark to kill the articles."

Jonathan went silent. "He said you did. That you never signed the contract. That you threatened to sue us if we ran the articles."

But she'd signed the contract. Mark told them to kill the series? Why would he do that? Unless…

No. She was not going to fall for it again. Never again.

But why would he give up the notoriety and fame that would accompany writing for a high-profile magazine like *TMM*? Why?

She closed her eyes and listened to her heart. No matter what, she couldn't deny Mark his success.

"Jonathan, listen to me. I *want* you to run the series."

"Look, Lara, we've already canceled them."

"I signed a contract."

"No, you didn't."

She'd given the signed contracts to Mark. He'd never turned them in. He canceled the articles because of her!

"Overnight me a contract. I'll sign it. I want you to run the first article in your next issue."

"Are you sure?"

"Positive. Obviously we just got our wires crossed here. I promise there's no problem with me writing for *TMM*. Gives me a chance to reach more readers."

"Fantastic! I'll have the contracts drawn up and sent to you immediately."

"Good. And Jonathan? Do me a favor. Don't tell Mark about this. I want it to be a surprise."

When she hung up, she wandered through the house, perplexed as hell by what she'd found out.

Mark had given up his dream for her. He'd given up fame, money, everything. But why would he do that unless his feelings for her were genuine?

Did she dare put her heart on the line again?

* * * * *

Mark opened the issue of *Total Man Magazine* that Jonathan had overnighted to him.

What the hell was Jonathan thinking? He was through with *TMM*. Did they give him a subscription as a consolation prize?

He was about to toss it across the room when words on the cover caught his eye. He blinked and looked again.

He Said/She Said! All About Sex From Opposing Sides Of The Mattress!

Shit! Goddamn, Jonathan! He yanked his cell phone out and quickly dialed Jonathan's number.

"Hey, sport," Jonathan said. "You surprised?"

"Are you insane? What the hell were you thinking running that feature?"

Jonathan laughed. "Calm down. I have a signed contract from Lara McKenzie and her written go-ahead to run the feature."

"What?"

"You heard me. I would have told you, but she made me

promise to keep it a surprise. Hey, you two got something going on or what?"

"Uh, no. She told you to run the articles?"

"Yup. I gotta run to a meeting. Let's talk on Monday about the next series of articles. You're back on board, Mark. And top management really likes your writing. They want to talk to you about doing more work for us."

"With Lara, you mean."

"Well, the feature with Lara is great, but you're a damn good writer. They have a few other things in mind for you to work on solo. I'll be in touch next week."

Mark stared at the phone as if he'd just had an out-of-body experience. That call hadn't just happened. No way in hell would Lara have agreed to run those articles.

She hated him.

Didn't she?

But if she hated him, why did she call Jonathan? And more importantly, why did she ask Jonathan to keep them a secret?

Hope filled the empty void he'd been carrying around for a month.

She loved him. That had to be it.

But why? She shouldn't love him. God knows he didn't deserve it. The first time he'd fallen in love and he'd fucked it up badly. He'd hurt the one person he cared about more than anyone else.

He had to see her, had to ask her why she told Jonathan to print the series.

And maybe, just maybe, if he groveled hard enough, she'd give him another chance.

He shook his head as he jammed things into his overnight bag. Mark Whitman, the guy who'd never fallen in love, was just about to get down on his knees and beg forgiveness from the one woman who'd managed to capture his heart.

* * * * *

Lara grinned at the cover of *TMM*, their feature highlighted in big bold letters.

She chewed her lip, wondering if Mark would be angry with her.

Should she call him? Drive up to New York and try to see him? She'd never taken a chance like this before. Shouldn't with him of all people. But what her head told her to do and what her heart wanted to do were two different things.

He'd stopped the articles because he loved her. Really and truly loved her. She had to believe that to be true. She mattered to him more than money or fame or contracts or *TMM*.

The doubts pounded away at her. Those nagging voices that told her she wasn't loveable. She was plain, a geek too filled with smarts and not enough beauty.

She pushed the doubts away. One thing she'd learned from Mark was tenacity and never giving up.

She jumped when the doorbell rang. Nancy said she might drop by today. But when she pulled the door open, it wasn't Nancy standing there.

Her heart stopped, remembering the very first time she'd seen him. His cocky smile had unnerved her, his wicked grin had disarmed her, and his gorgeous body had awakened the woman in her.

"Hi, Mark."

"Hi, Lara."

They both seemed at a loss for words. She couldn't tell from his blank expression how he felt. "Did you see the feature?"

"Yeah. Can I come in?"

"Oh. Sure. Sorry." She stood aside while he walked by. The sweet scent of him that still lingered throughout her house filled her senses with an aching need to touch him.

"Lara, why did you have the feature run?" he asked as soon

as she shut the door.

"Because you had it pulled."

He frowned and shook his head. "I don't understand."

"I don't either, really. Why did you kill the articles?"

"Because I'd already hurt you enough. There was nothing I could do to take back what I'd done, how I'd deceived you. Except to pull the feature."

"You lost a ton of money. And a chance for fame, too."

His gaze focused on the carpet. "It's only money, Lara. I can live without money, I can live without fame."

She waited. He looked up, his eyes warm and filled with an emotion she dared not name.

"But I couldn't live without your love."

She closed her eyes, waiting for the doubt, the disbelief, to creep into her heart.

It didn't. The only thing there was her love for him.

"I love you, Mark."

His eyes widened. "I don't deserve it. I'm sorry, Lara. I should have told you from the beginning. Then, after I started to care for you, I didn't know how to tell you without losing you. So I lied."

"Don't do it again. I can take anything as long as you're honest with me."

"I was a different person then. You changed me."

"Oh, I did not."

He stepped forward and threaded his fingers through her hair. She died at his touch, wanting him, missing him so much she was starving for him.

"Yeah, you did. I never thought I was the kind of guy to fall in love. My career, making it to the top in my field, that was always first. But then I met you, and you drove me crazy. I didn't want to, but I fell in love with you. And that means more to me, you mean more to me, than any money, any contract, any job I'll ever have."

Her heart was going to burst. "So now what?"

"Now we take it day by day. Open and honest. I don't know where we're headed." He grinned and added, "I think I have a pretty good idea where I'd like our relationship to go, but that's up to you."

"No, it's up to us." She curled her arms around his neck and kissed him lightly, then harder, pouring out her love for him with every touch of her lips against his.

His kiss, his touch, his mouth, told her everything she needed to know.

When he swept her into his arms and carried her to the bedroom, he said, "One thing. Bob's gonna have to go. And anyone else you have hidden in your nightstand. Any hands-on sex you get from now on has to be with my hands—on you."

"Whatever you say. Of course, if I kept Bob and the others around, I might treat you to a little show."

He stopped dead in his tracks. "You'd let me watch?"

Desire opened with her, just like her blossoming love for Mark. "All in the name of research, my love."

"Then show me."

Not too long ago she'd have been too embarrassed to show anyone how she masturbated. But now, with the man she loved, the idea excited her. Her nipples tightened as she leaned over and pulled Bob out of the nightstand. Moisture already gathered around her pussy, her clit throbbing in anticipation.

She slipped off her clothes and lay back on the bed. Mark pulled a chair up next to the bed, folded his arms across his chest, and watched.

With a quirk of her brow, she smiled at him, then turned on Bob. Just the sound of the whirring got her hot, but not because the vibrator was her only way of release. Not anymore. Now it was due to the man she loved watching her intently. She wanted to please him, excite him, turn him on like he turned her on. Big time.

Dipping the vibrator between her legs, she ran it along the folds of her sex, keeping her gaze trained on Mark. His eyes darkened and she slipped her gaze down to his crotch, watching the bulge there grow larger with every passing second. When she met his eyes again, she grinned and slipped Bob inside her.

"God, babe, that's hot," he said. He stood and approached the side of the bed and sat down next to her. He reached for her breasts, circling one nipple, then the other, with just the tips of his fingers.

Desire sparked hot in her womb and she pulled Bob out a little, then thrust it inside her wet pussy again. A moan escaped her lips when he plucked at her nipples, then bent down and covered one aching crest with his mouth.

The sensations were indescribable. Heat, sparks of intense pleasure and the feeling of tight, coiling need deep in her cunt.

"Fuck me, Mark. I want your cock inside me."

He stood and quickly undressed and she realized how very lucky she was to have a man like him in love with her. So much had happened in such a short period of time, and she was grateful she'd taken the chance to get to know him. Now, the thought of not having him beside her every day made her ache in a different way.

But that ache was soon replaced by a different one as he pulled Bob from her pussy and knelt between her legs. Swiping one finger along Bob's shaft, he drew her juices from it and slipped his finger in his mouth. Her pussy pulsed at the visual of him tasting her.

"Sweet," he murmured, then slipped Bob inside her again, thrusting in and out gently.

"Oh, God." The sight of him fucking her with her vibrator was incredibly erotic. She lifted her hips to give him access to her pussy. When he began to circle her clit with his thumb, the tight knot of desire coiled, then burst. She cried out, flooding the vibrator and his hand with her warm cream.

Mark continued to thrust the vibrator gently in and out until she felt the tingling sparks of renewed desire. Then he withdrew it, a wicked gleam in his eye.

"Turn over and get on your hands and knees," he commanded.

She did as he asked, ready to feel his cock buried to the hilt inside her quaking cunt.

"I kind of like this ménage thing with Bob," he teased. "I think I'd like to see him up your ass."

She whimpered at the thought of it, anticipation making her back up toward him. She pulled the lube from the nightstand drawer and handed it back to him, waiting impatiently while he coated the vibrator with the gel.

"First I want in," he said, then thrust his cock between her swollen pussy lips, burying it deep and hard. Her pussy pulsed around his thick heat and she moved back, fucking the length of him.

"Oh yeah, baby, that's good. Now let's have Bob join us."

He spread the cheeks of her buttocks and applied the lube to her anus, all the while continuing to pump his cock in and out of her drenched pussy. She wasn't going to make it. Already she felt the impending quakes of orgasm. But then Mark pulled his cock away to coat her ass with more gel. She felt the invasion of the vibrator as he eased it gently and slowly into her anus, pushing past the tight barrier until it slipped completely inside her.

"I'd love to have a picture of this," he murmured, leaning over to press a kiss to her back. "This vibrator shoved all the way in your ass, and my cock about to fill that sweet, hot cunt of yours. You make me crazy, Lara, do you know that? I've never known a woman as sexually uninhibited as you."

She'd never known she could be so uninhibited. Until she met Mark. He brought out the wildness in her like no one ever had before.

He probed her slit with his cock head, then slipped his shaft inside, filling her completely.

The sensation was like nothing she'd ever experienced. Her ass and pussy filled with cock, rubbing against each other as Mark thrust, then withdrew, alternating his pistoning drives with that of the vibrator in her ass. The sensations were too much to bear and she flew over the edge, screaming and fucking her ass against him and the vibrator as she came.

"Ah, Christ," he muttered, then buried his cock deep and shot streams of hot cum into her pussy, his fingertips digging into her hips as he pressed against her and held on, shuddering while he came.

After withdrawing the vibrator and collapsing next to her, Mark pulled her against him, cradling her against his chest.

Lara fought back tears. This was perfection, everything she'd ever dreamed or fantasized about love. The fact it had come true was amazing, overwhelming, and more like a dream than a new reality.

"So, was it good for you, babe?"

She laughed and leaned up to search his face. He winked. "It was okay."

"Okay? Just okay? I'll give you okay, woman! We've got more research to do, ya know. I promise you'll be gushing soon over how much more than 'okay' our sex life is."

She laughed hard, until he covered her mouth with his and gave her a hell of a lot more than "okay" sex.

He gave her love, his heart, his body and more than she could have ever dreamed of.

Also by Jaci Burton

A Storm for All Seasons 1: Summer Heat

A Storm for All Seasons 3: Winter Ice

A Storm for All Seasons 4: Spring Rain

A Storm for All Seasons: Ice and Rain *(print only)*

Animal Instincts

Bite Me

Bound to Trust

Chains of Love: Bound to Trust

Devlin Dynasty: Fall Fury

Devlin Dynasty: Mountain Moonlight

Devlin Dynasty: Running Mate *(also available in the* Primal Heat *print anthology)*

Dolphin's Playground

Dream On

Ellora's Cavemen: Legendary Tails II (*Anthology)*

Holiday Bound

Kismet 1: Winterland Destiny

Kismet 2: Fiery Fate

Kismet 3: Aftermath

League of 7 Seas: Dolphin's Playground

Lycan's Surrender

Magnolia Summer

Mesmerized (*Anthology)*

Midnight Velvet
Out of the Darkness (with C.J. Burton)
Passion in Paradise 1: Paradise Awakening
Passion in Paradise 2: Paradise Revival
Passion in Paradise 3: Paradise Discovery
Tangled Web (with C.J. Burton)

About the Author

In April 2003, Ellora's Cave foolishly offered me a contract for my first erotic romance and I haven't shut up since. My writing is an addiction for which there is no cure, a disease in which strange characters live in my mind, all clamoring for their own story. I try to let them out one by one, as mixing snarling werewolves with a bondage and discipline master can be very dangerous territory. Then again, unusual plotlines offer relief from the demons plaguing me.

In my world, well-endowed, naked cabana boys do the vacuuming and dishes, little faeries flit about dusting the furniture and doing laundry, Wolfgang Puck fixes my dinner and I spend every night engaged in wild sexual abandon with a hunky alpha. Okay, the hunky alpha part is my real life husband and he keeps my fantasy life enriched with extensive "research". But Wolfgang won't answer my calls, the faeries are on strike and my readers keep running off with the cabana boys.

Jaci welcomes comments from readers. You can find her website and email address on her author bio page at www.ellorascave.com.

COFFEE, TEA OR LEA?

By Ann Wesley Hardin

ଌ

Dedication

ꟹ

For Marjorie,
whose hilarious "Would you rather…" scenarios at dinnertime inspired Joe, one of my favorite characters ever.
And for Caroline, whose unbridled enthusiasm always surrounds and energizes me.
Without you two I'd be nothing, I tell you. Nothing.

Trademarks Acknowledgement

The author acknowledges the trademarked status and trademark owners of the following wordmarks mentioned in this work of fiction:

Barbie: Mattel, Inc.

Jack Daniel's: Jack Daniel's Properties, Inc.

Joe Cool: United Feature Syndicate, Inc.

Lycra: E. I. du Pont de Nemours and Company

Prada: Prefel S.A. Corporation Luxembourg

RoboCop: Orion Pictures Corporation

Smithsonian: Smithsonian Institution Trust Instrumentality

Wheel of Fortune: Califon Productions, Inc.

Chapter One

ஐ

Coop Masterson, federal air marshal and Lea Harding's worst nightmare, barreled up the airplane aisle, nine millimeter drawn and aimed. At her.

No. Not at her. At the asshole who had her in a headlock with a knife at her throat. The asshole who was dragging her toward the cockpit, spittle spraying her earlobe as he screamed at the air marshal who had, in three short hours, become her nemesis.

She supposed she should feel more warmly toward the hottie who was about to save her skin but Coop had pissed her off earlier. Once pissed, Lea tended to stay pissed until a damn good reason not to be presented itself. This had not yet happened.

Mr. Spittle tightened his grip. His forearm dug into her windpipe and she coughed. "Take it easy, buddy."

"Shut the hell up!" He wrenched her backwards and lost his balance. They tumbled against the carpeted bulkhead. Lea was not one to complain about rug burns on her back but she sure wished she could have more fun getting them.

"Freeze or I'll cut her throat!" the hijacker barked.

Coop kept coming. Looked like Lea was to be the sacrificial lamb.

Nice to know.

She clawed at Mr. Spittle's arm and claimed her reward—a new wrinkle engraved by the blunt tip of the hard rubber knife. Just one little twist and her kneecap would line up snugly against his balls. Except Coop would be mad if she acted against procedure.

She wheezed for breath. Whoa! Were those stars in her eyes? Coop had a stellar presence but Lea didn't think her sudden lightheadedness could be blamed on his looks.

Okay. Frick procedure. Lea curled her body inwards and shoved her knee into the promised land. With a soft oomph, Mr. Spittle folded into a heap at her feet. Still fueled by unsympathetic survivor's instinct, Lea eyed him coldly. That ought to teach him to mess with her! She blew damp bangs off her forehead, brushed her hands together and, turning, set them on her hips as Coop tripped over Mr. Spittle and slammed into her.

"Get the hell off me," she screeched as she hit the bulkhead for the second time.

"Shit," came his tight response.

A heady groping session followed. Lea shoved her hands against a rock-hard chest. Mingling scents of testosterone and power washed over her and every feminine cell in her body sashayed to attention.

Get a grip. You can't stand him. Remember?

Coop yanked his head back, gray eyes raining smoldering ash. "Goddammit, Lea! You were supposed to wait for me during this drill."

They unclumped their bodies and Coop sprang away like she was a bed of hot coals.

"You were too slow. I couldn't breathe!" She brought a shaky hand to her chest and slipped a finger inside the unbuttoned neckline of her white blouse. Wincing slightly, she felt certain she'd have a significant bruise by this evening. Wonderful. She had a date too.

Coop stiffened in alert, gaze flicking along the line of her exposed collarbone. Longish shaggy blond hair framed his unusual face and made him appear more like a medieval knight than a hired killer.

He wasn't what Lea would consider handsome. In fact, when she broke him apart, he wasn't even attractive. But somehow it all came right in the montage of his face.

When they'd been introduced this morning at the bookwork segment of the terrorism training class, her first reaction had been a hearty hubba hubba. After all, what could be sexier than six feet of sleek muscle assigned to protect and defend?

And those eyes—gray with yellow flecks like some intergalactic half-breed. Lea found herself getting lost in them again as they narrowed.

"I heard you gasp before you kneed him."

Her chin went out. "My point exactly."

"If I heard you gasp, you could breathe."

"That was a death rattle." She was all for keeping the skies friendly and safe, but not if it cost her life.

"You went against procedure. Again."

So much for "thinking outside the box". Which had been Coop's verbal instruction in dealing with threatening passengers. Babe-alicious or not, the man was a walking oxymoron.

With an accent on the moron.

Why did Pan Air always insist on hiring Gestapo instructors? "So it's *procedure* for flight attendants to die?"

"To hijackers it is."

He had her on that. But still. This was a training session. Not real life. She opened her mouth to tell him to lighten up. Before she could, the vanquished Mr. Spittle rasped something at her feet. Coop bent down.

"Too hard."

"I know, man." Coop slapped him on the shoulder. "I told her to ease up."

"Me…too…hard," Mr. Spittle gagged. He pointed to Lea and then formed the universal choking signal with his hands.

Coop pressed the bridge of his nose between two fingers.

"I told you," Lea taunted.

Mr. Spittle hauled himself up and staggered to a seat. He plopped down heavily, red faced and breathing hard. Lea experienced a moment of supreme admiration when he sent her a lopsided, pain-filled grin.

"Guess I got too into my role," he said. "Sorry about that."

She patted his shoulder. "I'm sorry too. I almost blacked out."

Mr. Spittle let fly a hefty sigh and leaned his head back. The action caused her gaze to focus on a sharply hewn jawline, full masculine lips and pretty darn nice blue eyes. Suddenly, she didn't mind the spittle quite so much.

"Too bad you didn't," he said. "Might have required mouth-to-mouth."

"Wouldn't that've been a shame." She smiled. Mentally, she tallied her dates for the upcoming month. Friday after next she had free. She thought. "You'll have to make it up to me."

A derisive snort from her left had her turning to Coop.

"This is a war game, not a mating game," he bit.

Leave it to RoboCop to spoil the moment. How else did he expect her to meet men?

Sure, being an international flight attendant had its perks—like regular access to the rich and famous, world travel, a decent salary—but most times the pickings were pretty slim when it came to single men.

Lea did all right. More than all right according to her best friend Kira Grayson. But though Lea had no interest whatsoever in marriage, she wanted to settle in with someone for some serious serial monogamy. Wouldn't you know that seemed too tall an order?

Lea sighed.

Nothing on God's green Earth would make her mother, Muriel, happier than Lea presenting a signed, sealed marriage certificate. The extra income would make that satellite dish Muriel had her eye on—in order to watch more *Wheel of Fortune* reruns—possible.

It was not going to happen though. Lea didn't need yet another financial dependent. After sending her parents a monthly check, she had barely enough left for car payments, her little brother's college fund and, oh yeah, food. Good thing she'd invested some of her beauty contest prize money in a condo several years ago. No mortgage.

And boy had the guilt gods had a field day with that. Were it not for the fact that she'd sprouted a spine in the last five years, they'd be sharing her tiny, but precious, condo with her. As it was, she lived blissfully alone. And that was the way it was going to stay.

She must've directed one hell of a sourpuss at Coop because he frowned, glanced at his watch and said, "Take five, everyone." Delivering one last malevolent glare, he stalked to the back of the plane.

"So, how about it?" Mr. Spittle was saying.

"Huh? What?" Lea flicked her peepers into high beam and directed them at him. The desired effect. Mr. Spittle puddled in his seat.

"You and me, Friday after next," he murmured.

There was a God!

"Sounds great," she cooed. "Let me find some paper and I'll give you my number." As she spun into the galley, she spotted Coop baring his teeth at her from down the aisle. Lea batted her eyelashes at him and he turned away. Good riddance. Now if only the hairs at her nape would relax.

While she searched the metal cabinets for a pen, she wondered why Coop had taken such an instant dislike to her. Usually the opposite occurred. But this time, the minute she'd slid her Prada rip-off under the seat at her desk, arranged her notebook and clicked her official Pan Air pen, it seemed he'd already formed a judgment against her.

At first, she'd attributed his threatening stare to his otherworldly eye color. But as the session droned on, and he answered all her questions in an über snide tone, she'd realized it was personal. Unused to men who didn't like her, she'd adopted a copycat attitude and things had gone downhill at warp speed.

So here they were—him able to shoot straight at full gallop from thirty paces, and her armed with rubbery chicken entrees.

"Here you go." She slipped Mr. Spittle her number. "You already know I'm Lea. Lea Harding."

"Jake White." He extended his hand. "So, come here often?"

She shook his hand and laughed out loud. He was cute! "Wish I did. This is a hoot and a half."

"Tell me about it," Jake chuckled. He peered at her phone number. "You live on Long Island?"

Lea nodded. "Long Beach to be exact. It's close to the airport. I like it."

"I would too." He appraised her with a fresh gleam in his eyes. "Too pricey for me, though. I'm in Easton, Pennsylvania. Even that's getting expensive."

"Things are tough all over." Lea shrugged. These days she didn't brag about her clean sweeps in pageants and the modeling career that followed or mention how well her real estate investment had done. Men tended to get the impression it was just dumb luck, and want her or her property for a showpiece.

Not that she hid her looks. Quite the opposite. A girl had to use her God-given gifts. But she'd been burned enough to realize that once men knew she'd been a publicly acclaimed babe, nothing else about her mattered.

Not straight As in college—the first diploma to ever grace her family's walls. Not her single-minded pursuit of a career that took more ability than the artful application of lip-gloss. Not of her strength in finally saying *no* to her parents' sweet but simple ambitions for her. None of that entered the equation once they learned she'd been crowned Miss New York.

Flock you, Charlie.

She'd gotten this far on her own terms and she planned on getting further. As soon as her brother Joe didn't need her to front his tuition anymore. Only four more years. *Law school here I come.*

"Still," Jake said. "How'd you manage a condo on Long Beach? Did you win the lottery?"

Was Lea imagining things, or did Jake lick his lips at the prospect? "I bought a flood-wrecked repo ten years ago. Sunk every penny I had into it."

"Oh." His voice had grown small. Her joy sagged a little until she remembered he'd asked for her number before he knew about the condo.

"The mildewy smell is mostly gone by now."

He grinned and all was right with the world. "Have to say this is a first. Dating a girl who nearly put me out of commission."

"Feeling better?" she asked with a quick but pointed glance at his lap.

"Should be right as rain by Friday after next."

He thought he was going to get some on the first date? Lea's smile froze on her face. "Whoa. Whoa. Back up a second, Jack."

"Jake."

She knew that. What she didn't know was where the hell he'd gotten the idea she was easy.

She loved sex. Loved sex. A day didn't go by when she didn't think about it twenty or thirty times. But she never slept with a guy on the first date.

Must be the smeared lipstick from the tussle with Coop. Lea pulled her purse out from under the seat and unearthed her compact and a tissue.

"Leave it. You look nice that way," Jake intoned.

Hoo boy. She had her work cut out for her.

"Time's up." Coop boomed in her ear. "Everyone to the back of the plane. Lea, take your place in the galley."

Lea glanced at her watch. Five minutes to the second. Figured.

"Communicus Interruptus," Jake said.

Okay. That was funny. Maybe Jake would be worth a shot after all. After a lifetime of photo shoots, Lea'd grown adept at fielding unwanted advances.

Rising, she straightened her blouse. Coop's slitted gaze swept her from bottom to top. Whatever his opinion of her personally, there was no mistaking the tiny ember in his eyes that exploded and splattered over the cabin when his gaze settled for a microsecond on her breasts.

He must've been preprogrammed at the factory to like big boobs. She wondered briefly what else he was preprogrammed for and a hot trickle of desire dripped into her abdomen. Lea didn't usually take to A-types like Coop, but their inherent drive for excellence in everything they did interested her immensely. Too bad they didn't even come close to liking each other.

* * * * *

Coop watched the frolicksome antics of Ms. Ditz-n-Glitz and Jake with one eye. The other one he kept on his paperwork as he shoved it into his briefcase and prepared to abandon ship. At the last minute, he pulled out a purchase order and scrawled "athletic cups" in capital letters across the front. This he kept in his fist and planned on dropping it off at Pan Air headquarters before hightailing it home.

The last half of the class had finished without incident. But the stress of policing Lea and trying to second guess what stunt she might pull this time had taken its toll.

Prior to today, Coop had a weekly standing appointment with a masseur. Now he considered building a guesthouse behind his pad for the guy. He rolled his neck and felt the stab of a burgeoning spasm between his shoulder blades. To think retirement had been at his fingertips.

He'd enjoyed his twin diesel cabin cruiser for exactly two weeks before the urgent call from Pan Air for a *Security Specialist* had lit up the line. Like the stupid prick he could be, he'd taken it on, gotten caught up in the altruistic idea of passing on his hard-earned knowledge, maybe saving a few lives along the way… He hadn't planned on having to pound that wisdom into the thick skull of a calamity waiting to happen.

He looked at her and a sound akin to chalk on a blackboard screeched in his brain. The vibration skittered down his spine and thumped in his crotch. The feeling momentarily amused him. Did he need a cup just to look at her?

She was a ball buster on wheels. Delivering misery and oxygen deprivation to the organs of every male within pheromone-sniffing distance. It didn't surprise him in the least that her knee had a built-in rifle sight. He'd met her type before, too many times in too many places. All he wanted for his life now was peace and quiet. Calmness and serenity. Boredom with a capital B. The complete opposite of how he'd formerly made his living.

Too bad Lea Harding scared the shit out of him.

It wasn't just because of her looks, which, he had to admit, rocked—nearly six feet of leg, slim waist and just-fucked red hair—it was also her brittle attitude. As if she'd been there, done that and not only got the wet T-shirt but wore it proudly.

What hardships could a cosseted, perfumed and powdered airhead like her have possibly endured? An emergency midnight foray to the nail salon?

She'd certainly never fought for her life or anyone else's. Yet someday she might. And it was Coop's freshly minted responsibility to prepare her for that.

He was royally screwed.

Shit. She was headed his way. He briefly considered deploying the inflatable escape chute and taking a flying leap. Better yet, he could toss her down it and watch the legs and hair tumble into a wad at the bottom.

Well, wouldn't you know. The thought of her lying breathless and spread-eagled on the tarmac gave him a hard-on the size of Florida. He quickly sat down and pulled his briefcase over his lap. "What do you want now?"

She gave a little snort and kept on trucking. "Keep it in your pants, *Cooper*. I've got to pee."

Blood and heat clamored out of his dick and into his face. Nobody used his full name and lived.

He pinched the bridge of his nose between two fingers. Of all the cabins in all the airplanes in all the world, he had to walk into hers.

Chapter Two

"Oh my! This plane is big. It's big, Lea." Muriel Harding turned to her daughter and laid a shaky hand on her arm. "Where do I sit?"

"Come on, Momma," Lester Harding said. "Lea's got work to do. We'll find it." He squinted down the aisle. "Someday," he added.

"There are numbers on the ceiling," Joe Harding said, casting a glum look at Lea. "If someone hasn't booby-trapped the plane already, we'll find it."

"Hush, Joe." Lea resisted the urge to clap a hand over her little brother's mouth. "Comments like that will land you in jail."

Actually, she was surprised he wasn't already there. Surprised he'd made it through security with all the metal rings he had piercing his nose, lips and eyebrows. His hair alone could classify as a deadly weapon. All he'd have to do was aim one blackened spike at someone's jugular.

"I'm already in jail," he complained. "I still live at home, remember?" His black leather motorcycle jacket squealed as he leaned negligently against a first-class seat.

"Only for a couple more months."

He rolled brown eyes that carried the weight of the world. "If I don't die before I get to college."

Was there such thing as a Drama *King*? Lea patted Joe's shoulder and turned toward her father. "You're in row twenty-four—"

"Maybe between all three of us, we can count that high," Joe put in.

Muriel giggled. "You're such a card, Joey."

"Yeah. A regular Ace of Spades," Lea said.

Joe sighed.

Lea watched them amble down the aisle, trying to feel excited about this family vacation to Hollywood. She loved them with everything she had in her. And would do anything for them. Anything.

Liking them, sometimes, was the hard part.

Tickets to a Wheel of Fortune taping lay hidden in her billfold. A birthday surprise for her mother, who watched it religiously. Lea couldn't remember precisely when this obsession began. But it seemed like Pat Sajak and Vanna White had been pseudo family members her whole life. She found herself thinking of them at odd moments and wondering what they were up to, and memories of their faces and voices seemed sometimes to mingle and merge with actual recollections.

Talk about scary.

She supposed it filled some mysterious void in her mother's life. Living vicariously through the contestants rejuvenated her. Hadn't it been that way with Lea's modeling career too?

She wouldn't have called Muriel a stage mother. But she clearly recalled the rush of adrenaline her mother got from go-sees and photo shoots. And Muriel always took it personally when Lea failed to get a job. Was Lea not beautiful enough? How could she not be exactly what they were looking for?

Desperation for the paycheck that followed the shoot might have been one of the reasons she felt that way.

Lea's parents hadn't had a whole lot to smile about in recent years. Poor health and a string of unfortunate investments had resulted in her father losing his job and most of his savings.

A burst of friendliness had resulted in Joe's birth and the family budget got stretched past its limit.

Her dad had managed part-time work for a while, but debts had mounted quickly. It soon became clear that financial solvency rested on Lea's slim, teenaged shoulders.

The burden had taken its toll. She was tired. She wondered when it would ever be her turn for some excitement. To be free of all constraints on her time and her money. To be footloose and fancy-free.

The Wheel of Fortune taping wasn't *exactly* her idea of a good time.

Except her mother would be so happy. Lea smiled and the giddy anticipation of Mom's reaction made it seem worthwhile.

Mostly, anyway.

She sighed. Almost time to meet and greet the rest of the passengers. She straightened her navy blazer and took her place at the door in time to see a dreadfully familiar form striding down the jetway. An angry afterburn singed a path through her limbs—RoboCop's signature calling card.

Apparently, when he wasn't leaping tall buildings in a single bound, Coop had an easy gait. Loose and self-assured. The relaxed demeanor of a man packing heat. He wore faded jeans and a sueded cotton shirt.

"Look what the cat dragged in," she muttered.

He stopped on the threshold and took her measure. They stared at each other in a heavy silence that crept slowly enough for beads of sweat to form on her upper lip. She hastily licked it off and those alien eyes focused on the action. He seemed to have momentary trouble swallowing.

"Request permission to come aboard," he finally said in a low voice.

Clever. But what was he doing, flirting? She tossed him a sharp look.

Nah.

Still, she sucked on her wet upper lip to keep from cracking a smug smile. "That all depends on what your business is here. To spy on me?" Pan Air's Quality Assurance geeks regularly ran rat patrols. She'd never seen a Security Specialist onboard before, though. The position was brand spanking new.

Coop drew back his shaggy head and peered down a slightly off-center nose. "What if I am?"

"Spy away." She spread both arms. "I always follow Pan Air Procedure to the letter." It was true too. She was a company gal.

"I know. It's *my* procedure you seem to have trouble with."

"I wouldn't if it made any sense."

His expression turned weary. "Don't start with me. The past two days have been a bitch."

The two days he spent training her. The fine hairs on her back went up. "Who's picking a fight now?"

Joe materialized between them. "Mr. Harding doesn't have a pillow."

She clenched her teeth and laid a hand on his arm. "Not now, Joe."

"But Mr. Harding said—"

Joe never called them Mom and Dad.

"Later, Joe."

Joe looked at Coop with the deadest expression Lea'd ever seen. "Deep vein thrombosis can kill you," he offered in an even deader voice.

"Not on short, domestic flights," she protested. To no avail. Joe repeated his fatalistic declaration.

It was all she could do not to clock him but good. His little obsession with death and dismemberment was wearing thin. *Please don't say it, Joe. Please don't say what I think you're going to say.*

Coop considered him quietly for a moment. "So I've heard."

"You've got to get up and walk around every hour."

"That's what I've been told," Coop said pleasantly.

"If there's turbulence, you're doomed."

Coop shrugged. "Yeah, but you wouldn't have to eat airplane food."

Joe cocked his head, a tiny flare of interest in his eyes. People usually flinched and edged away.

She closed in. "Joe, get back to your seat. Now. I'll get Dad's pillow later."

Joe brushed off her clawing fingers and returned his attention to Coop. He opened his mouth to say more.

No. No. No! "I'll grab a pillow, Joe." *To smother you with.* "Help me find one."

Too late.

"Would you rather die of deep vein thrombosis," Joe asked, "or stand on the wing during takeoff until the wind ripped the flesh off your face?"

Lea closed her eyes tightly. Her fingernails dug so deeply into her fists she thought for sure they'd pop out the other side and give Joe yet another "Would You Rather" scenario. His favorite conversational gambit.

Holding her breath, she cracked one eye only to see Coop stroking his chin and gazing thoughtfully toward the ceiling. Her other eye opened and she said, "Feel free to ignore him."

She was the one being ignored.

"Flesh," Coop said. "I could use a new face."

Joe's somber gaze wandered around Coop's visage for a minute before he nodded. "Yeah. You could."

Coop grinned and Lea felt the floor undulate like a surface wave in an earthquake. Good God, he was hot when he smiled! She realized in the entire two days she'd spent with him, he never had. Not once.

She knew she wore a schmucky, doe-eyed expression and no way in hell did she want him to see it. For perhaps the first time in her adult life, she cast around for ways to keep the focus on Joe. "They let him out on a weekend pass this time. For taking his meds like a good boy."

Joe looked at her as if she'd sprouted a spare head. She couldn't blame him for his confusion—she never teased him anymore. When had she stopped? A shard of nostalgia pierced her heart.

As if realization finally struck, Coop's head swiveled toward Lea and a long finger pointed at Joe. "He's your brother?" Coop's gaze shot from one to the other several times. With each glance, his eyebrows rose higher and higher.

"We share some genetic material," she admitted.

"That's…" Coop's teeth and lips formed an "F" before he caught himself. "…interesting," he finished.

"Tell me about it." She rolled her eyes and noticed with relief a line forming on the jetway behind Coop. She pulled him gently out of the way. "Now if you two don't mind, I have work to do."

Coop snapped out of his daze and hustled Joe down the aisle. "Where are you sitting, pal?" he asked. His deep voice merged with the muffled clacking of rolling luggage as he added, "I'm in twenty-four D."

* * * * *

Did Mile-High Barbie curse softly just now behind his back? Coop could've sworn she had. Whatever. The new development slouching into seat twenty-four C beside an anxious-looking older couple devoured his attention. Could these average everyday folks be the parents?

He stowed his duffle in the overhead bin across the aisle and the alleged mother glanced at him. A hand snaked up to pat a hairstyle that, while shorter and less fussy, boasted the same fiery color. The possible father kept his gaze firmly focused on the luggage wagons outside the window but Coop noticed a familiar nose.

He settled into his seat and grinned. If appearances did not deceive, the flight wasn't going to be as boring as he'd thought.

Despite Lea's abundance of irritating qualities, he had to admit this accidental excavation of her roots was entertaining indeed.

Just watching Joe trying to get comfortable was a hoot and a half. The quills emerging from the back of his head engaged the seatback in a duel of wills. Who would win?

Coop thought he'd bust a gut. It'd been a good long while since he'd enjoyed an airplane ride.

In the old days he would've been working. Watching the cabin without appearing to. Listening to conversations with half an ear. Waiting for disaster to get up and use the lavatory.

Not this time, baby.

This flight was all about relaxation. A long weekend of nothing but surf. Hanging ten by himself—one with the waves. Yeah. It felt good already.

"They just loaded our bags, Momma."

"Oh thank heaven."

Funny how people worried so much about luggage when there were far more unpleasant things to contemplate. Not that Coop personally had ever run into any of them.

Teige had.

Coop shifted in his seat as his brother's name did a once-around-the-park in his brain. A murky image of a young soldier inserted itself and two fingers formed a vee as he shouldered a military backpack and disappeared into the bowels of a transport plane. A three-year-old's rare glimpse of the sibling he'd scarcely known.

The plane lurched and began backing away from the airport. As had been Coop's custom for years, he popped the spout on his water bottle and tilted it into a silent toast before taking a swig. *This one's for you, buddy.*

Maybe not exactly this time, since Coop didn't police the skies anymore. But hell. Tradition was tradition. He didn't see any point in giving it up now.

Pity party over. He stowed the water bottle in the pouch on the seat in front and checked on Joe's progress. The boy had rolled a blanket into a neck pillow and appeared to be resting comfortably. Smart kid.

Joe caught Coop's eye and his mouth drooped into a defeated envelope. "Twenty percent of all accidents occur during takeoff. Ten percent of the people die each time."

"You can increase those odds by switching seats with someone at the last minute," Coop replied.

Joe's lips lifted so slightly Coop thought maybe he imagined it.

Lea breezed between them and Coop was blown backwards in a scented jet stream. "Seatbacks up, please. Sir, your seatback needs to be raised for takeoff…"

Coop got a swift glimpse of tight skirt over luscious ass as she leaned across a row to check a child's seat belt. "I'm sure your sister loves hearing those stats," he said.

"She almost became one."

A long, exposed, nylon-slicked thigh slowed the progress of Joe's words to Coop's brain. "Huh?"

"Lea was in a crash."

Coop jerked his head around. "She was?"

Joe nodded.

"Not with Pan Air."

Joe shook his head. "With a puddle-jumper. They went out of business afterwards."

It could only be one airline. The industry was small and bad news spread like ragweed. "Colony?" He glanced back at Lea. She'd been in the Colony debacle?

"Colonoscopy. Yeah. She got a cheeseball plaque for saving thirty lives." A touch of pride thickened Joe's monotone.

Coop remembered it clearly. An engine had dropped off during the takeoff roll and the plane had skidded into another one waiting to cross the runway. Both planes had burst into flames, yet no one died—largely because of the crew's expertise.

Lea had been there? He tried to wrap his mind around it.

"She had nightmares for a while."

"I bet she did."

"She would've quit except Mr. and Mrs. Harding need her money."

"No shit?"

"She wants to be a lawyer but she has to pay for my school first."

A lawyer? The Powder Puff Girl?

Color him an asshole. Didn't the old man always tell him not to be too quick to judge? It was a flaw that had followed him his whole life. Made him suspicious and wary. Made him a damn fine air marshal, in fact.

Still. He'd been dead wrong about Lea.

She *had* fought for her life. No wonder she took no prisoners. He should've recognized where her attitude came from.

And no wonder she thought he was a class "A" jerk. What could he possibly teach her that she didn't already know? Hell, she could even disarm a terrorist—that had been clearly and graphically demonstrated. His balls still ran for cover at the memory.

Coop's head nearly exploded. He felt awestruck as he watched her walking crisply back up the aisle. Towards him. Admiration swelled in his chest and something else swelled in his crotch.

Lea Harding had more to her than met the eye. And suddenly, what did meet his eye didn't look quite as distasteful as it had a New York minute ago.

She passed him without a return glance and slid into a jump seat near the galley. The engines revved and the plane started to roll. He watched her tighten the harness over a delectable pair of ta-tas.

Buckle up, sweetheart. The flight plan he'd filed for her had been fundamentally revised. Coop braced himself for a bumpy ride.

Chapter Three

ᘓ

Lea chirped buh-bye to the last deplaning passenger and gathered her things. Joe and her parents had been given express instructions to meet her at baggage claim, so she was momentarily free. Of course, she had to worry whether they'd listened properly. Tearing them away from Coop had been a trial unto itself.

What could they have possibly found to discuss so raptly for five hours? Scratch that. She already knew. She'd gone back there as often as time allowed and had tallied fifteen references to Wheel of Fortune, five Would You Rathers and one arm-hair-raising invitation to lunch.

She also could've sworn she'd seen Joe smile. But that was too far out to contemplate so she'd blamed it on a wayward eyelash.

Her only hope now, as she hastily clicked down the LAX concourse, was that Coop had taken her pointed *Hasta La Vista, Kemosabe* as a clue and ridden off into the wild blue yonder.

Hi-yo Silver Bird. Away!

With a sigh of relief she skipped off the escalator, wound through the carousels and found her family milling. With no sign of Coop.

Muriel immediately bombarded her. "What a nice man. So handsome! How do you know him? Is he single?"

"He works for Pan Air, and I have no idea if he's attached, Mom. I'm surprised you didn't wheedle it out of him."

"He isn't," Joe said.

Muriel's mouth formed a capital "O". Lea patted her arm. "Forget it. I'm not interested."

"Why ever not?"

"He's got a superhero complex." *And an ego the size of Manhattan. And a bullying attitude.*

And he doesn't like me.

"He said if I wanted to I could go surfing with him tomorrow," Joe offered.

"Oh no, Joey. That's too dangerous," Muriel chided, casting a mortified look at Lester.

Mr. Harding folded his arms across his chest and regarded Joe. "I'll have to agree with Momma on this one."

"I know. Sharks," Joe muttered. But Lea caught a shred of yearning in his eyes before he dropped his gaze to the floor.

Her heart skipped. He wanted to go! Joe didn't care enough to want or ask for anything. But he cared about this.

"Besides," Lester argued, "this is a family vacation."

Joe nodded.

"It's okay with me, Dad," Lea put in quickly. "Joe wouldn't be interested in doing what I've planned for tomorrow, anyway."

This would be good for Joe, she thought. Never mind that she disliked Coop, it was plain that Joe enjoyed his company—as much as he could enjoy anything. It also seemed apparent that for whatever reason, Coop liked Joe as well. The kid could use a friend.

Lester pinned her with a stern eye. "He could get maimed or killed."

"Coop's an ex-air marshal, Dad. He knows fifty ways to save a life." That couldn't be admiration in her tone.

"And one hundred and fifty ways to take one," Joe said, his voice definitely full of admiration.

"But our plans," Muriel protested. "Lea worked so hard to pay for this."

"Actually, these were free." Lea pulled the Wheel of Fortune tickets from her purse and fanned them out for her mother to see. The resulting whoop of unadulterated joy had heads turning and Lea grinning as her mother tackle-hugged her. "Happy birthday, Mom."

Lester rocked back on his heels and said, "Well, what do you know?"

Joe slumped and turned away.

Lea sensed this was no ordinary sulk. Something deep inside her brother had been hinging on this excursion with Coop. Had it been hope? *Real* hope?

Her heart took an express elevator to her toes. What kind of lamebrain would think Joe would be remotely interested in more Wheel of Fortune? Had she gone soft in the noggin? She hadn't been thinking of him—about what sort of activity a down-in-the-mouth eighteen-year-old boy might prefer.

But apparently, Coop had. He'd caught on faster than a speeding bullet and had flown to Joe's rescue. Far be it from her to upset the Man of Steel's quest. Because now she felt certain he *had* made Joe smile.

She set her jaw.

Joe was going surfing with Coop. No matter what she had to do to get the parents to agree.

* * * * *

"You want me to what?" Lea screeched later in her parents' hotel room.

"If you don't go, Joe doesn't go." Muriel tilted her head in a *neener neener* type way. "We hardly know the man," she added slyly. "He could be a child molester."

"That's ridiculous!"

Muriel raised her eyebrows and lifted her chin. "It is not."

Lea seethed. "Joe's a man! He should be out here with his friends. Not us. He's perfectly capable of fending off unwanted advances. Male or female."

"Not a powerful man like Coop."

Lea plopped down on the bed, head in hands. No way in hell would she spend a day, *on the beach,* with Coop Masterson. First off, she hated the beach. The mere thought of all that sand in her thong made her chafe. Secondly, she didn't have the vaguest idea how to surf. Not that Joe did but he'd always been more athletically inclined than she, and he seemed to have a desire to learn.

Thirdly, she couldn't stomach the airless, creepy darkness of the ocean, where stringy things swept out of the void to straddle her leg and death took no holidays.

Even though she lived at the shore, her idea of a perfect day at the beach involved looking at it from her deck. Warm, dry and shaded. With a venti latte in her hand.

"I didn't bring enough sunblock," she lied, proud of her little trump card. Her mother had always been protective of Lea's fair skin and had made her wear the stuff from the time she could toddle.

In thin-lipped reply, Mrs. Harding reached into her open suitcase and tossed a janitorial-sized bottle onto the bed.

Curses!

Joe meandered in and sat next to her. "Come on, Lea. It might be fun."

She raised her face and looked at him. He put a hand on her shoulder and the tortured plea in his eyes nearly undid her. She hadn't seen him so vulnerable in…forever.

"Besides," he said. "Do you really want to go to Burbank?"

Lea shuddered. Her gaze strayed to the TV screen where Vanna playfully turned letters. "I suppose you could give mine and Joe's tickets to someone else at the door," she murmured.

"It'd be easier to give away two," Muriel sing-songed.

Suspicion streaked through Lea. "You've given up the idea of a *family* vacation too easily. This isn't a plot to hook me up with Coop, is it?"

"No." Muriel's nose twitched. She'd never been a decent liar.

Lea stood up and poked a finger into her plump chest. "Cause it's Not. Going. To happen."

"Fine. Fine." Muriel threw up her hands. "But you still have to go if Joe goes."

Joe came up beside her and his grip on her shoulder tightened. Her spine turned to mashed potato. She held up a hand, curling her fingers into a fist until only her thumb and pinky stuck out. "Let's hang loose, Mongoose."

And Joe smiled.

* * * * *

First thing in the morning, Lea and Joe met Coop at the beach. The night before on the phone she'd steadfastly refused his offer to pick them up. She needed this last shred of control to get through the day. At least with her own car she could split whenever she wanted, and she would if his instruction today turned out to be as obnoxious as his instruction last week.

She tooled into the parking lot at Paradise Cove and braked to pay the fee. Twenty bucks. How ridiculous. She waved the bill out the window. The attendant took one look at her and told her she'd already been paid for. Squinting through the bug juice on her windshield, she spied Coop watching for them.

Dressed in bright orange and turquoise board shorts, with a skin-tight, white Lycra T-shirt and water shoes, he looked like Joe Cool incarnate. His shaggy hair was thick and stringy from the salt air and Lea had the sneaky suspicion he'd already rode more waves this morning than most mortals did in a whole day.

Catching sight of them, he waved and jogged right over and some of her animosity faded at his obvious eagerness. Maybe he had a human side after all.

Joe scrambled out of the car. "Hey."

"Hey, buddy." Coop slapped him on the back. "Ready to catch a wave?"

"Can't wait." Joe actually rubbed his hands together in glee. "Where do I get my gear?"

"Go check my rental truck. The green one over there. I got you covered."

Joe trotted off. Coop's gray eyes slid over to Lea and lazily made the sign of the cross around her body, leaving no areas unblessed. By the time his gaze locked with hers, she felt her lips begin to slacken and part.

"Thanks for treating us," she murmured. "I didn't expect you to."

"No problem. I told the guy to watch for a punk rocker and his groupie."

She laughed out loud and smacked him on the arm. "You did not!"

"Did too," he chuckled. "Hey it worked."

"You're going to pay for that, you know," she teased.

A brief, awkward silence descended. She got the impression he'd bitten back a raunchy reply.

"So how you doing?" he finally asked softly, as if they'd just woken up in a tangle of sheets.

She couldn't stop a smile, or the little head bob she usually reserved for men she liked. "I'm good."

"Me too."

Was that her bikini bottom melting off? An ordinary greeting never sounded so full of possibility.

He stepped in closer. Her stomach did a somersault. "I didn't peg you for the surfing type. What made you tag along?" His fingers tapped an erotic soft-shoe on her palm.

Okaaaay. This wasn't the same man. This was, apparently, Good Coop. Or, she cleared her throat and amended, Hot-to-the-touch, Tasty as Sin, Totally Rad Bad Coop.

Flashback to the groping session during training and how his hands had felt on her—sure and strong and knowledgeable. Would she feel those hands on her again today, as he helped her balance on the board, caught her when she fell? Would warm, wet and slippery flesh collide in the waves?

Enough of that. "My mother made me." She bent to rub an imaginary ding in the rental car. She certainly wasn't going to lose her head over Coop and his ability to deliver an incendiary hello.

He seemed to hesitate a second, as if waiting for something more, then she sensed his attention shift to Joe, who had returned with some Lycra T-shirts.

"What're these?"

* * * * *

"Rash guards. Put one on and give the other one to your sister."

There she stood in her itsy bitsy bikini, without makeup, her hair in a lopsided donut—looking for all the world like an unretouched centerfold—and telling him her mother made her come.

Her mother.

Coop didn't know quite how to feel about that. But he sure as hell knew he didn't feel good.

He'd spent a fevered night going bonkers wondering why she'd decided to accompany Joe. His rationalizations had ranged from the practical--she felt protective about sending her baby brother off with a stranger, to the sublime--she wanted to see *him*. He never once thought her mother made her do it.

Talk about kicking his balls off the rail, into the corner pocket.

It didn't dampen his raging lust for her, but he sure wished he hadn't wasted a whole fucking night fantasizing about something that was far from imminent. He could've used that time to strategize.

Just went to prove he could never let his guard down, never assume she might be as crazy for him as he was for her—at least until she issued a definite and unmistakable invitation. The problem was getting her to do that.

His babe radar had picked up a bleep and he could tell she was warming up to him. But he was also savvy enough to know she couldn't be steamrolled. He'd have to lure her in. Show her who he really was. So far she'd only seen professional Coop and she didn't think too highly of him. Today he'd show her his flipside.

And lookie here. An opportunity already. She was struggling with the tight spandex rash guard.

"Let me help."

"I can do it."

"Come here."

With a petulant stomp, she obeyed. Coop took the shirt and bunched the fabric up around the neck opening. Stretching it out as far as it would go, he gently slipped it over her head.

His hands itched to help more as she slid her arms into the short sleeves and tugged the shirt over her voluptuous torso, but he resisted. There would be plenty more opportunities to touch her once the actual surfing began. He tried not to drool.

"Thanks," she said. "These are harder to put on than they appear." She wiggled around, trying to get comfortable in the super snug fit.

"Wait until it gets wet and you try to take it off." She'd need his help then. Yes!

"Seems like more trouble than it's worth."

"You'll be happy to have it later on," he said. "Without it you'd go home with a raw stomach."

"Ugh." She grinned impishly. "I'll take mine medium rare, thank you very much."

God she could be cute. "Let's head out."

* * * * *

As they picked their way over the sand towards the ocean, it struck Lea what a thorough and gracious host Coop was. He'd provided everything they needed without bragging or making them feel as if he'd gone to a lot of trouble. But he had. It must've taken hours to get everything together, not to mention a giant wad of cash.

Realizing this, the firm, perfectly rounded ass bobbing in front of her suddenly became overwhelmingly attractive. And the long, sinewy tanned legs, she noticed, had exactly the preferred amount of hair. In fact everything about Coop seemed to have been painted in entirely different colors this morning, giving him an irresistibly magnetic glow.

Stopping near the shore, he turned to catch her staring. He did a double take when he spied her expression. "You all right?"

She swallowed and nodded. "Fine."

He reached for her surfboard and laid it out on the sand, crouching next to it. "You looked like you'd seen a sea monster. Don't be scared. I'll be with you all the way."

All the way. Yeah baby. That sounded bo-dacious. "I'm not scared."

"That's my girl." A big grin split his face and he patted the board. "Come over here and get on your knees, woman. I'm going to show you a thing or two."

Her jaw dropped. Well, if he was going to spend the day injecting innuendo into every word he said, she'd play along. Might as well join him in his frisky mood.

She sashayed over and dropped to her knees at the same time he stood up. Peering up at him from crotch level, she cooed, "Fire when ready."

He stared dumbstruck for a moment before a deep rumble rose from his diaphragm. Throwing back his head, he roared with laughter.

At the sound, an atomic burst of happiness lit her from within. She'd forgotten how good it felt to make someone laugh. Forgotten what it was like to have fun for fun's sake. This was exactly what she'd been pining for. To laugh and get down with a sexy man. Could she do it with Coop?

Two hours later she knew she could most definitely do it with Coop. He'd patiently taught them how to paddle, duck dive and pop up to a standing position. Not once did he raise his voice or display any of the irritating condescension she'd grown familiar with.

Quite the opposite. He'd made the experience hysterical—shaking his head in mock frustration when she lost her balance and fell, telling Joe to go for the pansy-ass waves for now and generally behaving as if teaching them, but not surfing himself, was the best holiday. Ever.

What a guy! Lea'd found herself liking him more and more as the morning progressed. And falling more and more under his sensual spell.

Lying on her board now, with him standing waist deep beside her, his hand at the small of her back near her ass, she silently willed him to go lower. Her butt cheeks quivered in anticipation.

Fifteen minutes ago, Joe had headed down the beach with a gaggle of teens to do some boogie boarding, leaving her alone with Coop. Now was her chance to feel him out—to discover if some serial monogamy sounded interesting.

"Here comes a good wave," Coop announced. "Go for it." He smacked her rear and gave her a push. Contact!

"Aye aye, Cap'n." She paddled toward the wave and turned to face the shore. Within a moment the water swelled beneath and took the board. Everything Coop had taught her suddenly gelled and she tucked in her knees and stood up, arms thrown wide. A giddy sensation of flying overcame her and she giggled crazily, shifting her weight to keep balanced.

She became exquisitely aware of Coop's regard—as if he was holding his breath, silently rooting for her with everything he had. The momentary distraction was all it took. The nose of the board flipped up and she tipped over backwards, plunging into the foam with a squeal.

Another wave smacked her as she surfaced, taking her under again. She floundered for air, and suddenly she was thrown back in time.

Into a plane.

Full of black, toxic smoke.

Which way should she go? There was no way to tell.

Don't inhale. There's no air. You'll die.

Panic danced a jig on the rim of her soul. She wanted to open her mouth and scream but it was locked.

Out of the darkness two hands found her and plucked her into sunshine. "Breathe!" Coop ordered, grabbing her cheeks in one hand and squeezing them to force her mouth open. "It's safe now."

With a sputter, oxygen filled her lungs. She gulped it down, gasp after gasp, while Coop held her like a baby and stroked her hair.

"I'm okay. I'm okay," she managed at last. "Just lost it there for a minute."

He rubbed a thumb under her eye. She hadn't realized she'd been crying.

"I wasn't worried," Coop said gently. "You've proven you can handle yourself."

She looked into his eyes and saw he knew exactly where she'd been in those terrifying seconds. She knew where he learned it too. Joe was such a little snitch.

"You seem to know how to handle me too," she said, touching his face.

He softened then tensed and let her slide to her feet. His gray eyes turned black as they searched her face intently. She moved in closer, letting her breasts brush his chest, using body language to deliver an engraved invitation. His head bent lower. She raised hers. Then he yanked her hard against him and kissed her madly.

His hot, open mouth sucked every inch of her face, devouring her lips, forcing them open so his tongue could invade the hidden, needy recesses of her being. His hands gripped her waist until she slid her own hands up his back, wrapping her arms around his shoulders and clinging for dear life. Then he dropped a palm to her ass, kneading and rubbing and tucking her pussy in tightly against his stiff, swollen cock.

"I want to handle you," he murmured against her mouth. "In every way possible."

"I want you to too."

"Like this?" A finger slid up the front of her thigh and underneath her bikini bottom. He stopped and pulled his head back to gaze at her. "Like this?"

The ocean lapped against her back as she rose and sank with incoming waves, secluding she and Coop from curious onlookers. "Yes. And more." The words breezed out on a sigh. Instead of locking lips with her again, he watched her face as his finger inched closer.

"You sure?" he asked. "Once I start, I'm not stopping."

"I'm sure," she whispered.

At the moment of contact, her whisper turned into a moan. Two more fingers joined the other at her labia, parting them tenderly while the middle one searched for her clit. Then came the slow rubbing while she sucked on his tongue. His wet lips surrounded hers, accepting the promise she gave him—for later.

His tempo increased and the sparks started flying. She wrapped both legs around his to allow better access. A blistering yearning consumed her, shocking her with the intense realization that she not only craved a good hard fuck, she craved it from Coop. The physical connection felt so natural she knew it was inevitable. And the fact that she liked him so much blew her mind to smithereens.

Lust had never gobbled her so completely, and when she came—burying her mouth in his shoulder to muffle her sounds—it was with a thermonuclear blast so unexpected she would've slipped under the brine again had he not been there to save her.

Chapter Four

ꟗ

"Lea!" came Joe's frantic call from the shore. "Lea! I saw your surfboard go airborne. You okay?"

Frustration tore a hole in her gut. "I'm fine," she yelled back and waved, trying gamely to pull her shattered self together. Coop's forehead fell heavily against hers and she heard him quietly curse.

"I know," she said in a low voice. "But thank you."

His chest heaved. "You're very welcome," he said through his teeth.

"Come out. I'm starved," Joe howled.

"Not quite the sort of eating I had in mind," Coop quipped and desire re-ignited her flesh.

"I'll taste better after I wash the salt water off."

"Really?" he complained as she grabbed his hand and started wading back to land. "I kind of like the salt."

Hoo boy, was she in for some mind-altering sex.

"I don't object to it myself," she purred.

A guttural groan ripped the air. "What do you say we ditch the punk and find a table for two?"

"You want to talk?"

"Yeah, I'm fucked up that way."

Would wonders never cease? Yet another quality she wouldn't have guessed. A tiny alarm sounded in her brain. Men who wanted to talk were usually serious men. The settling down types. At Coop's age and station, that might be what he had in mind. Wouldn't be a bad idea to establish some ground rules from the get go—no marriage, no babies, no frills.

But they'd have fun, fun, fun 'til a law school took this lovebird away.

As they hit the reef, Lea noticed that Joe wasn't alone. A small, dark-haired girl hovered uncertainly nearby, chewing a lip and looking utterly adorable in a bright yellow one piece.

Coop noticed too. They exchanged glances. "Joe's in trouble," Coop muttered.

"My thoughts exactly," Lea said. She gazed at her little brother and joy exploded in her heart. He seemed so happy—at least for this day—and she had Coop to thank for that.

He also looked way better without the spikes. The ocean had washed away the goop and his black hair fell in glistening waves to a set of fine shoulders. One of his new friends must have given him a puka shell choker. It contrasted nicely with a developing tan. Maybe this girl was the one in trouble.

"Hey, glad you're okay. This is Kim. Can she eat lunch with us?" Joe tripped over his words like a puppy on ice.

"Hi." Kim lifted a hand in shy greeting.

"Hey, Kim," Lea said. "And sure she can stay for lunch. Once we figure out what we're doing."

They all looked at Coop. "Don't ask me," he shrugged. "I only packed a cooler full of sandwiches. It's in the truck."

Without another word Joe and Kim trotted up the beach. When they thought they were out of sight, Kim reached out and they hooked fingers.

Coop grabbed Lea from behind. She wrapped his arms around her waist and snuggled a cheek against his. He nibbled down the side of her neck and she shivered with delight.

His lean, powerful body felt so good against her back. An emotion she couldn't quite name bubbled through her—coupling with desire, turning her on and providing a safety net all at the same time.

How strange.

"Coop," she asked. "What made you change your mind about me? I thought you didn't like me."

"I didn't."

She blew him a raspberry. "I didn't like you either."

"Do you like me now?"

"I'm starting to."

He chuckled and explored her earlobe with his tongue.

"Really. What made you change your mind?" she asked.

He pulled his mouth off her ear and spun her around to face him. "Your family told me all about you, and I liked what I heard."

"Joe told you about Colony."

He frowned and nodded.

"Is that what did it?"

He stroked her arms thoughtfully. "There was more to it than that. But yes, it made me admire you. I thought you were a hollow ornament before then."

"How poetic." She snorted.

"I thought of it myself."

"Would you have still been interested in *handling* me if I had been a hollow ornament?"

"No."

She had her answer. Like her, he was looking for more than a weekend fling. Something more than her appearance attracted him, and he had no idea about the condo.

Did he? Well, that hardly mattered now.

As long as he didn't expect an enduring future, the deal was sealed as far as she was concerned. She gave herself a mental high five. Serial monogamy here we come.

* * * * *

As Coop drove them back to Lea's hotel he recognized that he was completely and thoroughly fucked. One by one she had shattered his ignorant expectations—about her and about women in general.

Piece by piece she'd disassembled his heart, putting it back together in a way that blinded him to every other woman on the planet.

Living or dead.

When he'd held her sobbing body, when he'd heard laughter from her delectable mouth, when he felt her shudder with ecstasy he himself had given, he felt…honored.

She was the bravest person he'd ever met, aside from his brother. She took care of her whole family, shouldering an enormous financial burden. Watching and worrying over Joe like a mother.

Quite simply, she floored him. His life as he knew it was over.

She was mouthy, opinionated, strong and independent. She was high-maintenance beauty—a thoroughbred who, like the fragile horses, could break down at any moment.

In short, she embodied every quality that took a shitload of work to sustain. Just when he thought boredom would rule his days.

No wonder she'd scared the crap out of him when he met her. If he'd only known what lay in store, he'd have switched seats on that airplane. But then he'd never have known Joe either. And Joe reminded him so much of Teige.

Teige the Fatalist. Teige the Resigned. Teige the Dearly Departed.

Coop felt a burning need to save Joe from the same fate. Though Coop had scant memory of his much-older-brother in the flesh, he had a trunk full of letters Teige had written him from Vietnam. Ever the pessimist, Teige had instinctively known he wouldn't get out of there alive. So he'd spent every free second he had committing to paper the brotherly advice and instruction he wanted to impart.

A packet of letters for each stage of Coop's boyhood development. He'd read them all obsessively. Still did when he needed to connect with his only sibling.

Therein lay Teige's bravery. In the thick jungle of battle, with blood pooling at his feet, he'd thought only of the helpless toddler sleeping safely in his crib—and how that toddler would miss him.

Nothing Coop would do in his life could measure up to that brand of heroism. He hadn't even been on *one* of the four planes that fateful September when he was desperately needed.

But Lea had been in one of the hairier crashes in history. And he wanted to make her life easier, to reward her accomplishment. He wanted to take care of her in the way she took care of everyone else.

"I hope Joe's having a great time," she said from the passenger seat of his truck. "Mom's going to be mad I let him take the car and run off with a strange girl."

"She'll get over it." He hung a left into the hotel parking lot and snagged a spot. "At his age my hobby was running off with strange girls."

"Back in the dark ages, the world was safer."

Killing the engine, he turned and grabbed her, pulling her in for punishing kiss. "I'm only thirty-five, Miss Priss." Releasing her, he asked, "How old are you, anyway?"

"Old enough to know better than to hang with the likes of you," she said.

"I think you're thirty. Dirty thirty."

"Busted. Here I thought I still had a youthful glow."

He grinned. "You're radiant. Not unlike uranium."

"And this from a man hoping to 'get some'."

They smiled at each other while Coop's dick grew harder and harder. Yeah. He was looking to get some all right. Bummer she came here with her parents. Kind of put a damper on things.

"I guess we better head in and see what Mom and Dad are up to," Lea said. "You want to join us for dinner tonight? They'd love to have you."

"Sure," he said. He liked the parents. Listening to Muriel drone on about Wheel of Fortune had been surprisingly relaxing. It'd supplied a much-needed break from his usual inner sturm and drang.

His own parents, while loving, were much more demanding. If he zoned out for a nanosecond, he'd miss a question or a comment and they'd freak. By contrast, Mrs. Harding reminded him of white noise. He just had to be careful not to doze off.

They hauled out of the truck and strolled hand in hand to Lea's room. He followed her inside, barely restraining the urge to toss her onto the bed and crawl all over her.

Getting tumbled by waves all day agreed with her. She looked breezy, natural, uncomplicated and incredibly hot, making him wonder if he should encourage her to ditch the cosmetics.

Hell, what the fuck did he care? He liked her both ways. He was beginning to think he'd like her any way at all.

The message light on her phone blinked. She crossed the room to the cherry bedside table, dialed the indicated number and listened with a frown. Hanging up, she turned to him, blue eyes suddenly bright and round.

"S'up?" Coop asked.

She stood there looking stunned.

"Everything okay?"

She nodded, mouth opening and closing. Finally she said, "They ditched us. They checked out and went to a B&B up the coast."

Whoa! Instant hard-on. "You're shitting me."

"No." She shook her head in wonder. "They had so much fun together at Wheel of Fortune they decided to make this trip into a romantic getaway."

Coop laughed his head off. "I never thought of a game show as foreplay."

"You don't know my parents." She pressed a hand to her forehead. "I can't believe this."

He sat down on the bed and bounced to check the springs. "Well now, that leaves us at a loose end. Doesn't it?"

She dipped her head and peered at him from under the awning her fingers formed, a slow smile curving those shell-pink lips. "Maybe I'll give Joe a call on his cell and get an ETA."

He grinned. "A most excellent idea."

* * * * *

Come on, come on, she silently begged. Be there, will ya? The idea of a whole night in bed with Coop made her hornier by the second.

Joe picked up on the fifth ring. "Hey."

"Hey. Get this," she said without preamble. "Mom and Dad took off for a second honeymoon. They said they'd meet us back in New York."

There was a dead hush. "This is a joke, right?"

She twirled the phone cord. "No joke. We're on our own. Anyway, I wanted to see what you're doing tonight. Coop and I—"

"Spare me the details." Joe chuckled. "Don't worry about me. I'm at Kim's house. We're going out with the rest of the gang later. Don't know when I'll get back."

The rest of the gang. Joe spoke as if he'd known them for years. It was the wonder of teens, she thought, to hook up so quickly. And sometimes recklessly. "Joe, be careful. I mean, don't let them talk you into anything—"

"It's not like that. They're Cal Tech students, Lea. Kim's dad teaches there."

Her mouth dropped open. What could her goth brother possibly have in common with a bunch of geeks?

"We're going over to the dorms later. They're throwing some sort of astronomy party."

"Sounds, um, interesting."

"Don't ask. And don't worry."

"Wow. Well, okay then. Have a great time!"

"I am. Just leave a message when it's safe to knock on your door," he said wryly.

"Will do." She hung up and plopped down beside Coop on the bed. He reached over and started scratching her back. "Did you ever see the movie *Moonstruck*?" she asked.

"No."

She leaned an elbow on his thigh, undulating her spine to center his blunt fingernails between her shoulder blades. Man, that felt good. "Well, one night there's a full moon, and everyone in Cher's family has a romantic interlude with someone they shouldn't be with."

"And that relates to us how?"

Ten fingernails scratched her now—all over—making her want to purr. "Tonight has that magical quality, like in the movie. My family is off having experiences they've either never had or haven't in years."

"The only difference is you and yours are with the people they *should* be with," he said.

"You think?"

His scratching turned to massaging and he said, "Oh, I think." She swiveled around and he lifted her onto his lap so they were facing each other. "There's no doubt in my mind that I'm the man you need to be with right now."

Mr. Right Now. Yup. She had to agree. "I'm not so sure," she said. "Prove it."

Securing her legs around his waist, he stood up, hands cradling her ass. She clung, giggling, to his shoulders as he carried her into the bathroom and turned on the shower. While the water heated he set her on the countertop and unhooked her bikini bra.

"I intend to, and when I'm done with you, you'll be sure."

Lea leaned back against the mirror, spreading her arms, submitting herself to his visual worship.

His open palms roamed her torso tenderly, cupping and kneading her breasts, sweeping down between them to span her waist. And all the while his gaze followed their path with glittering wonder, his eyes alternately darkening and sparkling as he explored her, creating a map in her mind of the places he found alluring and those he found astounding.

"You're so fucking hot," he groaned. "I can't believe you're real." His head dipped and tactile lips fondled a nipple. Lea moaned and threaded her fingers through the salt-thickened knots of his mane.

He slid his hips between her legs and her arms fanned out to rest on his silky broad shoulders. He ran his hands up her back, arching her into him, clutching her head to deliver lingering, succulent kisses to her lips.

"Tangy," he muttered.

"It's the seawater." She'd never been seduced so reverently, so erotically. Time slowed to a crawl as her limbs grew sluggish with desire.

"I want to lick it off you." His lean body inched closer. His mouth blazed a fiery line down her neck and throat, hot tongue flicking gently across her collarbone.

"The shower…" she said.

"What about it?" His forehead rested momentarily under her chin as he tilted his head the opposite way to continue the sensuous assault on the other side of her neck. Through moist clouds of need, a sense of awe overcame her at how perfectly his face fit into the mold of her jawline. She wanted to cradle his head there, hold it and bond it to her, feel his hot spurts of breath forever.

"I should wash," she said.

"Saltwater has minerals, you know."

"And whale pee."

He chuckled. Her hands slid down his arms, wedging between their bodies to stroke his hard abs. Sucking in a tense breath, he lifted his head to gaze at her and moved slightly away. "Touch me, Lea," he commanded. "I need to feel you touching my cock."

"Gladly," she whispered, smoothing her hands along his waistband and tucking her fingers inside. His smooth muscular buttocks filled her palms and she felt them tense in anticipation. With torturous leisure, she dipped her head and untied the laces at his crotch with her teeth, lowering his board shorts until an enormous engorged penis popped out. "My, my," she purred. "What have we here?" Before he could answer she sucked his velvety head into her mouth.

Wind whistled through his teeth and he shuddered. The briny taste of the Pacific mingled with his own unique flavor on her tongue. The musky scent of desire wafted into her nostrils and her pussy responded with an answering drool. She slid off the counter and onto her knees before him.

"Lea," he gasped. Then suddenly he was on his knees too, pushing her down to the area rug on the floor.

Steam billowed from the shower, surrounding her in a sticky hot wetness that seemed to intensify the flavors and aromas of their passion. Though he was no longer in her mouth, it seemed she could lick the air to taste him and that her open pores were receiving his very essence.

"I want to suck on you while you lick me," she said.

"Great minds think alike." With that he rolled onto his back and pulled her on top. She circled to straddle his face, ass in the air like a stretching cat, and took him fully into her mouth while his tongue lapped her up.

If she'd ever had physical boundaries, Lea'd forgotten where they were. Coop's lips, tongue and fingers laid siege on all her defenses. She felt him spread her wide then pull her down over his face. He caressed and sucked on her labia as if he were kissing her mouth, and his tongue snaked inside her vagina in the most intimate of French kisses.

Ooo la la!

Finally, the tip of his tongue found her clit and she rose on her elbows, closing her eyes and abandoning all attempts to please him simultaneously. The awesome sensation of his warm, slippery attack on her center had her gyrating and shouting in surrender. He hung on tight and his lips clung to her like a vacuum as his tongue delivered stroke after stroke.

The need to orgasm became a distilled, excruciating pleasure. She fought against the jolting waves, sucking his cock back into her mouth, wanting to bring him along with her for the ride.

He groaned and gripped her thighs tightly as she slid her teeth along the rim of his head and drew them back over the seeping fissure at the tip. The flavor of his pre-cum dissolved on her tastebuds and she swallowed the length of his shaft in preparation for the flood that would follow.

Without warning, he lifted her off his body. Confused, her gaze flew to his and glimpsed a raging inferno in its depth. "Not yet." The command came out on a gasp. He was slicked with moisture and sweat, rock-hard abs coiling as he reached for her and tucked her underneath him. She gazed up at him and almost screamed from yearning for his rigid dick between her legs.

On all fours, he crouched over her like a wild animal, inspecting every inch of her face with his eyes. "I want to come inside you."

"I have condoms in my makeup kit," she squeaked. "Right there on the counter."

He rose up on his knees and rummaged in the bag, giving her an opportunity to stare at his flawless, naked body. Curly golden brown hair covered well-formed pecs and funneled neatly down his stomach to his crotch. Except for his chest, his legs and his arms, his body was hairless, tanned and silken—perfect male beauty in the flesh—and about to be hers.

Without effort, he tore open the foil package and secured the condom on its proper place. Dropping to all fours once again, he nipped at her nose. "Your choice. On the floor, in the shower or in bed."

"How gentlemanly," she teased. While erotic before, the misty confinement of the bathroom was quickly becoming overheated and claustrophobic. She considered the shower and the soap-slick slide of flesh on flesh.

"Any day now," he said.

"Bed." As great as the shower could be, Lea wanted firmer footing the first time out. How could he thrust into her as hard as she craved if they had to be afraid of slipping?

The short pause in activity sent her hormones into a temper tantrum. Kissing hungrily, they got up and stumbled to the bed, taking only enough time to crawl under the covers before they lunged for each other and tangled into a writhing knot.

Coop poised his cock for blastoff. Unable to bear his absence another second, she wrapped her hand around the shaft and guided him to the brink, arching her hips and crying out as he plunged deeply inside.

Shockwaves of ecstasy rode the slipstream behind his thrusts. He filled her completely and she felt every centimeter of him rubbing against her, tantalizing the magical G-spot, ramming hard against her back wall as if trying to barge through a door.

And with each lunge, her barriers gave another inch. Sex with Coop felt somehow different from all her previous partners. Her physical and emotional nerves seemed raw and exposed, and he capped each one like the master marksman he was.

"Oh, God, Coop. Just like that. Yes. Just like that." Spreading her legs as wide as they would go, she clutched his clenched buttocks and pushed him deeper. He tucked one shoulder under her knee and lifted his chest slightly off hers, bracing his thighs against her ass for leverage. Through the open tent formed by the sheet, she watched his cock pump into her.

He arched his back and watched it too for a moment. "I like watching myself disappear into you," he said. Then he slid his arms under her shoulders and grasped her face in his hands. "Scream for me. I want you to come screaming." His speed increased and he pounded into her, shifting his weight with each thrust so she was inched up the pillows.

A moan tore from her throat at the powerful sensations rocketing through her. Every nerve in her vagina begged for mercy, throbbed for release. Her body and soul writhed to escape the onslaught.

And suddenly, she broke free, punching out through a ceiling of frantic need, into an invigorating sky of delight, shouting his name and relinquishing herself to the all-consuming orgasm gods.

With a guttural roar, he followed. Yanking her tightly against him as he continued to thrust until every last drop had been spilled. By the time he finished, she was shaking and spent. Soaked in sweat. Panting.

Yet still, the aftershocks of absolute orgasm surged through her body. And her mind.

Only then did she remember he'd wanted dinner first, a discussion, perhaps a real relationship…

Chapter Five

ஐ

Could he propose and not seem like a desperate schmuck? If this was the kind of sex he could expect for a lifetime, he was *so* at the altar.

Though not one to act in haste after repenting in leisure too many times—when it was right, it was right. He hadn't reached thirty-five without the experience to tell quickly whether a situation would work. This one had success stamped all over it.

In the surprise move of the century, Lea embodied everything he'd dreamed of. Yearned for. It still blew him away how badly he'd misjudged her at first but he planned on making up for it—many times, in many different positions. A smile spread slowly over his face. He closed his eyes. Bliss. Pure bliss.

If they were married, he could lighten her financial load, help send Joe to college, even send *her* to college—compliments of a dot com windfall that, while not excessive, provided a comfortable monthly income. She'd be stupid to reject such an offer. And Lea wasn't stupid. Besides, now he knew exactly how much she liked him.

It's in the bag, Masterson. In the bag.

He had something she desperately needed and it wouldn't be long before she fell as crazily into love with him as he was with her right now. But how soon could he spring it on her?

Maybe after a few more romps in the sack. Hell, they had all night. By tomorrow morning she'd be begging *him* to get married. He'd make damn sure of that.

Lea snuggled beside him under his arm and started fiddling with his chest hair. Her slender, feminine fingers felt like breath against his skin, twirling the short hairs into a garden of whorls. He ran a hand up her arm, finding her tussled, flaming hair, and let his fingers slide through the silky strands before resting against her cheek.

It struck him that he'd reacted to her like a horny moose—fucking first and asking questions later—a departure from his current, more mature style of actually dating beforehand. He felt a little ashamed. But she didn't seem to mind. Quite the opposite. "How are things going for you?" he asked.

"Can't complain."

He felt her lips curve against his shoulder. Cool. She was smiling. "Hey!" He flinched when she gave him a little nip. "Don't you want to know how I'm doing?"

She lifted her face and grinned. "Oh, I can tell."

He bussed her nose. "Wench." Flopping his head back onto the pillow, he pulled her in tightly. One of her legs slid between his and he shifted to trap it. Her body felt luscious and ripe. He could eat that smooth, plump ass for lunch. At the idea, his gut rumbled.

"We need to eat," she said, and rolled over to grab a menu off the bedside table. "Takeout, or room service?"

He spooned her and peered over a creamy shoulder to see the choices. "What about getting dressed and going out?"

She turned her face and sent him a sidewise glance. "You're one class act, you know?"

"You make me want to be a better man," he quipped.

Something flickered in her eyes and a small frown line appeared over her nose. His heart lurched, and he felt confused for a moment, but the sensation passed. If he had one iron-clad rule, it was to never second-guess what a woman might be thinking. Maybe the cheesy movie line irritated her.

"Not that I have much room for improvement," he added and was rewarded with a cocked eyebrow.

"At least not in one area," she said.

His chest swelled with purely masculine pride. He'd gotten her off good. He'd gotten off good. What could possibly go wrong now? "What's it going to be?"

She seemed to be thinking hard over this one. He didn't mind dinner in bed, but a romantic evening out sounded appealing too.

* * * * *

A stomach full of dread made Lea resist the idea of a romantic dinner with Coop. Candlelight encouraged talking, gazing deeply into each others' eyes, more talking. Wine loosened lips. And loose lips sank ships.

He had honor and commitment engraved on his forehead. She'd glimpsed it already in the way he'd focused in his job, the way he'd focused on everything—from surfing, to Joe, to her. But it had crystallized during their lovemaking, becoming a tangible thing between them. She felt like she could physically hold his feelings in her hand. And they weighed too much.

What was she going to do? She could continue to play with him, pretend to be unaware of his emotions, but if this relationship already felt serious around the edges, what would it feel like in a few more weeks?

She didn't want anyone needing her. Couldn't handle more responsibility than she already had.

But…she liked him so much. Her heart wilted in her chest. He was so wonderful, so fun.

So honorable and committed.

When had she begun to view those as bad qualities? They weren't bad qualities. They just weren't what she wanted in a boyfriend.

Well, she'd take honor. Honor was desirable. Commitment was the bugaboo. But she was getting ahead of herself here. She did, after all, want a *temporary* commitment. Maybe she misread the whole situation and that's all he wanted too. The only way to find out was to talk.

Hoo boy.

"Let's go out."

"Atta girl."

He seemed pleased with her decision. It amazed her, the difference between the Coop she'd met a few days ago and the one pulling her to her feet right now. He even looked different—more relaxed, handsomer.

Happier.

Part of her hoped it hadn't been her influence alone that satisfied him so deeply. The other part wanted to seize ownership and shout it from the Hollywood Hills. But for all she knew, this could be the real Coop, with or without her. Why did the prospect of him being equally happy either way make her sad?

"Into the shower with you." Once again, he scooped her up in strong arms and carried her, laughing, into the bathroom. She'd never indulged in the female fantasy of being toted off into the sunset. It'd never particularly appealed to her before. But Coop made it seem downright delicious.

Whoa! Freudian moment. She might have lapsed into self-analysis if Coop hadn't chosen that precise second to set her down in the hot spray and run soapy hands across her breasts.

Interesting. Besides killing without leaving a mark he could perform bloodless lobotomies too. She willingly surrendered her last brain cell.

"I wonder if they make edible soap," Coop asked, standing back to view her sudsy body. "You look like a giant ice cream sundae." He slipped a few fingers between her legs and massaged the perfumed bubbles into her sensitive flesh. She slumped against him, rubbing herself off on his torso and enjoying the scrubby texture of his hair on her stomach.

"Now that is something worth investigating," she said and added, "With you around, I don't need a body brush."

He reached for the shampoo bottle and squirted some into his palm. Then he grabbed her hand and gave her a healthy dollop. "Wouldn't be a bad way to start our days." He spread the fragrant liquid across the crown of her head, curled his fingers through her hair and started kneading her scalp.

Taking the hint, she followed suit on him and became fascinated at the evolution of his mane from mangy scruff to soft, silky waves. No, this wouldn't be a bad way to start their days—all fifteen hundred of them. Plus or minus.

They took turns rinsing and spewing water at each other. "Batter up." She snatched the soap and sudsed Coop's body, paying extra special attention to one particularly cherished region. "Mr. Majestic here has had quite the workout."

Coop's deep guffaw made her smile. "Mr. Majestic?"

"That's his new name." He deserved it too. Lea'd never seen a penis of such perfect proportion. "When I get home, I'm calling the Smithsonian. They need to make a cast."

He laughed even harder. "I'd nominate your breasts but women the world over would commit suicide."

"Men will enter monasteries."

"Plastic surgeons will offer public stock."

"The statue of David will crumble."

"So will *Playboy*."

They leaned against the tile in hysterics. Coop reached over and cupped the back of her head gently. "You're the most beautiful woman I have ever seen," he said softly. "Inside and out. Lea, I'm fall—"

No! She kissed him to shut him up. She didn't want to hear. Didn't want it to end. But she couldn't string him along either. She *did* have a conscience.

He gripped her so tightly it hurt, kissing her as if the universe was collapsing. But the ache from his bone-crushing hold couldn't compare to the ache in her heart. This would probably be her last encounter with Coop. Life surely did suck sometimes.

She hoped she had the capacity to let him down easy. She'd never been famous for tact. Yet he deserved it. He deserved so much more than she could give.

He certainly deserved one last screaming fuck. Biting back her dismay, Lea stepped up to the plate.

With brutal emotion they coiled around one another. Spray from the showerhead pelted her skin. Its punishing pinpricks provided a measure of relief, as if she indulged in self-flagellation for what she was about to do. Tears stung the backs of her eyes, and she felt grateful that the flush of genuine desire and the heat from the water might camouflage any redness they caused.

"Lea, I want you in my life," he said roughly. "I want to take care of you."

"Take care of me now," she answered.

He entered her in one strong thrust, backing her up against the wall and draping her leg over his arm.

"Harder," she demanded. She wanted him to bruise her. Wanted to wake up tomorrow unable to walk.

"No." His body shuddered as he eased up. "We did that last time. This time is the real deal. I want to show you how I feel."

"Coop—"

"This is what it could be like. Every day." His velvety smoothness caressed her inside. His fingers flicked like butterflies across her skin.

While her body screamed for an all-out assault, the tender, fleeting wisps of his touch set up a frantic craving, telegraphing a message to hidden places. Places she'd never been sure existed. "I want this every day," she whispered.

"So do I."

"But—" she gasped as he angled her hips, flowing in and out of her completely and with measured grace. "Not forever. It can't be forever."

"Sure it can," he said. Wet lips covered hers. Tongues meshed, lapping the hot water that sluiced down their faces and into their mouths.

He pressed his slick body closer to hers, hemming her in, giving her no way to escape. His strong, gentle hands kept her ass in a firm grip as he pumped into her with a hypnotically even rhythm.

She had no choice but to cling to his shoulders as keening ecstasy snuck up on her. She would miss this lean body, the way he'd glance at her in surprise at something she said, his deep laugh. She'd miss his effortless understanding of Joe and his unselfish, nurturing nature—all these fine qualities she hadn't realized existed a few days ago.

Helpless gasps of pleasure hissed out between her teeth.

Something about Coop told her these qualities were genuine. He couldn't fake the brand of sincerity he offered any more than he could fake being a world-class lover. No question he was the perfect man. Except he had lousy timing.

A vortex of rapture whipped over her, and she felt herself spasm around him in a death grip. He caught his breath, gripped her and brought them both noisily over the top with the tiniest, subtlest movements. She thought for sure she would lose her mind. If she'd ever had one to begin with.

* * * * *

"I'm getting the Cajun tuna. You?" Coop asked.

Lea glanced up from her shrimp cocktail appetizer and stared at him. "Sorry?" The bright turquoise of her skimpy sundress made her eyes look like enormous blue gumballs.

He grinned and leaned over the table, taking her hand and lacing fingers. "Anybody home? You've been quiet the last hour. I asked what you were getting for dinner."

"Oh. Yes. Um—"

"Remind me to search the shower for your brain when we get back tonight." Okay. That got a smile. Albeit a small one.

But no smartass comeback.

Dread laced his blood, making his stomach clench and sending gushes of adrenaline through the pipeworks. He felt like a goddamn chimp with his lips pulled back over his teeth.

Something was up with her, and it wasn't good. She hadn't made eye contact for more than a second since he'd left to get dressed and returned to pick her up. When he'd kissed her, her lips felt dry and tight.

Coop hadn't exactly been dumped numerous times in his life, but the times he had been left a lasting impression. He could practically hear the bell toll.

He tried to convince himself he was imagining it. She could be thinking about a thousand different things right now—including how desperately in love she was. He wouldn't know for sure until she opened that luscious yap and spilled. But a little fucking voice told him to eat now while he had the chance. Later on he'd be too knotted up.

"I'll have the mahi-mahi." She closed the small menu and pushed it aside, leaning an elbow on the table and fiddling with a shrimp.

He nodded. "Sounds good."

She didn't reply.

"I thought later we could take a spin over to Santa Monica pier and walk around," he said.

"Okay."

He rolled his eyes and let out a tense breath. A young waitress materialized by the table to take their dinner orders. When she left he tried again. "I'm having a great time." Or at least he had been. What had caused Lea's somber mood? Had he made a left when he should've swung a right? Coop thought back over the day.

Everything had been fine until they made love. And he felt certain he'd done a bang-up job with that assignment. No way could she have faked all those orgasms.

Could she? He snuck a glance at her and a mental shudder quaked him from head to toe. Not a chance. No one was that good an actress.

Then came the shower and some conversation while they made love. Afterwards, everything had changed.

He recalled he'd almost told her he'd loved her and she'd stopped him. He'd told her he wanted her in his life and she'd said *not forever*. A cold finger jabbed his heart.

Bada-fucking-bing.

Not forever. What had she meant, precisely? He knew for a fact there wasn't another boyfriend unless he counted Jake White, the fake hijacker. Only one way to find out. "Are you going to sulk all night or are you going to tell me what's wrong?"

Across the table, she sat ramrod straight and drew a deep breath. When she met his gaze, hers appeared stony. "Coop, I really like you—"

"Whoa!" *Shit.* Things were worse than he thought. He held up a hand. He'd never sat still for the *it's not you, it's me* convo and he wasn't about to start now. "Lose the bullshit. I like you too. What's the real problem?"

Curvaceous lips thinned into a tight line. Coop noticed her hand tremble slightly as she reached for a water goblet. He could smell her anxiety all the way across the table.

"I think eventually you'll want more than I'm willing to give," she said levelly. "In fact, I think you already do."

Breathe, Masterson. He rested an elbow over the back of his chair and idly examined his fingernails. "Depends." He looked straight at her. "What are you willing to give?" Best to know the enemy face-to-face.

"Four years."

Not the answer he'd expected. But fuck, he didn't know what the hell he'd expected. "Four years?"

"Coop." She rearranged her silverware, concentrating so hard on making the bowl of the spoon even with the point of the knife he nearly flung it across the dining room. "I don't want to get married."

Play it cool. "Who said anything about marriage?"

"I'll never want to get married."

He swallowed. Hard. Was his head bobbing from side to side like the village idiot, or did it just feel that way?

"I don't want babies. I've had a lifetime of responsibility already and I can't tolerate any more."

And men the world over complained about women's indirect communication styles. Leave it to Coop to unearth the most direct female known to humankind.

Could he deal with her restrictions? Children he might be able to do without—if he had no other choice. But he really wanted a wife. He really wanted *her* for a wife. At least someday. "What responsibility? I'll take care of you. I'd love to take care of you. You've earned it."

Her gaze fluttered and swept the room. When it returned to him, it'd grown heavy with worry and sadness. His chest tightened. He thought about her parents and how Joe had told him that they depended on Lea for financial support.

"I'm sure my father felt the same way about my mother. But things happen. People change. They become disabled…"

"You're worried you'd wind up taking care of me?"

She nodded and bit a lip. "I'd start to hate you. I don't want that to happen."

He grabbed her hand and clenched it tightly. "Look at me, Lea."

She obeyed.

"I'm not your father. I have money set aside, disability insurance—"

"It's not just about financial support, Coop. It's the emotional support too. I don't have anything left to give. I'm used up."

"You need someone to recharge you."

"I want to play for once."

"I can do that." He smiled but she didn't smile back. "You've been through a lot, Lea. I'm aware of that. Hell, you're a hero. And heroes deserve a hero's reward. I want to give you that."

"Why?"

He released her hand and sat back. Why did he want to give it to her? Because it was something he himself would never know? Because Teige had never gotten it? Because he loved her, or at least felt the stirrings of what would surely be the love of his life? "A lot of reasons."

"Name one."

Best not to bring up the love thing again. "Because my brother died in Vietnam." She drew back in surprise as he leaned into his tale.

"I'm sorry. I didn't know."

He waved her apology aside. "Maybe some assholes would've spit on him when he got back, but his brother would've given him his due."

"So you feel you *owe* it to me?"

"And Joe." He shook his head to clear it and felt a searing burn behind his eyes. Pressing two fingers against the bridge of his nose, he sniffed and looked back at her. "Joe is like a reincarnation of Teige—the hopelessness, the resignation."

She blinked and her eyes widened. "This is all about Joe, then."

"No!" His fist came down on the table harder than he intended, shaking the wine goblets and sloshing some precious liquid on the tablecloth. "It's about you and Colony and Joe and… Shit, Lea. I haven't done a damn thing in my life that can compare."

A heavy silence descended.

"But you want to." She looked at him as if she'd found him stuck to the bottom of her shoe. "You really do have a savior complex."

"So the hell what? I'd like to help you. I'd like to help Joe."

"And I'd like to teach the world to sing," she snapped. "You can't base a lifetime relationship on wanting to rescue someone, Coop. Believe me, I know. I wanted to save my family too. And I did. And the more I gave the more they took until I feel so trapped I'm ready to chew my leg off."

"That's not going to happen." *Was it?* "There's more to this than just saving you." *Wasn't there?* "We have something." He'd felt fairly certain they did.

Until now.

What if she was right?

No fucking way was she right. He knew what he wanted in a woman and it was sitting right in front of him. Sure she had true grit but that was the hardened sugar shell guarding the delicate fanciful confection he'd glimpsed underneath. Not terribly important in the grand scheme of things.

Except he'd disliked her before he found out about Colony.

But hadn't they gotten to know each other fairly well? As an air marshal, he'd become adept at reading subtle clues. She'd displayed many of the qualities he wanted in a wife. Of that he was sure. Seemed she would take some convincing, though. Okay. She was worth it. He could wait. He could be convincing. He had four years.

"What? What do we have, Coop? From my point of view we have the hots for each other. We have fun together. But beyond that…" She trailed off and her last sentence blew out on a bleak sigh. "I don't need someone to watch over me or a lover who sees me as a project and you're already getting too serious about me. Maybe we should just end it now."

* * * * *

For a moment he looked as if he'd been sucker-punched. Confirming the depth of the feelings she'd thought he'd had for her and causing a searing regret to flame through her heart. She really didn't want to hurt him.

But then his gray eyes chilled and narrowed and the yellow flecks inside them swirled like a hypnotist's wheel. "Let's not be hasty, babe," he said smoothly. "Four years is a long time. People change."

"Yes, they do."

He nodded and she got the sensation of being in a car showroom with a slippery salesman.

"We'll probably crash and burn," he continued.

"I couldn't agree more," she said.

"Why not have some fun first?"

Well, what do you know? Seemed the bullshit was oozing freely today. Lea couldn't say for certain what exactly tipped her off, but over the course of the day she'd noticed Coop watched her face extra closely whenever he teased her. Or, she supposed, lied to her. "I didn't fall off the turnip truck, *Cooper*."

"What?"

She almost laughed. "Stop with the innocent act. I see right through you."

He made a horrified face and this time, she did laugh. "Cut it out. I'm trying to break up with you." Aghast, he pointed a finger at his own chest. More giggles. "This is a solemn moment. So stop joking."

"Don't I at least get a pity fuck?"

"I gave you one already."

"You did not."

"Yup. In the shower."

"That was no pity fuck, m'dear."

The waitress appeared and hovered uncertainly at Lea's elbow. She and Coop sat back while the silent, red-faced girl plunked the plates in front of them and ran like the wind.

"I thought California girls were more sophisticated than that," Lea commented.

"She must be new," Coop said. "So what about my pity fuck?"

"I don't know. You just want to hang around in case I change my mind and decide to get married."

"Maybe so. But maybe I also want to take what I can get while I can get it. So far, what I've gotten has been pretty good."

"What I've gotten has been pretty good too."

His gray eyes illuminated from within and he smiled at her with uncharacteristic tenderness. Some of her resolve melted in the face of such pure and open appreciation.

He wasn't going to be easy to shake. And her half-hearted attempt to spare him tonight had only served to make him dig his heels in deeper. Lea had to admit she admired a man who had a stubborn streak. Still, he had to realize that her hand was not up for grabs. She never intended to be responsible for another human being's welfare and happiness again. For as long as she lived.

"Then we have an understanding," she said. "You'll hang around to have sex with me for a while and won't come crying for more when I kick you out."

He extended a bare hand strong enough to bend steel, and she took it in hers. "We have an understanding."

Great. She'd won this little battle. So why did she feel like such a big fat loser?

Chapter Six

ℰ𝒪

Two weeks later Lea stood in the middle of the living room of her childhood home—surrounded by her parents, Joe and Coop—with her hands cradling her slack-jawed face.

"We said we're selling the house," Muriel repeated.

Lea had known things had changed during their bizarre long weekend in Hollyweird. Muriel and Lester had morphed into people she barely knew anymore—going out on dates, pinching each other's asses when they thought no one could see—but this was ridiculous. Selling the house? "Where are you going to live?" she squeaked.

"The Pattersons want to get rid of that RV that's sat on their driveway for years. We're buying it and we're going to see the world." The triumph in Muriel's voice set Lea aback. Her mother'd never been the type for the open road. Yet she seemed as excited as a pirate heading out on a high seas adventure.

"Coop said the RV was in good shape," Joe said. "Mom already bought a satellite dish for it."

Coop had the good grace to look sheepish when Lea glared at him. "Just needs new tires," he said.

"But—"

"No ifs, ands or buts, Lea," Lester said. "The real estate agent was here yesterday and she said we could get close to a million for this house. The property alone is worth that."

"A developer is going to tear this dump down and build four mini mansions," Joe said.

"My, my, are we going to have a tag sale or what?" Muriel sang, and actually danced a little jig. Lea didn't know whether to feel elated or horrified. What the hell had happened to her parents? Had the pod people finally taken over?

"Guess Long Island property value has risen a tad since nineteen seventy-five," Coop said.

"Damn straight, my man." Lester grinned, giving Coop a high five.

Lea nearly fell down. Recovering, she snarled at Coop. "This is my family's future we're talking about."

Coop merely smirked.

Muriel sidled up next to Lea and squeezed her. "We'll give you some of the money for your law school tuition. After all, you kept us in this house all these years." She squealed and clapped her hands. "Looks like your dream is that much closer, honey."

A sparkler of joy lit Lea's heart even as she saw Coop stiffen out of the corner of her eye. But quicker than a blink, reality intruded. "That's a wonderful thought, Mom. But Joe needs the money first. I already have a job and he's just starting out."

Coop released a steady, long breath. It peeved her that he would be relieved her dream had to be put on hold yet again. How come she always came last? You'd think if he cared about her, he'd want her to grab what she wanted out of life. All he cared about was getting laid.

Well, so did she. It'd turned into their favorite pastime.

She looked over at Joe affectionately. He'd gone to Los Angeles a disgruntled kid and come home a promising young man. The friendships he'd formed right there on the beach were solidifying through instant messaging, e-mails—and a new and improved cell phone calling plan. His friends were on a brilliant path at Cal Tech, and Lea could plainly see they'd had a good influence on Joe. His current, healthy surfer look was merely the outward manifestation of the changes that'd taken place inside. She felt so damn proud of him she could explode. And he would continue to come first in her life until he didn't need her anymore.

A giant glob formed in her throat.

"I have an announcement too," he said almost shyly. All eyes turned to him. Coop sat down and folded his fingers into a pyramid at his sexy mouth. "I've made up my mind and no one is going to change it."

A hush fell over the room and Lea had a blinding vision of what would come next. Even as Joe said the words, she was reaching out for him, grabbing at his arm, trying to keep her baby brother close and safe. With her.

"I'm going back to California," Joe said in a rush. "I can stay in a house some of my friends rented. They're getting me a job as a waiter so I can go to community college and maybe get into Cal Tech in my sophomore year."

"Cal Tech?" Lester whispered. "Son, only smart kids go there—"

Joe held up a hand. "Kim's father and I were talking about surfing, and he said I had an understanding of the physics involved that went beyond anything he'd ever seen."

"Joe!" Lea blinked back tears and covered her mouth.

"He said if I applied myself, I might get a scholarship to study surfing. I could travel around the world."

"Oh my good Lord," Muriel breathed.

"But it's too late for me to get in this year. So I'll go to community college instead."

"Joey," Muriel said. "There's more to getting into a fancy school than that. The money…well, honey…I don't think even your sister could afford that."

Joe looked at Lea with huge, gleaming cocoa eyes. "That's the best part. She doesn't have to pay for it. I'm going to. I'm going to work and I'm going to get scholarships based on my aptitude scores and my grades in college."

"Aptitude scores?" Muriel wrinkled her nose. "You never took those tests, Joey. Weren't you sick or something?"

"I got sick this year but I'd already taken one in my junior year. It blew chunks because I wanted to improve my score."

"Tell them what you got," Coop said.

Joe shrugged. "I got a fifteen fifty-three. Sucks. Kim and everyone got sixteen hundreds."

"Why," Lea said in a shaky voice. "Why didn't you ever tell us?"

"What was the point?" Joe threw his arms out in a desperate, helpless gesture. "Nothing interested me. I didn't want to be a geeky rocket engineer or stuck in some gay lab at a pharmaceutical company. I didn't know what else I could do with my life."

"So you chose nothing."

He nodded and let his head droop. "I guess I let it get me down. But surfing with Coop…" He trailed off and gazed over at Lea's lover. "It opened a whole new world. And then when I met Kim and the gang, and talked to her dad, and hung out at Cal Tech…" His voice thickened. "I felt like I'd come home."

"Oh, Joe."

"I belong there, Lea."

"Yes," she sighed. "I think you do." She yanked him in for a tight, teary embrace.

"So you're free, sis. I release you from your obligation. I should've done it a long time ago."

Damn it. She didn't want to wreck her face by blubbering. She and Coop were going out later and she didn't have time to take another shower. A few deep gulps against Joe's sleek shoulder steadied her for the moment.

"We release you too, honey," Lester said. "You've done your job and we're all fine now. It's your turn."

"Daddy!"

"Lester's right, dear. Give us a hug and go out with Coop. This is the first night of the rest of your life."

* * * * *

The rest of her life. Lea glanced over at Coop as he parked the car in her spot in front of the condo and hopped out to open the door for her. Tonight's revelations were too fantastic to take in. Both Joe and her parents going off on their own. Not needing her anymore. She was free.

Free.

The word rang like Christmas bells in her head. The money her parents offered as payback for her sacrifices, while not enough to allow her to quit Pan Air, was certainly enough to let her go part time. If she paid off the car loan she'd have no debt, only taxes and maintenance on the condo. Flying part time would definitely cover those expenses. And, combined with a brutal study load, would leave little time for Coop.

Did he know what was coming? Hard to tell by his face. He looked far too pleased with himself as they strolled up the walkway to her front door. Nothing about his attitude reflected a man on the verge of getting the axe.

"I never thought the day would come," she ventured, crossing the lush blue carpeting of the living room and stopping in the kitchen to crack a beer for Coop. He came up behind her and slid his arms around her waist, gliding his hands up to her breasts for a squeeze.

"In the nick of time." He pressed erotic kisses across the nape of her neck. "You were getting frustrated. Total breakdown was imminent."

She laughed and wiggled out of his grip, handing him the beer and filling a glass with ice and tap water for herself. "You're telling me."

"Funny how that happens." He tossed her a glance without quite meeting her eyes, and the schooled expression on his face as he half-sat on the kitchen counter raised her suspicions.

"Did you, by chance, have anything to do with this?" she asked.

His eyebrows shot up briefly before knitting into a frown. "What?"

She let a silent moment pass while she sipped her ice water and stared at him. Coop started swinging the leg that dangled off the counter. "My parents," she reminded. "Selling the house?"

He coughed. "Are you accusing me of educating Lester and Muriel about property values?"

"Somebody did."

"I don't know anything about one-acre tracts in Riverhead."

With a snort, Lea lunged at him and shoved him off the counter. "You're so full of shit."

He threw his head back and roared. She pounded on his chest halfheartedly until he put down his beer and dropped a kiss on the top of her head.

She felt like kicking herself in the ass. If she'd had half a brain, she would've advised her family to sell that property long ago. She'd been so stressed that the obvious solution to their financial dilemma had escaped notice all these years. Yet Coop had seen it instantly. It galled her a little. He made it look so easy. As if *savior* was his middle name. Maybe it was. Maybe that was a good thing after all. No one had ever lifted a finger for her. No one.

She hated herself for liking it.

"What about Joe?" she accused.

Coop held up his hands and she swung out of his embrace. "I had nothing to do with Joe. He made up his own mind."

"I disagree. You had everything to do with Joe. If he hadn't met you he'd still be a depressed washout. You showed him a different world."

Coop cocked his head and wrinkled his nose in a curiously self-deprecating gesture. "Maybe."

Did he not think he'd helped? "I'll always be grateful." *Time to say thank you and buh-bye. And maybe return some of Mr. Spittle's unanswered calls.*

"How grateful?"

"Very grateful." *Shut up!*

"Grateful enough to help me out with a recurring fantasy?"

Lea crossed her arms and placed a finger against her lips. She shouldn't even be considering it. "Depends on the fantasy." Who said that?

"Wait right there." Coop bolted out to his car and returned with the overnight bag he habitually kept in the trunk. He'd left it in her bedroom once and gotten a clue when she pointedly handed it to him the next evening. There'd be no jockey shorts and shaving kits in her bathroom. Not now. Not ever.

"Whatcha got?" she asked.

He unzipped the duffle and pulled out a colorful box. It took her a moment to read the label. "Fruit roll candy?"

"Better known as edible underwear," he leered. "I want you to eat them off me, but even more, I want to eat them off you."

This would only encourage him to think he had a chance. No way could she, in good conscience, indulge him. "Let me get this straight. I'm supposed to sheath Mr. Majestic in this and peel it off with my teeth?"

"Gently." He cringed.

"Oh, with utmost care, I assure you." She unwrapped a sheet and mentally measured it against Mr. M's impressive girth. "Not sure this is going to fit."

"It stretches when it gets warm."

"You would know?" Why did the thought stick a hatpin into her heart? It wasn't as if he was a virgin. And God knew she wasn't. But doing something with Coop as fun and inventive as fruit rolls lost a lot of luster when he had something to compare the experience with.

"Actually no. But I usually take a box to the beach when I surf." He hung his head and peered sheepishly at her. "A closet addiction. You ought to know by now that I wouldn't chew fruit rolls off just anyone."

Yeah, she did know. Part of the problem. It made Coop seem special. As if they'd broken new ground together not only in bed but emotionally as well. The result? She felt closer to him. Valued. And she suspected he felt the same way about her. Perhaps more so.

Just one dilemma after another. On one hand she didn't want to give up what they had. On the other, she had plans for herself that didn't include anyone else. She didn't want to have a bond with him. Yet one had mysteriously formed. And the longer she strung this thing out the tighter it would get. Until one day she wouldn't have the wherewithal to leave.

Time to cut loose.

Now if only he'd stop looking at her as if she already wore a candy sarong and he'd just flown in from Planet Lo-Carb. Was she really so heartless as to fuck his brains out tonight and give him the heave-ho in the morning?

His capable hands grabbing her said *yes*. She was a heartless bitch who could never say no to Coop's lovemaking no matter how cavalierly she planned on dumping him later.

Oh well. She'd deal with the bitch factor tomorrow.

Coop swept her up against his chest, carrying her into the bedroom and laying her gently onto the soft damask coverlet.

With silken movements, he spread her legs with his, hovering above while tenderly unbuttoning her blouse. "In the three weeks I've known you, you've gotten more beautiful," he said huskily. "How can that be possible? I'll never get used to looking at you and touching you."

"That's what good sex will do for a woman," she said, half-wishing he wouldn't be quite so free with the compliments. Making love with him was like being worshipped. She reveled in it but was increasingly concerned she'd become accustomed to him and unable to accept anything less. The Earth didn't grow many world-class lovers anymore. She had the passport stamps to prove it.

"I read the other day that a fulfilling sex life can take seven years off a woman's appearance," he said, tracing a fingertip between her breasts and down to her bellybutton.

"Is that so?" she asked. And undid his button fly.

"Scientific fact. I can make you look twenty-three."

She undulated as he pinched a nipple and grabbed it between his teeth, grinding them ever so gently to send shockwaves straight into her pussy. "This is just another one of your ploys."

"Not a ploy." He slid her shorts off. "A reason."

"To keep you around?"

"That's right. Tonight I'm going to give you many good reasons why you still need me." The heated tip of his tongue danced a tango in her pubic hair. Her back arched and she gripped his head, fingers tangling in the thick mess of hair. He found her clit and her legs shot into the air, heels finally settling on his shoulders and slipping down the length of his broad back.

"I don't *need* anyone," she gasped.

He stopped his assault and looked into her eyes. "Maybe not, but you *want* someone. And that someone is me. Doing this." He tore open a handful of fruit roll packages and ripped them into smaller pieces. Placing a small square on each of her nipples, he pinched them together to form protective pyramids. Then he quickly twisted a few into a belt and looped it around her waist while she watched in fascinated anticipation. Lastly, he draped a full sheet over the belt, covering her pubis.

Was she crazy, or did every woman deserve a man who knew how to make a fruit roll bikini? Suddenly, it seemed like one of life's basic necessities.

Yet not.

"You're awfully sure of yourself," she said.

"Have to be. Around you."

"Then don't be around me."

He groaned and rocked back on his knees. "You're not going to make this easy for me, are you?"

He had an amazingly good attitude about this whole dumping issue. "Nope." She rolled away and stood up as he reached for her and his eyes narrowed at the sound of her nervous giggle. "I am so out of here," she said, and shot around the king-sized bed towards the door.

For a big guy, he moved fast. Lea underestimated the distance and he lunged over the bed and captured her by an ankle.

"Gotcha," he growled. She squealed, kicking out of his grip so he lost balance and nearly slid off the mattress. Giggling uncontrollably, fruity bikini bottom flapping, she sped into the living room with him hot in pursuit.

He caught up with her as she made a break for the patio doors leading out to the deck. Facing southwest over the beach, the last orange glow of the summer sunset cast vivid spears of color across scudding clouds. Lea stopped shy of running out and spied Coop behind her in the reflection off the glass.

"Breathtaking," he murmured in her ear.

"Mmmm." His warm breath tickled her neck. "I never get tired of the beautiful sunsets around here."

"What sunset?" he asked. "I was talking about you."

Good one. She turned to make a smart-aleck retort and he captured her against him, the swelling of his cock an irresistible temptation.

"Your skin is luminous," he said, flicking his tongue along the side of her neck. She nuzzled into the rough texture of the five o'clock shadow on his chin.

"It's the light."

"You sure? I thought maybe it was me. And your need for this—" he cupped her pussy in a strong, kneading hand, parting the folds of her labia and slipping a finger into the hot, wet recesses of her tingling vagina.

"That too," she sighed, and a faraway voice warned her she was in serious trouble.

He'd engineered her family situation so she'd be free to go to school, knowing she'd leave him when she did. Why? Was he trying to make her feel obligated? To be so grateful for her freedom she'd keep him in her life? He'd known where this evening was headed before it'd even started and now he was pulling out the stops to get her to stay with him.

Leaning slightly away from the assault his lips and teeth were making on her collarbone, she tried to focus on the task at hand. "It's not going to work," she managed as his head lowered and he attacked the candy pasties.

"It's working fine," he surfaced with a chewy red strip between his teeth and grinned. "Yummy."

"No, not that. This. Your plan."

"What plan?" His stained tongue left sticky trails between her breasts and down her stomach. Kneeling in front her, he nipped at the candy loincloth. "Right now my only plan is to have dessert."

He was intentionally misunderstanding. Looking down, she had the sensation of being gnawed on by a hungry lion. The color and texture of his hair combined with his opened mouth chasing and capturing the fruit leather gave her a giddy sense of wild danger… And when he went for the waistband of the sweet skirt, she nearly lost all resolve and begged him to take her right here and now, for as long as they both should live. But that would never happen.

Not on her watch.

In search of glucose, his lower teeth grazed her clit. Her entire body shuddered, and, like a predator sensing weakened prey, he honed in and repeated the action. Before she could say "fuck off", those same lower teeth carved a property line around her and, adding insult to injury, the upper teeth joined in, gliding along the incredibly sensitive tip, surrounding it, claiming it and driving her stark raving mad.

If Coop was going to make love to her to serve his own purposes, she'd let him. She had her own agenda to serve and she could feel it cresting between her legs.

The end of his tongue flicked between the gentle cage of his teeth around her clit. With deft, brief lashes, he whipped her into a writhing frenzy. Flick after flick until she pressed back against the patio door, her head beating a pagan rhythm against the glass that matched the pounding throb of approaching orgasm.

Then he stopped.

"No," she cried. "Don't stop."

"Turn around," he commanded.

Without waiting for compliance, he spun her to face the exploding sunset, yanked her ass closer and rammed his hard cock into her.

Spine arched, she staggered forward and pressed her palms on the door. Coop supported her from behind, gripping her waist with a ferocity he hadn't displayed before in bed. Her mind jumped back to his authoritative presence in the classroom. She realized as much time as she'd spent with him the last two weeks, she'd forgotten to reconcile the two sides of his nature—friendly, playful Coop and merciless hunter Coop, intent on bringing his prey to ground. He was a force to be reckoned with, the relentless hammering of his cock inside her his weapon of choice.

Wouldn't you know he had the one weapon she was defenseless against?

The tantric screaming of her pussy at being denied a good licking soon yielded to the war drum-beat of his thrusts. She bet if she read his mind, it'd be chanting, "You will succumb. You will succumb."

But she wouldn't. Coop might win the battle of sex, but he would not win the war. They had an agreement, dammit, and he would honor it if she had to make him.

Her pussy began to spasm as she strained for release. The first gentle electrical disturbances of an approaching storm wiggled through her and just as the giant jolt was about to crack, he pulled out.

Lea howled in protest. Her body screamed. Every cell felt clogged and heavy, thick and frustrated. "Coop!" she yelled.

He didn't answer. Instead he reached for another sheet of fruit and rolled it around Mr. Majestic. "Eat this off me," he said, and pushed her to her knees.

The sight of his enormous candy-coated cock amused her momentarily. But a higher level of horniness soon launched in her body as the head, isolated from the rest of the shaft, took on a whole new and delicious appeal.

She loved its perfect helmet shape. Loved the feel of it in her mouth—the silky texture and round softness. When naked, it was irresistible. Now, with its succulent coating, she might never let go.

And lookie here. Coop was right. It got pliable when warmed. Gummy pieces lodged between her teeth as she sucked and licked on the candy and its host. Her tongue rolled around his penis and into the crevices of her mouth, snagging stray pieces before they hit the back of her throat. When she found one, she glued it back to the larger piece with the tip of her tongue, until the whole contraption started melting away and she had to suck harder to keep the juice from running down her chin.

Her busy-beaver movements sent Coop into a moaning frenzy. His fingers gripped the sides of her head in a vise. She caught glimpses of him in the reflection of the patio doors, standing erect in his Greek-God magnificence, hips thrust out, head thrown back in unbearable ecstasy.

He was perfection.

In a stunning flash, she knew beyond the shadow of a doubt he had to go.

Now.

As much as she desired him, as much as she'd played with the idea of keeping him around for amusement, and as much as she liked him, he was a liability to her heart. One she could no longer afford to ensure against. The risk was too great. The price too high. Her resources, and her luck, had run out.

Calmly, she sat back on her haunches and let Mr. Majestic dangle in the chilled air.

"What the fuck—" Coop's eyes flew open and he glanced down with an almost comical expression of confusion.

"You have to go now," she said, swiping her sticky, wet mouth and rising to head for the bathroom.

"Whoa!" He caught her arm and swung her around.

"Let me go." She tried twisting out of his grip and should've known better. Wonderful. Tomorrow she'd have a nice Indian burn above her elbow.

He peered into her face long and hard, causing her heart to kick around in her rib cage. As well as she thought she knew him, there was a wild, unpredictable quality in his current demeanor, and she remembered quite well from past experience that most men didn't take kindly to blowjobus interruptus.

Swallowing thin strings of saliva cobwebbing in a suddenly dry mouth, she stared him down as long as she could but wavered for a microsecond under the laser heat from his gaze.

"I'll be damned," he said softly, letting her arm drop and folding strong arms across his chest. "You're scared."

"Don't be ridiculous."

"You're scared shitless because you're falling in love with me."

"I am not!"

"Then finish what you started." He issued the challenge in a low, menacing voice. When she nervously took a baby step away, he advanced a giant step.

"I am finishing it."

"I meant this." Without laying a hand on her, he stood suffocatingly close, towering over her with a psycho-erotic edge so broad she started itching to touch him. How silly—the ease with which he ruled her. She felt caught in a revolving door—trying to get away from Coop, only to have him lure her back full circle with his extreme brand of sexuality. "If there's no danger, then why not finish pleasing me and allow me to finish pleasing you. You tipped your hand, babe. You're falling. And if that happens, you can't waltz off into the sunset."

She could do anything she damn well wanted. "I'm not about to fall in love with you or anyone. I don't want—"

"The responsibility. You already told me. Here's a four-one-one. Love sets you free. It doesn't tie you down."

"Wrong."

"Prove it."

She rested a burning cheek against the cool glass patio door and watched the embers of the sun fizzle on the horizon. Coop pressed closer, his moist, fuzzy six-pack on her flank. The heaving of his chest matched the tumult in her mind. Matched her own panting body.

"See what we have, Lea," he cajoled, kneading her breasts and stroking her sweat-dampened hair. "You can't give this up. I can help you. Be a partner. We belong together."

She shook her head but the action blended with the general shakiness of her whole body and was lost on him.

No," she muttered, cleared her throat and then again louder. "No."

"Yes. I won't give you up."

"But you said—"

"I lied."

"Bastard."

He laughed.

"It's not funny," she shrieked. This time she would *not* be waylaid by his good humor. He had to understand she meant business. "I'm serious, Coop. Deadly serious." She turned and straightened, feeling spent and tired, as if she'd been erased and only the faintest smudges of resolve remained. Her weakness for Coop was slowly but surely sucking the life out of her.

He somehow found a fleece blanket, swaddled her into it and they stumbled to the sofa on wobbly legs where she said quietly, "Analyze *us* for a second. You wanted someone to save, to make a hero of yourself. Well, you achieved that. You saved Joe and you helped deliver me from my prison cell. You've done your job and can ride off into the sunset a happy masked man."

"It's not just about saving you."

"Yes it is! You don't love me. You love my family, and even more so, you love what you can do for us. This is really, in the end, all about you. Well guess what? I say it's all about *me* now."

"You're the one that's full of shit," Coop growled. "You're the most unselfish person I know. It's part of your basic makeup. You could've ditched your family, but you didn't. Why? Because helping them fulfills you. I'm not the only one who goes around saving people. You might hate hearing it, but you and I have a lot in common and running away won't change that. You're in the service industry for a reason—and as far as I know, you're staying there. Law is a service too."

"It's not about that, Coop. It's about education. Being self-reliant. I won't be a burden. Not yours. Not anybody's."

"Love isn't a burden, Lea. It's an honor, a privilege. And if you became disabled, I'd gladly support you."

"But I wouldn't gladly support you, Coop. I wouldn't love you for better or for worse. I'm a fair weather friend and there's nothing you can do to change that."

For once, he didn't say anything.

"You. Can't. Have. Me."

Dead silence. Head down, she glanced at him out of the corner of her eye and watched his jaw clench three times. As if sensing her scrutiny, he turned his face away, smacked his thigh and launched off the sofa. "So be it." At the speed of lightning, he dressed, grabbed his things and headed for the door. "You want to be alone, you got it."

The slam and shudder of the front door closing had a final quality that nearly throttled dinner out of her stomach. For a second, she lay there, wondering what to do, grieving for the sour way it had ended. The sick feeling didn't last all that long, however. And within a few minutes, she found the strength to haul herself to her feet and into the shower, where she spent the next half hour washing every last trace of him off and tamping down the swells of regret that threatened to engulf her.

Chapter Seven

ꟿ

A piercing wail echoed in the canyon between dreaming and waking, and Lea bolted upright with a startle. Scrabbling along the bedside table in the darkness for the phone that never rang anymore, she realized suddenly where she was and leapt out of bed to scurry down the narrow hallway of Kira Grayson's condo.

Jack Grayson oozed sleepily out into the corridor, thick brown hair a boyish mop, eyes puffy from new baby exhaustion.

"S'all right. I got it." Lea patted Jack on the shoulder and steered him back into his bedroom. She peeked inside at Kira—snoring gently—then high-tailed it across to the nursery.

A crescent moon-in-a-sleeping-cap nightlight provided dim illumination as she lifted Thomas from his bassinet.

"Ooooh. Shhhhh. I'm here," she cooed. "I'm here, baby."

The red-faced newborn hiccoughed, looked up at her and stuck a spastic fist into his mouth. Lea snuggled him into the crook of her arm and he instinctively turned his face towards her breast, rooting with his mouth for the comforting nourishment of mother's milk.

"Wrong booby," she told him softly and whisked him into the kitchen where she hastily heated a bottle of formula in the microwave. He made a wretched face when he caught her familiar yet undesirable scent and began to fuss again. The moment he opened his mouth, Lea stuck the bottle inside and he looked at her in astonishment for a moment before suckling like crazy.

Mumbling nonsense in hushed tones, she walked Thomas around the condo, stopping at each photograph on the wall, each window. Pointing out chairs and tchotchkes. Just as she had been doing for the past two weeks since Coop flew the coop. Since everyone had flown the coop.

Even as Kira squeezed tiny Thomas out into the world, Lea's parents had started packing. Her mother held the tag sale to end all tag sales, the RV went in for detailing and the family homestead had gone before the For Sale sign had been planted on the front lawn.

By the time Lea finished playing doula for Kira the parents would be long gone. First stop, Niagara Falls—a re-creation of their honeymoon thirty-one years ago.

Since given the boot, Coop hadn't tried contacting her. She'd reckoned on one more shot, but apparently, she'd used up her chances. He had, however, maintained contact with Joe and, as far as she knew, was currently helping him move out west. Right now, they were probably in the vicinity of Tucumcari, getting their kicks on Route Sixty-Six.

It pissed her slightly, how seamlessly he recovered. He simply carried on with his superhero existence, saving Joe and her parents without her consent, happy as a clam. It was Lea, in those low moments before falling asleep, who wondered if she'd ruined the best thing that ever happened, or would happen, to her.

If her family was to be believed, she had. They'd howled as if the four horsemen of the apocalypse had sat down for tea at the kitchen table. Lea'd felt awful. Joe especially had taken it hard, though he recovered quickly enough when Coop volunteered to drive him to California and show him a few choice surfing areas along the coast.

She sighed, gazing out at a thin string of yellow along the horizon. Nothing felt right anymore. Even her skin felt uncomfortable. Tight. As if she'd outgrown it. As if that could happen. *You numb-nut.*

With Thomas' bottle half empty, Lea settled into a kitchen chair to help him finish. Watching him grow and change in the two weeks since his birth, helping Kira and Jack during this vital but exhausting time in their lives had given her purpose. She wondered briefly if Coop had been right about her—that she had a deep need to serve—but rejected the notion almost immediately. She could walk away from this particular commitment any time she wanted. It was temporary. A time filler. Helping out a dear friend.

After her parents and Joe had developed lives of their own, she'd been at a loose end. Had too much time on her hands to think. She'd applied to several schools but quickly realized that, like Joe, she was too late for the fall semester. She'd have to wait until spring. She needed something to do with her spare time, didn't she? That's all this was.

Thomas fussed and she realized he was sucking air. Quickly, she shifted him onto her shoulder and rubbed his back to induce a hearty burp. Just as he let loose a resounding one, Jack and Kira stumbled into the room.

"He sounds just like you, honey," Jack grouched sleepily. Kira shoved him and he fell into a chair beside Lea at the table, head in hands, thumbs digging into his eyeballs. "Can't. Take. Much. More."

"Lightweight," Kira snorted, measuring out massive quantities of coffee grounds into the small percolator on her stovetop. Dressed in bicycle shorts and a well-worn tank top, the small bulge on her abdomen and the enormous nursing breasts were the only indication she'd ever been pregnant. "Lea's been doing all the work."

Jack stopped scraping his face for a moment and peered out at her through his fingers. "What have I done to deserve such devotion?"

Lea smiled. Although there'd been no love lost between them in the past, she'd recently begun to appreciate Jack. He was a great husband to her best friend and, with proper instruction, would make a wonderful father. "I'm not here for you, Jack-ass. I'm here for Kira."

Jack chuckled.

The aroma of fresh, strong coffee permeated the tiny kitchen and Kira set out three full mugs. Sliding into a seat beside Jack and opposite Lea, she said, "I don't think you're here entirely for *my* benefit."

Lea felt her smile stiffen on her face. "Whatever do you mean?" she asked through her teeth, lifting her mug to hide what she felt certain was a pretty scary expression. As close as she and Kira were, she hadn't mentioned Coop. Kira had gone into labor at the same time he left and had enough to worry about without Lea crying on her spit-up rag.

"Tell us about Coop," Kira said.

Lea's jaw dropped.

"Don't pretend you don't know what I'm talking about. You slept through a feeding and I heard you crying his name."

No kidding. Damn. The last few nights she'd dreamt about Colony, had woken up soaked in tears and sweat. No biggie. It happened once in a while. Apparently she'd invoked RoboCop this time. So what? "Nothing to tell. We had a deal."

Jack and Kira looked at each other. "Where have I heard this before?" he said dryly.

"We agreed to a temporary relationship. Until I got into law school," Lea said. "I thought it would take four more years. But things changed."

Kira chewed on a lower lip and stared at her until she felt her composure shuffle. Kira's eyes narrowed. "What happened?" she probed. "You want to talk about it?"

"No," Lea clipped. Did she? Nah. "He has a savior complex and he rode to my family's rescue." The words came out in a rush. "He thought he loved me, but he really has some sick need to pay me back for my alleged heroism on the Colony flight. He also wanted to deliver Joe from the plague of ennui. He mistook that need for love."

"Bullshit," Jack said. Kira turned and Lea looked at him.

"What do you know about it?" Lea snapped.

"I know what lengths a man will go to for the woman he loves," Jack said. "I also happen to know the many ways they'll cover up for the intensity of those feelings. Coop just thinks he wants to save you. I'm sure he's met a lot of women worse off than you. You got to him way down deep and he's in denial."

"No, he's not. He says he loves me. He tried to get me to stay with him."

"Did he let you push him away?"

She nodded weakly. "Sort of. He's driving Joe out to college right now. And he helped my parents sell their house. They got a million dollars for it and gave me some…" she trailed off, the enormity of what he'd done for her sinking in at last.

"In other words he set you free."

She gulped.

"Put your happiness before his own."

"Yes."

"And he didn't go away when you ordered him to."

"Not really." She blinked.

"That's not a savior complex, that's true love." Jack got up and dragged a loaf of bread, butter and a toaster over to the table. Lea rocked the baby in thoughtful silence during the few minutes it took him to scrape breakfast together for everyone.

"Maybe," she finally admitted. "But I don't want true love at this stage in my life. I don't want to be responsible for anyone's happiness anymore."

Jack stacked a plate and slid it in front of her. "Hate to tell you this, but Coop sounds capable of managing his own happiness. He let you win this round, but only on his terms."

"True." The stinker. She hadn't thought of it that way.

"I doubt he'll ever be dependent on you."

"How can you know that?" she asked desperately. "My parents—"

Jack swallowed a mouthful of toast. "I know what happened with your parents," he mumbled. "That was the exception to the rule."

"Coop could become an exception too."

"So you want to live out your life waiting for the other shoe to drop? That's what I was doing, waiting for Kira to dump me like my mother dumped me. Guess what? Kira's not my mother, and Coop isn't your father. You can have it all, Lea. He's waiting for you right now. You may as well enjoy his company. If it doesn't work out, what have you lost?"

Nothing. She had nothing left to lose. Everyone she cared about was gone, and instead of feeling ecstatic, she'd been miserable.

"Jack's right," Kira said. "Look at you, here every waking minute. You need to be needed, Lea. Life can be pretty empty without anyone who needs you."

"Mind your own business," she snarled. "I'm sorry." She handed the baby over to Kira and put her face in her hands. A sudden weepiness had crept up on her. Like empty nest syndrome or something. It would pass. She'd be lying to herself to say she didn't miss Coop. Or his cock, more likely. Maybe his crooked face too, his hearty laugh. Okay. Possibly his tenderness.

Damn.

She also missed Joe. Only gone a short while and an unbelievable pain in the ass while he was here, she missed his dreary insights and despairing outlook. Somehow, having him around to always confirm that the worst was indeed about to happen had a comforting quality. In one fell swoop, Coop had removed all that from her life. Maybe Joe's was better for it. But what about hers? What did she have to bitch about now? To whine and complain about? A girl needed balance in her life.

She also wondered about how effortlessly Coop had been able to change everyone's outlook. Why couldn't she have done that? What was missing in her that made her family cling despondently when clearly they were ready to move on? Had she somehow encouraged their dependence? Enabled them?

She bolted upright, realization sickening her so much she almost had to run to the bathroom to hurl. "Kira," she asked. "Did I make them stay with me? Did I have some dysfunctional need to take care of them?"

Kira and Jack exchanged wary looks, as if they'd been down this road before in conversation. Unbeknownst to her. Had they discussed her, analyzed her?

"Well," Kira hedged, "we always kind of thought you were a bit of a control freak. I thought maybe that's why you and Jack butted heads so much."

Shit.

Jack said, "Maybe you have a bit of a savior complex too."

Goddammit.

They were not right. They were not!

"You were the last one off the Colony flight," Jack added—accusingly.

"It's my job to be the last one off," Lea shrilled.

"What kind of idiot takes a job like that?" Jack asked. "The Coops of this world, and the—"

"Hold it right there. I get it." Once again, she buried her head in her hands.

"There's nothing wrong with you, Lea. Without people like you there'd be bedlam and mass destruction."

"You can shut up now."

"I think we all take jobs that reflect our inner purpose," Kira said. "I needed to prove myself. Jack needed to be in control. You needed to help people. So did Coop. Imagine what you could do together if you pooled your talents."

Explode in bed? Been there, done that. She cracked a smile. The first one in days—except for when caring for Thomas.

"What are you running from?" Jack asked. "Your family responsibilities? Or yourself?"

"I'm not running away. I'm taking a vacation." Damn the three of them for being right. Coop was going to be insufferable when he found out. If he found out. Did she have to tell him? Only if she wanted him back. Would he come back if she apologized?

As if reading her mind, Jack said, "Freedom's just another word for nothing left to lose. Take it from me. You don't have anything left to lose, Lea. Might as well go for it."

"What about my pride?"

"Pride is worth jack shit on the open market. Give Coop a call. You can't deny your true self. Trust me on this one."

Though she'd had her problems with him in the past, she saw the wisdom in his words. Yet another crow to eat. What the hell. It'd be good practice. "Jack, I've misjudged you. I'm sorry."

"Nah," he waved a hand. "You had my number. I was an asshole. But even assholes can be cleaned up."

"Go home, get some sleep and call Coop. In that order," Kira instructed. "I want a full and detailed report this evening."

Why did her image of home suddenly look like a scaffold?

* * * * *

"So, Lea's off helping Kira with the new baby. I figured she wouldn't last long without someone to mother."

Joe's voice sifted into Coop's shattered brain as he stared out the window at the Pacific Coast Highway, wondering if Jack Daniel's came in timed-release capsules and trying to sleep off last night's dose. "What d'you mean?" he mumbled. "She couldn't wait to ditch all that."

"That's what she says," Joe said. "Typical."

Coop shifted in the cramped passenger seat to get a better view of Joe's profile, curiosity—and Jack Daniel's—poking him with a sharp stick. "Typical?" he prompted.

"Oh sure," Joe said. "She's not happy unless she can bitch about her load. But let a day go by without someone needing her for something and she freaks."

Interesting. "Tell me more," Coop said.

"For a long time, I figured it was easier to let her have her way. I mean, I had nothing better to do. It wasn't until L.A. I saw something I wanted badly enough to break away."

"She let you go," Coop said in her defense. "She encouraged you."

"Yeah. But you should see the missed calls on my cell. She calls all the freaking time and leaves pointless messages. She's probably hoping you'll pick up."

He wished. God, he missed her—had been second-guessing himself the last two weeks. Had he done the right thing by leaving her that night? "No, she isn't."

Joe shrugged. "She noses around, trying not to mention your name. Like I'm stupid." He laughed affectionately. "She's into you."

"But she said—"

"I don't care what she said. I know her."

"And she's just as fucked up as everyone else?"

"That's what I like about you. You always get it."

No, he didn't always get it. Obviously. Though he liked to think he did. He'd missed this one by a mile.

Here he thought she was serious about leaving him when, according to Joe, she was having a temper tantrum. Like a toddler. Screaming *no* when she meant yes, just to prove she had control. It made sense in a twisted way. His gut agreed with Joe.

The things you could see when your dick was in semi-retirement. "Did all this happen after Colonoscopy?" he asked.

Joe presented him a startled look. "How did you know? We figured it was a phase. That she'd get over it. But it's been a long time."

"Not long enough," Coop said.

"How long does it take to get over stuff like that?"

"You don't. You learn to live with it."

"Dude."

Through the puddles of alcohol dehydrating his brain, the missing pieces of Lea's psyche suddenly dropped into place. "She could've died on the Colony flight. The chaos must've scared the ever-loving shit out of her." As well as the realization of what she'd sacrifice for others. Namely, her life. So now she wanted everyone gone. Because if she had no one to save, she wouldn't have to die doing it.

Coop gave himself a mental back-pat for the insight.

A spin on the classic fight-or-flight syndrome. Instead of choosing one, she'd acted on both, confused herself and no longer knew who she was.

He couldn't help her figure that one out. She was on her own. If Joe was right and it was her nature to be a caretaker—a fighter—then she'd return to her family and maybe even to Coop. On the flipside, if the trauma of the accident altered her on too profound a level, he might never see her again.

Damn, it was hard to go there.

However, in his favor, all signs were currently pointing to the former and for the first time in days, hope lit a match in his heart. But he'd seen post traumatic stress ruin more than one life, so he forced himself to temper that hope with a dose of hard reality.

If he pushed his slim advantage, would it blow up in his face? Might be best to lay low for a while and wait.

"You think she needs shock therapy?" Joe asked.

"Say again?"

"Never mind."

They fell silent as the miles ticked by.

Chapter Eight

ᘓ

For the second time in one day, a jarring noise awoke Lea and her hand shot out from under the covers to scrabble for the phone. Popping her head out as well, the late morning sun streaming into the window blinded her momentarily. She squinted at the caller's name on the handset and sat up.

Joe. Finally! Maybe Coop was there too. "Hello?" God, was that her voice? It sounded so soft and unsure. Everything about her felt soft and unsure after the wounding revelations at pre-dawn. Kira and Jack had managed to instill the doubt demons so thoroughly she could no longer say for certain what she wanted or who she even was. The only thing she knew for sure was that she desperately wanted to hear Coop's voice.

"Bad news," Joe said abruptly. "We're alive but—"

A massive surge of adrenaline galvanized her. "What happened?" she shrieked, cradling the phone on a shoulder and leaping out of bed. She knew it. Just knew it! Couldn't leave them alone for a second!

"Surfing accident. Coop's messed up."

Fear backhanded her so viciously she had to lean against the wall for support. "No!" Coop the Mighty? It seemed impossible. Surreal. Her vision went foggy.

"Shark attack. Coop went in to help."

Arrogant bastard. She'd kill him! *Please God, let him be okay.*

"He'll live but his shoulder's busted. Looks irreparable. He has a concussion. And, er, well, we don't know yet."

Relief vacuumed the air from her lungs only to be replaced with an urgency she hadn't felt since... Wait a cotton picking second. "How did his shoulder get busted?"

"Um, a board hit him?" Joe made it sound like a question.

"Oh." Her body went strangely calm. Something didn't smell right and it wasn't the uneaten sushi in her fridge. How could a board hit his shoulder hard enough to break it if he was in water deep enough for a shark? The last time she checked, waves were calmer out there.

"Can you come help?"

"Joe," she said. "Is this for real?"

"Come on! Jeez, Lea. You think I'd kid around about something like this?"

Yeah, she did. Slightly. The facts weren't matching up. "It seems weird," she said. "That's all."

"Turn on the news if you don't believe me," he said sullenly.

Feeling like a bad sister, she snatched the clicker from her nightstand and flicked on CNN. Stocks were down. Houses were up. A shark attacked a surfer out in Rocky Rights.

Mother Mary!

"I'm packing right now. Where are you?"

While Joe provided the address, she hopped into tan casual dress slacks and a cream silk blouse—her uniform when she flew on an employee pass. Today's flight schedule looped in her brain. At any given moment there were hundreds of planes en route to the West Coast. One of them would have a seat available. "I'll call you when I know which flight I'll be on," she said. "Can you meet me at the airport?"

On the other end of the phone, Joe hesitated. There came a muffled sound, as if he'd put his hand over the mouthpiece and she could've sworn she heard a car door opening and Coop's voice saying "Let's roll".

"Joe? You there?"

"Lea? I can't hear you."

"Joe!"

The line went blank.

Squirrely, rotten baby brother. Goddamnit! She threw the phone down and spun on her heel, glancing around the room as if her luxury bedding could provide some assistance. Was this for real? Or was Joe trying to get them back together using a screwball trick as old as dirt?

Muttering and tossing her makeup kit and a change of clothes into an overnight bag, she figured she'd find out soon enough. And if her suspicions proved correct, tonight's dinner would be Joe Fricassee.

But what if it were true? She froze. The image of Coop risking shark bites and fending off flying surfboards so a stranger could go home to his family heaved tears into her eyes and filled her heart with anguish and longing. She had no doubt he would step up to the plate in such an emergency. And it scared her silly.

He was like her. It was what they were drilled to do. But more than that, it was the material they were made of, and it couldn't be changed. Not without losing some substance, some balance, some essential quality that molded their entire personalities.

And what a beautiful personality he had. Irreplaceable. He lived outside of himself, strived for a greater purpose.

She plopped down on the edge of the bed and stared vacantly out the window. Oh God, she loved him. Loved him so much it killed her to imagine the world without him. Her world without him.

Sitting in the relative safety of her sunny bedroom, she knew with terrible certainty that one day she'd get another phone call about Coop. Probably from Joe, and probably minus such a bearable outcome.

She would regret disposing him. Maybe not today, maybe not tomorrow. But someday. Lea didn't want that kind of desolation in her life. She wouldn't handle it well.

As she rewound the tape of her existence since the accident, a keen, sympathetic awareness uncurled in her heart, exposing raw nerves, freeing awful memories and providing an unfamiliar sense of resolution. Suddenly she understood things about herself she'd denied for so long, understood what kept her parents together through the bad times, what Coop was all about. What drove them all. And what gave them the ability to feel so deeply.

Compassion for all living things. Dedication and a sense of duty.

Love.

She so wanted some of that.

If he was dead-set on living his life for others, she'd make it as pleasurable and easy a life as possible. She could do that for him. Wanted to do that for him. He deserved it, and she loved him.

Grabbing her suitcase, she strode for the door. If she had to fucking walk across the entire United States in her stilettos, she would do it. Superman needed his Lea Lane.

* * * * *

At the insistent knocking on the hotel room door, Coop cursed, turned off the shower and slung a towel around his hips. He hadn't ordered anything from room service, and no one knew he was here…

"Open up!" A strident female voice that could belong to *none other* came clearly through the thin door, and he froze mid-stride. What was Lea doing here? Her distressed tone sent adrenaline cantering through his system. Something was wrong. Joe? Couldn't be. The boy had just disappeared on some mysterious errand, leaving Coop time to wash the seawater off from this morning's fun-filled surfing excursion and get ready for the last short leg of the trip to L.A. It had to be something with her family, or—

Nope. No way. She couldn't be coming all this way to get him. Even if she wanted him back, he couldn't imagine her hightailing it across the United States in a needy rush. Her style, he suspected, would be to play it cool.

Still, she was here. His hand trembled as he reached for the doorknob. An unfamiliar feeling…fear? No, not fear…Hell yeah. Fear gripped him and made him pause for one last deep breath.

Opportunity was knocking. Literally. His future stood pounding and shouting on the other side of a cheap motel door. Most men would be delirious. Coop's arm hair stood up.

He looked down at his towel, willing clothes to appear on his body, or the instant hard-on from the sound of her voice to vaporize. No go. It sucked to be a lovesick schmuck.

He gave the doorknob a slight twist.

"Joe! Open the door! I need to see Coop."

His hand stopped twisting and he closed his eyes tightly. Damn. Coming from that sensual mouth, those words sounded sweet. *Remember this moment, Masterson. It's as close to heaven as your ugly mug will ever get.*

Now if only he could be sure he wouldn't blubber. He took another split second to compose himself, put one hand on his towel and swung open the door.

When she saw him, she froze—both fists raised and about to slam down on his head.

"One extra-large Coop for your viewing pleasure," he quipped.

Her blue eyes grew huge as she gazed at him in shock. Then the unusually soft light in them hardened and her lips thinned. "I'll kill the little turd!"

"What?"

"Where is he?" She stomped into the room.

"Whoa. Whoa! Back up a sec." He clasped her upper arm as she flew past, swinging her around in a swirl of blazing hair and eyes. "You said you needed to see *me*."

"Not until I roast that lying piece of shit on a spit." She yanked her arm free and ran a hand through wild hair. God, she looked gorgeous. He'd never seen her so mad, so emotive.

So free.

But he also noticed a puffiness around her eyes, as if she was tired or had been crying. Or both. Her face looked pinched and worried. Obviously, little Joe had told a whopper.

Curiosity got the better of him. This could be good. "What'd he tell you?"

"That you were hurt!"

"Hurt?"

"Maybe irreparably."

"Disabled?"

She nodded.

Hot damn!

"He said you got beaten up by a surfboard saving someone from a shark attack. He is so dead!"

And she'd come running. Because he needed her. She forgot that part but, for once, Coop got it. Talk about actions speaking louder than words. He finally knew what the hell it meant. He nearly fell to his knees at her feet.

But first she needed the truth. It might change her view. "That's not quite how it went down," he said with more conviction than he felt. He'd *almost* gotten beat up by a surfboard as he *almost* saved someone from a shark attack. *Almost* was the story of his life. And it might not ever be enough. Coop swallowed hard.

"I had a feeling he was lying," Lea huffed.

"He didn't lie."

She blinked at him with eyes so full something inside him switched on like a light. She cared for him more than she let on, perhaps more than she knew. He could see admiration in her gaze. But above it lay the unvarnished sheen of abject terror.

"Joe stretched the truth. There was no saving the day. I punched the shark and it swam away. End of story."

She moved closer to him and he got a faded whiff of perfume and something more—the vague scent of feminine concern and comfort. Of peace.

"Still, you put yourself out there, on the line." What *was* that in her tone? The aura of brittleness that normally surrounded her seemed fractured, allowing a soft, glowing light to filter through the cracks. Coop noticed her hands opening and closing by her side, her weight shifting from foot to foot, and he realized she felt unsure. She no longer appeared to be the confident, cocksure woman he'd fallen for.

"Coop," she whispered. "Someday you might not return from a rescue mission."

He shrugged and waved a hand. She grabbed it midair and laced long, gentle fingers through his. A shot of pure white joy powered through his veins.

"I might get a real phone call like the prank one Joe made." She pulled at him tenderly so he took a step closer, mesmerized by her metamorphosis, hoping with all the hope he had left that the emotion saturating her eyes was enduring.

"Heroism isn't necessarily a fatal disease," he croaked. Though it often could be. Did he want to risk it anymore?

"I can't take that chance, Coop. I didn't think I needed saving, but I do. From a life without you. Can you..." she faltered and his heart skipped. "Can you save me one last time?"

* * * * *

Now she knew why women swooned. As every shred of emotion vacated her body and swooshed out into Coop's ears, Lea thought for sure she'd faint. She hadn't wanted to feel this. Do this.

"What's in it for me?"

Her unfocused gaze locked onto his face. He was trying not to grin, the bastard. Frustrated amusement strutted into her hands, making her want to fist them and sock it to him. He had a bad habit of teasing her during heart-rending moments, making her laugh, lightening her load. How dare he? She smiled. "Fruit roll bikinis on demand?"

His face opened in an expression so bright she seriously needed her shades. "Let me see. Um. No."

Brute! "You're going to make me beg, aren't you?"

He folded strong arms over his chest. "Might be my last chance."

"Okay, then." She could do this. She had something serious to say but she deserved a hard time as much as he deserved his jollies giving it to her. He'd put up with a lot of flack from her, and she could tell he'd take her back gladly, if she'd let him have his fun. "What about undying devotion?" *And love?*

"From who?"

"An idiotic woman who is willing to do anything to show how wrong she's been. And," she cleared her throat, "and how scared."

His air of bravado wilted. "You had good reasons to be scared."

Her eyes filled up and he brushed away an errant tear with his thumb. At his touch, she rushed into his arms and he crushed her to him. Safe, warm and so secure.

"You don't ever have to be scared again," he said gently. "I've got your back."

"Oh, Coop."

"And your breast." He grabbed it. "And let's see, a leg too."

She giggled sloppily through her tears.

"What else you got for me here?" he murmured into her hair, letting his hands roam freely over the body he knew so well.

"How about this?" She pulled back and placed his hand over her heart. "It's flawed, hardened and broken, but it's the only one I have."

He slid two fingers inside the open neckline of her blouse, and she shivered at the feather-light contact. "I'll take your flawed heart and raise you one super ass," he said.

"It *is* a super ass." She undid his towel, cupped his naked cheeks and ground her hips against his. They stood face-to-face and heart to heart and she slid her hands up his lean waist to cradle his face.

"Everything about you is super," he said. "I missed you. Missed this." He began unbuttoning her slacks and as he did, some securely fastened parts of her soul broke free and escaped bondage.

She felt them fluttering in the air, flagging her down, trying to get her attention. But the chaotic flapping confused her and she couldn't tease out each feeling to fondle in her mouth and form the words to spit out.

I love you. Why was that suddenly impossible to say? She'd practiced on the airplane. Wanted to tell him. But now, standing in front of him with his eyes on her face, his body against hers, the words clotted inside her like pea soup. "Make love to me," she requested in a tiny voice. It was the best hint she could offer at this moment. "I don't know how to. Can you show me?"

"Not sure I know how to make love either." He peppered kisses along her forehead. "But I'd be willing to keep trying 'til we get it right."

"The supreme professional."

"Bet on it." Easing her slacks down over her ass, he pushed her panties off and helped her step out of the puddle of cloth on the floor. "Can love be made against the wall? Or would that be a breach of etiquette?"

Lea grabbed his hair and yanked his head closer to hers. Before their lips collided she murmured, "I believe it can be made anywhere."

She opened her mouth for him and he devoured her lips, sucking in the breath departing her body, making her part of him. His hunger for her swelled with each nip, each suckle and Lea realized why love making was referred to as consummation.

Coop feasted on her, feeding off her need for him, lapping at the scraps he'd made of her heart. As he roughly stripped her of the rest of her clothes, she knew any moment he'd be finishing her off and she would be irrevocably mingled with him.

She was relinquishing herself to the unknown, relinquishing control over the fate of her heart. Any time now, he'd be penetrating her and this time it would be more than physical.

Hell, who was she kidding? It'd always been more than physical with Coop. It had just taken her a while to acknowledge it. But conscious acknowledgements had power. A lot of power. And they didn't always make life easier.

As the twelfth hour loomed, her heart bloated with fear. Fiery, hellish images raced at her then yawned into a dark, gaping void that surrounded her and left her reeling on the rim of past experience.

Don't go in there. Look forward.

Sucking in a tense breath and tightening her jaw, she focused on Coop.

The fresh, soapy scent clinging to his shower-moistened body filled her nostrils and smothered some of the worries in her head. His big hands slid along her waist and he maneuvered her across the room in a delicate waltz punctuated with succulent kisses and gentle pinches on her flesh.

"One, two, three..." His smile curled against her mouth and, taking his cue, she giggled and bounced up on her toes. A low, sexy laugh vibrated his chest and he used her momentum to hoist her legs around his waist and pin her between the textured fabric wall and his body.

"This is nice," she whispered, wiggling against the wallpaper. The stark contrast between the scratchy, unyielding foundation at her back and his firm but giving silky bulk supporting her against it underlined his role in her future.

He *was* her future.

He pulled his head back and eyed her. "I think I'll put a hook here to hang you on when I'm not using you. Keep you out of trouble."

She snorted. "Like there'll ever be a time you're not using me."

"You know me too well." His head dipped toward her again and he rolled his forehead along hers, nuzzling noses and lips and caressing her face with his gaze.

She basked in the hot glowing light emanating from the gold-flecked gray of his eyes and became mesmerized by the movement inside them. No longer alien and vaguely threatening to her, now they seemed like a softly undulating soothing pool, beckoning to her after a long, weary journey with the promise of safety and rejuvenation.

"Ready for me?" He poked his cock against her slick opening and a guttural sigh tickled her throat. She felt like she could stay this way forever, suspended in anticipation, her labia cupping his velvety head like a protective helmet, aching to have him inside but not yet ready for his ultimate invasion.

"I can live without you, you know," she informed him with a sniff. Wisecracking was her last line of defense but she could hear the doubt in her voice.

His cock inched forward and his grip on her ass tightened until she could feel each one of his fingertips denting her flesh. "I was doing fine before I met you," he replied.

"I don't want to live without you, though." She nuzzled his nose. *Say it, girl. Just say it.*

He nipped hers and another two inches of cock slipped easily into the gate. "And why's that?"

Her lungs sucked air until her chest expanded almost painfully against his. Her heart thumped wildly and she could feel the stark, raw love in it clambering up her spine, through her brain and exposing itself in her eyes like a beacon atop a lighthouse. "I love you."

He thrust fully inside her and her moans ripped through the room. "Took you long enough."

"I'm slow," she gasped.

"That's not what it says on the men's room wall at Pan Air."

She smacked him and he hoisted her up higher over his cock, sliding deeper inside her to the end. She spread her legs wide and accepted his big, comforting body.

"I love you," he stated. "And I'll save you." He wet her lip with his tongue. "This one. Last. Time."

Epilogue

ည

Cramped in the backseat of the tinny Euro-car, Lea burrowed into her parka, closer to Coop, and peered out at the frozen Ukrainian landscape. Only she and Coop would make this insanely desperate journey to Russia in the dead of winter. If it hadn't been for that damn video, and a crooked little face that looked so much like his…

"You know," the massive, semi-female liaison turned in the front passenger seat and pinned Lea with a stern eye, "she's not an energetic child."

Lea nodded, a thick clump of fear tangling in her chest as she glanced at her husband.

Please God, give me strength.

Could she do this? She had little or no experience. Had no idea what lay down the road ahead and couldn't even identify the feelings torturing her at this moment.

The only thing she was sure of was the flood of pure love that'd smacked her when she'd seen that face. A little girl who needed her. Needed Coop. Needed a family…

Coop winked at her and pulled her tightly under the crook of his arm. "You'll make up for her lethargy," he muttered and Lea laughed and gazed into his twinkling gray eyes.

Had it only been two years? Already it seemed timeless. As if they'd always known each other, always been together. She could scarcely remember her life before him. Didn't want to bother. And it seemed her family didn't want to either.

Joe, solidly ensconced in his studies at Cal Tech and still dating Kim, never failed to scrounge enough time to hit the surf when Coop breezed into town. Her parents had looped around the nation and crisscrossed the states so many times they were currently planning their first foray overseas—and wanted Lea and Coop to join them.

Looked like that would have to go on the backburner for a while. So they could adjust to the tremendous turn their life was about to take.

"But she's healthy," the big Russian added. Her lips thinned and she faced forward again. "We're here."

The shit-brown stone institution loomed ahead with the menacing austerity of a state penitentiary. As they got out of the car and trekked through crunching snow to metal, cell-like front doors, nausea churned Lea's stomach.

They'd never even met this one-year-old. Had only seen her sad video amongst a sea of others. But her vacant blue eyes had held a tiny something as she'd glanced at the camera lens. A small spark, a fleeting glimmer. Something that had made both Lea and Coop jump and declare, "She's the one" at the exact same moment.

What had possessed them to look at the adoption video at a friend's house? Why had they sat there for hours, fast-forwarding, scanning faces, searching?

Searching for what? For someone to save? They'd made a pact not to do that anymore. Yet here they were, in a vast wasteland of shattered hope, doing precisely what they'd vowed never to do again.

What was wrong with them?

They filed into a putrid green room where a dozen cribs were scattered willy-nilly. The watery winter twilight leaking through a single smudged window provided no cure for the bilious environment.

"No wonder she doesn't move," Coop whispered. "Who could in this sewage tank?"

"My God," Lea choked.

They laced fingers and Lea clung to his solid strength and resolve. He had her back. Told her so every night before they fell asleep and showed her every day with his unique brand of attentive love. With Coop behind her she knew she could do anything. Be anything. And it was the most glorious feeling of all.

The matron marched purposely across the room and plucked Number One-Hundred-Thirteen from her crib. Perched on a well-padded hip, the baby turned towards Lea. Saucer-sized blue eyes flickered over hers, flickered over Coop's and back again, locking for a scant moment.

Should Lea reach out, touch the child? She didn't want to frighten her during this crucial encounter. "Tatiana?" she coaxed softly. "It's Mommy."

Coop's hand squeezed hers but he didn't say a word.

"Momma," the matron repeated. "Momma." She pointed at Lea.

Silence.

"Papa," the matron said.

Blank look.

Coop's arm slid around Lea's waist and she realized he was shaking. More than shaking. Her body felt suddenly heavy and she spread her feet to stay upright. Coop was leaning on her. Using her for support.

He was scared shitless!

"It's okay." She swept her free hand along his cheek, gently turning his face so he would look at her. "It's okay."

At her touch, he closed his eyes and sucked in a tense breath. His forehead rested on hers momentarily then he swallowed and straightened and pointed to his chest. "Papa," he declared.

Tatiana stared at Lea.

Stared at Coop.

Then held out her arms.

Also by Ann Wesley Hardin

Layover
Miss Behavior
Out of this World

About the Author

They say there are eight million stories in the Naked City, and I think Jaci Burton wrote every single one of them. I don't know. She must've sneezed and missed a deadline because here I am at Ellora's Cave, and I couldn't be more thrilled.

Addicted to love? You bet. As well as all its sensual side effects. Great sex comes in many packages and I prefer mine wrapped in laughter, irony and sweet, edible substances. When not writing at the computer, I can be found in a fencing salle, cruising Internet auctions for vintage airline memorabilia, yelling at my children to let mommy write, or working my schleppy nine-to-fiver. When I grow up, I'd like to be a full time Ellora's Cave writer, but until then, I'll just frolic in the outskirts of the Naked City.

Bon Voyage!

Ann welcomes comments from readers. You can find her website and email address on her author bio page at www.ellorascave.com.

TWICE UPON A ROADTRIP

By Shannon Stacey

ꟸ

Dedication

ഗ

To my sons for being totally amazing, despite having a mother who talks to invisible people.

To FY and BB, because I would be so lost without you all.

To Briana St. James, editor extraordinaire. Thank you.

And to Stuart, who vowed to love me for better and for worse and meant it, who ignores the dust bunnies, and who never once said I couldn't do it. Without you, this book simply wouldn't exist.

I love you, now and forever.

Trademarks Acknowledgement

The author acknowledges the trademarked status and trademark owners of the following wordmarks mentioned in this work of fiction:

ACME: Jewel Companies, Inc

Aerosmith: Rag Doll Merchandising, Inc.

Barbie: Mattel, Inc.

Barney: Lyons Partnership, LP Rhenclid, Inc.

Better Homes and Gardens Channel: Meredith Corporation

Boston Red Sox: Boston Red Sox Baseball Club Limited Partnership The Jean R. Yawkey Trust its General Partner

Boy Scouts: Boy Scouts of America

Cadillac: General Motors Corporation

Cinderella: Disney Enterprises, Inc.

Disney World: Disney Enterprises, Inc.

El Camino: General Motors Corporation

Ford Taurus: Ford Motor Company

Garfield: Paws, Incorporated

Harley: H-D Michigan, Inc.

Hershey's Special Dark: Hershey Chocolate & Confectionery Corporation

Keds: SR Holdings Inc.

MG: MG Rover Group Ltd.

NASCAR: National Association for Stock Car Auto Racing, Inc.

National Geographic: National Geographic Society

Reebok: Reebok International Limited

Sara Lee: Saramar, L.L.C.

Sheetrock: United States Gypsum Company

The Twilight Zone: CBS Broadcasting Inc.

The Weather Channel: Weather Channel, Inc.

Viagra: Pfizer Inc.

Chapter One

ꭍ

For a Thursday it had been one hell of a bad day.

Jillian Delaney navigated across the grocery store parking lot, cursing her rotten luck. It wasn't a Monday or a Friday the thirteenth. She hadn't broken a mirror, walked under a ladder or tripped over a black cat. There was simply no explanation for the words that had come from her boss's mouth.

She stopped the cart and let it rest against her hip while she opened the back door. The cart slipped and she cringed as the shopping cart gouged a trail across the cherry red fender of her new car.

"Damn," she hissed, examining the wound. Could this day get any worse?

The Fates only laughed at the foolish question and split the bottom of the plastic bag in her hand. Groceries showered the pavement. Two cans of vegetables hit the asphalt with metallic thuds before splitting up and rolling in opposite directions. A can of soup ricocheted off a can of tomato paste. And the jumbo thirty-nine-ounce can of coffee landed on her foot.

Jill let loose a short, frustrated scream and threw the torn bag into the car. Tears burned her eyes, but she concentrated on her anger. She was *not* going to cry in the grocery store parking lot. She would cry when she got home, then comfort herself with the one-pound bag of chocolate she'd just bought. One by one she picked up her canned goods and pelted them into the backseat. Half bounced back at her—par for the course today.

Some idiot had stolen her promotion. For four years she coveted that job, waiting for Mrs. Bright to retire. Now some out-of-towner with a fancy résumé—she wasn't even *from* New Hampshire—had swooped in and pulled the rug out from under her. In two weeks, somebody else would be the head librarian at the Carlson Memorial Library.

Jill swore and kicked the fender, leaving a nice little dent right below the scratch. *In for a penny…* She kicked it again.

Pain exploded in her toes. An anguished growl tore from her throat and she sat on the edge of the backseat. With one hand, she rubbed her bruised toes while the other hand massaged her temple. Maybe a good, public cry was inevitable, because her day was getting worse by the second.

A pair of men's Reeboks stopped in front of her. "Hi there. Is there a problem?"

Geez, do I look that bad? Or maybe the screeches of outrage had given her away. She stood with a weary sigh.

The man occupying the Reeboks smiled at her and she completely forgot what she was going to say.

His tall frame was a tad bit thinner than she usually liked, but he still managed to fill out his worn jeans and Red Sox T-shirt pretty well. Her gaze skimmed over his clean-shaven jaw, his sensually curved lips. He had thick, mahogany-hued hair she would bet curled like mad if he didn't keep it trimmed short. And those dark chocolate eyes…

Jill pressed her lips together to keep from grinning like an idiot. Spring was most definitely in the air, and it had been a while since spring had sprung. "I'm fine—really. Thanks for asking."

"I, uh…I appreciate the groceries but I bought my own," he said, waving toward his own cart.

"What?" Wasn't it just her luck to bump into a cute guy whose elevator didn't go all the way to the top? If only she was more superstitious, she'd have a clue what she'd done to bring this on herself. Had she spilled salt at lunch and not tossed it over her shoulder? "Look, pal, I'm not in the mood for any games right now, so if you move your cart I'll just leave, okay?"

"That's my car."

"What? I don't…" She looked over her shoulder and the

words died on her lips. Her travel mug was red, not blue. And her center console hadn't been that organized since it left the dealership.

"This isn't my car!"

The man smiled at her—cautiously, as if she might bite. "Like I said, it's my car. But there's a lot of them out there, so it's an easy enough mistake."

The tears welled with renewed vigor and she flicked her wrist at the freshly abused fender. "I beat up your car."

He bent low to examine the damage and, despite her distress, she couldn't resist a quick peek at his ass. *Nice. Very nice indeed.* Too bad it had taken her less than a minute to make a fool of herself in front of the best-looking fish she'd seen in the sea lately.

"It's fixable. I doubt it will cost more than what my insurance deductible is, so there's no sense in going through them."

"Please don't call the police. My brother-in-law is the chief and I'll never live this down."

"No need for cops. We can exchange info and I'll let you know what the estimate comes to. You *will* pay for it, right?"

"Of course," Jill muttered while she dug in her purse for a pen.

She didn't look forward to tightening her belt another notch. The damage she'd done to her credit cards in anticipation of her promotion was substantial. "My name is Jill Delaney. Here's my address and phone number."

He took the slip of paper she handed him. "Jill Delaney?"

"Yeah, it's all right there." She leaned into the car to gather up her loose canned goods.

"You're the children's librarian?"

How does he know that? She jerked back and smacked her head on the roof of the car. "Ouch!"

Real concern furrowed his brow. "Are you okay?"

She rubbed at the spot, wincing against the pain. "No, I am not okay. I'm having the worst day of my life!"

"I'm sorry. I—"

"No—the second worst day," she continued after a shaky breath. There were those pesky tears again, and she blinked them back. "The worst day will come in two weeks when I have to meet the bitch who stole my promotion."

She stopped rubbing her head and looked at him as a horrible suspicion wormed its way into her mind. "How did you know I'm the children's librarian?"

"I'm Ethan Cooper," he replied, extending his hand. "The bitch is my mother."

She knew her jaw dropped, but she couldn't help it. Of all the people she had to run into right now, why did it have to be him? Humiliation surged from a trickle to a raging flood. She felt reason slipping away, as it always did when she embarrassed herself.

Angry words bottlenecked in her throat, fighting to be first. "I don't... Son of a bitch!"

He jerked back, giving her a startled glance. "You're just a ray of sunshine, aren't you? They let you work with children?"

She blew upwards at the blonde wisps forever escaping her ponytail. "I can't believe this is happening to me! Do you know what your mother did to me?"

"My mother didn't do anything to you." He looked confused and maybe a little angry. "There was an opening for a job she's qualified for and she applied. The trustees hired her. It has nothing to do with you, sunshine."

The bastard made the endearment sound like an insult. It was an insult. Normally, it would make her feel all warm and fuzzy inside. But right now she just wanted to stomp on his toes.

"I know it had nothing to do with me. But that was *my* promotion. I worked so hard—"

Jill swallowed the rest of the sentence and started throwing her groceries back into her cart, muttering words she didn't care if he heard. "Nothing to do with me... I waited four years... She's not even from here."

Ethan leaned over her shoulder to peer into the car. "Do you need a hand with those?"

"Please just leave me alone. If you're nice to me I'll start bawling right here in the parking lot."

He held up his hands. "Look, sunshine, I—"

She stood and put her hands on her hips, looking him in the eye. "Stop calling me *sunshine*."

His narrowed gaze didn't flinch away from hers. "It's better than some of the other names that have crossed my mind in the last two minutes."

"You don't even know me," she protested.

He crossed his arms, dragging the hems of his T-shirt sleeves up over his biceps. Very nice biceps, too. She tried not to look, but it wasn't easy. And those shoulders...

He didn't speak again until she made herself look up. "You don't know my mother, but you called her a bitch."

"She stole my job."

He threw up his hands. "I don't have time to talk in circles with a crazy woman—"

"Crazy?" Just who did he think he was?

"Fine—she stole your job. We're horrible people and there's a massive conspiracy out to get you. Happy? Now get your shit out of my car so I can go home."

Fury tied Jill's tongue so all she could do was turn around and start piling cans in her arms. She was going to start crying any second, and she didn't want to add that to her list of already pathetic behavior. For every two she picked up one fell and she finally just dumped what she had into the cart and threw the rest in, one at a time. Of course a can had rolled under the car, so she got down on her hands and knees to fish it out.

Her fingers closed over it just as Ethan Cooper mumbled

something above her. She struggled to her feet. "What did you say?"

"I said I'll be sure to tell my mother she can look forward to working with you."

The sarcasm was as thick as cheap mascara and she glared at him. "You know what? Fine—I quit."

She swung her cart around and walked away, her chin thrust in the air. *Oh God, where did I park my car?*

"Wait," he said, and her heart lurched in her chest when he grabbed her elbow. "You can't quit."

"Why not?" she demanded, wondering even as the words left her mouth if she'd gone insane. He was right. She couldn't quit her job. She had bills to pay—a *lot* of bills.

His hand was warm through her thin sweater, making her flesh tingle. She shook it off. She didn't take chemistry in school, but she knew it when she felt it. And Ethan Cooper was the last man on Earth she wanted to share any kind of sexual chemistry with.

And oh boy, did she ever feel it. Why was this happening to her? Why couldn't she have met this guy at a bar, or at the damn laundromat? Instead of sharing a drink, they were having a pissing match in the middle of the grocery store parking lot.

And she'd just quit her job. "Your mother is very capable from what I understand."

"She is, but she hasn't even started yet. What is she supposed to do without you?"

Jill refused to back down from his anger. "Melinda—the page—knows my job almost as well as I do. She can be the children's librarian."

She thought of the upcoming summer reading program and squelched a pang of regret. She'd promised the kids a sundae party for any who met their reading goals.

Well, Melinda could shelve books like a whirling alphabetizing dervish and knew the Dewey decimal system by heart. Surely she could scoop ice cream.

Still, there was that file full of grant forms to fill out and fundraising letters to send. And performers to book. And she so loved to watch the kids' faces during the puppet show.

"And what are you going to do?" he asked, dragging her thoughts away from the to-do list that wouldn't be hers to do anymore.

Good question. "I'm going to travel. I want to see the world."

She was amazed she even managed to say it with a straight face. Wanting to see the world was one thing. Paying to see it was an entirely different story. Maybe a *little* vacation wouldn't hurt, though.

Ethan chewed the inside of his lip, and Jill was fascinated by the way the muscles in his jaw worked. It really was too bad he was the promotion thief's son. Those Reeboks would look damn fine under her bed.

"So that's it?" he demanded. "You don't get your way, so you quit?"

He made her sound like a petulant child. Maybe she was acting like one—just a little—but she was having a *really* shitty day. "That's right. I'm quitting my job and I'm going to see the world. And I'm going to find the man of my dreams so he can sweep me off my feet."

The corners of his lips twitched. "Good luck."

Okay, that hurt. "I'm leaving now. Have a nice life."

"Why didn't you quit three weeks ago?"

Jill took a deep breath and blew the hair out of her eyes again. If he disliked her so much, why wouldn't he just go away? She couldn't hold the impending emotional meltdown at bay much longer. "Why would I have quit three weeks ago?"

He hesitated and the answer hit Jill like a wrecking ball. "They hired her three *weeks* ago?"

He nodded. "We've already rented her condo and moved her in and everything. She wouldn't have come up from

Connecticut without a concrete offer."

Disappointment and rage battled for Jill's emotions. "Why did they wait until today to tell me?"

"Maybe the trustees thought you might react like *this*," he suggested.

Jill's cheeks grew hot and she clenched her jaw to keep any more juvenile comments at bay. Then she just turned and walked away.

Those three weeks were the icing on the cake. After the years she'd been there, they hadn't had the respect to tell her straight out. She couldn't—*wouldn't*—work at the library anymore.

"Hey, Jill?"

"What?" she shouted, spinning back to him.

"Your groceries?"

Humiliation kept her from looking him in the face when she walked back for her cart. She pushed it up the row, then down the next until she found her own car—the messy one with the red travel mug.

Loading the loose groceries into the backseat, she came to a decision. She was going straight from here to the bank. And then she would take the best trip her savings account would buy.

* * * * *

"This oughta be good."

Jill rolled her eyes at her father's bemused smile. It was the same smile he gave the clowns on stilts at the Rotary Club circus, or his son-in-law when he had a power tool in his hand. Her life was a disaster waiting to happen and he was going to laugh his butt off when it did.

Her mother, on the other hand, didn't look a bit amused. "Don't you think you should get another job before you go running off?"

"I'm not running off. It's just a vacation."

"When the going gets tough, Jillian gets going…in the other direction," her father muttered, then he chuckled.

Why he chuckled was beyond Jill. Maybe it had been funny the first sixty thousand or so times he said it, but it got old sometime around her fourth grade year.

At that moment her sister, Liz, and her tribe of heathens exploded through the back door. Shit. They must have gotten the exhaust fixed. Jill cursed herself for not hearing the beat-up minivan pull in the driveway—it was too late to run and hide.

Three boys ranging from two to eight took off in the direction of the TV room, leaving in their wake one muddy sneaker, two coats, a baseball and one very sticky sippy cup. Her five-year-old niece stayed behind and yanked the hem of her dress up to her chin.

"Lookie my panties, Auntie Jill."

Jill oohed and aahed over the pink and purple hearts until little Bethany took off after her brothers. Last time it had been little ruffled panties with "Saturday" embroidered across the butt. On a Tuesday. It was little wonder Bethany was Jill's favorite.

"What does her teacher think of Bethany showing off her underwear?" Jill asked Liz, who slumped into a kitchen chair.

She shrugged. "It's kindergarten. As long as the kids don't pee in them, the teacher doesn't care if they flash them around."

"I saw a T-shirt yesterday I wanted to buy for her. It said *I'm too sexy for Barney* on the front."

Liz snorted and took the coffee cup their mother handed her as if it was the fabled mead of Valhalla. "You better not. So…what's up?"

"She quit her job," her mother answered before Jill's brain had even processed the question.

Liz shook her head mournfully. "You'll be sorry."

Jill mouthed the words as she said them. She thought about making a fast break for the exit, but it wasn't worth the effort. They knew where she lived.

You'll be sorry and *I told you so* were the basic staples of conversation for Martha Delaney and her older daughter. Her younger daughter didn't need to use them, since they were usually aimed in her direction.

Mom quickly brought Liz up to speed on the situation, which sounded far less reasonable in her mother's tone of voice.

"Vacation?" Liz asked in a voice that dripped disbelief. "To where?"

Nowhere she had to fly to, unless she could come up with a much better plan for glue and feathers than Icarus. Her bank account didn't reflect any of the frugality that had been her New Year's resolution—for three years running.

"I don't know yet."

"Don't you think you should get another job first?"

Jill resisted the urge to stick out her tongue at her sister—barely. "If I get another job first I'll have to work for months, maybe even a year, before I get vacation time."

"And you quit because somebody else got Mrs. Bright's job?"

"Yes, it's about my dignity, thank you."

Her mother slapped a plate of cookies down on the table. "Unemployment is very dignified."

Dad shoved a cookie in his mouth just in time to stifle another chuckle. Jill ground her teeth and reminded herself that this was a man who thought Archie Bunker would have been the comedic genius of the century if only he'd burped a little more on television.

A scream ripped through the small house and Jill's brain like a banshee on crack.

Liz didn't even flinch. "Is there blood?" she shouted in a voice that would drown out Aerosmith's woofers.

Murmurs in the negative floated into the kitchen, so Liz shrugged and returned to her coffee.

Not for the first time, Jill wished there was some way she could capture the essence of her niece and nephews and market it as birth control. She didn't need the FDA to tell her it was effective.

If Jill even thought her biological clock was winding up to tick, all she had to do was think about Liz to make it freeze up like a cheap computer. Her sister looked so…tired all the time.

Not a second went by that she wasn't running, fetching, feeding, washing, wiping or yelling. Jill never had any aspirations of greatness, but she sure as heck had aspirations of a life.

"I can't believe you got into a pissing match with the woman's son. In the middle of the parking lot, no less. And you dented his car?"

Her dad shook his head. "I told you you should have bought that yellow El Camino from Fred. No mistaking that sucker for anything else."

"Yeah, that would have solved all my problems," Jill said, earning herself *a don't use that tone of voice with your father* look from her mother.

She shouldn't have mentioned Ethan Cooper at all. She could have told them she quit right after she learned about the new children's librarian. Instead she'd ranted about the entire episode, only leaving out the accelerated heart rate that wasn't totally due to anger.

The man was scrumptious. Arrogant and smug, but scrumptious nonetheless.

"This is just like the time you left Poor Eddy at the altar," Mom said.

Jill groaned. The Delaney family didn't subscribe to the water-under-the-bridge philosophy. Bygones were never bygone.

"Absolutely," Liz agreed. "If things get a little rough, get out of the way of the door."

"She's always been that way," Dad added. "When the going—"

"I'm still in the room," Jill shouted. "And it's not the same thing. I wasn't ready to get married, so I saved Eddy and myself from a life of misery."

All three of them snorted in long-practiced unison. Though Jill had given up on her dreams of finding secret adoption papers a long time ago, there were still times—like now—when she was certain the Delaney family had found her on the doorstep.

Her parents and Liz were conservative, sensible people who worried and debated every side of an issue before making a decision. They even read the nutrition labels on cans. Jill took a more…unstructured approach to life.

"Back to the issue that's actually relevant," she said firmly. "I'm going to take a vacation. I want to spend a little quiet time by myself and consider my options—decide what I want to do with my life."

To practice asking "Do you want fries with that"?

"Where are you going?" Mom asked as she took the nearly empty plate of cookies out of Liz's reach.

Somewhere cheap was the only thing that came to mind, but she managed not to say it out loud. Fiscal responsibility was another dominant Delaney gene she'd missed out on.

It wasn't easy being a totally broke black sheep in a family of peroxide blondes.

* * * * *

"Is that you, Ethan? I'm in the kitchen."

He smiled and tossed his keys on the TV. Those were the same words his mother had said to him every time he walked in the door since his first day of kindergarten. Her kitchen was the center of Debra Cooper's universe—even in her new condo.

"It's me." He walked down the short hallway, then stopped short. "What on Earth are you doing?"

His mother was standing on a chair, stretching to hang a bright yellow valance. One end of the curtain rod was up, the other end was still in her hand. How many times had she swatted his butt for standing on chairs? It was *dangerous.*

"What does it look like I'm doing?" Her wink took the edge off the question.

"Why didn't you wait for me? You shouldn't be climbing on chairs. You could fall. You could break a hip or something."

She hooked the rod on the bracket and hopped off the chair, landing on sure, Keds-clad feet. "I'm not ninety, Ethan. And I swear you worry more about my hips than my obstetrician did. I take my vitamins every day—the extra calcium ones. Which you know since you ask me about them every day."

"I know, but—"

"And you better not have any of those disgusting nutritional shakes in there," she interrupted, pointing at the grocery bag he set on the table. "I'm not drinking any more of them."

"I'm just watching out for you, Mom. I don't like you being alone." Not for the first time, Ethan wished he had a few sisters. Preferably at least one with a spare bedroom. He hated her living by herself.

"Do you really think your father did all this for me?"

Ethan felt a small pang in his chest, just as he always did whenever he thought of his dad. He'd passed away a year ago and it wasn't getting any easier.

"He didn't," she answered for him. "I took care of the inside of the house and you. Everything else was his job. He didn't hang my curtains and he certainly didn't count my vitamins."

He knew that. But he also remembered his father clapping a hand on his shoulder and saying, "You're the man of the house while I'm gone, son. Take care of your mother for me."

Those words had echoed through his mind as they laid his father to rest and he couldn't shake them. Sure, he knew it was only something fathers said to sons to take the sting out of being left behind with their mothers. He knew his mother was still healthy and vibrant.

And she was all he had left. She and the memories of his dad. He hadn't been able to take care of his wife, or protect his business, but he wouldn't let his father down.

Ethan gripped her shoulders and kissed her cheek. "I'm sorry. I just... I worry about you."

She smiled and patted his arm. "I have nosy neighbors and thin walls. And I've got my cordless phone and this surveillance collar of yours. I'm never truly alone."

Ethan laughed and started taking groceries out of the bag. "It's not a surveillance collar. It's a necklace. If you fall—"

"And break a hip?"

"—you can press the button on the pendant and the rescue squad will come. It's better to be safe than sorry."

"I swear those were your first words. *Beddah safe ven sowwy,*" she said in a high baby voice.

Nothing wrong with being cautious, he thought. It was a philosophy that served him well. Not with his ex-wife or vice cops, but other than that, it usually worked for him.

"Mrs. Bright phoned while you were gone," his mother told him. Ethan didn't even blink—he was used to his mother changing subjects at will. "The children's librarian called her and quit this afternoon."

A picture of the woman from the parking lot popped into his head. She hadn't wasted any time, surprisingly. Somehow he hadn't thought her that decisive.

"I met the woman. You should be glad to be rid of her."

His mother pinned him with that maternal, lie-detecting look. "Did you have anything to do with her quitting?"

"Of course not!" Ethan could feel the heat in his cheeks. He hated that. All his life he'd responded to any accusation with a guilty flush, even when he was innocent. If a polygraph technician ever so much as asked him his name he'd flunk for sure. "She thinks she should have been promoted instead of the library hiring you."

"That's understandable. I'd feel the same way."

"Don't you think you're being a little too reasonable?"

"Why? She was there four years and the only reason they hired me was my master's degree. The state is trying to phase out trained-on-the-job librarians."

Ethan slammed the deli drawer shut and closed the fridge. "That doesn't excuse her leaving you high and dry."

"It's not personal, Ethan." Content the curtains were straight, she returned the chair to its place. It knocked against the table and he winced.

The year he was ten, Ethan and his father spent the entire summer refinishing the cherry monstrosity. It looked out of place in the tiny, bright kitchen, but he was glad she hadn't left it behind.

"Ethan." His mom laid her hand on his arm and he blinked a few times before smiling at her.

"I was thinking about when Dad and I refinished this table for you. I miss him."

"So do I, sweetie. I swear my feet get cold at night just from missing him. You need to date more."

Ethan shook his head. That was quite a leap, even for her.

"There must be some nice young ladies in this town," she continued.

He hadn't met any nice young ladies yet. Only a blonde, not-so-nice young basket case. His lips twitched as he thought of the way her hair kept falling across her eyes, and his hand clenched at the memory of wanting to sweep it away for her.

Then his cock twitched at the memory of her sweet ass presented to him while she picked up her groceries. On paper her height and weight probably listed as average, but there was nothing average about how they added up to Jillian Delaney.

Her legs were long enough to really wrap around his waist. And when she'd bent over and her shirt lifted, the little bumblebee tattoo at the small of her back had damn near driven him mad.

Ethan had to step sideways to stand behind a chair, hiding his erection. He needed to get a grip.

But, damn, she'd been hot. Tousled blonde hair, blue eyes and hips made for holding on to. She was a damn fine package except for that matter of her not being on the same planet with sanity.

Hooking up with a frazzled iceberg was something his half-sunk ship of a life didn't need. His priorities were simple—mother first, his own life next. The sexy blonde was on her own.

"After you're settled in and comfortable in your job," he said. "Then I'll go back to Connecticut and see about selling the house. At some point I'll figure out what I'm going to do after that."

"Good. In the meantime, I thought it might be nice for us to take a little trip before I have to start at the library."

Ethan looked down at her too-innocent face. His mother hated to travel and she absolutely refused to fly. Images of a tacky singles cruise flashed through his mind. "What did you do?"

"I joined the senior center today and signed us both up for the Spring Fling bus tour. We're going to Orlando!"

Chapter Two

ꙮ

Ethan laid his head back against the bus seat, closed his eyes and tried to breathe through his mouth.

He wasn't going to let his mother forget this trip for a good long time. She owed him big-time, but he couldn't think of anything worth being stuck on this damn bus for.

He inhaled for a weary sigh and instantly regretted it. A wave of smells he could only partially identify assaulted his sinuses. Mothballs. At least a dozen different brands of drugstore perfume. Menthol. Stale cigarette smoke. Arthritis cream. It was going to be a very long trip.

"God help me, what did I do to deserve this?"

He knew that voice. Ethan's eyes flew open and he stared at the woman staring right back at him.

Jill… That was her name. He'd found himself thinking about her at odd times during the week since the parking lot incident and more than once he'd awakened with her face on his mind and a raging hard-on.

This was the *last* place he'd ever expected to see her.

His dick tried to stand up and wave hello even as his mind registered the potential awkwardness of Jill and his mother sharing a bus. Plus he'd dreamed up some particularly hot fantasies starring her, and he wasn't sure he could look her in the eye without blushing. It was like an awkward morning after without the night before.

"What are *you* doing here?" she demanded.

Ethan shook his head, wondering if his mother would notice if he crawled across her lap and jumped out the emergency exit window. "I'm taking my mother on this trip.

What are you doing here?"

She narrowed her eyes, her cheeks rosy. "I'm taking a vacation," she mumbled.

Ethan threw back his head and laughed out loud, attracting the attention of almost every person on the bus. Jill's cheeks flushed deep strawberry. He watched her look around for any empty seat besides the one across the aisle from him.

"This is your big plan?" he scoffed. "The senior center's bus trip to Florida?"

"Shut up," Jill hissed.

"I didn't realize when you said you wanted to see the world, you meant Disney World."

Her blue eyes—almost the color of her well-worn jeans—shifted to him, then away again. "I volunteer at the center, not that it's any of your business. There was room for me and it sounded like fun. How did *you* get around the seniors-only rule?"

"My mother convinced them to make an exception because she's new to the community. She can be very persuasive." The fact that he was even on this bus illustrated what an understatement that was.

The stubborn mother in question shifted next to him and leaned forward. "Are you going to introduce me to the young lady?"

Lord, I know it's spring, but a freak blizzard would be good right now. Anything to get him off this bus. "No. She's moving on."

"Ethan Ulysses Cooper, there's no excuse for being rude!"

He heard Jill snicker and looked up in time to see her mouth *Ulysses?* He shot her a black look and clenched his mouth shut. The next time he fantasized about her they were going to play bondage games so he could put a gag on her.

Jill was jostled from behind by a man in red plaid shorts and black knee-high socks. "Sit down, missy."

Ethan smiled at her indignant expression, but it faded when

she sat across the aisle from him. "It's a big bus, sunshine."

"And it looks full back there," she snapped back. "I'm not about to fight my way back up to the front."

"Who is that, Ethan?" his mother insisted.

"I'll tell you later," he muttered.

Some vacation this was turning out to be. It had sounded okay at first. A nice trip to Orlando with his mom before she settled into her new job and he went back to Connecticut.

Somehow his mind had glossed over the senior center's part in the bus tour. His mother wouldn't be retiring anytime soon, but joining the center was a good way to make new friends with similar interests. His mother making new friends was good—Ethan spending days trapped on a bus with them was not so good.

But she had signed them up for the senior center Spring Fling tour, and it was too late to do anything about it but have a good time and take very shallow breaths.

She'd had his best interests at heart, of course. It would do him good to get away for a while, she had said. He needed to have some fun, she said. And since his ex-wife had run his business into the ground before running off with an undercover vice cop, he had nothing better to do.

Pain arced across his temples and he leaned his head back. Closing his eyes again, he prayed this purgatory on wheels would get moving soon. Spending seven days in the company of his mother, her new friends and the nut from the grocery store was bad enough. He didn't need Betty along for the ride as well, even in his thoughts.

After six years of marriage, the bitch had cleaned out their personal accounts and his business account, then stuck a goodbye note to the fridge with his Garfield magnet. His appearances in divorce court and bankruptcy court were scheduled six hours apart and she married her overly macho—probably corrupt—vice cop the second the ink was dry.

He was surprised he'd even been able to keep the car,

which he'd left off at the auto body shop the previous day. Jill's check for several hundred dollars had cashed and the man promised it would be as good as new when he returned. At least one thing was going right.

The bus lurched under him and started to move away from the center at a crawl. He tried to block out the vacation planning and bingo reliving going on around him. If he could sleep for most of the bus ride, he just might survive.

And then what? He had no idea what he was going to do with the rest of his life. Working every day, coming home to his wife and planning for the children he wanted to have had flown out the window when Betty left. Now he had to figure out how to fill the gaping hole she left behind.

The concept of dating scared the hell out of him. He'd met Betty at college and, as the single friends of two couples, they'd naturally gravitated into a relationship. Dating before then had been very casual.

Jill Delaney was the first woman to kick his pulse into high gear since the divorce. Sure, she was attractive and she probably had to be fairly smart to do her job—her *former* job. But if he had a type, she wouldn't be it.

The bus picked up speed as the driver merged into highway traffic. Ethan told himself to sleep, but images of the blonde across the aisle played across the backs of his eyelids like the screen of a seedy XXX theatre.

If only he was a fuck 'em and leave 'em kind of guy. A few hours between the sheets with Jill Delaney would get her out of his system. Then he could move on without a backward glance.

He sighed and shifted in his seat. It was going to be a long trip.

* * * * *

Jill adjusted the rock-hard pillow behind her neck, wishing she could sleep.

The bus was dark enough now, but the cacophony of snores

grated on her nerves. She had tried to read, only to turn off the tiny overhead light when the passenger lucky enough to nab the window seat grumbled.

She had run out of things to distract her from the man sitting close enough to reach out and touch a long time ago.

His restlessness had kept her on edge well into New Jersey. It annoyed her to no end that her nerves leapt to attention at his every movement, that her lungs seemed determined to breathe in rhythm with his.

She would make a point of dating more often once she got home. Having her body strain toward Ethan Cooper like a dowsing rod pointed at the Pacific was wearing on her nerves.

Part of it was his damned cologne or aftershave or soap—whatever the hell it was. Even over the all-you-can-smell buffet that was the bus, he smelled masculine and hot and just a little bit spicy. If she didn't get away from him soon, she'd be straddling his lap and licking her way from his neck down. And she didn't even like him. What the hell were her traitorous hormones thinking?

Yes, she definitely needed to get out more. Or at least stock up on batteries. She'd need a little release by the time she escaped the scent across the aisle.

When they had stopped for dinner just past Baltimore, the driver told them it would be a couple of hours yet before they reached their hotel. They would stop again in North Carolina, in deference to the age of the passengers and be in Orlando the following day. It certainly wasn't a destination that had ever topped her wish list. Sure, when she was a little girl she dreamed of seeing Cinderella's castle, but that had faded long ago. Now it was only a hot, crowded tourist attraction.

Orlando? Where had all her money gone? The question that had filled her mind for days finally dragged her attention away from the rise and fall of Ethan Cooper's chest.

After working for seventeen years she should have had enough saved to live it up at Carnival in Rio de Janeiro or explore the Amazon Basin. Mardi Gras would be fun. Even white-water rafting in Colorado. Something more glamorous than the senior center's Spring Fling tour.

Although bamboo shoots ruining her manicure couldn't make her admit it to Ethan, this was the only trip she could afford. And heaven only knew what she was going to do when the vacation was over. She had no job, no money and a pretty hefty car payment to boot.

She shouldn't have quit her job. It wasn't the first time her pride had gotten her in trouble, and it probably wouldn't be the last. But it would be the first time she left herself in danger of being homeless.

Her sister's *you'll be sorry* echoed in her mind like some kind of gloomy Ghost of Future Mistakes. Not too far in the future, though. She was already sorry.

It was, contrary to the Delaney family's opinion, a far different situation than when she'd left Poor Eddy at the altar several years before. *Poor Eddy.* She hated the way that had become his name in her family—almost one word.

No doubt they thought breaking her engagement and quitting her job were both simply random acts of impulsiveness and wounded pride. They didn't understand. It wasn't anything as simple as pride that had made her leave Poor Eddy standing at the altar, no doubt checking his watch every thirty seconds.

Liz thought her life was wonderful. She couldn't see it the way Jill did. Her sister had given up everything for her husband and children, and she didn't see the way they drained her of energy. They sucked the life right out of her like rabid vampire brats. Her dreams of being a photographer for *National Geographic* magazine were dust, and she worked at the portrait studio of the local department store.

Jill didn't want that. Standing in front of the mirror, gazing at herself in the pouffy, white wedding gown, she had panicked. Her life flashed before her eyes—childbirth, diapers, runny noses, ungrateful teenagers, gray hair—and she bailed.

But that was different. This *was* pride, and she was going to have to swallow it to get her life back in order. There wasn't much out there for jobs right now and she didn't think dishing out fast food would allow her to keep both the apartment *and* the car. She'd rather go on that reality show that made contestants eat buffalo balls, but she had to beg for her job back. And the woman she had to grovel to was sleeping soundly two seats away.

She glanced over at Ethan, knowing he was her biggest hurdle. No doubt he had a lot of influence on his mom, and if he'd related the disaster in the parking lot, she was toast. His head was back against the seat and his breathing was slow and soft. She couldn't tell if he was asleep or not.

"Hey," she whispered. Nothing. He didn't even stir.

She told herself she'd be doing him a favor by waking him. Otherwise, he'd be awake all night in a motel room with the Weather Channel.

"Hey," she said again, a little louder. She reached across the aisle and nudged his arm.

He opened his eyes and turned his head. His hair was a little tousled and he blinked slowly as he came fully awake. A sleepy smile tugged at the corners of his mouth.

That's how he'd look in the morning, after a night of lovemaking. She had to fight the urge to squirm in her seat when she imagined waking up to those dark chocolate eyes and that little secret smile.

But he was fully awake now, and in the dim light, she could see he didn't look very happy. In other words, he looked pretty much the same as the last two times she'd talked to him.

"I'm sorry about the other day," she said.

"You woke me up to tell me that?"

Way to go, Einstein. But she had to do this before she lost her nerve. "I don't want you to think I'm a bad person. I was having a really horrible day when we met in the parking lot."

"I noticed. And you spread the joy well, too."

"I'm really sorry."

Ethan nodded and leaned his head back again. He closed his eyes, a sure sign he didn't want to talk anymore. But Jill wasn't done. She had to try.

"Hey," she whispered again.

"What?" he said in a low growl.

"Did you tell your mom I called her a bitch?"

He tried to stifle a laugh and it came out a snort. He looked over at her again. In the darkness, she could see the gleam of his teeth as he smiled. "No, sunshine. She's nervous enough about her new job without being insulted before she even starts."

Sunshine. The tongue-in-cheek comment didn't rankle nearly as much as it had in the store parking lot. But the sarcasm was still there. "I had only found out an hour before I…ran into you. It was still pretty fresh. And it's not like I knew her—or you."

"Don't worry about it."

So, he hadn't told on her. That was a good thing. But he must know how his mother felt about having her children's librarian quit out from under her. "She's nervous?"

"Yes," he said in a clipped tone.

Jill waited, but he had nothing else to say. Apparently, his moment of amusement was over. He wasn't an easy man to talk to. She took a deep breath, determined to get it over with.

"Do you think she'd take me back?" she whispered. Damn she hated begging, or anything remotely resembling it. "I really need that job."

He didn't react the way she half-expected. Instead of derision or disbelief, he considered her question for a long moment. *Please, please, please.*

"I don't think so," he finally replied, and her heart sank as she imagined how she would look in one of those cute visors with a fast food logo on the front. "She needs somebody dependable."

"Hey, I'm dependable," she protested. *Well, maybe not all the time.* Not when it came to weddings or getting passed over for promotions. Or baby-sitting—how was she supposed to know her nephew's favorite pastime was shoving things up his brother's nose? Why would any child want to do that? Better yet, why on Earth would the other child let him?

"As long as you get your way," he said, and she heard the censure in his voice. "My mother doesn't need to deal with somebody who throws a hissy fit and quits whenever she's mad."

When the going gets tough, Jillian gets going…in the other direction. The joke was less funny every time her subconscious coughed it up. But maybe not as exaggerated as she thought. Still…a hissy fit?

Turning away from Ethan and his scathing judgment of her, Jill cursed herself—again—for getting herself into this predicament. Leaping before looking was an old habit and she never knew how to climb back up. It was easier to walk away in a different direction. But not this time. She needed her job back and she had to get by Ethan to get to his mother.

The bus shifted and she looked out the window. The driver was pulling off the highway onto a darkened exit ramp. The hotel where the group had reservations should still be a couple of hours up the road and she wondered why they were stopping.

She glanced over at Ethan, but he didn't appear to find anything amiss. He looked over at her and shook his head. "I'm not asking her, if that's what you're after."

"What?"

"For your job back. I won't ask my mother for you."

Jill sighed. "I didn't really think you would. Why do you think he pulled off the highway?"

He shrugged, apparently not too concerned about the unscheduled detour. Or if he was, he had no intention of sharing it with her. That wasn't surprising. The man had probably never been frazzled or uncertain a day in his life. She hated people like that.

The driver pulled into a run-down gas station and stopped. A bearded man walking to an old pickup veered toward the bus when it came to a halt. Straining, Jill could hear the two men talking.

"We're closed up, mister."

"I need some air in those back tires," the driver argued. "I think I got a leak."

"Machine's over there. You got quarters, then you got air. Gas pumps are shut down and I'm going home."

"Just the air."

The attendant walked back to his truck and drove off. There was a sign on the building pointing restroom seekers around back, and Jill grabbed her purse and stood up.

"I need to use the bathroom while we're here."

"There's a bathroom at the back of the bus," Ethan muttered without looking up.

"No, there's half a closet with an oversized tin can—one shared by about fifty geriatric digestive tracts. And I'd like to wash my face and pee without my knees up around my ears."

He almost smiled. Jill held her breath, but his lips only twitched ever so slightly.

"It's probably locked, and they're closed," he said.

"Locked? In this place? I doubt it."

"You can't go back there alone."

She waited, fairly confident he would do the right thing. When Ethan rolled his eyes and stood, Jill smiled. Chivalry might be dead, but it wasn't buried.

Then he stretched and every erogenous zone in her body stood up and joined the chorus. She tried not to watch—masochism wasn't her thing—but the sight of his muscles twisting and tensing under his T-shirt was too tantalizing to miss.

When he twisted at the waist, a low growl of pleasure vibrating in his throat, Jill had to press her thighs together. A small ache settled in the small of her back and throbbed in time to her long-neglected pussy.

His T-shirt pulled out of his jeans over one hip, revealing just a sliver of skin. She wanted to press her lips to that spot, to push the fabric up and away from the snap. She could practically hear the sound of his zipper.

Before some appreciative sound could escape her lips, she turned and snatched her small purse off the seat. The only thing worse than lusting after this man would be having him know she was doing it.

* * * * *

Ethan followed Jill up the dark aisle. He paused on the bottom step and saw the bus driver engrossed in untangling the air hose.

"We're going to use the restrooms," he called. The driver waved a hand in response without looking up.

Away from the air-conditioned comfort of the bus, the warm and slightly humid night pressed in on him. It was a far cry from the spring chill they'd left behind in New Hampshire.

But not anywhere near as sizzling as the look Jill had given him. He wasn't so wrapped up in stretching he missed the interest—more like blatant lust—that flashed across her face before she turned away.

And it wasn't faked—he was sure of it. That was no "fuck the boss's son to get the job back" move. She had practically devoured him with her gaze and, if her lust was an act, it deserved an Oscar.

His heart rate was up and a fine sheen of sweat coated his flesh. The almost forgotten tingle of anticipation rippled through his nervous system. It had been a long time since a woman had wanted him—given him *the look.*

Even Betty had shown a marked disinterest in him during

the last year or so of their marriage. More than likely she had already fallen into the pumped-up arms of her vice cop by then.

Lingering humiliation added more heat to his already flushed skin and Ethan banged a mental U-turn. His frayed emotions could only handle one woman at a time. And as he followed Jill around the back of the gas station, every last inch of him was focused squarely on the gently swaying behind in front of him.

Jill wore a pale pink T-shirt tucked into tight jeans, and Ethan let his gaze roam over her ass, down her legs then back up again. His blood was nearing the boiling point when she stopped and looked over her shoulder at him. Her blue eyes watched him, questioning.

He nearly boiled right over until he realized he had followed her right past the men's bathroom to the door of the ladies'.

"You're not coming in with me," she said.

"Oh. Wasn't paying attention, I guess."

He held her gaze captive with his own, trying to return the look. She only cocked an eyebrow at him and waited. *Damn, I must be more out of practice then I thought.*

He turned and went back to the men's restroom, locking himself in with a sigh of relief. Maybe Jill's missing his signal was for the best.

She wasn't what he was looking for in a woman—he wasn't even sure he *was* looking. The problems Betty had caused were still reverberating through his life and Jill reminded him a lot of her. Impulsive, temperamental…hot.

Ethan leaned over the sink, careful not to actually touch the questionably-colored porcelain and turned on the cold tap. What he needed was an icy shower. Better yet, skip the shower. A tub of ice cubes might help if they didn't melt the second he sat down.

Almost without conscious thought, he released the snap of his jeans and tugged at the zipper. A quick adjustment of cloth and his aching cock was free. He sighed with relief, but it wasn't enough. If he didn't blow off some steam, he was going to explode before they reached Virginia.

He closed his fingers around the length of his cock and he groaned with pleasure. It had been too damn long since he'd buried himself in a woman.

He imagined Jill in the neighboring room, washing her face. Rushed, she would splash water on her shirt, soaking it until her nipples stood out against flimsy fabric. He ran his fingertips along the underside of his erection as he imagined sucking those nipples through wet, pink cotton and his whole body shuddered.

Placing his free hand on the mirror, he leaned his weight against that arm and relaxed his knees. His skin tingled and the almost immediate quickening in his balls told him it had been way too long.

Conscious of the time restraints, he fast-forwarded through peeling off her jeans and pushing aside the crotch of her white lace panties. Definitely white. His strokes quickened as he positioned the head of his cock against her welcoming cunt.

And she let loose with an unholy, wall-shaking scream of terror.

Ethan jerked his head up and his hand froze. That wasn't right.

Chapter Three

ꙮ

What the hell was he thinking? He wasn't the kind of guy who jerked off in slimy gas station bathrooms.

Jill yelled again and he shook off his lingering need. After hurriedly tucking his twitching cock back into his pants, he yanked open the door and ran the few steps to her door.

"Help!" she screamed, pounding on the other side.

"Jill? What's the matter?" Had she hurt herself? The bus would have a first aid kit, not that he had any clue what to do with it. He hoped like hell the driver did.

"It's stuck! The door is stuck!" He could hear a note of hysteria creeping into her voice. "Ethan? It's dark! The light blew when I hit the button for the hand dryer. I can't see!"

That was it? The door was stuck? He took a quick second to tamp down his laughter, then leaned close to the door. "I'll get you out, so calm down. And back away."

There was silence for a few seconds before she called, "I'm clear!"

Ethan backed up several paces and eyed the door. The wood was ancient, no doubt the reason it was stuck. No sweat.

He took a deep breath and started to run, dropping his shoulder at the last second.

He hit the door.

Bounced. Dropped like a stone.

Pain exploded in his shoulder. Groaning, he clutched his arm to his chest and stared up at the door. It hadn't budged.

"What was that?" Jill called. "Ethan? *Ethan*?"

"Give me a minute!" he shouted. The agony was already

abating to a throbbing ache—hopefully a sign nothing was broken.

"Ethan Ulysses Cooper!" Jill shouted and he snarled at the door. Yet another thing he was going to get even with his mother for someday. "You get me out of…oh, wait."

He heard a metallic click and the door swung open. Jill almost stepped on him. "What are you doing on the ground?"

"Don't ever call me that again," Ethan growled, pushing himself to his feet with his uninjured arm.

"Why are you just sitting—" He saw understanding dawn in her eyes. "Good grief! You tried to break the door down with your shoulder?"

Ethan glared at Jill, daring her to laugh. The battle not to waged on her face, but she managed to press her lips together and restrain herself to a smile.

"Thanks for trying," she said. "I guess you'll be mad when I tell you there were two locks on the door, and I only remembered to undo one."

Damn right he would. He rolled his eyes and started walking back around the building. There was probably one hell of a bruise blossoming on his upper arm and shoulder thanks to her stupidity. A physical reminder to keep his eyes off her ass and his mind out of the gutter where Jill Delaney was concerned.

"The lights went out and I panicked," she called after him, and he could hear her hurrying to keep up.

Ethan only shook his head and kept walking—until he turned the corner. His gaze swept the parking lot as disbelief surged through him.

Jill stopped next to him and he heard her gasp. "The bus is gone!"

* * * * *

"I can't believe they left without us." Jill looked up at

Ethan. He didn't look back. There was not a doubt in her mind he was placing all the blame for this latest turn of events in her lap. "The driver will come back for us, right?"

The glare he gave her could have chilled Death Valley at high noon. "I don't think so."

Fear curled into a tight ball in her stomach. "Don't be ridiculous. He can't strand us here. How could he even leave without us?"

"I told him we were going out back and he waved. He must have forgotten."

"Yeah, but—"

"Everybody else on the bus was asleep," he continued. "And we didn't hear the bus leaving because you probably chose that moment to practice your Jamie Lee Curtis imitation."

Jill folded her arms across her chest and stared at her feet. "I was scared. There was no light, and…it's pretty nasty in there."

Ethan said nothing. He just rubbed his shoulder and stared up the road in the direction the bus would have taken. Jill sighed. Things seemed to go from bad to worse when they were together and she wasn't sure which of them was the jinx. Probably her.

"Maybe your mom will wake up before they get too far," she said hopefully.

"That would be nice, sunshine," he said. "But my mother took a pill to help her sleep. She's a nervous traveler, which is why she dragged me on this cursed trip. And this wasn't a scheduled stop. By the time he's gone a few miles up the road, the driver probably won't even remember what exit he took."

The small knot of fear tightened like strings of Christmas lights. "You mean I'm stuck here? For how long?"

"No, we are stuck here," he gave her a tight smile, "but not for long, I hope."

"Do you have a cell phone?" Problem solved. Everybody

had a cell phone. Except her, of course, because she kept losing them.

"No, but there's a pay phone over there. What's the name of the motel we're supposed to stop at tonight?"

How the hell did the only two people on the planet without cell phones wind up stranded together? She must have done something pretty horrible in a past life.

Jill looked over at him and shrugged. "I don't know. My itinerary's in my suitcase—on the bus."

He shook his head slowly. "Of all the people to be—"

"Hey! I didn't memorize the damned thing. That's the driver's job. And why don't you know?"

He stared at her for what seemed like minutes, but she didn't look away from his dark eyes. His sudden burst of laughter took her by surprise. "Touché, sunshine."

Relief swept through Jill and she smiled. At least he wasn't going to strangle her right here at the gas station.

His laughter tickled her, easing the knot of anxiety in her belly. It wasn't deep and rumbling, as she'd expected, but a little higher and very infectious. Maybe this wouldn't turn out so badly after all.

"So…now what?" she asked when his amusement faded.

"Now we see if that pay phone has a directory with it and you can call all the motels until we find them."

Jill groaned as they walked across the parking lot. It was her fault they missed the bus, she supposed, but she hated making phone calls.

"I bought a prepaid phone card so I could call home for my messages," she said, digging it out of her purse. "I'll use that."

Fortunately, they found a tattered, oil-stained phone book and flipped through the motel pages. None sounded familiar. Ethan sat on the curb and leaned back against a tree. "Have fun."

She cast him a sour glance before she began the endless task of dialing numbers. The 800 number to access the card, then 1 for English directions, then the twelve-digit card number, then the motel number. "Do you have reservations for a senior tour group tonight?"

No luck. She repeated the entire process again. And again and again. Ethan emitted a tiny snore and Jill reached her foot out to nudge him. If she had to this, the least he could do was stay awake.

She dialed the next number in the directory, beginning to fear that the tour group was probably out of the area the book covered. Trying to get more listings from information wasn't her idea of fun.

The line was picked up with a curt "hello," followed by a rapid-fire recitation of what she assumed was his name and the hotel name. She didn't catch a word of it, but she had the listing in the book marked with her thumb.

"Do you have reservations for a busload of senior citizens tonight?" she asked without much hope.

He grunted something unintelligible, followed by computer keys clicking in the background. A pause. More clicking.

"Yup. Got 'em."

Jill almost squealed in the poor man's ear. "You do?"

Ethan sat upright and watched her intently as she spoke. "I need the name of your hotel and driving directions, please. We were separated from them."

She scribbled down the directions he gave her on an old receipt and thanked him profusely.

"You found them?" Ethan asked when she had replaced the dirty receiver and wiped her hands on her jeans.

"No, I thought we'd just stop in and say hi." His lips thinned into a grim line and she regretted her sarcasm. "Yes, I found them. Sorry."

They stood and looked around for a minute, finding only darkness in every direction. Without thinking, Jill took a step closer to Ethan. She was glad he was with her—even if he was being a jerk.

Aii-eee…aii-eee.

Jill jumped a foot. "What the hell was that? Was that an alligator?"

"I don't think alligators chirp."

"Have you ever *talked* to an alligator, Mister Know-it-All?"

Ethan rested his hand on the small of her back. Every nerve in her body snapped to high alert, focused on that slight hollow just above the waistband of her jeans. His palm radiated a heat that funneled straight from the point of contact up her spine and then back down to the sorely neglected area between her thighs.

Ohmigod. She focused all her energy on not doing something stupid, like throwing her arms around his neck and kissing him until his toes curled. He was just trying to comfort her, and she couldn't repay him by attacking him. Could she? No, that would probably be rude.

He looked down at her and she prayed he wouldn't notice the effect his touch had on her. If he was going for a calming effect he'd missed by a mile or two.

"So…how do we get there?" he asked.

"I don't know," Jill whispered, thankful her voice seemed to be in the proper working order considering how the rest of her body was going haywire. "I found them—you figure out how to get there."

She followed his gaze to the row of junks lining the parking area, awaiting repair or the tow truck to the junkyard. "What? You can't be… We can't *steal* a car!"

"Relax, sunshine. Even if I wanted to it wouldn't be one of those. Grab that phone book again and let's call a cab or something."

His hand left her back, and Jill sighed. It was for the best, she thought. Another few seconds and she might have knocked him to the ground and had her way with him. Considering the fact he didn't like her very much, she couldn't see that making his night any better.

After punching in another round of numbers, she discovered the only cab company in the directory was closed. According to the answering machine recording, they wouldn't reopen until seven the next morning.

"Guess we're not in the big city anymore," Jill said, sitting down on the curb with an air of defeat. "Now what?"

The words had barely left her mouth when they heard the purr of an approaching engine. Ethan sprinted to the road and waved his arms. At the last second a small, red convertible veered into the parking lot.

Jill walked over to stand next to Ethan, who was talking earnestly with the driver, a tall man wearing a polo shirt and a skeptical look.

"I'm headed that direction," he was saying thoughtfully. "And it's only about a half-hour out of my way."

"We'll pay you," Ethan insisted. He looked at Jill. "How much cash do you have on you?"

"Um…forty dollars, I guess," she replied, privately fuming. She didn't know why it surprised her that *she* would have to pay the guy. After all, Ethan blamed her for everything, so he probably figured it was her responsibility.

They looked back at the guy, but he was looking at Jill—or rather looking her over. She moved closer to Ethan, trying to send the guy a message, even if it was the wrong one.

"Only got the two seats," the man said, waving at the empty passenger seat in what Jill now saw was an old MG. "Your ol' lady will have to ride on your lap."

"She's not my—" Ethan paused. "That'll be fine."

Jill took a step back. "I am *not* sitting on your lap."

Just the feel of his hand pressing against her back had triggered an intense hunger for an orgasm, but Ethan was *not* on the menu. There was no way in hell she could survive this without making a fool of herself. She took another step back, shaking her head.

He grabbed her elbow to stop her retreat. "We've been here at least an hour. Maybe even longer, and how many cars have you seen go by?"

He had a point. She could either sit on his lap or camp out in front of a rundown gas station—alone. There was no doubt in her mind Ethan was leaving in the MG, with or without her.

"Maybe we could..."

"There is no maybe, sunshine," he interrupted. "I'm leaving. Are you coming with me or not?"

She cast him a sullen look. "I don't have a choice, do I?"

The man in the car took the two twenties Jill handed him and tucked them into his pocket without a word. She wasn't surprised. Even though he was only going a half-hour out of his way he was charging them forty dollars, so a thank you was probably too much to expect.

"I'm Rip, by the way," he did say. He caught her questioning look and grinned. "Slept a lot when I was a young'n."

She watched Ethan lower himself into the tiny car and shook her head. *This is not a good idea*, she thought to herself over and over. She would barely fit, and after the way her body had reacted to his hand simply touching her back...

Ethan extended his hand, not looking any happier about the prospect of her on his lap than she felt. Well, he deserved it after the way he had treated her, didn't he? She hooked her leg over his and lowered herself over him.

* * * * *

Ethan bit back a groan when the full weight of her bottom nestled over his crotch. She twisted on his lap, pulling her other leg into the car. Suddenly, spontaneous human combustion didn't seem so far-fetched anymore.

She yelped when he grabbed her hips and shifted her roughly, moving her off of his frustrated, half-hardened cock and onto his thigh. The last thing he needed was for her to feel how much their present predicament aroused him.

Despite their predicament, it was taking every ounce of his willpower to keep his hands off Jill. He'd been doing fairly well, too, other than touching that sweet little hollow at the base of her spine, but he wasn't sure he'd make it out of this car still able to walk.

Jill closed the door and Rip fired up the engine. The old car roared to life, sending a vibration through his body that didn't help in the least. He closed his eyes and tried to think about his mother—how she would react to discovering she had lost him. Then he tried to picture his ex-wife. Anything that was anti-sex.

It didn't help. He hadn't noticed until this moment how good Jill smelled. Even after a day on the bus, surrounded by myriad of aromas, she still carried a hint of spicy and tantalizing perfume. Her shampoo was faintly fruit-scented and the combination made him think of the tropics…

Palm trees, rolling waves. Endless stretches of white sand. Jill's naked body stretched before him on a beach towel, sand clinging to her pale skin. He imagined Jill's tongue licking the ocean salt from her lips while her hands ran over her breasts, offering them to him. He tipped the umbrella drink in his hand, dribbling piña colada over her nipples. The chill of the drink would harden them, making them perfect targets for his lips, his tongue. The gentle scrape of his teeth. He imagined her fingers tightening in his hair while she moaned his name.

Ethan moved down her body, marking the trail for his tongue with his drink, until finally he reached her pussy. He poured the cocktail over her swollen clit, then pressed his mouth to her. The piña colada mingled with her sweet cream, and he lapped at the paradisiacal drink like a man dying of thirst.

When she came, flooding his mouth with coconut-flavored ambrosia, he pulled away from her and poured the sweet island drink over his throbbing cock. "Lick it off, baby."

"Did you say something?" Jill's voice jerked him out of the delicious daydream like a verbal bungee cord.

He muttered something in the negative and thanked his lucky stars she couldn't see his face.

Enough of that. The woman was nothing but trouble—a kind of trouble he didn't need. What kind of idiot didn't even recover from one woman's fickleness before considering a tryst with another just like her?

The kind of idiot he saw in the mirror every day, apparently. That surprised him. Walking into trouble with his eyes wide open wasn't his usual style. Better safe than sorry. That was him.

They hit a bump in the road and Jill shifted, landing squarely in his lap again. This time he couldn't hold back the moan. Luckily, he didn't think it could be heard over the roar of the British racing engine.

"Sorry," Rip said in his direction. "These beauties ain't Cadillacs, you know?"

"Yeah," Ethan responded through gritted teeth.

Jill squirmed, trying to regain her former position, but he stopped her with a hand on her back. "Just sit still," he hissed.

"I'm trying," she said, and he could hear the tension in her voice.

Pity outweighed common sense. This couldn't be any more comfortable for her than it was for him. He slid his hand up her back and over her shoulder to pull her back against him.

She stiffened for a moment, and then relaxed against his chest. "Are we almost there?"

Ethan stifled a bizarre urge to bury his face in her hair. "Not even close, I'm afraid."

His hand rested comfortably on her hip now and he thought maybe he would survive this ride with his dignity intact. As long as she didn't squirm anymore.

Jill tilted her head to whisper privately. "I'm really sorry about this, Ethan."

Her breath tickled his jaw. He shivered, praying she wouldn't notice. "Don't worry about it, sunshine. It'll be over soon enough."

She laughed and the sound shot through his body and straight to the traitor between his legs. He stiffened, unable to move Jill without attracting more attention to his sudden discomfort. *Geez,* he thought. *I haven't been this embarrassed since the eighth grade.*

He knew the very second she became aware of his arousal. She stilled and her breath caught. He waited, afraid to make any move, and a little curious about what she would do.

If she wasn't interested or—God forbid—she was downright disgusted, he'd just have to pass it off as an involuntary response to physical contact. Technically, that was true enough. He just wouldn't tell her how badly he wanted to bury said involuntary response inside of her.

It seemed like forever before she lifted her face higher. "Too bad this car doesn't have a backseat," she whispered for his ears only.

Ethan's inflamed senses exploded. It had been too long since he felt this kind of desire and anticipation, and he had to exercise considerable restraint not to pull up on the emergency brake, stop the car and bend her over the hood.

He had to appease his hunger with what little he could get. He ran his hand over her back, her ass, then traced the line of her bra strap across her back. The ride seemed endless and by the time Rip pulled into the motel parking lot, Ethan's need had grown so painful he wasn't sure he'd be able to walk.

He practically pushed Jill up and out of the car, then managed to climb out himself. All he wanted to do was check in, assure his mother he wasn't lost anymore and then take Jill—anywhere and any way he could get her.

They said nothing on the way into the office, but he was intrigued by the rosy flush of her skin. Was she as eager to be with him, or was she regretting her brazenness in the car? He couldn't summon the courage to ask her.

A young man wearing a weary smile and nametag that read *Hello, my name is Donnie* greeted them. "Howdy folks, what can I do you for?"

Ethan stepped up to the desk. "Can you tell me what room Debra Cooper is in, please? She's with the senior tour group."

Donnie shuffled some papers, and then clicked through endless computer screens. A clock on the wall ticked off the seconds and Ethan's pulse pounded in time. If Donnie didn't click a little faster, he was apt to embarrass them all by taking her right there on the lobby floor.

"I'm sorry, sir. I do have the individual names of the tour group, but Debra Cooper is not listed."

Frustration—of several varieties—made his tone harsher than he intended. "Look, she's got to be here. She's with the senior tour group from New Hampshire."

Understanding lit Donnie's face. "That explains it. We've only got one group here tonight and they're from New York."

He looked at Jill and watched her eyes widen. He didn't even have to ask. She hadn't confirmed it was the *right* tour group when she called. He exhaled, and his lungs weren't the only thing deflating.

"Sorry, mister. You've got the wrong motel."

Chapter Four

ꙮ

Jill winced when Donnie said the words, mentally kissing her orgasm goodbye. Sex? Heck, at this point she'd be lucky if he ever spoke to her again.

She was wrong.

"New York?" Ethan demanded. "You didn't ask if it was the *right* senior group?"

His derisive tone made her sound like an imbecile and her chin lifted automatically. "I didn't think to."

His expression changed from disbelief to downright menacing. "You didn't *think* to? Didn't you think that small detail might be kind of important?"

As always, embarrassment fueled her temper and she shouted at him. "I was tired and upset! And you weren't any help. All those damn numbers I had to call while you just sat there. We could have taken turns at least."

He opened his mouth to speak several times, then shook his head. He didn't need to speak, his face said it all. He was cursing the day he'd ever met Jill Delaney and she knew it.

She fought the urge to cry with grim determination. She wasn't going to take *all* the blame for this. He should have called himself if he was so perfect.

But it hurt so much when he looked at her like that. Feeling the hard length of his cock under her ass had given her a thrill the likes of which she hadn't felt in years, but it would be nice if he could at least *try* to like her.

"Now what?" he muttered, and she got the impression he was talking more to himself than to her. That was fine with Jill. She didn't have much to say to him, either.

"It's too late to keep going," Ethan continued. "Even if we managed to locate her tonight, we're both too tired to drive. And who knows if there's a car rental place around?"

"There's one around the block," Donnie said. Jill felt a quick flash of relief, but it died when he said, "It's closed up for the night, though."

"She's probably close by," she said hopefully. "Maybe the bus driver stopped just up the road a bit."

"We don't know that for sure and, as Donnie here pointed out, we have no way to get there," Ethan snapped, and she stuck out her tongue when he turned back to the desk. "We need a couple of rooms, I guess."

Donnie clicked his way through the computer screens again, then smiled at them. "We have one room available—a king-size bed with a view of the pool."

"I said we need a *couple* of rooms," Ethan repeated. "As in *two*."

The night clerk's smile faded a bit. "I'm sorry, sir, but we only have one."

One room, one bed—two people. She watched Ethan drop his shoulders and shake his head. *Great. Won't this be cozy?*

Despite her best effort to hold it back, laughter suddenly shook Jill's body. Ethan turned and gave her a cold, questioning look that only made it worse. Tears blurred her vision as she covered her mouth, trying to stop it.

"What exactly is so funny?"

Jill shrugged, unable to find the right words. She wasn't sure there were any words because she didn't even know where the laughter came from. The only thing she knew for sure was that she and Ethan were going to be spending a lot more time together than either of them had anticipated.

And the look of horror on his face when Donnie told him there was only one room available had been her undoing. Just minutes ago he'd been so hot for her she'd thought Rip was going to get one hell of a show for his forty bucks. And now, when the perfect arrangement for spending the night together had presented itself, he looked as if he'd stepped in a fresh pile of cow shit.

Ethan threw his hands up. "Fine. We'll take it. Jill, you have a credit card, right?"

Her good humor evaporated as quickly as it had appeared. "Why do I have to pay for everything? As you so joyfully pointed out, I recently quit my job."

A hint of redness crept up his neck. "I don't have my wallet. It's in my mother's purse."

Jill gave him a much-exaggerated look of shock. "Oh my, Mr. Perfect Planner. You mean you didn't foresee this little problem?"

"Very funny," he said in a clipped tone. "It hurts to ride for a long time with a wallet under your butt."

"It does," Donnie agreed, nodding at Jill.

"I know all about riding around with a lump under my butt," she said, and she had the pleasure of watching Ethan's face flush a deep crimson.

"Do you want to sleep tonight or not?" he growled.

"Fine." She dug in her purse and pulled out the single credit card she had with her. The rest of her cash, traveler's checks and credit cards were in her suitcase. She'd been terrified she'd forget her purse somewhere between New Hampshire and Florida and be left with nothing.

She slapped the credit card into Ethan's palm, filled out the form and handed him their room key. After Donnie gave them directions to the room, he wished them a good night with a suggestive smile. Judging by his tone she was surprised he had enough restraint not to wink at them.

"Yeah, sure," Ethan muttered under his breath as he practically pushed Jill down the hall. "A good night, my ass."

She thought about apologizing, but decided against it. It was just a coincidence that bad things happened to him when she was around. If he didn't understand...tough. A few screwups on her part didn't merit righteous arrogance on his part.

By the time Ethan let her into their room and closed the door behind them, her temper had redlined. "Who the hell do you think you are?"

The room was hot and stale. He went straight to the air conditioner. "Why don't you do me a favor and be quiet for a while?"

"No, I won't." She felt a moment of satisfaction when the ancient unit coughed and sputtered to life, blasting him with dust.

Ethan swore and lifted the hem of his shirt to wipe his face, giving her a view of smoothly taut abs. Jill swallowed hard, balling her hands into fists as her panties grew annoyingly moist. The urge to touch him was back with a vengeance, but she fought it.

How the hell could she want to straddle him and strangle him at the same time? He frustrated her more than any person she'd met recently, and here she was wanting to run her hands over his stomach?

She wanted to free his erection from his jeans and torment him as he'd tormented her in the car. Her imagination conjured an image of Ethan squirming as she ran her tongue over the head of his cock, refusing to take him deep against her throat. She could almost hear him begging.

"Can this day get any worse?" was what he actually said.

"Don't ever say that out loud," Jill warned, tossing her purse onto the nightstand. "You need to lighten up. Your blood pressure must give your doctor nightmares. And keep him in yachts."

He turned on her so fast she took a step back. "Lighten up? Lady, do you know why I came on this trip?"

Not good. He was back to calling her *lady* again. "I guess because your mom wanted you to come."

"That's right—my mother who hates to travel and who has had a lot of upheaval since my father died last year. She *needs* me."

Jill gazed into his dark eyes and saw the anguish behind the anger. It occurred to her that his worry over his mother must have been in the forefront of his mind all night—except for that brief, delicious distraction in the MG, of course. And she had foiled him again. He was blaming her for more than inconvenience. She was keeping him from taking care of his widowed mother—a task he obviously took very seriously.

Which was sweet, even if it *was* keeping her from having that orgasm. Any guy who loved and cared for his mother so much had to be pretty decent.

"I *am* sorry, Ethan," she said quietly, thinking maybe she did owe him an apology after all. It wouldn't kill her and it might make him feel a little better.

"You should be."

Or…maybe not. "She'll be fine with the tour group. The guide will take care of her."

"With the same attention he gave us?" His anger was almost a physical presence in the room. "I'm supposed to take care of her, not strangers."

For a split second, Jill wondered if she should be afraid of this man she barely knew. He was little more than a stranger, no matter how much her body might want to shimmy up against his. But there had been plenty of opportunities for him to lose his temper in their short acquaintance. He could have blown his top when she mucked up his fender. Or when she locked herself in the bathroom, which had actually caused him physical pain. He hadn't really lashed out even when she called his mother a bitch.

Wow, have I done anything at all right? She definitely had her work cut out for her if she was going to rehabilitate his opinion of her.

"I didn't do any of this on purpose."

Ethan towered over her and smirked. "Didn't you? I saw the way you looked at me on the bus."

Damn, he caught her. Embarrassment made her voice harsh. "You think I sabotaged our vacation just so I could have sex with you?"

Was that a flicker of uncertainty in his eyes? "Are you denying you want me?" he asked in a husky tone she'd never expected to hear come out of his mouth.

Jill's skin prickled with heat and she shoved him back with both hands. He tripped and sat down hard on the edge of the bed. She walked toward him, her finger pointed accusingly at him.

"What about you?" she demanded. "What about when we were in Rip's car, huh? What was that about?"

She couldn't take her eyes off his mouth. His jaw relaxed and the corners of his lips turned up just a bit. Right now it looked utterly kissable. Dragging her gaze up to his eyes, she was jolted by the smoldering heat that wasn't there just a second ago.

Ethan reached out and snagged her belt loop, hauling her toward him. "You want to know what that was about? I was imagining you naked on a tropical beach, spread out on a towel like an all I could eat buffet."

Jill's legs quivered like two overgrown gummi worms at the image of Ethan's head between her thighs with her fingers tangled in his hair. She didn't fight him when he hooked his hands behind her knees and pulled her forward until she straddled his lap.

"And what, exactly, was I doing naked on a beach?"

"You were licking piña colada off my cock, actually."

She wasn't sure which surprised her more, the words coming out of Mr. Uptight's mouth, or the rush of wet heat between her thighs. But one thing was sure—kissing off her orgasm might have been premature. *Yes!*

"I...I don't even like you," she said, just so they were on the same page. Not that it mattered. Her mind may not like him very much, but her body was about to pounce on him.

He grinned and ran his hands up her sides, over her breasts. "I don't like you either."

Jill moaned, damning her nipples for hardening at his touch. They could at least make him work for it. "And I don't... My life is such a mess."

Ethan forced her to lean back and bent his head, licking the hollow at the base of her throat. She almost came right there and then. "And my divorce hasn't been final long and my mother's lost—or I am. What does any of that have to do with this?"

She was sure that all had a lot to do with this, but she'd be damned if she could remember what.

"Look, sunshine," he said. "We're both more or less adults here."

"More or less?"

He ignored her indignant interruption. "Why not enjoy ourselves instead of spending the entire trip sexually frustrated?"

"You mean, like vacation sex?" Hot, naked and sweaty sex just for the sake of hot, naked and sweaty sex? No strings? What a bargain.

"Exactly."

His breath was hot and ragged on her moistened flesh. *Do I really want to do this?* Now was the time to stop—to take the coldest shower of her life. She knew Ethan wouldn't take *no* well at this point, but he'd already shown himself to be a fundamentally decent guy and she had faith he would stop if she asked him.

But Jill wanted him—wanted him so much it scared her silly. She didn't even *like* him. But his lips traced a path of fire up her neck and she plunged her fingers into his thick, mahogany hair. "Will you still hate me in the morning?"

His chuckle vibrated across her flesh. "I promise."

Jill put her hands on his shoulders and pushed him back until he was lying on the bed. She only broke eye contact for the split second it took to yank her T-shirt out of her jeans and pull it over her head.

Ethan's gaze left as hot a trail as his mouth when it moved over her skin. He stared with a raw hunger that made her feel like the sexiest woman on the planet. Like a goddess. She moved her hips slowly, grinding the crotch of her jeans against his. She could feel the constrained length of him through the denim and she shivered with anticipation. He sat up and nipped at her nipple through her lacy bra, but she shoved him down again.

Jill couldn't remember the last time she had felt like this. Couldn't remember if she even had ever felt like this. Her body ached for his touch. And yet she was afraid she would shatter if he put his hands on her.

Which was ridiculous. Vacation sex was shallow and meaningless. It was only about the pleasure, and she'd better remember that.

"You're a beautiful woman, sunshine," he said in a low, husky voice that sent a tremor down her spine. He reached for her breasts, but she pushed his hands away.

"If you start singing 'You Are My Sunshine', I'll have to gag you."

He grinned wickedly. "That might be interesting."

"Why, Mr. Cooper!" Jill exclaimed in a mock-Scarlett voice. "How scandalous!"

Slowly—very slowly—she ran her fingers under her breasts to the small clasp nestled between them. She felt him tense between her thighs and saw the bead of sweat on his forehead.

His tongue flicked over his lips. "I want to see the rest of you—*all* of you. Right now."

She simply smiled, very deliberately opening the clasp with a faint click. His eyes never left her fingers. She snapped it shut, and then opened it again. *Click…click…*

In the blink of an eye, Ethan flipped her to her back and Jill laughed at the growling sound he made. He pushed back the flimsy fabric of her bra and stared down at her breasts.

His hungry look was so intense Jill's amusement slipped away. She pushed her hips up against his, urging him to move…to do *something*. She needed to come, badly.

And he knew it, the bastard, and took his sweet time. He nipped at her jaw and his tongue blazed a hot, wet trail down her neck. His mouth brushed over her collarbone, and his kissed the hollow at the base of her throat. His teeth grazed over the soft skin there and a groan of impatience escaped her.

Finally he turned his attention to her breasts. His tongue toyed with her nipples, lavishing equal attention to each, until she thought she would scream. She clawed at his shirt, trying to pull it up as his hands worked at tugging her jeans down over her hips.

Ethan pulled back from her to divest himself of his clothes. The shirt she hadn't been able to get over his head went first, and then he went for the snap of his jeans. Jill held her breath as the zipper rasped and he pushed the denim down. By scooting a little sideways on the bed, she was able to reach out and caress the length of his cock through his boxer briefs.

He kicked his jeans the rest of the way off and knelt on the bed. "If you keep doing that I'm going to come. I'm too close, and I want to be inside you."

She reached for the nightstand and fumbled in her purse for a little foil packet, which she set next to his knee. After a moment's pause and the crinkle of packaging, he grabbed the bottoms of her jeans and pulled them off with one hard yank. Her cotton panties followed.

The abruptness and her sudden nakedness made her gasp and Ethan grinned down at her, looking for all the world like a pillaging pirate right then. He certainly didn't look like the white-collar office slave she was sure he was.

Then he got very still, and his grin faded. He looked for all the world like he was struggling with some moral dilemma, and boy, was she going to get pissed if he'd suddenly decided vacation sex was on his list of no-nos.

"Now's the time if you're having second thoughts. You're sure you want to do this?" he asked, and she almost laughed at the desperation on his face. She was half-tempted to say no just to see him suffer.

But that would only prolong her own suffering. She wanted him *now*. "I'm very sure that if you don't fuck me right now, I'm going to tie you to the bed and have my own way with you."

Jill didn't even have to time to admire the hard planes of his body, the impressive swell of his erection before he lifted her hips, forcing her knees apart. He pressed against her, teasing her clit until he gleamed with her juices. Then he plunged his cock deep into her, filling and stretching her, and she didn't care anymore. She'd explore him at leisure later.

He filled her completely and Jill could feel her muscles tensing already. She'd been dreaming of Ethan's cock pounding into her since the first time she saw him, and it seemed far too long to wait. But better than she'd ever imagined. She hadn't expected the tenderness.

Each slow stroke brought her a breath closer to release. She felt his hot, ragged breath on her neck and caressed the taut muscles of his back as he fought for control. He was going to make sure she came first, and that knowledge alone was nearly enough to send her over the edge. He moved his hips, grinding his shaft against her clit before burying himself deep in her again.

"Jesus, Jill," he groaned into her neck. "Your cunt is so hot. I wish I could fuck you forever."

His words inflamed her, and she raised her hips, meeting each stroke and taking his cock to the hilt. She gasped when he grabbed her ankles and draped them on his shoulders. He tilted his hips, and the angle and depth of his penetration sent her over the edge.

He quickened, pounding into her, and she matched his

rhythm, the hot friction sending wave after wave of pleasure pulsing through her body.

She felt him jerk against her, pulsing inside of her. She cried his name as her body gave in to his with exquisite intensity.

Ethan collapsed on top of her and they were silent for a few minutes, trying to catch their breath. Jill idly ran her fingernails up and down as his back, smiling when a slight aftershock shook his body.

"Oh damn," Ethan whispered.

Jill stiffened. *Here it comes.* Now he would roll away, sorry he'd gotten himself involved in a one-night stand with the kind of woman who'd have a one-night stand—not his usual type, she'd bet. *Just, please not yet.* "What?"

He lifted his head from her breast. "I forgot the best part."

She frowned even as his lips turned up in a smile. "That wasn't the best part?"

"No," he whispered just before his lips touched hers.

The kiss was gentle and Jill felt the *uh-oh* echo deep into her soul. Their breath mingled and it felt so…right. Damn, that wasn't good.

Ethan lifted his head and stared down at her, his chocolate eyes serious—questioning. She didn't have any answers so she wrapped her fingers in his hair and pulled his head down. Her kiss wasn't gentle—she pushed him, devouring his mouth with her own.

He rolled, dragging Jill with him. She straddled his hips, her lips still crushing his. If she couldn't come up with answers, she'd simply take his mind off the question.

Chapter Five

Why the hell did I have to go and kiss her?

Ethan opened his eyes, squinting against the ray of sunshine that slipped between the heavy drapes and fell across his face. Jill's body pressed against him, soft and warm, reminding him of how her lips felt under his own.

He could tell himself the sex—both times—was just for fun, but that kiss...

There was nothing playful about it. Even now, the feelings kissing Jill had stirred in him made little beads of sweat pop up on his forehead.

It wasn't the insatiable lust he felt for the woman curled against his side that bothered him. It was the unfamiliar, unwelcome feeling of completion. Suddenly, despite the chaos of his life, all his ducks were lining up and he felt something alarmingly close to contentment. *That* bothered the hell out of him.

Allowing the feeling to take root in his heart or his mind because of the sex would be a huge mistake and he knew it. Contentment with Jill Delaney was out of the question—so far out of the question it was nearly an oxymoron. Even if he could put aside the fact that she was the oil to his water, she had made it quite clear she was only out for a little fun.

She'd certainly succeeded there. Sex had never been more fun. And the sudden resurgence of desire so soon after release had been a pleasant surprise. It had been a while since he pulled off that little trick.

The phone rang, its old-fashioned blare nearly stopping his heart. Before he could stop her, Jill reached out and snagged the receiver.

"Hello," she said in a low, husky voice that made his customary morning stiffness a bit stiffer. "Oh…hi, Mrs. Cooper. Yeah, he's right here."

No, no, no. Could she have made it any more obvious they were in the same bed? He swore under his breath. Jill passed the receiver over her shoulder and closed her eyes again.

He took a deep breath, then greeted his mother. "Are you okay, Mom?"

"Am *I* okay?" she shouted, and Ethan jerked the receiver away from his ear. His mother was fairly loud in person—she was absolutely deafening on the telephone. "Where on Earth did you get to? I've had the hardest time tracking you down."

"We got off the bus to use the restroom and the driver left without us. This motel had reservations for a tour group, but it was the wrong group."

"Oh yes, the driver is very sorry about that."

Jill murmured something unintelligible and stretched like a well-fed cat. His mother's voice faded into the background while Ethan watched, mesmerized. He bit back a groan when the sheet slid down over her firm breasts, then forced his gaze away. His mother was practically in the room, for goodness sake.

"Ethan, you did use a *condom*, didn't you?"

"What? Mother…what?"

"Did you find a condom somewhere?"

Ethan knew there was no chance he would ever be able to scrub his mother's chipper voice saying…that word out of his mind. And this was Jill's fault, dammit. If she hadn't come into his life, he could have gone to his grave without ever having discussed birth control with his mother.

"I do have your wallet dear, and I'm sure you didn't go stocking up on them to take a trip with me and my old fogey friends. You know how much I want grandchildren—like all my friends had *years* ago—but I hope you're smart enough not to fool around without birth control."

Ethan gripped the receiver. "I am *not* going to discuss contraception with you."

The warm lump next to him giggled and he slapped it in the vicinity of its ass. He felt like a damn teenager busted necking on the couch, and she was laughing? She deserved more than a slap on the ass. What she needed was a good old-fashioned, facedown over his lap spanking.

An image of her ass, slightly rosy from the palm of his hand and sorely in need of a kiss to make it better, almost made him drop the receiver. He rolled over to face the wall. He was turning into a pervert after one night with the woman.

"The young lady who answered the phone—she was sitting across from you on the bus?" his mother asked, once again embarrassing the hell out of him. Now he had an inkling of how boys felt when their moms walked in and caught them with Dad's magazines.

"Yes, that was her."

"That's funny," she mused. "I somehow got the impression you didn't even like her."

He didn't know how to respond to that. Did he like her? Of course. He'd certainly enjoyed her company last night. But did he *like her* like her? He didn't know. She hadn't stopped aggravating him long enough to find out.

When in doubt, change the subject. "We're near a car rental place, so I'll rent one and meet you at the hotel in North Carolina, okay?"

Jill's sex-tousled hair emerged from under the sheet and he looked over his shoulder at her. "You mean *I'll* rent a car."

"Wonderful," his mom said. "Kenny can't wait to meet you."

Her words penetrated, distracting him from the fetching picture Jill made. "Kenny? Kenny who?"

"Kenny Sanford—my new gentleman friend."

Gentleman friend? What the hell did that mean? And how

fast did the guy move? Considering his mother had been in a sound, chemically-induced sleep when he got off the bus with Jill, pretty damn fast. "You've got a boyfriend already?"

"Don't take that tone with me, Ethan Ulysses Cooper."

"Don't call me—"

"The bus driver is waving at me," she interrupted. "He said we can't wait for you here, so I've got to run. Bye now, dear."

"Wait! Let me grab a pen so I can take down the name of the hotel in North Carolina," he said.

He started to throw back the sheet, then froze. There on the desk—on the far side of the room—were the small pad of paper and stub of pencil stamped with the hotel name. What kind of place put them as far as possible from the phone?

Jill's skimpy panties were the only article of clothing within reach. Those wouldn't do—red wasn't his color. And at some point during the incredible night, they had kicked the blanket off *her* side of the bed.

Sauntering naked across the room wasn't exactly his style. He could steal the sheet with a hard jerk, but that would leave Jill sprawled naked on the bed. The last thing he needed was that kind of distraction with his condom-endorsing mother chattering away in his ear.

Maybe he could sneak over there and back before she even noticed. Ethan glanced down to find her staring up at him, her hands tucked behind her head and an amused smile curving her lips. She looked over at the pencil then back at him, daring him to go get it.

The little minx. Bunching as much of the cheap fabric as possible into his fist, he gave it a hard yank. His breath caught in his throat when the sheet tore away, leaving her bare.

He tried not to look. He really did. His mother was practically in the room with them. Preaching safe sex, no less. He wrapped the sheet around his waist, then looked down. It didn't hide a thing.

"Did you learn how to make tents like that in the Boy

Scouts?" Jill asked before she rolled onto her stomach, her delectable bottom shaking with laughter.

"Ethan?" his mother yelled in his ear, dragging him back to the task at hand. With the cord stretched to within an inch of its life, he wrote down the information she read off to him, then promised to meet her at the hotel as soon as possible.

Ethan walked around the bed to hang up the phone, and then slapped Jill hard on the butt. She yelped and turned over, somehow managing to snag the sheet on her way. Pulling as hard as she could, she managed to get almost all of it before he recovered.

He jerked it back, dragging Jill with it. When she was close enough he caught her arms and hauled her up against his body. The sheet slipped to the floor unnoticed. His kiss was hard and punishing.

"I don't have any more—"

"No, don't say it!" he interrupted. *Good grief.* What could be worse than forever associating the word *condom* with his mother?

"Don't you have one in your wallet?"

"Yes, but my wallet's on the bus, remember? I wonder if room service stocks them. I wonder if they even *have* room service."

"I bet we can have some fun without one," she whispered against his lips as her fingers trailed down his stomach and closed around his cock, driving thoughts of hotel services right out of his mind.

Ethan looked at her soft, warm mouth and groaned. "That's a fool's bet."

* * * * *

Jill smiled and let his hot flesh glide across her palm. She wasn't ready to leave this room and their agreement behind quite yet.

Ethan was already fully erect and she closed her fingers around him, squeezing lightly. His hips rocked, urging her to stroke him. She loosened her grip, allowing him to fuck her curled fist while she kissed and licked her way down to his nipples.

She played with him, nibbling at his chest and lightly stroking his cock until he growled in frustration and put his hand on her shoulder to guide her lower. Jill knelt in front of him, still running her fingers ever so lightly over him.

"What do you want?" she asked in a low voice, eager to hear him unleash the Ethan the rest of the world didn't get to see.

"I want you to suck my cock," he said through gritted teeth, holding himself still as if too much eagerness might scare her off.

"I wonder if room service would deliver a piña colada. A nice creamy tropical drink would be soothing, don't you think?"

Ethan put his hand on the back of her head and pulled her toward his throbbing cock. "I've got creamy for you. Just open wide."

She flicked her tongue over the head, licking at the drop of fluid gathered there. Then she pulled away and sat back on her heels. "I think you should ask me nicely."

Ethan threw back his head and groaned, making her want to laugh. He was so much fun to torment. She licked her lips and waited, peering up at him through her eyelashes.

"Please, baby. Please take me in your mouth."

She rose back up onto her knees and put her mouth to the head of his cock. With her tongue she teased for just a moment, then she took him deep into her mouth. With each thrust her saliva lubricated him and she let him push a little farther, until finally she had him nearly to his balls.

"Oh…sunshine," he groaned. "Fucking your mouth is almost as sweet as fucking your pussy."

She moaned a little, feeling herself grow wet with desire at his words, and the vibration made him buck against her, ramming his cock into her mouth. She let him slip out from between her lips, then traced a line with her tongue from the head to the base of his penis. His entire body shuddered when she nuzzled his sac, gently nipping at his balls with her teeth.

"Do you like that?" she asked, stroking him firmly with one hand.

"Oh yeah." He tightened his grip in her hair, pulling her mouth back to the head of his cock.

She teased him some more, alternating between running her tongue around the head and drawing him completely into her mouth. His fingers flexed against her scalp and she knew he was getting close.

She caught his cock in a tight fist, using the moisture her mouth left behind to lubricate his flesh. She sucked him into her mouth, using both her hand and her lips to pleasure him. His hips moved against her, and he pressed at the back of her head, holding her close.

She quickened her rhythm, sucking a little harder. He pumped his cock into her mouth, groaning. Then he jerked, filling her mouth with his salty come. She pulled back enough to swallow, then took him deep into her mouth again. He pulsed, emptying himself, and then gently pulled her to her feet.

Capturing her in his arms, he fell backward onto the bed, taking her with him. She nuzzled his chest and he kissed the top of her head. "That was…incredible."

Her heart swelled at the contentment she heard in his voice. He'd given her an amazing night of sex, and it thrilled her to be able to please him as well as he'd pleased her.

He squeezed her and chuckled into her hair. "You're such a pervert. I might just have to keep you around a while longer."

* * * * *

"It was *my* credit card," Jill said an hour later, trying to snatch the keys away from Ethan.

"I'm driving." He unlocked the passenger door, then moved around the white Ford Taurus.

"Are you still mad about the T-shirt?"

Ethan looked down and plucked at the fat, orange cat adorning his chest. "Did you have to get Garfield?"

Frankly, she'd barely noticed the cat since he pulled the T-shirt over his head. The way the white cotton stretched over his shoulders and back was far too distracting. The man either pushed some serious files or spent a lot of time at the gym.

"What's wrong with Garfield?" she asked.

"Get in the car."

When he got in and started the engine, the meaning was clear. Get in or get left behind. She slid into her seat and snapped her seat belt closed. While he concentrated on pulling out of the lot and finding his way to the highway on-ramp, she stared out her window.

"I'm a grown man," Ethan said when he'd merged into traffic. "Did you pick this one purposely to make me look like an idiot?"

"Look, it was a convenience store, not a department store, okay? It was either Garfield or a shirt listing the top ten signs you may be a redneck. I looked, but I couldn't find one that listed the top ten signs you're an asshole."

She expected him to ignore her, but he glanced over at her. "When I was a kid my best friend in the world moved away. He gave me a cool Garfield magnet as a goodbye present."

Crap. Jill wondered if they made an asshole-identifying T-shirt in her own size. "I'm so sorry. Now seeing Garfield reminds you of loss and saying goodbye?"

Ethan snorted, and she thought he would spray coffee all over the steering wheel. It was a close call. "Do they give degrees in daytime talk show psychobabble, or can you practice without a license?"

"I guess you know which part of my anatomy you can

plant those lips on, don't you?" Jill fixed her gaze on the tree line, watching them whip by in a blur. She should have bought a book in the gift shop. Even the mild queasiness brought on by reading in the car would be better than arguing with Ethan for the rest of the trip.

"Why, did I miss a spot?"

Her head whipped back around and she saw that his face was as crimson as hers felt. It was obvious he couldn't believe he'd said that and amusement bubbled in her throat. "No, you hit all the right places."

Ethan kept his eyes on the road as they were swallowed up in awkward silence. Jill couldn't think of a single thing to say about the night—and morning—they'd spent together that would make either of them feel more at ease.

Considering that the fireworks they usually set off weren't of the passionate sort, she was surprised they had turned out to be so compatible in bed. *Compatible?* Heck, he would have knocked her socks off if she'd been wearing any.

She'd never been so completely and thoroughly pleasured before, even after a do-it-yourself orgasm. Ethan had kissed all the right spots. He'd run his tongue over her most sensitive flesh until she thought she'd die from the sensation. And he hadn't even tried to stick his tongue in her ear. It was like she'd managed to summon her own sexual genie.

"I hate this T-shirt," Ethan grumbled again and she smiled at his weak attempt to cover his embarrassment. A sexual genie with issues, of course. "Sometime between milking my bank accounts dry and running off with a cop, my wife stuck a goodbye note to the fridge."

Ouch. No wonder he was cranky. "With your Garfield magnet?"

He nodded. "She was a lot like you."

"Excuse me? I've never left a Dear John letter stuck on anybody's fridge." She hadn't left Poor Eddy so much as a Dear John memo—just left him waiting in his tux. But Ethan didn't need to know that.

"No, but you're beautiful and fickle and unreliable, just like her."

Jill's temper flashed from matchstick to napalm blast in a nanosecond. "Maybe you should have made that comparison *before* you fell into bed with me, don't you think?"

"Why?" He looked at her for a moment, anger shadowing his eyes. "It didn't mean anything, right?"

It was a good thing the jumble of emotions that question evoked bottlenecked in her throat, because Jill had no idea what might have popped out of her mouth at that second.

The son of a bitch had her over a barrel and he probably knew it. She couldn't agree it meant nothing or she'd prove his point for him. Satan would need snowshoes before that happened. And she couldn't disagree without confessing that the night just might have meant more to her than she let on.

"I don't go around falling into bed with every guy I meet," she said after a deep breath. *There, that was noncommittal.*

"Then why do you carry a—" he paused, seemed to shudder, "—protection in your purse?"

Awareness fell on Jill like a ton of bricks. Ethan was provoking her purposely, picking a fight so he wouldn't have to talk about anything personal.

He didn't want to let her in—wanted to keep her at a distance. What better way than making her angry enough to give him the silent treatment. She would try not to take the bait.

"My sister gave them to me as a hint I need to date more. We were at my parents' house at the time, so I shoved them in there and forgot about them. And you have one in your wallet," she pointed out, smiling sweetly at him. He ignored her, but he didn't have to answer. Redness crept up his neck. "And you were married."

"And the...*thing* probably expired sometime during the Reagan administration."

"Oh shit…the expiration date."

Ethan almost pinballed between an eighteen-wheeler and the guardrail. "*What*? How old were those things we used last night?"

"Condoms!" Jill shouted. "Why can't you say it? Condom, condom, condom!"

"Shut up!" He steered the Taurus across the slow lane, over the rumble strip and brought it to a skidding stop in a cloud of roadside dust. "You drive. I need a nap. You can't drive me insane if I'm sleeping."

"Wanna bet?" she mumbled, shifting over to the driver's side while Ethan walked around the car.

She watched him move, his shoulders stiff with aggravation. She got a secret thrill, knowing what he looked like under those clothes—what the hot, smooth flesh of his back felt like.

She knew that lightly running her fingernails over his back, right below where a belt would ride, made his entire body shudder with want. She knew he liked to wrap his fingers in her hair. And she knew he kissed like a god. That damn kiss…

He got in, oblivious to the pheromones she had to be pumping out. After putting his seat back, he closed his eyes. Jill put her seat belt on, letting the engine idle while she watched the clock.

A full minute passed before he growled and looked up at her. "What are you waiting for?"

"You forgot to buckle up."

"Oh for…" He snapped the latch and closed his eyes so tightly she was surprised it didn't hurt.

Jill rejoined the flow of traffic and then set about passing as many vehicles as she could. She had to hit the seek button at least a dozen times before she found a radio station she liked. The wrinkle between Ethan's brows deepened each time the music changed. She found the Top 40, set the volume control at six and sang along as the miles sped by.

She was disappointed when Ethan started snoring. The man could sleep through anything. And she would, too, if she didn't find some coffee soon. The caffeine from her two morning cups was expended long ago. He really should have known that a single woman who bought her coffee in the extra-large cans would require more than two cups, but he'd insisted they get on the road.

While she concentrated on overtaking a minivan with luggage strapped to every conceivable surface, thoughts of the night—and morning—she spent with Ethan crept into her mind.

One thought sprang to the forefront and Jill felt as if her stomach had dropped into the Marianas Trench. She may have injected some much needed passion into her life, but she'd also shot herself in the foot.

There was no way she could ask Ethan to help her get her job back now. Not without looking as if she was trading favors, so to speak, and she had no doubt he would jump straight to that conclusion. Thinking she faked it to get her job back would give him another excuse to treat her like crap.

Truthfully, the library hadn't crossed her mind at all during the night. Now there was no sense in worrying about it. And she wouldn't.

She could find a new job, and she didn't have to sling burgers. She could work at the home improvement warehouse, directing customers down the wrong aisles. Or she could work at the supermarket—maybe as the lettuce sprayer. That would be pretty hard to screw up, even for her.

And Ethan would go back to Connecticut and do whatever boring and uptight thing he did there. Like she needed another person in her life judging her and finding her wanting. But she'd miss the way he looked at her right before he kissed her. She'd miss the way he smiled and tucked her stray strands of hair behind her ears so he could see her face.

She sniffed and punched the radio's seek button again. It had to be the country music. Somewhere around the Mason-

Dixon line it invaded the airwaves, full of broken dreams, purloined pickups and exes in Texas. It was no wonder she was feeling just a slight bit teary-eyed. She'd *really* miss the multiple orgasms.

The hours and miles flew by, and still Ethan slept. He snored, but very softly, and his face was so relaxed—with that little tug of a smile at the corners of his mouth—that she just kept driving. She tried to tell herself that she just didn't want to listen to him bitch at her for a while, but she knew there was a part of her that just liked glancing over and watching him sleep.

Until the time for lunch came and went and he showed no signs of stirring. A girl had to eat. Especially a girl who'd been up half the night tussling with Mr. Stick-In-The-Mud's wild side. And if she didn't get caffeine soon, she was going to have the mother of all meltdowns.

As she passed an RV, she saw an exit coming up fast. *Coffee.* At the last second she rocketed the Taurus across traffic and it leaned hard onto the exit ramp. She'd missed the signs, but every place sold coffee, and most offered warmed-over pizza or microwaveable burritos. She'd top off the gas tank, too.

All she needed was a gas station. The off-ramp ended at an unmarked junction and she shrugged. Every highway exit led somewhere, right?

Eenie meenie minie mo. Jill turned right. She could taste the coffee already.

Chapter Six

Ethan knew something was wrong the second he opened his eyes. Jill's hands strangled the steering wheel and she blasted him with a thousand-watt smile. The flash of white teeth didn't blind him to the panic in her eyes.

What the hell did she do now? The question ran through his mind, but he had a sinking feeling he already knew the answer.

"Where are we?" he asked, returning his seat to the upright position, nearly clotheslining himself with his seat belt in the process.

"I stopped for coffee and gas, but they didn't have any food. I'm getting back on the highway now."

Ethan stared through the windshield at the narrow, winding road and dense trees. Not so much as a dotted yellow line marred the pristine backcountry look. "How long have you been *getting back on the highway?"*

"Um…almost an hour."

"You got us lost." He should have known better than to fall asleep and leave her unattended. The woman needed a *do not operate heavy machinery* sticker slapped on her forehead.

Shaking his head, he reached down and picked up the unopened, lukewarm paper cup he assumed was meant for him. He ripped off the tab and gulped half the tepid liquid before he tasted the sugar. Shuddering, he made a mental note to tell her he liked his coffee light and unsweetened before the next caffeine stop.

He unfolded the small map Jill had bought in the gift shop. With him navigating, they'd be back on the highway in no time. "Which exit did you take?"

"I don't know."

"What did the sign say? It must have had a town name or route number listed." Jill wouldn't look at him, and the unpleasant sensation growing in his stomach wasn't from the sugar. "What did it say, Jill?"

"I didn't actually see the sign," she answered reluctantly, before the explanation spilled out of her in a rush. "I really wanted some coffee and I had to go to the bathroom, but I was passing one of those big RVs and at the last second I saw an exit and took it. I never saw the signs."

Ethan forced himself to remain calm, despite his growing certainty he'd be traveling from New Hampshire to Florida by way of Colorado. "How about the signs before that one?"

"I didn't read them." She must have heard his muttered curse because she threw up both hands. "How hard is it to go from New Hampshire to Florida? You go to the ocean and take a right."

"Both hands on the wheel!" Ethan crumpled the useless map and tossed it into the backseat. "If it was that easy, we wouldn't be lost. And you read the signs so you know where you are if you get off the highway. Why are you so nonchalant about this?"

"Why are you so uptight about it?" she snapped back. "It's just a detour, Ethan. We haven't been zapped into the Twilight Zone."

"Speak for yourself," he muttered.

That had to be it, he thought. There was no other explanation for the chaos that had swamped him since Betty stuck her goodbye note to the fridge. All his careful planning had been flushed so fast he could still hear the giant sucking sound in his head.

But even that paled in comparison to the havoc Jill was wreaking on his life. She damaged his car, stranded them, dressed him in this ridiculous T-shirt and got them lost. And she threw into the mix the most mind-blowing sex of his life.

Ethan glanced over at her, trying not to notice the way her seat belt emphasized her breasts. She chewed at her lower lip. As he watched her teeth scrap over the rosy surface, just as his own had done merely hours before, parts of his anatomy that should have been exhausted throbbed.

He swore under his breath and stared at the passing trees again. Was there any part of the woman that didn't turn him on? He was acting like a fifteen-year-old! No, that wasn't right. Even watching Candy Parker suck her eraser in algebra hadn't made his toes curl the way simply breathing the same air as Jill did.

But she didn't figure into his plans for the future. Ethan had to see his mother settled into her new life, and then he had to find one for himself. Becoming infatuated with a gorgeous woman who wasn't ready to settle down would only add up to a giant headache.

Amazing sex did not a lasting relationship make. No doubt while he was busy trying to get all his ducks in a row, Jill would be tossing them up in the air yelling, "Fly! Be free".

This is just a fling, he reminded himself. A sizzling fling he didn't want to end, but a fling, nonetheless. No doubt, Hurricane Jill would blow out of his life just as suddenly as she'd blown into it.

"Did you piss off a Gypsy as a child or what?" he asked, desperate to break the silence before his thoughts could get him into any more trouble.

Her giggle was high-pitched and nervous, as if she couldn't decide whether or not he was teasing. "I am *not* cursed. I've screwed up a few things in my life, but believe it or not, my life wasn't this bad until you came along. Maybe you're the cursed one."

He guessed being divorced, bankrupt and AWOL from the senior center's Spring Fling tour might count as cursed, but flaming matchsticks between his toes wouldn't make him admit it. "What kind of screwups?"

She shrugged. "My attempts at baby-sitting my sister's kids

usually end at the emergency room and, until I got the job at the library, I didn't have a great employment record. And I left my fiancé at the altar."

She mumbled the last sentence, almost as an afterthought, but he didn't miss a word. "Why doesn't that surprise me?"

Jill took her eyes off the road to give him a sharp look. "Avoiding the biggest mistake of my life—and his—does not make me irresponsible. I know that's what you're thinking."

"Keep your eyes on the road." Ethan choked down more of the too-sweet coffee. "Refusing when he first proposed would have been the responsible thing to do."

"I thought I wanted to marry him."

Why the thought of Jill marrying some faceless other man made him want to crumple his paper cup was a mystery. After all, if Jill was busy playing happy homemaker, he'd be well on his way to five days and four nights of fun in the Sunshine State.

"What made you change your mind?" he asked, but what he really wanted to know was what the other guy had been missing.

* * * * *

Jill ignored the question. They were approaching an intersection and she strained to read a clump of signs nailed to a telephone pole. Ed's Bait & Ammo was off to the right. To the left they could find used truck parts, free kittens and Loretta's Luscious Locks.

"Go straight for now," Ethan told her. "But if I see a sign that reads *Mayberry – 12 miles*, I'm driving."

She didn't bother to argue. Since neither of them had any clue where they were, his guess was as good as hers. And this way, if they ended up in the Texas panhandle, it would be his fault.

She also got an extra few seconds to think about his question. Ethan had a poor enough opinion of her without hearing a detailed account of everything she'd ever done wrong.

And her reasons for leaving Poor Eddy at the altar were none of his damn business. Even if they had been headed for a serious relationship—and he'd made it clear they weren't—he didn't have the right to pry into her romantic past. Such as it was.

Cursed by a Gypsy, Jill fumed. She wished she knew how to give him the evil eye. That would teach him a thing or two about curses.

"So why did you dump your fiancé at the altar?" Ethan asked again.

"Because I'm foolish and irresponsible," she snapped.

"I'm sorry, sunshine," he said, resting his hand on her thigh.

The tingle that shot through her lower body surprised Jill. Not only because her body wasn't sharing her mind's currently very low opinion of the man, but also because she thought the tingle-prone parts of her body would be a bit numb after their workout.

"I know I've been in a rotten mood," he continued, "but being stranded, separated from my money and now lost does that to me. Not to mention my mother's off keeping company with some guy named Kenny."

"Kenny?"

"I don't know—some guy on the bus. So, if we're going to be stuck in this car driving around the backwoods of North Carolina—at least I *think* we're in North Carolina since it's almost dinnertime—we should get to know each other."

She knew he had a birthmark shaped like a toadstool on his ass. What else did a girl need to know?

"Okay," she said. "I like action movies and walks not in the rain. My favorite color is '79 Corvette red and my favorite food is macaroni and cheese."

"I meant…" He turned and frowned at her. "Your favorite

food is macaroni and cheese?"

Jill reached down and removed his hand from her thigh. "I suppose that's irresponsible, too?"

"No, I liked macaroni and cheese…when I was twelve."

"It's a very versatile dish. You can add hamburger to it, or chopped ham. You can even add broccoli and sautéed chicken and you have a casserole." She couldn't tell if that was a gagging sound he made, or if he was simply clearing his throat. "What's your favorite food?"

"Broiled swordfish."

"Figures."

"What figures?"

Jill gave him an angelic smile. "Not only are you a stick in the mud, but you're a food snob, too."

"Keep your eyes on the damn road." He shifted his body so he half-faced her. "Now that you've insulted me—several times—tell me about this near miss at the altar."

She may as well come clean about it. His opinion of her couldn't sink much lower without a wake of dead bodies popping up.

"I thought I wanted to marry Eddy. I really did. And then…" she paused. It was so hard to put into words.

"And then what?"

"I was standing in front of the mirror in my wedding dress, and I was so happy and so excited."

"That's usually a good thing, sunshine."

"Liz—my sister—looked happy and excited, too, when she got married. For a little while, and now her life's in a total rut. I don't want that."

He was quiet for a minute and she wondered if he was thinking about his ex-wife. Did she leave because she was stuck in a rut?

"What makes you think her life's in a *rut*?" he finally asked.

"Maybe she's just in a content place."

Jill rolled her eyes. He would side with her sister. "I wish you could see the pictures Liz used to take. She wanted to be a photographer for *National Geographic* magazine—and she could have. She was that good. Now she takes pictures of screaming kids at the department store."

"Is she happy?"

She risked another rebuke by taking her eyes off the road to frown at him. "How can she be happy? She gave up all her dreams. Now she knows every day she has to do the same thing over and over and the biggest mystery in her life is whether it's her son or her husband that keeps peeing on the back of the toilet. She sacrificed everything."

Ethan drained his coffee cup and she saw him shudder. It must have cooled more than she expected while he was sleeping. "Maybe it was worth it to her, sunshine. She's got a family she loves and a good job. Maybe it satisfies her to take a bunch of fussy kids and capture one smiling moment their parents can treasure forever."

"Now you sound like my mother. Are you going to lecture me about my sex life, too?"

"Well...actually, I'm kind of happy with your sex life...for now."

Jill stifled a giggle when his cheeks flamed her favorite color. The man was so uptight he embarrassed *himself.* "For now?"

"Yeah. For now."

A little ache settled in Jill's chest, but she told herself it was coffee-induced heartburn. She wasn't looking for *serious,* she reminded herself, so *for now* worked.

She didn't want a white picket fence or two and a half kids. Baking was for Sara Lee, and microwave directions were her best friends. Her dust bunnies multiplied so fast they must have leporine Viagra stashed under the couch.

Ethan was the kind of guy who expected his wife to qualify

for a spot on the Better Homes and Gardens Channel. He was Ward Cleaver in jeans and sneakers. Heck, he probably got his taxes done *before* April fifteenth every year. She didn't need that kind of pressure.

Ethan cleared his throat. "So having a family would keep you from living out your dreams?"

"Absolutely! It's hard to live your life to the fullest when you have a houseful of people demanding food and clean laundry and…more food. And how are you supposed to tour the Amazon with a baby? They have piranhas and snakes and stuff."

Jill felt his gaze on her profile, but she resisted the urge to turn and look at him. She didn't have to justify her life to him. He wouldn't understand anyway. She'd bet ten dollars Mr. Domestic even owned an apron with *Kiss the Cook* printed on it. His idea of adventure probably extended to putting extra lighter fluid on the barbecue.

"Yeah," he said in a sarcastic voice that grated on her nerves. "I can see how having children would really clash with being a children's librarian."

Jill clenched her teeth. She was this close to opening the door and pushing him out.

She could find her way to the hotel alone. Maybe. And even if she couldn't, she'd rather drive around in circles than listen to Ethan criticize her life for one more second.

Of course having children didn't interfere with working at the library. They didn't interfere with work—only the fun stuff. When she had enough money saved, she was going to travel. She would see the world, taste adventure—without a baby carrier slung around her neck like a noose. Then she would think about a family.

Reminded of her pitiful finances, Jill grimaced. The numbers on her credit card statements were larger than the numbers on her bank statements and now she was unemployed to boot. At this rate Jules Verne would have to tinker with her biological clock by the time she was ready to have kids.

"I wasn't going to work at the library forever," she said. "Just until..."

"Until some wealthy patron was so grateful the new Stephen King book was in he swept you off to a life of grand adventure?"

"That's it." Jill yanked the wheel and pulled the Taurus into the long grass that passed for a shoulder. "I am so tired of your attitude."

The car shuddered to a stop and she threw it into park. She hit the button to release Ethan's seat belt, and then before he could react she reached across him and opened his door. "Get out."

* * * * *

"Are you insane?" Ethan waved his hand at the windshield. "I'm not letting you abandon me in the middle of nowhere."

"I signed for this car. I paid for this car. And I want you *out* of this car."

"I was only teasing you, sunshine."

"Well, I'm not teasing you, little black raincloud. Out."

She couldn't be serious. After all she'd done to him? No way was he letting her ditch him on the side of the road.

"All you've done is insult me since we left the motel—since we met," she continued. "I am *not* a bad person and I'm sick of you trying to make me feel like one."

Guilt wormed its way into his thoughts. He'd been a jerk all morning, and taking out his frustrations on Jill wasn't really fair. Even if his most recent problems *were* her fault, she was stranded, too.

"I'm sorry—"

"You said that about ten minutes ago, then you started right in again."

True. But he meant it this time. "You'd really leave me here in the middle of nowhere with no car, no money, no identification?"

"Flighty, stupid people do that kind of thing all the time." He could tell she tried hard to hide behind a jaunty tone, but he could hear the hurt behind the words and it made him feel about two feet tall.

"I never said you were stupid."

"You implied it."

Ethan groaned and leaned his head back against the seat. He'd been married long enough to know he couldn't argue with what he hadn't said.

"How about we make a deal?" he said, ready to brace himself if she tried to shove him out the door and drive away. "If you don't dump me here—lost and penniless—I promise I'll be nice. And I'll ask my mother to give you your job back."

That got her attention. Jill stared at him, gnawing at her lip, until he was convinced she wanted him gone more than she wanted to pay her rent.

Ethan cursed the new sneakers he wore. If he had to walk, the blisters would be hell. "Well?" he prompted.

"I don't want my job back." But she did. He could see it in her eyes.

"You told me on the bus that you did—that you *need* it. Why did you change your mind?"

"Because…because we had great sex."

He frowned, letting her words tumble around his brain, hoping they'd line up in some way that made sense. "So, you *would* want your job back if the sex was *lousy*?"

Jill's cheeks burned and for one second Ethan was sure she was going to push him backward out of the Taurus. "Of course not."

"Then what exactly does incredible, mind-blowing, super-hot sex have to do with your job?"

Jill blushed, but she didn't look away. "It might seem like I was trying to get my job back by having…delicious…breathtaking sex with you."

He watched her mouth—watched her lips draw each syllable—and for one insane second wished they were still stuck in that motel room. His plans be damned. That mouth had brought him to knees. Literally. And the memory was a little hazy, but he thought he might have actually begged at some point.

Then her words sunk in. The questions slammed into Ethan like a baseball bat. Did she offer her body in exchange for her job? Had she seduced him just to get him on her side?

Of course she had, his bruised and battered ego agreed at once. He wasn't the kind of guy who inspired mad lust in women. He was boring—a stick in the mud, as Jill herself had said. Several times. If he weren't, his wife probably wouldn't have run off with a testosterone-overloaded adrenaline junkie.

But he thought of the way she had come to him in the motel room. He remembered the feel of her lips under his—the catch in her breath when his tongue slid across hers. The woman simply wasn't that good an actress.

While fully clothed, they were as compatible as ammonia and chlorine, but between the sheets they had the real deal.

"I never thought you did," he said.

Jill narrowed her eyes at him and he knew he was in trouble. "You were thinking it just now."

Guilt warmed his cheeks. He couldn't deny it. She wouldn't believe him anyway, especially with the damn guilty flush. "Only because you brought it up. It never crossed my mind until you said it."

"You're only saying that so you won't have to walk to Orlando."

Ethan almost laughed at her flippant reply, then he saw something flicker across her face. He couldn't decipher it. Hopefulness? Desperation?

Her comments about the screwups in her life echoed through his mind. Maybe Jill Delaney expected people to believe the worst about her.

"Sunshine, if my life were a bathtub you'd be the plugged-in hairdryer. You've done nothing but complicate my life since the moment we met. But I don't believe you'd do something like that."

He thought he saw a tear glisten in one eye before she turned her gaze back to the road. "Close the door and let's go."

His relief at not being tossed out of the car like an empty fast food wrapper was eclipsed by this new glimpse into Jill's personality. *Self-fulfilling prophecy*—a phrase he'd heard tossed around on those trashy talk shows Betty liked to watch. Probably the same shows that convinced her to run off and find herself—and a new husband.

Jill expected to mess things up. Her family probably expected her to mess things up. So, things got messed up. She'd come to expect it, and a cycle of trying and falling flat on her face was born.

Well, he'd promised to be nice to her. Maybe if he complimented her a lot—built up her confidence—he could help her break the cycle. At this point, anything that got them to the hotel and then on to Florida in one piece was worth a shot.

He glanced over at her, racking his brain for just the right compliment. Something that boosted her self-esteem—made her feel strong.

"You…umm…have beautiful breasts." *What?*

"What?" Jill turned to gape at him and he felt his face go red.

Ethan prayed she would hit a bump, causing his door to fly open so he'd go tumbling out. That had to be the most asinine thing he'd ever said to a woman.

"I…uh. Well, you do, dammit."

Chapter Seven

ꟷ

"Thank you," Jill muttered, trying to ignore the heat that pulsed into her face. Where on Earth had *that* come from? "And you have beautiful—"

"Don't! Just forget I said anything."

Laughter bubbled up in Jill's throat. "It's okay, Ethan. I wasn't going to say condom."

"Oh, God." He covered his face with his hands. "Don't say…whatever it was you were going to say."

Jill giggled and shrugged. "Okay. But they're so big. And round. And—"

"Jill!"

"Brown"

"Brown?"

"You have beautiful eyes, Ethan," she said, her shoulders shaking with silent laughter. The man was just too easy to wind up. *Wind him up—he walks, he talks, he has nervous breakdowns.*

"A restaurant!" Ethan shouted, and she heard the relief in his voice even as she hit the brakes and turned the wheel.

The restaurant was small, with a paint job older than any of their fellow Spring Flingers, but the parking lot was full. Hopefully that meant the food was good, because she was starving. She squeezed the Taurus into a spot and killed the engine with a sigh of relief.

A sign on the door told her the Nickel Hill Cafe took all major credit cards. At least she could pay for the meal. Rip was cruising around in his MG with all of her cash. She made a mental note to find an ATM and get a cash advance, since Ethan had so conveniently left his wallet on the bus.

It would serve him right if she bought herself a steak for lunch and made him wash dishes for a grilled cheese sandwich.

They could grab a quick bite to eat and ask directions back to the highway, which Ethan would write down. Then *he* could drive. Their fate would be out of her hands and anything that went wrong would be his fault.

Jill was surprised to find a table open, but most of the patrons were seated at a long counter nursing coffees. They hit the restrooms, ordered from a menu full of things that would go straight to her hips and fixed their coffee. Jill noted the lack of sugar in Ethan's and smiled. That explained the grimacing in the car.

He cleared his throat and she looked up. "I really like your hair like that," he said in a gruff voice.

She reached up and smoothed the messy ponytail. "Thank you."

The man was up to something—she just couldn't figure out what. She watched him squirm for a long moment. "You know, when I said you had to be nice to me or walk to Florida, I meant don't actively insult me. I didn't mean you had to fawn over my hair and my breasts."

From behind her came a male cough of choked laughter, followed by a female squeal of disgust and the rattle of dishes. Jill winced. *Oops.*

"Jill!" Ethan hissed. "Keep your voice down."

The waitress appeared with their fried lumps smothered in gravy, so she decided to let Ethan off the hook…for now. She'd figure out what he was trying to accomplish with his misguided flattery later. For now they concentrated on their plates, since they hadn't eaten since breakfast. Except for the candy bar she'd bought at the gas station for lunch. And since he'd been playing Sleeping Beauty and she was still hungry, she'd eaten his, too. The wrappers were hidden in her purse.

"Tell me about yourself," she said when the worst of the hunger had been satisfied.

He looked up from slathering real butter on a homemade roll. "What do you want to know?"

"Well, we'll start with the easy stuff and then I'll pry my way into your closet like you did mine. What do you do for a living?" She paused with her fork half-raised. "No...let me guess."

"I don't do anything right now," he reminded her. The tone of his voice warned her she was treading on very thin ice. "My ex-wife and her new husband apparently needed some start-up money and the household account wasn't enough."

Ouch. Way to pick an icebreaker. She felt as if she'd just thumped him over the head with a conversational sledgehammer.

"Okay, I'll guess what you did before she left. Accountant?"

He snorted. "Don't you think if I was an accountant I would have protected my money a little better?"

"A lawyer?"

"If I was I'd have gotten it back," he snapped.

Jill frowned. "An embalmer?"

"Of dead people?"

"If you embalm live people I'm leaving you here."

"Very funny. What makes you think I'm an embalmer?"

"Your people skills, maybe?"

He made a sour face, but Jill didn't care. His recent marital and financial disasters might make for a touchy subject, but she didn't think knowing his occupation was too much to ask.

"I refinished furniture," he grumbled at his plate.

That shut her up for a minute. *Refinishing furniture?* She was so sure he did something more academic, more...cerebral.

But then again, he was damn good with his hands. "What kind of furniture refinishing? Antique restoration?"

"Nope. Yard sale restoration."

Jill swallowed the last bite of the most delicious, calorie-laden meal she'd ever eaten and laughed. "You? Yard sales? I doubt it."

"So now I'm a second-hand snob, too?"

"You said it."

Ethan pushed away his plate and leaned back against the booth. "I used to work twelve hours a day helping people maximize their retirement dollars."

"Ha! I knew it."

"Then one day," he pointedly ignored her, "I saw an old bureau on somebody's front lawn. It was painted green and covered in stickers, but I could just see the ornate woodwork from the road. I paid ten bucks for it."

He paused while the waitress refilled their coffee cups, but Jill barely noticed. She was too busy noticing the way his face lit up just thinking about that ratty dresser. The planes of his face softened and his mouth relaxed into a half-smile.

It was a look she usually only saw when he was sleeping, and she let the warmth in his eyes wash over her. It didn't matter that the look was meant for furniture. She'd take what she could get. And that pissed her off to no end. He didn't need to be warm and smiling for vacation sex. He just needed to be hard and horny as hell.

But she couldn't quite stamp out the little part that yearned for it to be her that put that warmth in his gaze and the smile on his lips.

"It took me six months' worth of weekends to strip that bureau—four layers of paint. But the cherry underneath was warm and beautiful. I sold that piece for almost two hundred."

"Wow!"

Ethan chuckled. "Considering the hours I put into it—and the paint thinner—it wasn't as great a profit margin as it sounds."

"So you gave up number-crunching to form the Junk Furniture Rescue League?"

She surprised an honest laugh out of him. It was deep and infectious, pulling at her until she joined in. It felt so good to sit and laugh over coffee—almost as if they were a real couple.

Whoa! *There's no couple stuff going on here.* Miss Unemployed Spur-of-the-Moment and Mister Tall, Dark and Serious were simply killing some time together. Nothing more to it.

"It was almost three years before I had enough pieces done to throw away my ties and open the shop," Ethan was saying, and Jill forced her attention back to him. "Then I started building a reputation for restoring heirloom furniture that had been neglected for too long or painted over—and saving yard sale pieces."

The light in his eyes was dimming and Jill didn't fight the impulse to rest her hand atop his. "Can't you start a new shop?"

He jerked his hand away as if Jill herself had destroyed his business. "No. Betty took everything—the accounts, the deposits from customers, the money that was supposed to be paying suppliers. Reputation and word of mouth is the name of the game. I'm done. And we're done here. Let's hit the road."

Jill paid the bill while Ethan wrote down the directions from a local seated at the counter. She watched him, tall and handsome in his Garfield T-shirt, and wished the happy, fun Ethan could have stayed a while longer.

Then again, maybe the mercurial shift back to cranky, serious Ethan was for the best. It would be a lot easier to walk away from him in Orlando.

Her stomach ached suddenly and she cursed the overdose of fried dinner. Something just wasn't sitting right, that's all. It had nothing do with the thought of parting ways with Ethan Cooper.

She'd walk away from him just as she'd walked away from Poor Eddy. Relationships became marriages, which inevitably led to children. Even though casual sex was not her usual style, commitment was even less so. She'd shake his hand, say goodbye and lay off the fried foods.

They both hit the restrooms again, and then Jill met him back at the Taurus. His arms were folded across his chest and he looked a little smug for her taste. She'd screwed up again, and she hadn't been present for it. Even for her, that was rare. "What kind of person leaves the keys in the car?"

"I didn't," Jill replied, shaking her head in confusion. She wasn't a big-city girl, but even she knew better than that.

Ethan dangled the rental key chain in front of her. "Really?"

"I swear I thought I took them out." She patted her pockets and came up empty. Then she unzipped her purse and started to rummage through the debris.

"Why are you looking for them? They're in my hand."

She shrugged and yanked the zipper closed again. "I guess I just have an overwhelming desire for you to make a mistake every once in a while."

"That's your department, sunshine. Just thank your lucky stars nobody stole it."

"Fine. I'm sorry. So, punish me by not speaking to me for a few hundred miles. Please."

She yanked open the passenger side door and got in the car, ignoring Ethan settling into the driver's seat. She snapped her seat belt closed, then leaned her head back and closed her eyes. It was all on Ethan's shoulders now. He had the directions and he was steering the car. Since the man practically reeked of responsibility and common sense, they were home free. Nothing would go wrong now.

* * * * *

Ethan drove the winding route back to the highway with clenched teeth. Jill's sullen silence was wrapped around her like an iceberg, and the chilly atmosphere gave him throbbing temples to go along with his aching jaw.

He cursed himself for giving her a hard time about leaving

the keys in the car. His plan to be nice—to reinforce the things she did right—had lasted a whopping thirty minutes or so. Little wonder he'd never been offered his own talk show.

The worst part in Ethan's mind was the fact he hadn't even been angry. Humiliation was the emotion that struck hardest whenever he thought about Betty and the end of their marriage. It still embarrassed him and he'd shoved Jill away to keep her from seeing it. And she was mad again.

At least he was behind the wheel now. He didn't have to worry about being abandoned because he wasn't about to leave himself by the side of the road. But the silence was almost enough to wish he could.

Ethan nudged Jill with his elbow. "Once I see my mom and get my wallet, how about I take you out for a nice macaroni and cheese dinner?"

The arctic blast from her shoulder warmed a degree or two. "You mean…like a date?"

A date? Ethan prayed the gulping sound he made wasn't as loud as it sounded to his own ears. "I…I guess so."

He hadn't been thinking that far ahead when he made the offer. His subconscious must really want to see the woman again, even if his logical mind didn't think it was a good idea. But an invitation was an invitation, even if it was for toddler finger food.

"Isn't that what it's called when a man invites a woman to dinner?" Jill demanded.

Her testy tone rubbed Ethan the wrong way. Couldn't the woman even accept a meal without making a scene? "Maybe I just want to say thank you for footing the bill on this little misadventure."

"With macaroni and cheese? I paid for the motel room, this car, our gas, our meals, T-shirts…"

"A *Garfield* T-shirt! You should get just plain macaroni with butter for that. And I wouldn't have needed that motel room, this car, gas, meals or this damned shirt if *you* hadn't locked yourself in the bathroom, would I? And you said macaroni and cheese is your favorite food."

Jill threw up her hands. "Fine. Your thanks are accepted. No need to waste the eighty-nine cents."

Ethan took a deep breath, consciously easing up on the accelerator. If he didn't calm down, they'd be doing a hundred and thirty miles per hour before they even hit the highway—or a tree.

"I'm going to pay you back every red cent when I get my wallet," he muttered, half under his breath. "But I still wanted to say thank you."

What had possessed him to ask her out for dinner anyway? The smart thing to do was get to the hotel, find his wallet and repay her for his expenses. Then he could walk away and not look back.

He had no business dating anybody while his life was in shambles anyway. He wouldn't have time for a relationship in the coming months. And he had nothing to offer a woman but a storage locker full of cast-off furniture.

Any woman, but especially Jill. Her life was as messy as his own. She needed a man with a boat stable enough to withstand her constant rocking. And the only thing they had in common was unemployment.

But a part of him wanted to argue the point—to convince her to share one more meal together. He wanted to recapture the easy camaraderie they'd briefly shared. Before she had to go and get too personal, ruining everything.

But how personal was *too* personal once you've had sex? He didn't like thinking about Betty and her testosterone-laden new husband, but he had spent the night with Jill, for goodness sake. She had the right to ask a few questions without having her head bitten off.

"Look," he said in a shaky voice. "I like you, sunshine. A lot. And I'd just like to have dinner with you when we get to Florida. A nice, quiet meal—when we're not lost and stressed—

so we can get to know each other a little better."

She didn't answer, so he risked glancing over as he sped up the highway entrance ramp. "I'll even get you a steak to go with that macaroni and cheese."

"Skunk!"

"That's a little harsh—"

"No," Jill pointed out the windshield, "a skunk!"

Ethan hit the brake and yanked the wheel hard to the left. He heard Jill's head hit her window as he steered hard around the oblivious little stinker.

"Are you okay?" he asked when he'd taken a breath and merged the Taurus into traffic.

"Yeah," she said, rubbing her head and laughing. "I'm glad you missed him. The last thing we need is eau de Pepé."

"What in tarnation's going on up there?" a hoarse voice demanded from behind them.

Ethan saw the head pop up in the rearview mirror and his heart flip-flopped. Jill screamed and he hit the rumble strip at seventy miles an hour, the roar of the tires drowning out the man in the backseat.

The Taurus shuddered along the breakdown lane and Ethan winced as the rear bumper almost scraped the guardrail. He eased off the brake and let the car roll to a stop.

"Well, drop me in a field and call me Patty! I've been kidnapped!"

Ethan stared at the old man in the mirror, then at Jill. His heart felt like a hyped-up hummingbird in his chest and he clutched the steering wheel to keep his hands from shaking. *I'll never leave North Carolina alive.* He slouched way down in his seat, giving up.

"Where's your empty coffee cup?" Jill asked in an unsteady voice.

"If you need to throw up, just open the door."

"No, Einstein. You left your trash in the center console. This isn't our car."

The old man chuckled and stuck his head forward through the bucket seats. "No, sir, it sure ain't. My daughter rented this one while hers is getting fixed. Swerved to avoid a skunk and ran right into Velma Johnson's fruit stand."

Jill slapped Ethan on the arm. "I told you I didn't leave the keys in the car. This one's not my fault, pal."

He dropped his head and banged it on the steering wheel, the horn punctuating each whack. "Why is this happening to me? And aren't skunks nocturnal?"

If he believed in reincarnation, he'd bet the farm he was Jack the Ripper in his past life. Even being cursed by a Gypsy couldn't bring luck this bad.

"It's spring, so they're feeling rambunctious. Nice driving there, son," the man said, nodding enthusiastically between the seats. "What did you do with my daughter? Did you put her in the trunk?"

Jill laughed. She actually *laughed*. The woman was insane. "Nobody is in the trunk," he hissed through clenched teeth.

"As far as we know," she pointed out. "With our luck the guy who rented this car before his daughter was in the mafia and it's full of dead bodies."

Ethan shook his head. "And you had the nerve to call my *mother* a bitch?"

"Ah…newlyweds, huh? Ain't in-laws a pain in the patootie?"

Ethan and Jill both stared at the man, then shook their heads at the same time. "We're not newlyweds," they said in unison.

"Been married a while then, have you? I'm Joe, by the way. Joe Jackson. No relation."

"We're not married, either," Ethan said bluntly. Maybe the waitress spiked his gravy and this was all a dream. A bad one. "No relation to whom?"

"That shoeless baseball player. The one that comes out of the cornfield in that movie. Where are we headed?"

"Orlando," Jill replied.

"Great. Some sunshine sure does sound good to this old bag of bones."

Ethan was already shaking his head. The last thing this trip needed was an old guy with diarrhea of the mouth. There was busload of them waiting for him at the hotel. Assuming he ever made it there.

"I'm taking you home," he said, putting the car back into gear.

"I don't want to go back. Hey, I bet I got that Swedish syndrome! You know, where the kidnapped person wants to hang around with the kidnappers."

Jill was giggling again and Ethan shot her a quelling look. "We did not kidnap you."

Joe clucked his tongue. "That's funny, son. Down here when you take a body off to Florida without askin' his permission, we call that kidnapping."

"We didn't know you were in the car."

"Ignorance is nine-tenths of the law."

"No," Ethan put the car in gear. "*Possession* is nine-tenths of the law."

Joe slapped the back of Ethan's seat. "And you're in *possession* of my kidnapped behind."

Ethan picked up speed and merged again into traffic, hoping he'd get to stay there for at least five minutes this time. "Sunshine, keep your eyes peeled for one of those places the cops use to reverse direction."

"You get caught turning around in those you'll get in a mite bit of trouble, son."

"Yeah, well us kidnappers don't worry too much about piddly things like traffic tickets."

"No, but the stolen car might be a problem," Jill pointed

out, with a bit too much humor in her voice for Ethan's liking.

"How far up is the next exit?"

"Oh, about twenty miles," Joe said. "So, when's the weddin'?"

Chapter Eight

ഗ

Jill didn't try to hold back her laughter when Ethan growled low in his throat. She couldn't even if she wanted to.

This was, without a doubt, one-hundred percent his own fault. When she came out of the restaurant, he was standing next to a white Ford Taurus dangling the key at her. All she did was get in the car.

And that's why he's so mad. He couldn't blame their latest mishap on her. Sure, *none* of this would be happening if she had remembered that second lock on the bathroom door, but they would have been Orlando-bound if he'd picked the right car.

"There is no wedding," Ethan said in a no-nonsense voice. "We're not married. We're not engaged. We're not even a couple."

That hurt. He didn't have to sound so *absolute* about it. Of course they weren't a couple. Not counting their disastrous meeting in the grocery store parking lot, they'd known each other just a little over twenty-four hours.

She frowned. But they'd had sex and in her book that must make them *something*. And how could the sex between them have been so incredible if it was meaningless? Maybe she wasn't cut out for vacation sex after all. "We're just friends. Friends who have sex."

Ethan made a choking sound and gave her a look that could have torched an asbestos fire suit.

Joe's boom of laughter faded into a chuckle. "Those are the best kind of friends, you ask me. Tried to have that kind of friendship myself—with Sally Bowman, but she took up with some old geezer that got himself some Viagra. You tried that stuff, son?"

Jill hoped Ethan wasn't swallowing his tongue. He was still making that choking sound and his face was becoming a rather dark shade of red. She patted his knee. "Ethan doesn't need Viagra, Mr. Jackson. He did okay on his own."

Ethan glared at her. "Okay?"

She laughed at the affront in his voice. "Magnificent?"

"Better," he mumbled.

"Why were you hiding in the backseat, Mr. Jackson?" Jill asked Joe, letting Ethan off the hook.

"Wasn't hiding, missy. Was having myself a nap. That daughter of mine likes to run the roads before she's gotta pick the grandkids up from school. She dragged me right along with her. Decided to grab some shuteye and next thing I know I'm dreaming about wreckin' at the Daytona 500."

"Are you married?" she asked. If she could keep the conversation close to something resembling normal, maybe Ethan wouldn't succumb to a stroke before they got back to the restaurant.

"Was married sixty years," Joe replied with a touch of sadness in his gravelly voice.

"I'm sorry. When did she pass away?"

"Pass away?" Joe snorted. "The old bag ain't dead. She ran off and left me."

"Oh." Jill didn't know what to say. How did she end up stuck in a car with two men whose wives had run off and abandoned them?

"I should have gotten me some of those snore strips," Joe said.

Jill shook her head, sure she had misunderstood him. "Snore strips?"

"Sure as shootin', missy. The old bag complained for sixty years about my snoring, then she up and left me."

"My wife left too, Mr. Jackson," Ethan said quietly. "I'm quite sure the lack of snore strips had nothing to do with it."

"Y'all call me Joe. What did you do to make your wife run off?"

"She left me for an undercover cop."

Sure, he doesn't bite Joe's head off when he asks questions. She heard bitterness in his voice, but he didn't sound angry. Maybe it was a guy thing.

Joe shook his head, which was still poking out through the bucket seats. "At least yours left you for some excitement. My wife ran off with the guy who delivers the weekly papers. Guess he was delivering something else, too."

Jill felt bad for Joe, but she couldn't help wondering about Mrs. Jackson's side of the story. Had she escaped a lifetime of unhappiness, or did the woman just want some hot sex in her golden years? Marriage seemed to her like a prison sentence. On the other side of the bars, the single people enjoyed life while wives were left with the monotonous domestic equivalent of making license plates day after day.

But she always thought there was some kind of cut-off in a marriage. If you made it a certain number of years, it was a done deal. Apparently not, if sixty years didn't qualify. How can something as final and *binding* as marriage be so precarious? she pondered.

She glanced sideways at Ethan, wondering what it would be like to wake up next to him every morning for sixty years. A pleasant feeling washed over her, followed almost immediately by panic.

Oh my goodness, was that warm and fuzzy? It couldn't be. She felt like strangling Ethan Cooper sometimes. She felt lust for Ethan Cooper a lot. Sometimes she even liked him. But she could not, under any circumstances, allow herself to feel warm and fuzzy about Ethan Cooper.

"Yup, I learned some good lessons from that go 'round," Joe was saying. "When I get hitched again, I'm gonna get some of those snore strips. And I'll take out the garbage, too. Women don't like doing that."

Jill snorted. "Women don't like unrolling smelly socks, either. Or falling in when the toilet seat's left up, or pulling the remote control out from under the couch cushion for the thousandth time."

Joe looked at Jill, then at Ethan and shook his head. "Run, son. Run as far and as fast as you can."

"I'm trying, believe me," Ethan muttered.

"Excuse me?" Jill said, indignation burning her cheeks. "Do I need to remind you that you promised to be nice to me? Or have you decided you're in the mood for some exercise?"

Ethan laughed and slapped her knee. "Sorry, sunshine, but this isn't your car. You didn't pay for it. You didn't sign for it. Since I stole it, it's *my* car."

Jill opened her mouth to tell him exactly what he could do with *his* car, but her words were drowned out by shrill sirens. She looked in the sideview mirror and her heart nearly stopped when a car raced up behind them, lights flashing.

"It's the law! Make a run for it!" Joe yelled. "Put the pedal to the metal, boy!"

* * * * *

Ethan flipped on the turn signal and eased his foot off the gas. Putting the pedal to the metal was not an option. With his bad luck charm buckled in beside him, no doubt he'd cause a fifty-car pileup if he tried to outrun the police.

"Step on it, boy!" Joe shouted. "That's Sheriff Dodd and Deputy Parker back there. Dumber'n a box of rocks, both of them. Put your blinker on left, then turn right. That'll lose 'em!"

"I can't turn," Ethan growled. "I'm on the highway."

He coasted the Taurus onto the shoulder and came to a nice, easy rolling stop. Leaning forward, he reached for his back pocket.

His empty back pocket. Anxiety cranked up the heat in his stomach when he remembered his wallet was tucked safely in his mother's purse. He closed his eyes. Took a deep breath. He was in a stolen rental car with a lunatic and the old man they had kidnapped. And he had no identification. There was no way in hell he would even think *can this day get any worse?*

"This ain't the time for meditatin' son. We can still get away. Wait for them to get out, then step on it."

Ethan glared at Jill, who was barely managing to contain her laughter. "Do something about Patty Hearst back there."

"Like what? I forgot my ACME Kidnapping Kit this morning. No duct tape."

"Smart-ass." He watched the sideview mirror as the patrol car came to a stop behind them. There were two men in the car, but only the driver got out.

He was the tallest man Ethan had ever seen, weighed less than Jill soaking wet and had an Adam's apple the size of a baseball. He also had a pretty big shotgun cradled in his arms.

"Make sure you speak up, son," Joe said. "Junior Parker's deaf as a crow-eaten cornstalk."

Jill giggled and Ethan glared at her. She put up her hands in a defensive gesture. "No ears, get it?"

He hit the button to lower the window. "I don't know how you can see any humor in this."

She put her hand on his knee, which did little to calm his nerves. "Relax, Ethan. This is all a misunderstanding. They're not going to put us on the chain gang for—"

The unmistakable sound of a round being jacked into a pump-action shotgun interrupted her sentence, along with his heartbeat.

Joe whistled between his dentures. "Holy sh—"

"Attention, kidnappers!" Deputy Parker shouted. "Put your hands out the window where I can see them."

Ethan leaned close to the door and rested his wrists on the door, his hands in plain sight of the deputy. At least if he threw up, he could stick his head out.

He heard the whir of power windows, and then Joe's hands appeared alongside his. He assumed Jill had done the same.

"Not you, Joe Jackson," Deputy Parker yelled. "You go on and get out of the car."

"You'll never take me alive!" Joe shouted, and Ethan thumped his head down on the door between his arms. "I'm going to Orlando with these folks."

"You ain't going anywhere but back to your family," Deputy Parker argued. "Bobbi Jo's damned near turned the whole town upside down. You know how she is when she's upset."

"Why do you think I'm going to Orlando?"

Moving in slow motion to avoid startling the deputy, Ethan lifted his head to look at Joe. The rear windows didn't lower all the way for safety, so the old man's fingers curled over the glass. He grinned at Ethan, who shook his head.

"I'm glad you're having a good time, but that man has a loaded shotgun pointed at my head. Will you please explain to him that this is just a misunderstanding?"

Before Joe could respond, Deputy Parker took a step closer to the Taurus, mindful he didn't get taken out by any of the cars passing them. "You there—driver."

"Yes, sir?" Ethan replied in his most respectful tone.

"Get out of the car, slowly and come back around to the trunk."

He pulled his arm in to open the door.

"Hey!" Deputy Parker pulled the shotgun butt to his shoulder. "Keep your hands where I can see them!"

Ethan thrust both his wrists out again. He glanced down, then back at the deputy. "With which part of my body do you think I'm going to open the door?"

That stumped the officer for a moment. Ethan waited patiently, not about to make any sudden moves. He could hear Jill breathing a little faster than normal behind him, but he wasn't about to risk turning to check on her. At least she'd stopped laughing.

"Just reach right down and use the outside door handle," Deputy Parker instructed. "Step on out, letting the door open as you go. That's right. Now put your hands on top of your head and come on back."

During the short walk, Ethan looked at the big man still sitting in the passenger seat of the patrol car. He appeared to be sleeping, which surprised him. This was probably the most exciting thing to happen in this area since NASCAR.

"Lean over the trunk and spread 'em," Deputy Parker ordered.

Disbelief filled Ethan's mind, giving a disconnected-from-reality feeling. That had to rank right up there on the list of things he'd never expected to hear directed at him. "Deputy, I—"

"You got the right to remain silent."

"Okay."

"You got other rights, too, but I can never remember what in blue blazes they are. Sheriff Dodd's got the card, so he'll read them to y'all when he wakes up."

Ethan placed his palms flat on the trunk and spread his legs. A passing car honked. It never looked as humiliating on those reality shows, he thought.

When nothing else happened, he risked a glance over his shoulder. The deputy was frowning at the shotgun cradled in his arms. It was pretty clear the man had no idea how to frisk him while holding the gun.

"I don't have any weapons on me," Ethan said, figuring the more helpful he was, the easier the whole process would be. "And nothing in my pockets."

Deputy Parker scoffed. "Yeah, I'm gonna believe a kidnapper. I didn't just fall off the turnip truck last night."

"I'll frisk him for you," Joe shouted, hanging his head out

the window like a Golden Retriever.

"Joe!" The deputy was starting to sound frazzled and that made Ethan nervous. Confused, half-deaf lawmen with lethal weapons had that effect on him. "You get on out of the car now."

While Joe got out of the car, Ethan looked through the back window and met Jill's gaze. She wasn't laughing anymore, but her amusement was still evident. This was a big joke to her.

Well, they'd see how funny it was when she was the one spread-eagled over the trunk of the car with a steadily streaming audience of camera-wielding vacationers.

Ethan forced himself to take a deep breath. If he didn't relax, he'd blow a blood vessel right here on the side of the highway.

Jill's right, he told himself. Once the cops stood still long enough to hear their story, they'd be free and on their way. Nothing to be stressed about.

* * * * *

"You go on and see if Sheriff Dodd's coming around," Jill heard Deputy Parker say.

Ethan had shut off the car. Even with the windows down, it was stifling without air conditioning and she had a strong urge to pant. Ethan might be bent over the trunk at gunpoint, but at least he had a breeze.

"Can we hurry this up a little?" she called. Her question was rewarded with nothing but a hard, warning glare from Ethan. The deputy didn't give any indication he'd heard her.

"Get on up," Joe was saying to the sheriff, "before Parker goes and shoots himself in the foot."

Jill watched the big man haul himself out of the car, then walk over to exchange a few words with his deputy. Her eyes met Ethan's and disbelief flooded her when Sheriff Dodd handcuffed him and read off a list of his rights.

They weren't going to let them explain? She was sure if they'd just listen to the story, they'd all be sharing a laugh in no time. Really, what were the chances of two rented, white Tauruses ending up in the same backwater diner's parking lot at the same time? It could have happened to anybody.

The sheriff hauled Ethan away from the trunk. "Junior, you go and get the woman out while I put this one in the car."

Deputy Parker walked around the passenger side of the car and Jill had to swallow twice to clear the lump in her throat. She'd never seen a shotgun so up close and personal before.

"Come on out, nice and slow," he instructed, keeping the gun pointed enough in her general direction to make her pray she didn't sneeze.

"Officer, I can explain—"

"You got the right to remain silent, too." He snapped handcuffs around her wrists and panic almost made her wet herself. She was *in custody*!

"But I don't want to," she argued in a high-pitched voice she'd never heard come out of her own mouth before. "I want to clear this up."

"She giving you trouble, Junior?" the sheriff demanded.

Jill watched Sheriff Dodd push down on the top of Ethan's head and stuff him through the back door of the cruiser. He had a blank look on his face, as if he couldn't believe this was really happening. Can't blame him, she thought. He'd probably never had so much as a parking ticket.

The sheriff slammed the door closed and started back. "I'll take care of her while you search the car."

"Don't you go opening that trunk without a warrant, Junior Parker," Joe shouted. "There just might be dead bodies in there."

Jill watched in disbelief as the sheriff slid down the front of the cruiser and came to rest with his head on the front bumper. Seconds later a raucous snore shook his body.

"What's wrong with him?" she asked the deputy.

The tiny man gave her a sideways look. "Who's Jim?"

"No," Jill pointed at the car, "what's wrong with *him*?"

"That ain't Jim," Deputy Parker shouted. "Lady, that's Sheriff Dodd, like he said. You got dead bodies in that trunk?"

"No! No, it was just a joke. I was kidding around about how maybe the person who rented the car before Joe's daughter was in the mafia and…" Jill let the sentence trail off. She wasn't making a lick of sense and he probably couldn't hear her anyway.

He leaned in close, sniffing at her face. "You been drinkin' today?"

"I wish."

Deputy Parker nodded. "We all do a little drinkin' when we fish, ma'am, but you can't be drivin' around after. Especially in a stolen car with a kidnapping victim. We got laws in this state."

"I wasn't driving!" Jill yelled. "*He* was."

The deputy looked over at the patrol car. "From the way he keeps smilin' in there, I'd say he's even more drunk than you."

Jill looked closer at Ethan. Yes, he was smiling. But not in an amused way. More in a *they're coming to take me away, haha* kind of way.

"Ain't neither of them been drinkin', Junior Parker," Grandpa Joe hollered out the front window of the cruiser. "You let them go now."

"Now, Joe, you done been kidnapped. I reckon you ain't in your right mind at the moment. Soon as Sheriff Dobbs comes 'round we'll get you on back to your family."

"Any idea when that might be?" Jill asked.

"Oh, any time now. If he gets too excited, he just conks out for a while. He'll be fine in a few minutes and we can get y'all down to the jailhouse."

This wasn't funny anymore. Remembering to shout, she said, "Look, Deputy, this is all just a misunderstanding."

"What's to misunderstand? You took a car that don't

belong to you. That's grand theft auto. And you took ole Joe with it. That there's kidnapping. What about that don't you understand, ma'am?"

Well, when he put it like that... "We thought this was our rental car. We didn't mean to steal it."

"Tell it to the judge."

The judge? A picture of herself, standing on a platform in an orange jumpsuit with her hair tangled and greasy flashed into her mind. This couldn't go all the way to trial. Could it?

The deputy escorted her past Joe and the sleeping sheriff. She was careful not to trip over the man's legs. They'd probably add assaulting an officer of the law to the list of charges against her.

Deputy Parker opened the back door and helped her sit backwards on the bench seat. Then he pushed down on the top of her head and said, "Swing your legs inside the vehicle, ma'am."

The door slammed shut. She turned her head, and she and Ethan simply stared at each other until Joe opened the door and pushed his way in.

Shoved up against Ethan, Jill took a second to register that she was, in fact, handcuffed in the back of a police car. And there was no chance of convincing herself it was all a nightmare. The handcuffs pinched her wrists hard enough to wake her from a coma.

"I'm gonna ride with y'all," Joe informed them in an unbearably cheerful voice that made Jill wince. "Just waitin' on Sheriff Dodd to wake up and call the tow truck."

"Why can't they simply each drive a vehicle back?" Ethan asked, beating her to the question.

"Oh, the sheriff can't drive. He gets a little excited and falls asleep, he might run the car right into a tree. Junior Parker drives him everywhere. And they gotta impound that one—search for contraband and stuff."

"Contraband?" Jill repeated. "Do they think we're

smuggling aliens, too?"

The old man gave her a sideways look. "Now, girl…you start goin' on about little green men, they're likely to send you over to the county hospital before long."

"No, I meant…never mind."

Jill leaned her head back against the seat and closed her eyes. Even in the air-conditioned cruiser, the heat from Ethan's body was incredible. She let herself wonder for a second what it would be like to curl up next to him in bed on a cold winter's night.

Heavenly, she decided. Without thinking, she shifted, resting her head on his shoulder. Instead of pulling away, he leaned his cheek against her hair.

"We'll get this all straightened out back at the station," he murmured. "I'll take care of it."

And he would, she thought. Some of the tension eased from her body. Ethan would take care of her. Funny how she didn't feel even a bit claustrophobic at the thought.

Chapter Nine

ꕤ

The bars swung closed with a clang worthy of The Gong Show. *Hooked – exit, cell right.* Ethan took a step back from the door, the bitter taste of anger burning his throat. This simply couldn't be happening to him. He'd never even had a speeding ticket, and now he was locked up?

"I want to use the phone," he yelled at the deputy's retreating back.

"You can't go home," Deputy Parker yelled back.

"No, I..." It was too late. The man was already gone.

Damn. How was he supposed to call a lawyer if he couldn't use the phone? While it was true most of his knowledge of criminal proceedings came from primetime television, he was sure that one phone call was within his rights. So was a lawyer.

Somewhere between the fingerprinting and the photo session, he'd realized that an attorney might make a better advisor at this point than Jill. Her *don't worry, it's just a misunderstanding* attitude wasn't getting them very far.

He scrubbed his face with his palms. It was early evening now. After an hour and a half wait for the only tow truck in the area, which apparently had a bad starter and was hit or miss, they arrived at the small, brick jailhouse. That's when they discovered the process had only begun. Now, with ink-stained fingers and no shoelaces, he tried to resign himself to a long wait. And to the possibility there would be no placing of bail and cushy hotel bed tonight.

But he wanted to call a lawyer, and then he needed to call his mother. There was no telling what ideas the woman would get into her head when he didn't arrive as promised. She'd probably either think he was lying dead in a ditch somewhere, or had run off to Vegas with Jill.

Too bad she hadn't spent less time worrying about whether or not he had a condom and more time wondering if he had bail money.

"Are you mad at me?" Jill asked in a small voice, breaking into his thoughts.

Ethan peered through the bars at the cell across the wide hallway. She sat on the narrow cot, her arms wrapped around drawn-up knees. Her face was pale and, though he couldn't be sure from this distance, he thought her bottom lip was trembling.

Hell yes, he was mad at her. And himself. And Joe Jackson and the sheriff and his deputy and that dumbass bus driver. He was pretty pissed off at everybody he'd ever met. But this one particular incident wasn't really her fault, and even if she was responsible in a roundabout way, he couldn't kick her while she was down.

He sighed, letting his forehead rest on the cold bars. "No, sunshine. I'm not mad."

"It's okay if you are. This is the worst trouble I've caused yet."

She was rocking back and forth ever so slightly, and Ethan felt a pang of worry. He'd been so wrapped up in his predicament, he hadn't even given a thought to how scary it was for her. She was a pain in the ass, but as far he knew this was a first for her as well. "You didn't cause this. Like you said, it's just a misunderstanding they haven't given us a chance to clear up yet. And I'm the one who took the wrong damned car."

He expected her to perk up at his admission of fault, but she said nothing. "Hey, sunshine, if I can get them to let us use the phone, is there anybody you want to call?"

"Sure." She laughed, but it wasn't a happy sound. "My family's probably huddled around the phone right now, waiting for me to call and ask to be rescued from my latest scrape."

The way she said it made it clear this was a phrase she'd

heard a lot in her life. Jill's scrapes had no doubt given her mother plenty of stories to share with her friends over coffee. He wondered if it had ever crossed their minds they'd flushed her self-image down the toilet.

He added her parents and her sister to the list of people he was pissed off at. And Kenny Sanford, too, just because who knew what the opportunistic gigolo would get up to with yet another unsupervised night with his mother. Then he got mad at himself for behaving like a child where his mother was concerned, but dammit he was her child.

"Sheriff Dodd!" he bellowed in the direction of the front office.

He had to shout three more times before the man appeared. His eyes were narrowed and his pace was slow, as if he was expecting masked accomplices to leap out of the shadows at any second.

Ethan hoped the excitement of walking to his cell wouldn't put the sheriff to sleep. The man kept a suspicious eye on Ethan, but leaned close enough for him to speak quietly.

"Look, we're not really criminals," he said earnestly. "Neither of us have any weapons or the power to bend bars. Is there any chance of letting us share a cell?"

Sheriff Dodd shook his head. "I didn't just fall of the turnip truck, you know. Not supposed to put suspects together. Don't want to give y'all time to get your stories straight."

"There aren't any stories. Just one simple explanation, which your Deputy Parker is supposed to be verifying. We'll be out of here in no time, but in the meantime, Jill's scared and I'd like for you to move her in here."

The sheriff considered the request while Ethan watched the vein throb in his forehead, hoping the decision wouldn't prove too overwhelming.

"I guess there's no harm in it," Sheriff Dodd said. "But no hanky-panky, you hear?"

Ethan snorted. He hadn't developed any incarceration

fetishes that he knew of. "No problem."

"One of my deputies is over at Bobbi Jo's house right now, trying to get a report from Joe."

That cheered him immensely. Once Joe explained the whole situation, they'd be free in no time. They'd all share a good laugh and they could still make it to the hotel in time to make sure his mother wasn't being romanced out of her bingo money.

"The ornery ol' cuss won't say a dang word," Sheriff Dodd continued. "Just keeps repeating his name and social security number over and over like a broken record."

"He what?" When had his life become a comedy skit? "Any chance I could call him—let him know I'd really like for him to…confess?"

"It's just gonna have to wait, seeing as how I've got an important meeting to get to." The sheriff hitched up his gun belt. "I'm the Grand Masked Master of the Nickel Hill Raccoon Lodge."

Ethan laughed. Sheriff Dodd's gaze hardened. "Oh. You're serious."

"As a heart attack."

"What sort of things do you guys do at a Raccoon Lodge?"

"I'd tell you, but then I'd have to kill you."

Ethan waited, not even blinking, for the sheriff to laugh. Or at least break a smile. Nothing. A shiver of fear tickled his spine.

Great, he thought. *I'm afraid of a man who falls asleep when he breaks a sweat.*

"Do you get to wear a hat?" Ethan pictured the sheriff in an authentic Davy Crockett raccoon cap. Still no smile.

"You sassin' me boy?"

"No, sir."

Sheriff Dodd stared at him long enough that Ethan got nervous. Were his eyelids drooping? Was it possible to nod off standing up with your eyes wide open?

"I'll get your girlfriend," the man said finally, grabbing the big ring of keys off his belt.

"She's not my…okay."

She wasn't his girlfriend, but she was something. He wasn't sure what, but now didn't seem to be the time to argue about it.

* * * * *

Relief gave Jill a much needed burst of energy when Sheriff Dodd unlocked her cell. She practically skipped to the door.

"See, Ethan," she called over to him. "I told you they'd understand."

"You quit moving so fast," the sheriff ordered, looking a bit red about the ears.

Jill stopped like a kindergarten freeze-tag champion. No way could this man take a siesta when she was so close to freedom. "Okay. Is there any paperwork involved?"

"Well, normally in a prisoner transfer situation there would be, but seein' as how you're only going across the hall, we'll skip it."

"Across the hall? You're not letting us go?"

"No, ma'am. You got some mighty serious charges against you. I'm just moving you over with your boyfriend."

"He's not my…okay."

Jill felt like an inmate who'd spent ten years digging a tunnel with a broken spoon, only to find herself in the prison cesspool. Freedom—so close, yet here she was, still stuck in a steaming quagmire of trouble.

She was docile, following Sheriff Dodd to Ethan's cell, standing quietly while he unlocked it. But it was hard because all she wanted to do was throw herself at Ethan and let him hold her. She wanted him to tell her again that everything would be okay. Because it certainly wasn't looking that way right now.

"Thank you," she whispered to the sheriff when he swung the door open.

"No hanky-panky now, you hear? Your boyfriend wanted you over there with him, but he promised there'd be no monkey business."

Tears gathered in her eyes as she stepped into Ethan's cell and his waiting arms. She didn't even wince when the door clanged shut behind her.

"How are you holding up?" he whispered into her hair.

"This is even worse than the time my nephew flushed my sister's prized African Violet down the toilet while I was bawling through Steel Magnolias for the fiftieth time."

"But not as bad as..."

"What do you mean?"

"Spending the afternoon in jail can't be the worst thing that's ever happened to you."

Jill pulled out of his embrace so she could frown up at him. "I'm not sure I like the sound of that. I don't go around accidentally triggering nuclear meltdowns, you know."

"I know, but something must have happened to you that was...less pleasant than being arrested on a felony charge."

"Well, there was the time I was trying to show the neighbor how to light up his...uh, gas with a cigarette lighter and set a stack of old newspapers on fire, which was too close to the gas can and I blew up my dad's first Harley. That was much worse."

Ethan nodded mutely for a second. "I should say so. But see—now you can look on the bright side. It could be worse."

Jill managed a little laugh. "I guess you're right."

He led her over to the small cot and they sat side by side. It would only be comfortable for about ten minutes.

"If you don't mind my asking," he said, "how old were you when you blew up the motorcycle?"

"Eight. And it was two weeks before Christmas."

"Ouch."

"That's what my behind said."

"So you've always been disaster-prone?"

"Yup." This wasn't the most cheerful conversation to have in a jail cell. She was looking for comfort, not depressing memories piled onto a really bad day. "I broke the television and the stereo learning to walk."

Ethan laughed long enough that she sidled away from him. Not too far, since the cot was only about five feet long, but she made her point. If he didn't change the subject, she was going to have the sheriff transfer her back to her own cell. At least she didn't have to share the cot.

"They should have had sturdier stands," she muttered. "And who keeps old newspapers and gasoline right next to a Harley?"

Ethan reached over and physically hauled her back against his side. It was a caveman move that had her heart beating double time and her hormones paying attention. "Maybe all this stuff happens to you because you and your family expect it."

"Oh, now who got a psychobabble license out of a cereal box?"

"I'm serious. It's like a…self-fulfilling prophecy thing."

Jill's eyes widened. "I think you're right! Right before I got on the bus I kept thinking *what if I get stranded and then kidnap an old guy who's not related to Shoeless Joe Jackson while stealing a car?* And it came true."

"Smartass."

"Since you figured out why Lady Luck throws me the rejects, have you figured out how to get that stick out—"

"I am not uptight," he interrupted quickly. "And we're talking about you, not me."

"I'm done talking."

They sat in silence for what could have been fifteen minutes or an hour. She wished, not for the first time, that she'd quit leaving her watch in the dish next to her kitchen sink. There was no clock in the cell, and at the moment that vexed her more than the steel urinal hanging on the other wall. Although that would probably change. Soon.

Ethan scooted back on the cot so he could rest his back against the wall, somehow managing to take her with him. Leaning into his chest and shoulder was too comfortable to resist, so she let herself relax against him.

He was so solid, and she couldn't help but feel secure in his arms. It was nice not to have to suffer through this latest disaster alone. Of course, if not for him she wouldn't be sitting in the Nickel Hill jail, but right now, with his arms wrapped around her, she couldn't bring herself to care.

"Why did you ask Sheriff Dodd to bring me in here with you?" she asked when she couldn't stand the quiet for another second.

"There aren't any pillows, so I thought if you just lean back against the wall, I can lay my head on your lap and take a nap."

"Oh no you don't." She laughed and slapped his leg. "You heard the man—no hanky-panky."

"Since when does sleeping count as hanky-panky?"

"When it's done with your face in the general vicinity of my crotch."

He was getting better. The color in his cheeks only reached bubble gum pink on the mortification scale. She'd have to start working harder to keep him on his toes.

"Have you ever noticed," he asked, "that the more upset you are the more wise-mouthed you get?"

"Nope." Like she'd never been told that before.

"You do. And judging from the last few minutes, you're nervous as hell."

"Yeah...well, I'm on a first name basis with the emergency room staff, rescue squad, police department and poison control people back home, but I've never been charged with a felony before."

He chuckled against her hair. "It's not on my resumé,

either."

Resumés. Jill winced. She'd been trying not to think about how desperately her resume needed updating before she could start looking for a job.

How on Earth could being incarcerated not be her biggest problem? Even if they released her right now and put her on an express bus back to New Hampshire, her life would still be a mess.

There was no hope for it. She would have to ask Liz for help and swallow more than one dose of *I told you so*. But her sister worked for the department store and what good were family connections if they couldn't get you a minimum wage job?

Ethan's offer to help her get her job back was tempting, but she couldn't bring herself to take him up on it. No matter how much he claimed the sex didn't factor in, she couldn't believe it had nothing to do with his decision. And facing his mother after she'd quit once would be hard enough without having had vacation sex with the woman's son.

That was assuming the offer was even still on the table. Criminal law wasn't her forte, but she was pretty sure felons weren't supposed to work with children.

Approaching footsteps wrenched her attention back to the here and now. They both sat up straight and she felt Ethan breathe a sigh of relief.

A short, well-rounded woman in a June Cleaver dress came around the corner balancing a heavy tray. Jill's hopes nose-dived. This didn't look good for getting out anytime soon.

"I'm Missus Carter," the woman said. "I own the cafe over yonder and Sheriff Dodd asked me to bring y'all some supper."

Ethan got to his feet so fast he almost dumped Jill on the floor. "Did he say anything about letting us make a phone call?"

"No, he didn't. And ya'll need to stay where you are or I'll give this to my dog."

The tray looked heavy and Jill held her breath while the

woman figured out how she was going to slide it through the slot in the bars. They'd already had supper, but there were two coffee mugs on that tray and one spilled drop of that precious liquid would be the last straw.

"Would you like help with that, ma'am?" Ethan asked.

"You just stay back. Young lady, you come take it."

Mrs. Carter finally managed to fit the overflowing tray through the slot in the bars. Jill took it, letting the heavenly odor of strong coffee fill her senses.

But as she turned and handed the tray off to Ethan, another thought struck her. As much as she needed to re-caffeinate her veins, she had another pressing problem. Maybe one this woman would understand.

"Mrs. Carter, I need you to do me a favor."

The woman's mouth pursed in immediate disapproval. "If you need something you should ask Sheriff Dodd."

"It's kind of personal. I can't pay you right now, unless you'll take a credit card, but I'll mail you a check as soon as I get to Orlando."

The woman shook her head. "I didn't fall off the turnip truck last night. I ain't taking no check from a felon."

"*Alleged* felon."

"What the *hell* is a turnip truck?" Ethan shouted.

She ignored him. "I'll send cash. Please. I need some clean clothes."

Mrs. Carter considered the plea for a few seconds, and then sniffed. "I reckon I could take a look around the church basement. Jeb's been collectin' stuff for the big rummage sale next month. Might be something to fit you in one of the bags."

"Oh, that's…great. Maybe something in orange velour?"

Mrs. Carter sniffed again and Jill wished she could reach out and shake the words back out of the woman's ears. "Wait, I—"

"I don't need your snippy attitude, young lady. You wait

'til tomorrow and you'll be dressed in orange, all right. An orange jumpsuit."

She walked away and Jill wanted to throw herself down on the cell floor and kick her feet. Her mouth had just cost her clean underwear.

"Way to go, sunshine. You managed to piss off the only person who was actually going to help us."

One…two…three…four… She gave up. She'd have to count to at least five thousand to cool her temper and her coffee would get cold.

Ethan sat on one end of the cot and put the tray down in the middle. Jill sat on the other end and lifted the lid on her plate. It was that deep-fried, gravy-smothered feast all over again.

Her mouth watered in response. If Mrs. Carter always did the cooking, life in prison might not be so bad after all.

Chapter Ten

ꟈ

Sometime during the night, Jill pulled Ethan's elbow out of her rib cage for the umpteenth time and cursed him for being such a nice guy. She might have been lonely and scared in her own cell, but at least she didn't have to share a cot.

The insensitive sleeper in question mumbled incoherently then rolled onto his back. For a second Jill was certain she was going to fall, but Ethan hauled her with him. She sprawled atop his body with her head on his chest, surprised by how comfortable it was.

"Better?" he mumbled.

"Much."

When his arms wrapped around her back, she sighed and tried to go back to sleep. For an insensitive jerk, he could be a really nice guy.

Too nice, she mused as sleep clouded her mind. He made her think about profane words she had no business thinking about—like forever and permanent and *I do.*

Here was a man she could picture waiting for her at the end of a flowery, beribboned aisle. As her eyes drifted closed, Jill could almost hear the organist pounding out "Here Comes the Bride".

There was her mother, mascara-tinted tears of joy flowing down her cheeks. There was Liz, looking very big-sisterly in her matron of honor dress. There were Liz's kids, duct taped to the front pew.

Jill snuggled against Ethan, smiling as she walked down the aisle. She imagined the love shining in his Hershey's Special Dark eyes when he recited his vows.

I promise to love, honor and cherish you, for better or worse, in sickness and in health, day after day after day…every single day until we die.

A baby's cry ripped through her dream and Jill looked down. Gone was the bouquet. Gone was the pouffy gown. Gone was her waist.

Her subconscious conjured up a kitchen furnished with a beautifully refinished table and secondhand avocado appliances. Somebody—presumably Ethan—was hiding behind the morning paper. The baby in her arms was trying to gnaw his way through her shirt to a nipple that seemed to be pointing straight to her navel.

A little dark-eyed girl tugged on her pants. "Mama. Mama. Mama. Mama."

This was bad since she hadn't worn pants with snaps and zippers since the oldest—*of how many?*—was born. The worn elastic waistband headed south, threatening to take her too-comfy maternity undies with it.

Off in the distance a child laughed. Another shouted. A toilet flushed. A cat yowled.

Jill jerked and rolled onto the floor, the nightmare like a shot of one hundred proof espresso.

That answered any questions about her ability to see the future. The hounds of hell would win the Iditarod before she sentenced herself to that scenario.

It really was too bad, she decided. Ethan would probably make some woman a very good husband. Just not her.

"What's wrong?" Ethan asked, no doubt startled awake by her self-ejection from the cot.

"Nothing." What else could she say? *I don't want to let my guard down too much or I'll end up spending all my time calculating the unit price of diapers?*

She couldn't make any sense of it, so he wasn't likely to. Bemoaning the loss of waistline and sexy underwear after a decade of marriage wasn't exactly pre-first date conversation.

"Okay," he said in a voice that let her know he thought she was anything but that.

"Bad dream," she muttered. "Very bad."

Without saying another word she crawled back up on top of him, wiggled herself into a comfy position and fell back to sleep.

* * * * *

He heard her long before he saw her.

Lying on the cot, wondering if he'd been decapitated during the night because he sure couldn't feel anything below his neck, he listened to his mother give somebody holy heck.

"My Ethan would never even steal a car, never mind kidnap somebody. What would he want with an old man, anyway?"

Ethan cringed and tried to roll over. The paralysis wasn't total, because his fingers twitched, but he wasn't getting out of bed anytime soon.

A light weight on his chest lifted and Jill peered down at him, her eyes still half closed. "What time is it?"

"They took my watch," he replied. Not that he could have lifted his wrist high enough to look at it.

"Maybe they thought you'd try to hang yourself with it."

"I still might if they give it back in time. My mother's here."

Her blue eyes opened to full alert status. "Will she bail us out?"

"It sounds like she's going to try the harassment and intimidation route first. Did you sleep on top of me all night?"

"Half, at least. I was uncomfortable, so you pulled me up here."

"Remind me to never do that again."

Not that he'd have the chance, he reminded himself. They were fast approaching the end of the road—in more ways than one. And for some reason, despite her history of scrapes and the lack of feeling in his body she had caused, he wasn't looking forward to it as much as he'd once thought he would. Unbelievably, she seemed to be growing on him.

The voices were getting closer—coming down the hallway—and he heard Sheriff Dodd say, "Ma'am, I—"

"My son is not a criminal."

"Ma'am, I—"

"I want you to release him *right now*."

Ethan heard a sliding sound, a thump and a gasp before his mother shrieked, "Oh, good lord, I've killed a sheriff."

"Uh-oh," Jill said, leaping off him in a flurry of elbows and knees that left him gasping for air and with plenty of aching evidence that his body wasn't permanently numb.

"Do something, Kenny!" his mother yelled.

Kenny? That guy she met on the bus had traveled with her? Alone?

With a groan that came from the tips of his pins-and-needles-racked toes, Ethan managed to roll and shove his way to a sitting position. That was the last time he ever played a human mattress.

"Mrs. Cooper," Jill called through the bars. "He'll be fine. He's sleeping."

Very gingerly, Ethan stood and made his way to the cell door. Every muscle in his body protested at the sudden rush of blood and oxygen, but he didn't seem to have sustained any permanent damage.

His mother rushed to him and Ethan felt a rush of guilt. Her face was pale with worry and exhaustion, and her hands trembled as she reached through the bars.

"Ethan!" She grasped the sides of his face and pulled in his to the bars so she could kiss his face.

The metal was cold and none-too-soft against his cheekbones, but he let her do her maternal thing.

"I was so worried about you. I saw you on the news and I had to call around to find you and then Kenny and I came straight here."

She had to pause to take a breath and Ethan jumped in. "I'm fine, Mom. Really, it was just a misunderstanding."

"Maybe when the sheriff wakes up we can get out of here," Jill said.

Ethan heard a little click in his mind, followed by a thunk in his stomach. "You saw us on the news? What news?"

A man stepped over to his mother and rested his hand on her back. Ethan made a low growling sound in his throat that nobody seemed to notice. Damn good thing there were bars between him and this geriatric gigolo, he fumed.

"Ethan, this is my *friend*, Kenny Sanford. Kenny, this is my son, Ethan and his girlfriend..."

"I'm not his—"

Jill cut herself off, and he realized that the same thought had just occurred to both of them. His mom still didn't know the woman her son spent the last two nights with was the same woman who had left her high and dry at the library.

They were granted a temporary stay of introduction when Sheriff Dodd snorted a few times and sat up. He pushed himself to his feet, grumbling under his breath.

"Dadgummit. I hate it when that happens."

His mother left off squeezing his cheeks through the bars and threw up her hands. "It's a miracle!"

"I told you he wasn't dead," Jill said.

"Maybe you should ask if they're going to release them," his mom said to her *friend*, "since I nearly killed him."

The sheriff hitched up his gun belt. "Ma'am what I was trying to tell you before my unfortunate episode is I'm releasing Mr. Cooper and Miss Delaney right now."

Ethan breathed a sigh of relief. The nightmare was over.

"Miss Delaney?" his mother repeated. "Jill Delaney?"

Okay, the nightmare was *almost* over.

"Yes, ma'am," Sheriff Dodd said. "Bobbie Jo done told her daddy if he didn't 'fess up to the whole truth she was gonna put him in a home. The cheapest one she could find. Spilled his guts like filleted trout."

Ethan and everybody but his mother cringed at that tasty visual. His mother was too intent on sizing up Jill. He needed to distract her before somebody said something that spelled a second nap for the good sheriff.

"What do you mean you saw us on the news?"

His mother shifted her gaze to him, and then shook her head. "Some tourist passing by on the highway saw the ruckus and had his wife lean out the window with the video camera. They showed it on the news and I recognized you right away, even though you were handcuffed and blurry."

"Took us nearly an hour of phone calls to find you," Kenny added. "Then we had to rent a car to get here."

The sheriff cleared his throat like a congested bullfrog. "Y'all want out of there, or you wanna socialize for a while?"

* * * * *

Safe at last in their Orlando hotel, Ethan left his mother off at 219, glared at Kenny unlocking 222, tried not to watch Jill entering 226 and let himself into 225.

Cozy. The only ray of sunshine in this Senior Spring Fling monsoon was having his own room. Even if it was directly across the hall from Jill Delaney. Between the nap—very long nap—in the car and thinking about how much he'd like to have had the chance to see Jill on her hands and knees, he'd be lucky if he slept at all.

He'd wondered in the car if the vacation sex came to end when they reached their destination, or when they arrived back in New England. They hadn't really established clear terms. That got him thinking about all the ways he'd still like to have her, which got him hooked on an image of her ass in the air. His denim-constrained hard-on had him squirming all the way through Georgia.

But, logically, he knew it was over. They weren't going to have wild and free vacation sex with his mother, her *friend* and half the town's elderly community surrounding them. He'd go his way and she'd go hers. Maybe they'd bump into each other during his visits to his mom. Maybe they'd even get together for some macaroni and cheese and a few laughs. He didn't even want to think about it right now. Too depressing.

His mother had arranged for his suitcase to be delivered from the bus he'd spent so little time on to his room, but he didn't have time for a shower before they met for the group dinner that certainly hadn't been his idea. Once he got under that hot water, it was going to be a very long time before he got out again.

Instead he dug his newly recovered wallet out of his back pocket. Sitting on the edge of the bed with the free notepad and stubby pencil, he did a quick tally of what he owed Jill. He'd pay her later and that would be the end of it.

The end of everything. No more chaos, no more impulsiveness. No more Jill Delaney.

Ethan flopped down on the bed. There was a good reason why this was the end of the road for them. Several good reasons, he thought. He just couldn't remember a single damn one of them.

He took the time to peel off the Garfield T-shirt. The garbage can beckoned, but he dropped it on the floor next to his suitcase. He'd never wear it again, but he couldn't throw it away.

A door slammed down the hall, and he donned a plain white T-shirt and dragged a comb through his hair. Then he shoved his wallet back in his pants and double-checked that he had his key. An hour, hour and a half at the most, and he could retreat to his room. He wasn't really in the mood for socializing.

It didn't help when he walked into the dining room and

saw Jill and his mother already seated and laughing at something the dastardly Don Juan had said. They were his women, dammit.

"We're absolutely sure they returned the Taurus?" Jill asked as soon as he sat down. "The *right* Taurus?"

"Hello to you, too. I called the rental company myself," Ethan said. "I'm not about to leave anything to chance at this point."

His mother chuckled softly from across the table. "You never leave anything to chance—at any point."

Then why did he feel like his life had spun out of control and was about to hit the guardrail?

* * * * *

Jill wanted to laugh, but she already had a weird walking-on-eggshells feeling. The whole library promotion thing was lurking just below the surface and she didn't need laughing at the woman's only child as an icebreaker.

"So what's on the Spring Fling agenda for tomorrow?" Kenny said in the too-loud voice of one trying to smooth an awkward moment.

It didn't work, of course. If talking too loud cured awkwardness, Jill would have taken to carrying a megaphone with her a long time ago. But she could see the man was trying to be friendly, despite the fact he couldn't miss Ethan's sullen expression. He looked like a four-year-old pouting, for goodness sake.

"Epcot, I believe," Debra replied, then they were all quiet while perusing the vastly overpriced menu. Jill was disappointed. There didn't seem to be a fried lump anywhere.

"What do you do, Mr. Sanford?" she asked, when their orders were given and awkward silence ruled once again.

"Call me Kenny. And I make a pretty good living bilking lonely, widowed librarians out of their used book sale money."

Debra laughed first, then Jill joined in. Even Ethan chuckled when Kenny winked at him.

"My first job was forty-nine years of plumbing. Worked my butt off, built a nice little nest egg for myself. Looked around one day and realized I had plenty of money, arthritic knees but I'd never found myself a good woman."

He paused, then rested his hand on Debra's knee. "Until now."

Jill felt Ethan tense next to her and she hoped he wouldn't cause a scene. His father had been gone a year, which probably didn't seem like much to him, but Debra clearly enjoyed the man's company. And they did seem to have hit it off quickly. Love at first sight?

She glanced sideways at Ethan. They'd hit it off pretty quickly, too. Maybe they'd had a rocky beginning…and a rocky middle, but the attraction had been there from the start. The spark. And they'd experienced a lot in their short time together. But he didn't look at her the way Kenny Sanford looked at Debra Cooper, that's for sure. Only when they were having sex, and that wasn't enough.

"You won't find one better," Ethan finally told Kenny, but he didn't exactly sound as if he was ready to walk his mother down the aisle.

"So," Debra said with the air of one deciding just to jump headfirst into an icy pool. "Let's talk about the library."

Jill stalled by draining her water glass. "I, umm…"

"I'm not accepting your resignation. That's all there is to it."

Ethan chuckled and she kicked him under the table. He knew very well how she felt about getting her job back. It just wasn't right that she should get her job back because she was screwing the boss's son. Especially since said boss didn't know how very temporary the screwing was.

"Mrs. Bright accepted my resignation. And it wasn't really a resignation. It was more like quitting during a hissy fit, as Ethan described it."

"I've read your file, and on the day I report to work I'm unaccepting your hissy fit. You are too good at your job and I need you too much."

"Mrs. Cooper, considering my, uhhh, relationship with your son, I don't feel that it would be very appropriate to—"

"Bullshit," the older woman barked, and they *all* shut up. "Not a single person at this table thinks there is anything underhanded about your relationship with my son. It will be nice, actually. After Ethan sells my house in Connecticut, there will be enough so I can help you guys get a little house and he can do furniture while you work part-time for me and finish your degree."

Jill felt her face freeze and she was pretty sure her expression resembled the Mona Lisa as painted by Picasso.

Ethan stood up so quickly his chair nearly fell over. "Let's all hit the salad bar. The radishes looked really good and the sesame seeds..."

A little piece of her heart seemed to dry up and crumble away. She knew he didn't want his mother to know they weren't serious about each other—which was fine. But he couldn't have handled that a little more smoothly? It was now painfully obvious to everybody at the table that Ethan didn't see a future with her. And she'd known it, but it hurt to know that Debra and Kenny now knew it, too.

It hurt, period. She knew she wasn't—and didn't *want* to be—the domestic goddess Ethan would look for in a wife. She knew she wasn't his type, and that vacation sex was exactly that. But opposites were supposed to attract, dammit, and she wanted him to be attracted to her. Not her body. But *her*.

She sighed and followed them up to the salad bar. Another hour, tops, and she could hide in her room and cry herself to sleep. As long as her roommate, Mrs. Henderson, was asleep. The woman would talk to a hairbrush, for goodness sake.

She took a deep breath and put on her best public-servant smile. Her heart might be breaking but she wouldn't give him the satisfaction of showing it.

Chapter Eleven

Jill knocked as softly as possible on the door, but the sound echoed accusingly around her. Maybe he was asleep. He wouldn't hear the knock and she could pretend she'd never come.

She shouldn't have. Not after his mad rush to the salad bar at dinner. But she couldn't be so close to him and not touch him—one last time. A goodbye kiss, at least.

Ethan opened the door, clad only in a white hotel towel tied around his hips. Or maybe a goodbye quickie, even. She stared at the knot for what seemed like forever.

What was it she'd come to say? For the life of her she couldn't remember a single basic English word.

"Hey, sunshine. You lost again?"

That was one way to put it. "I, uh…I can't sleep."

"Did you try warm milk?"

It's really over. He'd told her it would be, but on some level she hadn't believed him. But when a scantily clad, sexy-smelling woman knocks on a man's door late at night and he suggests warm milk, the spark has fizzled out.

"No, I didn't. I tried counting sheep, but Mrs. Henderson's snoring kept scaring them off."

Ethan folded his arms across his bare chest and leaned his hip against the door jamb. That knot wasn't pulled very tight. She tried really hard not to look. "Maybe you're tense."

Tense. That was it. His lean, naked torso and smoldering dark eyes made her tense. She nodded.

"And the shower didn't help?"

She shook her head.

"Maybe a massage would ease some of that tension."

Was this *her* Ethan oozing sizzling male sexuality like hot fudge over a dish of soft serve vanilla?

She had to clear her throat before she could speak. "Do you know a good masseuse in Orlando?"

"No, but I've got a phone book in my room. You can let your fingers do the walking."

Think provocative, she told herself. *Blank. Blank.* "I used to do that with Barbie shoes when I was little."

"Okay." He tilted his head. "You used to do what with Barbie shoes?"

Was that high-pitched giggle coming out of her mouth? She slapped her hand over it, just in case. "Um…put them on the ends of my fingers and…walk them around. I liked the high-heeled, white cowboy boots the best."

"I'm trying to have sex with you here."

There was that giggle again. "I know. I'm just…"

Ethan stood straight again and lifted his hand to her face. His fingers traced a line from her temple to her chin and she turned her cheek to his palm.

"Why are you nervous, sunshine?"

She had no idea. Wasn't sex what she was hoping for when she knocked on his door?

No, a little voice in her mind whispered. Well…yes, some incredible sex wouldn't hurt. But that wasn't all. She just wasn't sure what else there was.

Ethan's hand curled around the nape of her neck, drawing her face toward his. Their lips touched and Jill stopped pondering any ulterior motives her subconscious might be harboring.

His icy mint toothpaste made her tongue tingle when it touched his and the tang of his shaving cream burned her nose. He nipped at her lip and she groaned.

Any lingering nervousness was devoured by her hunger for him. She reached down between their bodies and tugged at the knot. The towel fell across their feet.

"Maybe we should close the door," he murmured against her lips.

"Hmmmm?" It took a few seconds for his words to register. When Jill realized he was standing, shower-damp and naked, in the hall, she laughed. "You don't have a roomie, do you?"

"What if I do?"

Uh-oh. Sex with a geriatric voyeur wasn't her thing, but she had Mrs. Henderson, so her room was out. Did the hotel have a pool? Probably. And they kept an eye on it from the desk with a surveillance camera, no doubt. At least the clerk wouldn't be physically in the room, though.

"Get in here," he said, gathering up the towel with his foot and kicking it behind him. "Public displays of nudity aren't exactly my style."

"What about your roommate?" she asked in a fierce whisper as he pulled her into his room and closed the door behind her.

"Don't have one," he said. "I just wanted to see what plan you'd come up with if I did."

Jill laughed until Ethan ran his hands up her sides and under her arms. He lifted her, pulling her body slowly up his.

Wrapping her legs around his waist, she lowered her mouth to his. He was hard and suddenly the skimpy nightgown she wore wasn't skimpy enough. She wanted him inside of her.

"Put me down," she whispered.

"No." Ethan took a few steps to brace her against the door. He nipped at her ear, her jaw, her neck.

Jill sighed, leaning her head back against the door. When he blew softly across the trail of moisture his mouth had left, she shivered with longing. His cock pressed against her already drenched pussy, rubbing her clit through the flimsy fabric.

He rocked her gently, increasing the friction, and she melted. She was going to come before she even got the nightgown off.

"If you don't put me down, I can't get naked."

She barely managed to get her feet under her before he dropped her.

"You get naked while I get the…things," he ordered.

"Aye aye, Captain." She would have saluted, but she was too busy tearing her nightgown over her head. "When did you get more condoms?"

Ethan winced and Jill stifled a giggle. "I'm sorry. When did you get more Mister Happy rain hats?"

He sent her a look that would have been a lot more effective if the little happy guy in question wasn't bobbing like a conductor's baton. "I have never called it *Mister Happy*. And they had a dispenser at the jail."

"They had a condom dispenser?"

He flinched again, then waved four see-through packets at her. Her first thought was *four?* Then she wondered why a man so determined not to get any further involved with her would need condoms at all.

And her third thought—*pink?* "Who do you think ordered pink condoms?"

"Mrs. Carter?"

"Sheriff Dodd?"

Jill stuck out her tongue. "Ewww."

They laughed together for a moment, then stared at each other. She raised an eyebrow at him. "I'm over here. You're over there. And we're both naked."

"Turn off the overhead light and I'll meet you on the bed."

Jill hit the switch and tried not to watch Ethan donning the pink condom by the light of small bedside lamp. She knew without looking that his cheeks would be the same color as the condom. Prophylactic pink, she thought, then had to bite her lips to keep from giggling. Now wasn't a good time for him to think she was laughing at him.

She got halfway across the room before the lamp bulb blew. The darkness was complete. The crinkle of plastic paused, then continued.

"You are hell on light bulbs, sunshine."

She looked in the direction of his voice and the stifled laugh burst out of her mouth.

A glow-in-the-dark shaft of neon pink bobbed across the room toward the bed.

"May the Force be with you," she said in her deepest voice.

"Watch it, or Princess Leia can go crawl into bed with Mrs. Henderson," he growled. "Get over here."

"Yes, Jedi master. Please don't punish me with your big, pink light saber."

Before she could react, the pink wand leapt at her and Ethan caught her around the waist. She squealed in surprise as he dragged her onto the bed. The man must have eyes like a cat.

He ran his tongue over the hollow of her throat and the feline analogy fled her mind. No sandpaper there. Just hot, silky heat.

"I've wanted to do that all day," Ethan whispered, his breath tickling her moistened flesh. "I love that spot, and watching you swallow drove me nuts all through dinner."

She didn't want to think about dinner anymore. Grasping his glowing pink cock, she guided him toward her throbbing pussy. She wanted more moaning, less talking. And she wanted it right now.

"Not so fast, sunshine."

Ethan pulled away from her to get out of bed. He opened the blinds enough to let light from the parking lot shine in, then turned to look at her. She was stunned by the emotion she saw on his face. Desire, and maybe something else that she couldn't define. Or maybe she was just imagining that something else.

The whole rushing to get radishes episode was still too recent for her to believe he'd changed his mind.

"Now your light saber won't glow," she said, needing to lighten the mood a little. She was not going to cry. Again.

"I want to watch your face when you come."

"Then you'd better get over here or I'll start without you."

He was stretched out beside her in a second. "It's a good thing you knocked when you did. I was about five seconds from crossing the hall in my towel."

He slid his hand between her knees and lifted until her leg was draped over his shoulder, then cupped her pussy in his palm. Jill whimpered and lifted her hips, opening herself to his touch.

"What do you want, baby?" His whisper was harsh against her ear and the knowledge that he was nearly over the edge himself made her brazen.

"I want you to make me come."

"How?"

"I don't care how. Any way you want to. Just, please..."

He slid a finger into her pussy and she gasped at the sensation. His hands were slightly rough from his woodworking and the sensation was so deliciously different from his smooth cock. A second finger joined the first and her hips bucked.

His thumb slid over her clit, and the sensation was too much. She tried to pull her thighs together, to squeeze his hand, but he held her leg immobile. His teeth pinched at her inner thigh as he worked a third finger into her dripping cunt.

She couldn't speak as he slid his fingers into her, pulling them nearly all the way out before sliding them into her again. When he twisted his wrist, she cried out and sank her fingernails into his back.

"I had to jerk off in the shower," he said against her hair. "I kept picturing you on your hands and knees. I was fucking you from behind and my balls were slapping against your pussy."

She came then, her hips bucking against his hand while the strength of his arm kept her pinned. His fingers twisted inside her, the hardness of his knuckles stretching her, and she screamed into his neck. Her come flooded his hand and he didn't withdraw his fingers until the tremors of her orgasm had passed.

"Oh my." She sucked in oxygen, her breast brushing his chest with every breath. She'd have never guessed before the first time they'd made…had vacation sex, that behind the Mr. Uptight façade lived a very passionate and sexually aggressive lover.

He grinned and lifted his fingers to his mouth. "Very sweet," he whispered, before very slowly and deliberately licking her juices from his fingers. With his other hand, he grasped his cock, circling the thick base with his fingers.

Jill's breath caught in her chest. She'd never dreamed the sight of a man holding his cock, pleasuring himself, could be so…damn…arousing.

"Roll over," he commanded.

Scrambling to her hands and knees, her body already eager for more, she turned, presenting him with the view he'd pictured in the shower. His groan encouraged her and she rested her weight on her forearms, wiggling her ass at him.

"Come and fuck me now."

He slapped her ass—hard—and she gasped at the pleasure of that small pain. "Don't be bossy, sunshine."

She expected him to plunge into her, so the sensation of his hot mouth closing over her set her nerves on fire. He sucked gently and Jill had to rest her forehead on her hands. She spread her knees farther apart, totally opening herself to him. His tongue circled her highly sensitized clit, then plunged into her quivering opening.

Jill bit her lip, trying not to cry out. He tortured her exquisitely, dipping his tongue into her, then running it over her clit, sucking gently, then plunging it into her again. "Please,

Ethan. Please…"

She didn't even know what she was pleading for, but he must have, because suddenly his cock was there. He rubbed its head over her swollen lips, through her slick juices. Over her ass. Then he plunged into her cunt, hard and fast.

She screamed into the bedspread as the orgasm hit her instantly and with an intensity she'd never felt before. At that angle, his cock pounded so deeply it was almost painful, but so incredibly filling. His balls slapped against her sensitive flesh, just as he'd promised.

Ethan ran his hand into her hair, pulling ever so slightly, and she almost sobbed as the tremors shook her body. Her pussy clenched around his cock and she heard him moan.

Then he stopped moving. She was still beneath him, except for the rapid rise and fall of her chest as she tried to catch her breath. In her post-orgasm haze, she was a little confused. Had he come? She didn't think so. Finally, she lifted herself onto her forearms again, pushing back against him.

"Don't move yet," he ordered, his voice little more than a husky whisper.

"What's wrong?" What the *hell* was he doing?

"Not a fucking thing, sunshine. I'm giving my willpower a workout at the moment."

He was trying *not* to come yet. Jill giggled, which made her ass shake and he slapped her again. Her pussy clenched in response and he groaned. "You're killing me, here."

When he pulled out, Jill whimpered and tried to wriggle him back in. He flipped her onto her back and raised her hands over head, holding them there with one of his own. Pinned, she could only look up into his eyes as he moved between her thighs.

"Greedy little bitch, aren't you? Two's not enough?"

She shook her head. "It'll *never* be enough."

* * * * *

Ethan stilled, wondering if she had any idea how her words were affecting him. She was right. This *wouldn't* ever be enough. He would want this woman forever.

He released her hands and she wrapped them around his neck, pulling him closer. Reaching down, he placed the head of his straining cock against her sweet cunt. Jill shifted and he sank again into her soft heat. He clenched his teeth as his balls tightened and the muscles in his back rippled.

She urged him with her hips, but he refused to pound into her yet again. He moved slowly, his muscles trembling with the restraint. Her blue eyes watched his face, questioning, and he smiled.

He pulled back, almost to the point of slipping out, then ever so slowly pushed back into her. He never looked away from her face, their gazes locked as he tortured them. He could feel the quivering deep in her pussy, the tightening in her thighs. She was close again.

Jill closed her eyes as her breathing quickened, but he leaned down and pressed his lips to hers. "Don't close your eyes, sunshine," he whispered before running his tongue over her lower lip.

He quickened his pace, losing himself in her gaze. There was so much he wanted to say, but he didn't know how. Hell, he didn't even know if she'd want to hear it. So he let his eyes, his body, speak for him.

They came together, and he heard his name on her lips as he plunged into her, spilling himself into latex while her pussy spasmed around his flesh. He gripped her hips, pounding into her until he was spent, then he collapsed onto her.

He kissed her cheek, her neck. Her hair. Then her mouth. For what seemed like forever he lost himself in her kiss. Then he laid his head on her breasts and sighed. He'd never been so utterly content, and he was sure he never would be again.

Later, when they were curled together under the light

blanket, her head nestled against his chest, he hummed "You Are My Sunshine" into her hair. And as he drifted off to sleep, his subconscious registered that this could be the last time Jill ever fell asleep next to him. Pulling her closer into his embrace, he hooked his leg over hers, trapping her next to him. She wasn't going anywhere.

* * * * *

Jill blinked at the clock a few times, but the numbers didn't change. 4:06. She closed her eyes again. She'd never particularly cared to know what four o'clock in the morning looked like.

Ethan's body curled perfectly against hers. Close enough to feel the warm pressure of his back and hip, but not so close their skin would get sweaty and make obscene sounds when they pulled apart.

She opened one eye. 4:07. No fire alarm bells. No uninvited bedmates of the eight-legged variety. No surprise Hurricane Horatio battering the window. So why was she awake?

So she didn't have to hear him say, "Hey, it's been fun—maybe I'll see you around Epcot sometime" in the morning.

Jill groaned and threw her arm over her eyes. It was way too early to deal with this. Inner demons shouldn't rear their ugly heads before she'd downed her first pot of coffee.

Ethan had made it clear right from the beginning that Orlando would be the end of the road for them. Tonight was nothing more than a final hurrah—a farewell kiss run amok.

But, like an idiot, she'd gone and fallen in love with the man.

There. Brick wall torn down. Self-awareness achieved. Wouldn't Oprah be so proud of her? But it sure would be nice if the woman was hiding under the bed right now, ready to tell her what the heck she should do now.

What she should do was leave—just go home. Do not pass go, do not collect any more heartache.

But what she wanted to do was roll over, rest her head on Ethan's chest and leave it there for the next sixty or seventy years. Matching rocking chairs and the whole nine yards.

But the whole nine yards was precisely the problem. She couldn't handle that. What she wanted was a closer to two yards or so—three at the most. Okay, even four or five.

She'd give anything to spend forever with Ethan—just the way they were now. They could travel. Maybe she'd devote her life to getting him to bungee jump or cross the road ten feet from the crosswalk.

But Ethan wanted the whole shebang. The house. The white picket fence. Two and a half kids and a dog. And even if she was ready—and she suspected she might be getting closer by the minute—he didn't want them with her.

Slowly and silently, she pulled her leg out from under his and slid out of the bed. She was doing him a favor, after all. He wouldn't have to face that awkward *don't call me, I'll call you* moment.

After pulling her nightgown over her head, she stopped at the door and watched him for a long moment in the glow of the parking lot lights seeping through the blinds. His brow was unfurrowed and the corners of his lips turned up in a slight smile.

She almost went back to kiss him goodbye, but the tears were already running down her cheeks and she didn't want to wake him.

Chapter Twelve

ᘓ

Ethan muttered a good morning to Kenny, then pulled out the chair on the other side of his mother. He knew he was acting like a petulant teen, but there was no way he would get used to this guy.

He turned over his coffee cup and filled it from the carafe his mother passed to him. Inconspicuously, he looked around the dining room for Jill. When he woke up alone, he'd just assumed she'd be in the dining room, drowning herself in the strongest coffee she could cajole from the waiters.

"She went home," his mom said.

So much for inconspicuous. "What do you mean she went home?"

"Mrs. Henderson told me she packed up and went to the bus station early this morning. She's going back to New Hampshire."

She's gone? His mind shied away from grasping his mother's words. Jill couldn't be gone. She'd been snoring—in a cute way, of course—in his ear only a few hours ago. His chest started to ache and he fought the urge to press his hand there. If his mother got it into her head he was having a heart attack, she'd be mobilizing the Florida National Guard.

"Why did she go?" Maybe her family had left her a message on her room phone and she was needed at home, or she'd forgotten to feed her cat, or something. Anything but the possibility that she'd simply walked out on him in the middle of the night.

Without a goodbye, or a note, or anything? He couldn't believe he'd meant that little to her. He was even starting to think that…well, he didn't think she'd leave without so much as a kiss blown over her shoulder.

His mother only shrugged, but Kenny looked at Ethan over his coffee mug. "My guess would be *you*."

Ethan knew that, but he didn't like this gigolo plumber knowing it. "What's that supposed to mean?"

"Last night I got to thinking that maybe you and I should have a talk."

Oh, no no no. No no no.

"Nice use of the Force there, Luke."

Shit! He ran his hands through his hair. Not in a million years would he live that down. "I, uh…yeah."

Not in a million years could he explain it either.

"What are you talking about Kenny?" his mother asked.

Now he knew exactly how a deer felt when staring into the high beams of a half-ton pickup. And words weren't exactly lining up on the tip of his tongue to form a response.

"Nothing, pumpkin," Kenny said, resting his hand over hers, with a conspiratorial wink at Ethan. "It's a joke…a guy thing."

Pumpkin? Ethan wanted to gag. Or choke the sadistic bastard holding his mother's hand. Either one would do.

"Oh." His mother smiled and went back to picking apart her cinnamon bun. "Why do you think it's Ethan's fault? She didn't say a word to any of us."

"Did you see her face when the topic of she and your son getting a house together came up and Casanova over here recommended the radishes?"

Ethan's face heated when he remembered his ridiculous attempts to get Jill away from the table before she let his mother and her *friend* know they were having a week-long one-night stand. "She was uncomfortable talking about our relationship."

"No, she was uncomfortable that the mention of a future with her made you jump out of your chair like your ass was on fire."

He took a deep breath. Better to be thought a dog than a heartless creep. "We don't… It was just supposed to be a vacation fling. We were attracted to each other, but we're very different people. It was just a…fling."

To his everlasting amazement, his mother laughed and shook her head. "Sometimes I think that's how the best ones start."

"Mother!"

"Your father and I were total strangers when we met at the party of a mutual friend. We were playing some silly game and we were dared to, uh, spend five minutes locked in a closet together. We were married six months later."

That certainly wasn't the version his *father* had told him. But he'd think about it later. No, on second thought, he'd never think about it ever again.

"What should I do?" Ethan asked, and for some reason he looked to Kenny instead of his mother.

The older man shrugged. "Your mother's the first lady I've ever truly set my cap for, so I don't have a lot of experience here. But if it was just a fling for you, then let her go. She'll get over you. If it *was* more, then don't let her get on that bus."

They were all silent for several minutes. Ethan stared down into his coffee cup, already feeling the cold void Jill's absence left. He couldn't imagine going through even a single day of the rest of his life without her making things…interesting.

He pushed back his chair and started making his way out of the restaurant. His mother caught up with him just as he hit the hallway.

"Ethan! What is the matter with you?"

"I've got to go," he said, slowing so she wouldn't have to run along beside him.

"I know you don't really like Kenny, but he didn't mean you any harm. He was trying to help."

It took a moment for Ethan's brain to process her words, intent as he was on the excruciatingly long walk through the hotel corridors.

"It wasn't him, Mom. I've got to try to catch Jill before she gets on that bus."

"Oh." She smiled and tucked her arm under his. "I thought you walked out because you don't like Kenny."

Damn right he didn't like that widow-chasing gigolo plumber. "It's not that I don't like him. He seems like a decent enough guy. But you just met him and it's been like thirty-five years since you dated!"

"Oh, Ethan," She sighed, and it had a tone he remembered well from childhood. He was on his mother's last nerve and if he wasn't a grown man, she'd be swatting his ass all the way to his room.

"For goodness sake, child, we're just enjoying each other's company! Do you *want* me to spend the rest of my life alone, crying myself to sleep? That's if I even *can* sleep in the horrible silence after three and a half decades of listening to your father snore. I can't martyr myself to make you happy, Ethan."

They were almost to the lobby, but Ethan stopped. He just stood there feeling like shmuck. A pretty juvenile shmuck at that.

"I don't want you to be unhappy, and I know Dad wouldn't want you to be alone. I just really miss him."

"So do I and spending time with Kenny doesn't change that."

The lobby and the front doors beckoned, but he couldn't leave his mother like this. Hopefully buses to New Hampshire were few and far between. "I know I've been acting like a child—"

"Because you *are* my child."

"—but I'll do better."

She smiled and touched his cheek. "It seems to me you

have your own love life to worry about now."

No kidding. And he still had no idea what he was going to do about it.

"Go get her, honey."

Ethan kissed her cheek and, when she'd walked away, stepped into the lobby. He'd have the desk clerk call a cab and hope like hell the driver could get him to the bus station on time. But first he patted his back pocket to make sure he had his wallet. If he ended up chasing the damn woman all the way up the eastern seaboard, he'd need the money.

* * * * *

Sitting on a dirty countertop in a bus station bathroom, Jill sniffled into a wad of brown, scratchy paper towel. Some vacation.

Every time she thought of Ethan and the sweetly contented smile on his sleeping face, the tears started all over again. It was going to take a long time to get over the man. And somehow, she didn't think forever would be long enough.

Half a dozen deep breaths later she forced herself to look in the mirror. Great. Red eyes, red nose and red blotches of cheap paper towel burn on her cheeks.

"What the hell am I doing?"

"I don't know," said a voice from within a stall and Jill almost fell off the counter. "But when you're done could you pass some toilet paper under the door?"

"I thought I was alone."

"Obviously. I have a shy bladder. So until you figure it out and go off to fix whatever your problem is, I can't pee."

"I can't fix it," Jill said mournfully. Taking a full roll from another stall, she passed it under the other woman's door.

"Thanks. Why not?"

"There's this guy—"

"There always is."

"—and I'm in love with him. And the sex is amazing. You wouldn't even believe it."

"Probably not. So he dumped you?"

Jill sniffed and perched back on the countertop. "No. I snuck out while he was sleeping."

The voice behind the stall door sighed. "Was he *about* to dump you?"

"I don't know." She buried her face in a fresh handful of paper towel. It was a good thing it wasn't one of those air-dryer-only bathrooms or she'd be windblown as hell.

"He said it was just for fun," she continued between sniffles, "but I think maybe he's falling in love with me, too."

A disgusted sigh this time. "So I'm sitting here getting a bladder infection *why*?"

"Oh, I'm sorry." Jill slid to her feet, embarrassed by her selfishness. "I'll just go so you can, uh… I'll just go."

"Wait! You can't go without explaining why you ran away from a guy who's great in the sack and might actually be in love with you."

"But your—"

"I'll buy some cranberry juice. It's like turning off a soap opera halfway through."

Great. As Jill's World Turns. "Do you want me to put my fingers in my ears and hum for a few minutes?"

"My bladder will still know you're here. Now hurry up before somebody else comes in."

"Ethan wants a Fifties woman. Apron, pantyhose, perfect kids and all that."

"And you're not that."

"No, I—"

"But he's falling in love with you anyway?"

"I think so, but—"

"So you're in love with a man who's in love with you and the sex is great, but you're crying in a bus station bathroom?"

Jill scowled at the shredded paper towel. "Insane, huh?"

The silence spoke volumes, so she said, "There's an old saying in my family. 'When the going gets tough, Jill gets going—in the other direction'."

"We have an expression in my family, too—'if it ain't broke, don't throw it away'."

"Really?"

"No, but it sounded kinder than 'you're a dumbass'."

Oprah, she wasn't. Jill twisted the paper in her hands, trying to figure out how she'd screwed up so badly yet again. Maybe she *had* pissed off a Gypsy as a child. She didn't remember meeting any, but she'd gone to a few carnivals when she was young.

"Look," the woman said, "just because he *thinks* he wants Mrs. Cleaver, doesn't mean he does. Why else would he be falling in love with you?"

"What if you're wrong?"

"At least you'll know."

But how could she do it? What if he laughed at her, or gave her one of those humiliatingly scornful looks? She knew the rules when she went into the game. But sometimes he looked at her and she felt there was so much more he wanted to say. It was a crap shoot.

But Ethan Cooper was certainly worth stepping up to the table and rolling the dice for. Even having her love thrown back in her face was better than spending the rest of her life wondering if he'd loved her, after all.

She wasn't going to run this time. She was going back to fight for him, even if it meant getting her heart broken.

"You're right." Jill slid down off the counter and grabbed her bags. "I'm going back and I'm going to tell him I love him."

Jill pulled open the door, then paused. An unmistakable

tinkling sound came through the stall door, followed by a near rapturous sigh of relief.

"Thank you!" she called, then she started to jog toward the station's exit sign.

Twenty minutes later, she was not quite jogging through the front entrance of the hotel. If he'd already left for one of the parks, she'd never find him. And she wasn't sure her courage would hold up until closing.

She scoped out the elevators, looking for one already on the ground floor. There was one just sliding open. Before she could take a single step toward it, a man came out of nowhere and plowed into her. She stumbled backwards a few steps, the obscenities gathering on her lips.

"Jill!"

It was Ethan. The Fates had passed up a chance to kick her while she was down? Must be her lucky day.

He grabbed the suitcase out of her hand. "Why the hell did you sneak out of my bed?"

All activity in the hotel lobby came to a screeching halt and the guy who'd stepped into the elevator had the audacity to hit the door open button.

"Ethan, I…Because I love you."

"That's the worst damn reason I've ever heard!"

Jill blinked. This wasn't at all going right. She knew going in there was a possibility she was doing nothing but humiliating herself, but she hadn't expected it to be in public.

Ethan crossed his arms. "Hold on. You *what*?"

"I love you. I think….I'm pretty sure…probably. Definitely."

His face softened, and she held her breath. He was either really pleased, or trying to come up with way to soften the impending blow. "So why sneak out in the middle of the night? Why were you going home?"

"Because love wasn't part of the deal and I didn't want to

hang around for the rejection."

"Why did you come back?"

She took a deep, shuddering breath. This was hard. *Really* hard.

"Because I love you and maybe you don't love me because we haven't known each other very long and you don't seem like the type to believe in love at first sight which is okay but I couldn't leave without at least telling you that because I always run away and this time—"

Ethan grabbed her by the back of the head and covered her mouth with his, cutting her off her tumble of words. She sucked in a breath through her nose and tried not to think about how hard her heart was beating in her chest. It would be just like the Fates to strike her down with a massive coronary on the verge of a possible happily ever after.

He kissed her with force, and a wickedly delicious shudder ran down her spine. Then somebody coughed, and he broke it off.

"You were babbling, sunshine."

Jill could feel the stupid grin on her face, but couldn't stop. "If I babble some more will you kiss me again, because you know I babble when I'm nervous but maybe if—"

He laughed and kissed her again—just a quick one this time. "Let's go."

He pulled her back to the elevator, where the rubbernecker was still holding the door open.

"Out," Ethan ordered, and Jill felt a little thrill of pleasure at his tone. Sometimes he did the *Me, Tarzan* thing really well. The guy frowned, but stepped out of the elevator.

As soon as the doors slid closed, Ethan backed her against the wall of the car, pressing the length of his body to hers. "You were right."

"About what?" she asked, but she didn't really care. He was hard and the heat of cock against her thigh was distracting as hell.

His hand slid up her thigh, under her shorts, until he hooked the elastic of her panties with the tip of his finger. "I don't believe in love at first sight."

"Oh." Fucking a woman in an elevator certainly gave new meaning to "let her down easy." She braced her hands against his shoulders, ready to push him away.

"It was more like love at second sight." He kissed her again, slow and sweet, and she sighed as he nipped at her bottom lip. Their breath mingled and his finger still toyed with the edging of her undies. Damn herself for wearing them, anyway.

"So," she whispered against his lips, "just so we're clear this is a mutual thing then?"

The elevator stopped and Ethan withdrew his hand from her shorts as the doors slid open. A frazzled, sunburned couple half-hidden by the burden of theme-park shopping bags fought to fit through the opening.

"I'm a doctor, " Ethan said in an urgent tone. "I think this woman might have contracted a rare, communicable disease."

The couple fled, bags bouncing, and Ethan hit the door close button while Jill tried her best not to laugh. The elevator began its agonizingly slow ascent once again.

"So, where were we?" Ethan whispered into her neck.

"Your hand was—"

"I love you," he interrupted. "That's where we were. I love you and I have a feeling I'll spend a lot of time in the future wondering where we are and how the hell we got there, but as long as you're with me, who cares, and there's no reason I can't move to New Hampshire and we don't have to have kids until you're ready and—"

Jill threw her arms around his neck and gave him a fast, passionate kiss of her own. "You were babbling."

His hand crept back toward the hem of her shorts. "What do you think would happen if we hit the stop button?"

She shuddered when his finger brushed ever so slightly over her clit. "They'll probably call the fire department. Let's find out."

"They might call the police."

"I *dare* you to do it."

Ethan grinned wickedly and Jill's heart seemed to skip a beat. She was going to spend the rest of her life with this man.

He ran his tongue over her bottom lip and she moaned against his mouth. "On three. One…"

He slid his finger over the thin, wet fabric of her panties. "Two…"

"Three."

Epilogue

Six months later

ꙮ

He looked like James Bond without the shaken martini. When Jill took her first step down the aisle, he smiled and she had to rethink that. No actor playing 007 had ever looked as hot in a tux as Ethan Cooper.

She counted to herself as she took each step, bringing her feet together each time as she'd been instructed. *Don't strangle the bouquet. Keep my chin up. And don't let my heel catch in the hem of my satin gown.*

Finally, after what seemed like the longest walk of her life, Jill reached the altar and hung a left. As she turned, the organ player launched into "The Wedding March" and the bride appeared in the doorway.

Debra Cooper looked radiant in her simple ivory gown and she had eyes only for her groom. Kenny stood next to Ethan, looking nervous as hell except for the goofy grin lighting up his face. The Justice of the Peace cleared his throat, Ethan winked at his mother and Jill concentrated on not falling off her high-heeled shoes.

A few vows, a reception line, a cake demolition and several trips to the cash bar later, Jill finally managed to corner Ethan in an alcove under the stair of the bed and breakfast. She collapsed against him, exhausted from a week of pre-wedding insanity.

"Tired, sunshine?" he asked with his mouth resting in her hair.

"Mmmhmmm. How are you doing?"

"Good. Mom seems happy, and Kenny's a great guy."

Jill sighed and nodded against his chest. "And they love the rocking chairs you refinished for them."

They swayed silently to the music coming from the reception room for a few moments, before Ethan nuzzled her neck. "Can I ask you something?"

She lifted her head. "Yes, it's definitely time to sneak off to our room and have sex."

He laughed and lifted her off her feet. He made a show of staggering toward the stairs, and she clutched his neck. The first thing she noticed when he opened the door was the scent. The heavy, sensual scent of dozens of roses washed over Jill as Ethan set her down gently on the bed.

"What country is this?" she asked, utterly confused.

He frowned and wrinkled his nose. She had to admit he'd overdone the number of blossoms by quite a bit. "It's not really a country."

Jill lifted an eyebrow, waiting patiently. The game had begun months ago. Concentrating on their work left them little time or money for travel, so they saw the world in bed. They staged their desired destinations and tried to stay within the theme, with a varying degree of results. Antarctica, for one, had been a disaster. "So where is it? This one's your fantasy."

The blush she loved so much crept up his neck as moved behind her to unzip her gown. "The, uh…Rose Garden."

"*The* Rose Garden? What is that, like a Republican fantasy?" She tried not to laugh, but she'd never heard of anybody wanting to screw in a White House garden before. Although it had surely been done.

Ethan slipped the gown with its built-in bra from her shoulders, and she shivered with want when knelt behind her and covered her breasts with his hands. The smell of the roses was intoxicating, if a little overwhelming and she closed her eyes, blocking out the rented, overly feminine room.

"You can laugh at the roses," he whispered against her ear. "I couldn't find the country I was looking for, so I had to settle."

He moved away then and pulled her to her feet. The gown pooled on the floor, leaving her in nothing but a white thong and strappy white sandals. The thong was already damp, and she could tell by his mood that he was really going to make her suffer. He took great pleasure in thwarting her impatience.

"What country were you looking for?"

His smile was wicked as he moved to press his tuxedo-clad chest against her naked breasts. "I'd like to find a country that truly adores anal sex."

She laughed, but her panties went from damp to wet in a less than a second. The thought of that cock in her ass had her grinding her nipples against his tux. "How did we get from anal sex to the Rose Garden? Not that I'm complaining. It can't be as bad as the Amazon last month. Poison ivy on one's ass really sucks."

His laughter made his chest jerk against her taut nipples and she moaned. "The florist brought too many roses, so…"

His words died out when Jill backed away from him and sat on the edge of the bed. When she laid back on the white eyelet comforter, bent her knees and caught her heels on the edge of the bed, he sucked in a breath that made her smile. Talking time was over.

"That's, uh…not what I was going to ask you, by the way. Downstairs," Ethan said quietly.

Okay. Talking time was *almost* over. She'd just hurry it on its way. Lifting her hips, she slid the thong down and over her sandals. He caught it in midair and tucked it in the pocket of his tux.

Jill spread her thighs wide, making sure her chatty lover had an unobstructed view as she moved her hand over her wet pussy. She heard his deep, ragged breath and knew there would be no more talking. Nothing made Ethan hotter faster than watching her fuck herself.

She dipped her fingers into her own juices and drew moist circles on her hardened nipples. Ethan took a step closer, and shoved his hands into his trouser pockets. She kneaded her breasts, catching the nipples between her fingers. Only when Ethan shed his tuxedo jacket and started on the cummerbund did she return her attention to her throbbing pussy. He wasn't going to give her much more time.

She ran her fingertips over her clit, stimulating the bundle of nerves until she had to bite her lip to keep from begging him to fuck her right then. Ethan moved to stand between her thighs, his eyes never leaving her hands. She slid one finger into her own heat, then another, while gently rubbing her clit with her thumb.

"You are so fucking hot," Ethan said through gritted teeth, and she was surprised when he knelt in front of her. Normally he didn't join in until she'd brought herself to the first orgasm of the night.

He pressed his mouth to her, nudging aside her fingers and replacing them with his tongue. Jill squirmed on the bed, lifting her hips to his mouth. He plundered her with his tongue, then brought his own hands into play. He captured her left wrist in one hand, and with other, slipped something onto her finger. Only then did he lift his head.

Jill's heart stopped when she saw the diamond solitaire he'd slipped onto the ring finger of her left hand. Tears welled in her eyes, and she tried to blink them away, which was no easy feat while lying on her back.

"That's what I wanted to ask you downstairs. But you distracted me, as always. I love you, sunshine, more than you can imagine. Will you marry me?"

"Yes," Jill managed to say, but it was mostly a sob. "I love you too."

She captured his head and pulled him up her body until she could press her mouth to his. The taste of her own juices on his lips reignited the flames of arousal and she kissed him hungrily. His tongue slipped between her lips, and she barely noticed the sound of his zipper or the rustle of fabric.

He reached down between them and guided his cock into her, so quickly and deeply she gasped into his mouth. He rocked against her and she moved her hips as well, grinding her clit against him.

"I'm going to fuck you every chance I get for the rest of our lives," he promised in a low voice. "And you'll never have to worry about me straying because there's no pussy I want to fuck more than this one."

She dug her heels into his ass, forcing him to drive faster and deeper. Her fingernails bit into his back and she came, crying his name. Almost immediately he withdrew, and she moaned in protest. She wasn't done with him tonight.

He rolled her onto her hands and knees and she reached up to drag a pillow down from the top of the bed. This remained Ethan's favorite position, but after denting the Sheetrock over their bed at home, Jill had learned to cushion her head.

"You won't need that. I'll be gentle."

"Fuck gentle," she growled. "You're never gentle this way."

Ethan laughed and grabbed her hips. "You'd be disappointed if I was."

He was right. Jill was still blown away by the private, intimate side of her man. The side that not only didn't show, but that nobody even suspected existed. The side that whispered nasty promises in her ear. The side that gave her a case of facial rug burn she'd had to hide with makeup. The side that liked to jerk off when he knew she could see him. He could make her hot as hell with just a glance.

When the head of his cock slipped into her, Jill drove backward until his balls slapped against her. Ethan grabbed her hips, pounding her unrelentingly. She clutched the pillow, screaming into it as she came again. He slowed his pace, and she shuddered as her pussy clenched, gripping him with sweet, warm friction.

She tensed when he ran his palm over her ass, but the anticipated slap didn't come. Instead, he slid a finger over her clit, lubricating it with his juices before moving up to explore the object of his newest fantasies.

Jill forced herself to relax, rocking back and forth along his throbbing cock. He was close, she knew, and when he inserted the tip of his finger into her tight anus, his breath grew more ragged. She moaned as he pushed his finger into her, her nerves on fire with this new sensation. She pressed her hips back to meet each forward thrust of his cock and finger, and felt the tensing in her muscles.

"I think I'll wait until our wedding night," Ethan told her, panting with the effort to prolong their pleasure. "I've fucked you every other way. The night you become my wife I'm going to fuck your ass, sunshine."

"How very…Neanderthal of you," Jill managed to say before the orgasm rocked her. She screamed into the bunched pillow and felt Ethan's cock pulsing, his hips jerking against hers as he came along with her. His fingernails bit into her ass and he groaned her name. Her chest heaved with the effort of catching her breath and she grunted when he collapsed on top of her.

"I love you," he murmured into her hair, and Jill smiled at the tone in his voice. Sex was over and the perverted caveman would be hidden until next time. He never talked to her like that except during their lovemaking. "I'll be right back."

He disappeared into the bathroom for a few minutes, then he crawled into bed beside her. He captured her left hand, twirling the diamond with his thumb. "That wasn't the most romantic time to propose, I guess."

"It'll make a wonderful story to share with our friends, though."

The blush was almost instantaneous, and she laughed. "I thought it was perfect."

"You're perfect," he countered. "I love you."

"I love you, too." She kissed him, then tucked her head against his chest.

"And when the going gets tough?"

"Jillian's not going anywhere."

About the Author

Shannon Stacey was a two-time Olympic gold medal winner, basking in the glory of cereal box appearances, before giving up the athletic world to pursue her love of music. Her command performance of "Mandy" reportedly brought the Queen to tears, but an unfortunate incident with a habanero pepper forced her to turn her attention to other pursuits. After swimming with sharks off the Great Barrier Reef and scaling Mt. Kilimanjaro, she once danced the night away in a little bar known as Rick's Café Americain.

Okay, I got a little carried away there. All fiction. Although I'm pretty sure the Queen would cry if she heard me sing Barry Manilow. But I just love to make stuff up. My ability to veer away from the truth, and my horror of anything mathematical, made it pretty clear from an early age that I would be either a writer or a really bad accountant with a lot of good excuses. It wasn't clear until much later that my favorite stories would be about two people defying all odds to find their Happily Ever Afters.

I married my own Prince Charming in 1993, and we're the proud parents of a future Nobel Prize for Science-winning bookworm and an adrenaline junkie with a flair for drama. We also have two cats who refuse to curl up on my lap and keep it warm while I write. Fortunately, writing steamy love stories helps heat up the cold New England winters. I'm excited and honored that Ellora's Cave is bringing my stories to readers.

(That last paragraph—all true.)

Shannon welcomes comments from readers. You can find her website and email address on her author bio page at www.ellorascave.com.

Enjoy An Excerpt From:

BLIND JUSTICE

Available at www.cerridwenpress.com

༄

Three distinct shapes took form, Dylan leading the way as he strode up the walk. Even I couldn't mistake the Welshman. A ramrod six foot five, he towered over most men in a crowd. His head was a dark, wedged outline because, as I knew from long acquaintance with him, the dark hair was cut short behind. A silver streak flared back from a scar at his hairline, a relic of a long ago knife fight, and hung down over one side of an unlined forehead, above deep lavender eyes in a naturally tanned face.

Before he opened his mouth, I looked forward to his slight accent. A melodic, almost singsong pleasure of sound fought a losing battle with a west coast drawl.

Dylan Jones hadn't got where he was on his looks, best described as rugged or attractive. He made Lieutenant, Homicide Division, on the strength of his well-deserved reputation, renowned among the ranks as a damn good, street-smart cop.

Looking toward the bulky shadows, I inclined my head, just enough to answer his unspoken question. Recently I'd discovered I could converse with Dylan through some kind of thought transference, didn't know if it was some low-level telepathy or a desire to "see" things not always there.

I called myself an "onlooker"—seeing, as well as feeling, things that happened to others. I'd begun to accept I could see what happened as I read an object or a room. I was still trying to get a handle on this new gift so I could use the talent to help others. Now I found myself able to converse silently with the Welshman, something I didn't seem able to do with anyone else.

I sensed he was watching me, silently asking my opinion. Silently I gave him his answer. Yes, Dylan, there had indeed been murder. Yes, there had been abuse, the cruelty going on for many days. No, the man responsible had killed in that hellhole of a house, but he wasn't living there.

The perversions started with humiliating expletives and physical taunts while the victim was restrained. Soon she was forced to beg for mercy while enduring molestation of her most private and sensitive parts. The acts escalated when the killer found release in the "purification" beatings that left broken heads and limbs.

Eventually he reached a point he believed to be "restoration". He referred to it as "time to wrap it up", before dispatching the unconscious, battered woman.

He relished preparing and serving their last supper.

The abuse was his appetizer and main course.

For dessert, he took life.

It always surprised me when I thought of a suspect this harshly, but he may have murdered at least eight women, used their own trusting natures to snare them. Taken each one to his home, shown the unsuspecting a good time for a day or two, and held the poor creature captive.

Once he held the women prisoner, his true colors merged into one—black, the color of evil.

The pain I felt at the primary crime scene was both physical and mental. The victim's sorrow finally overwhelmed her when she realized she'd entered into a death chamber of her own free will.

The cruelty came from the suspect, the predator who lured these women to his home with promises of a pleasant evening—an evening that turned into a horrendous span of days.

Death occurred in a front room on the main floor. Any neighbor with half an ear should have heard the screams and cries of the victims and used the brains God gave them to report the strange happenings. Only the discovery of body parts in the alley behind the house tipped anyone to what had gone on. The suspect must have decided that keeping two bodies in his freezer at the same time made it too crowded. Not enough room for the next poor soul.

Dylan told me later that a city employee dumped an extremely heavy can into his trash compacter. Stunned to see a human arm, the garbage collector heaved his lunch into the grass beside the fence. Recovered, he'd dialed 911. His truck was taken into evidentiary custody. He took the rest of the week off.

By the time Dylan asked me to *read* the house, forensic experts had completed preliminary examination of the murder scene and given permission for limited access. Earlier, my uniformed escort and I began on the upper level. He told me we were instructed to follow a narrow path marked with tape on the floor, from the entrance door to another room facing the street. It was bright inside, illuminated by halogen lights erected by the investigators.

The squalid main and upper floors were littered with broken furniture, fallen plaster, piles of plastic bags and animal excrement.

I'd gagged, the putrid smell enough to repel the curious. Only vermin would consider it home. My policeman said even a surgical mask wouldn't help and placed a small jar near my hand, instructing me to take a dab of the mentholated ointment and wipe it beneath my nostrils. It would keep me from smelling the rot for at least a few minutes.

When we shuffled to where the final moments of each woman had been spent, he told me the investigators were surprised the killing room was so conspicuously clean and sparse in its furnishings. When he mentioned that, my mind immediately pictured an abattoir, dead animals hanging from suspended hooks. There was a small dining table, two wooden chairs, a mattress and two prominent fixtures. A high-backed easy chair sat in the center and a large freezer took up a short wall by the window.

I shivered, thinking about the freezer.

The suspect was the seemingly salt-of-the-earth, caring preacher Reverend Peter Thaddeus from the charismatic congregation around the corner. A man of the cloth. A supposedly religious man who should be helping to heal pain, stop cruelty and put an end to sorrow. Instead, he gratified himself with an extravagance of evil.

Somehow, one of the local newspapers got hold of the suspect's name and, trying for fourth estate sensationalism, had christened him the Preacher. The name stuck and even the Rocklynne Police Department personnel working the case referred to him that way.

As for me, the police wanted to be entirely sure they arrested the right man when they took him into custody. Dylan Jones asked, I complied. My *reading* confirmed everything they knew.

Many in the department considered me "that psychic broad". At least I'd heard myself called that by one of the detectives at the precinct house where I'd waited earlier today. He wasn't aware my hearing was acute enough to hear his muttered, disparaging comment. "That psychic broad" was thirty-one, a university graduate in the studies of art and, later, paranormal activities.

I considered myself a gifted psychic.

I'm also legally blind.

Why an electronic book?

We live in the Information Age—an exciting time in the history of human civilization, in which technology rules supreme and continues to progress in leaps and bounds every minute of every day. For a multitude of reasons, more and more avid literary fans are opting to purchase e-books instead of paper books. The question from those not yet initiated into the world of electronic reading is simply: *Why?*

1. ***Price.*** An electronic title at Ellora's Cave Publishing and Cerridwen Press runs anywhere from 40% to 75% less than the cover price of the exact same title in paperback format. Why? Basic mathematics and cost. It is less expensive to publish an e-book (no paper and printing, no warehousing and shipping) than it is to publish a paperback, so the savings are passed along to the consumer.
2. ***Space.*** Running out of room in your house for your books? That is one worry you will never have with electronic books. For a low one-time cost, you can purchase a handheld device specifically designed for e-reading. Many e-readers have large, convenient screens for viewing. Better yet, hundreds of titles can be stored within your new library—on a single microchip. There are a variety of e-readers from different manufacturers. You can also read e-books on your PC or laptop computer. (Please note that Ellora's Cave does not endorse any specific brands. You can check our websites at www.ellorascave.com or

www.cerridwenpress.com for information we make available to new consumers.)

3. ***Mobility***. Because your new e-library consists of only a microchip within a small, easily transportable e-reader, your entire cache of books can be taken with you wherever you go.
4. ***Personal Viewing Preferences.*** Are the words you are currently reading too small? Too large? Too... ANNOYING? Paperback books cannot be modified according to personal preferences, but e-books can.
5. ***Instant Gratification.*** Is it the middle of the night and all the bookstores near you are closed? Are you tired of waiting days, sometimes weeks, for bookstores to ship the novels you bought? Ellora's Cave Publishing sells instantaneous downloads twenty-four hours a day, seven days a week, every day of the year. Our webstore is never closed. Our e-book delivery system is 100% automated, meaning your order is filled as soon as you pay for it.

Those are a few of the top reasons why electronic books are replacing paperbacks for many avid readers.

As always, Ellora's Cave and Cerridwen Press welcome your questions and comments. We invite you to email us at Comments@ellorascave.com or write to us directly at Ellora's Cave Publishing Inc., 1056 Home Avenue, Akron, OH 44310-3502.

Ellora's Cavemen

Legendary Tails

Try an e-book for your immediate reading pleasure or order these titles in print from

www.EllorasCave.com

Cerridwen, the Celtic Goddess of wisdom, was the muse who brought inspiration to story-tellers and those in the creative arts. Cerridwen Press encompasses the best and most innovative stories in all genres of today's fiction. Visit our site and discover the newest titles by talented authors who still get inspired - much like the ancient storytellers did, once upon a time.

ELLORA'S CAVE
ROMANTICA PUBLISHING